Good Earls Don't Lie

ALSO BY MICHELLE WILLINGHAM

Secrets in Silk Series (Regency Scotland)

Undone by the Duke
Unraveled by the Rebel
Undressed by the Earl
Unlaced by the Outlaw

MacEgan Brothers Series (medieval Ireland)

Her Warrior Slave
"The Viking's Forbidden Love-Slave" in the *Pleasurably Undone* anthology
Her Warrior King
Her Irish Warrior
The Warrior's Touch
Taming Her Irish Warrior
"Voyage of an Irish Warrior"
"The Warrior's Forbidden Virgin"
Surrender to an Irish Warrior
"Pleasured by the Viking" in the *Delectably Undone* anthology
"Lionheart's Bride" in the *Royal Weddings Through the Ages anthology*
Warriors in Winter

The Accidental Series (Victorian England/ fictional province of Lohenberg)

"An Accidental Seduction"
The Accidental Countess
The Accidental Princess
The Accidental Prince

The MacKinloch Clan Series (medieval Scotland)

Claimed by the Highland Warrior
Seduced by Her Highland Warrior
"Craving the Highlander's Touch"
Tempted by the Highland Warrior
"Rescued by the Highland Warrior" in the *Highlanders anthology*

Forbidden Vikings Series (Viking Age Ireland)

To Sin with a Viking
To Tempt a Viking

Warriors of Ireland Series (medieval Ireland)

Warrior of Ice
Warrior of Fire

Other Titles

A Viking for the Viscountess
A Maiden for the Marquess
"A Dance with the Devil" in the *Bedeviled* anthology
"Innocent in the Harem" (sixteenth-century Ottoman Empire)
"A Wish to Build a Dream On" (time travel to medieval Ireland)

Good Earls Don't Lie

MICHELLE WILLINGHAM

Published by Montlake Romance, Seattle
www.apub.com

ISBN-13: 9781503939769
ISBN-10: 1503939766

Cover design by Michael Rehder

Cover illustration by Judy York/lottreps.com

Printed in the United States of America

For James—Your bright spirit and humor always make me smile. Thank you for bringing sunshine into each day. There's no doubt in my mind that you have the Irish gift of the gab.

Chapter One

Yorkshire

May 1846

His head was killing him. It felt as if a hundred horses had trampled his skull, and right now he tasted blood and dirt in his mouth. After a moment, Iain Donovan gathered his senses, clearing his head.

The last thing he remembered was riding toward the Penford estate. He dimly recalled having passed a grove of trees when, abruptly, he'd been knocked off his horse. A shattering pain had crashed over him, and he vaguely remembered voices arguing and shouting.

But no one was here now.

Iain tried to sit up, and blood rushed to his head, threatening a loss of consciousness once again. He reached out to touch his brother's signet ring, only to find it gone. A sense of fear rose up in him, and he uttered a foul curse.

No one knew him here. He'd never left Ireland before now, and this country was completely foreign to him. While his mother had taken his older brother Michael to London every Season, teaching him all the skills necessary to become the Earl of Ashton, Iain had been left at home. She had done everything in her power to ensure that he was the invisible spare, the hidden son of no importance.

None of that mattered now. He was the only heir left, and he intended to prove that he was a man of worth. He would rebuild Ashton and help his people—even if that meant traveling across the Irish Sea to meet with strangers.

The wind sent gooseflesh rising over his skin, and when he realized he was no longer wearing a shirt, he let out another curse. Who would do such a thing? The bloody bastards had seized the shirt off his back, devil take them all and eat them sideways.

The thieves had stolen not only the ring and the few coins he possessed, but his horse, his coat, waistcoat, and shirt—even the shoes he'd worn. A fine welcome to England this was. After leaving the nightmare of Ireland behind him, he'd thought that here, everything would be better.

Apparently not.

Iain rose to his feet and studied the land around him. It was a fair day, with the sun shining over rolling hills and meadows. He supposed he could walk the remaining distance to the Penford estate, for it was only a few miles farther. Though he didn't particularly like the idea of walking in his trousers and stocking feet, he had no other choice.

He grimaced as he followed the road leading toward Penford. All the baggage he'd brought from Ashton was gone now. He'd have to borrow clothes and shoes, and no one would possibly believe he was the Earl of Ashton. Without a coach, servants, clothing, or a signet ring, they'd think him a beggar at best.

His head was pounding from the mild wound, but more than the physical pain was a rising sense of panic.

Calm down, he ordered himself. He would tell the truth about his ill luck, and surely someone would believe him. Lady Wolcroft had visited Ashton a few years ago. Surely she would remember him. After all, she was the one who had invited him to visit when she'd learned of the troubles they had suffered with the famine. His mother, Moira, and Lady Wolcroft's daughter, Iris, had been good friends at boarding school. Moira had spent all her school holidays with Iris's family and was like another daughter to them.

But friendship aside, he couldn't suppress the rise of uneasiness. Aside from Lady Wolcroft and his tenants, very few outsiders even knew there *was* a spare, in addition to the heir. His gut twisted at his mother's disregard, but he pushed the anger back.

Despite the circumstances, his younger sisters were depending on him to save their estate. For Colleen and Sybil, he would not fail. *Could* not fail. The task before him was greater than any he'd ever imagined, but he was determined to prove his mother wrong and restore Ashton to its former wealth.

And so it was that Iain had decided to travel across the sea, to leave his familiar homeland and dwell among strangers. And most of all, to offer himself up in marriage, in the hopes of wooing a wealthy bride.

Most men would never dream of such a thing, but his pride had crumbled as surely as the estate of Ashton. His brother was dead, and his sisters needed him. He'd be damned if he'd turn his back on them, forcing them to wed strangers. No. There was a way out of this mess, even if it meant offering himself up as the sacrificial lamb.

With each step, Iain gathered command of himself until he was confident that he *would* be welcomed at Penford, despite his bedraggled appearance.

As he continued along the dry road leading toward the hills, he saw sprouts of barley and rye emerging from the soil. The sight was a sobering contrast to the rotting fields he'd left behind at Ashton. The blight had destroyed their potato crops, until there was naught left, save a crumbling castle and enough debts to bury the family alive.

His mother and sisters had gone to stay with their aunt in New York, while he managed the affairs at Ashton. He had no intention of abandoning the estate or the people who had called it home for all their lives.

For they were starving. Too many of them had watched their crops rot in the earth, and they had nothing left. No livestock, no money—nothing to trade for food. Hundreds had left in the hopes of finding work elsewhere, but no one wanted Irish refugees.

Iain knew that if he wed an heiress, his bride's dowry could help the tenants survive until the crops improved. And though he had little to offer, save his Irish charm and a decrepit castle, he had to try.

The road curved over a hill, and when he crossed the apex, he saw Penford within the valley. On the west side of the estate, he spied a lake, gleaming silver and gold in the morning sunlight. For a moment, he paused to enjoy the sight. The estate was near a village, though it lay in an isolated part of Yorkshire—not exactly the best place to find a wife.

But Lady Wolcroft had her own motives for bringing him here . . . and he would do anything necessary to form an alliance with the matron. She could bring him into her circles in London, introducing Iain to potential brides—and he was well aware that she had her own unmarried granddaughters. He would certainly consider the young ladies as marriage prospects before he left for London.

He continued the painful walk down the road, and when he turned the corner, he spied two adolescent boys on horseback. On *his* horse, Darcy.

Damn them all and may the crows feast upon their bones.

Iain didn't call out to them, for they could easily outpace him. Instead, he began running lightly, hoping he could overtake them before they noticed his arrival. The rocks dug into the soles of his feet as he ran hard, and he bit back the pain. Almost there . . .

"The horse is mine," one of the boys insisted. "I found him first."

"No, he's mine," the other boy glared. "I'm going to tell Father that he followed me home."

They couldn't have been more than thirteen, he guessed. Their thievery was likely adolescent mischief, and he fully intended to get every last one of his possessions back. He quickened his pace, but within seconds, Darcy grew skittish and neighed, alerting the boys to his presence.

At that, Iain shouted out, "Stop, both of you! That's my horse!"

"I told you we shouldn't have done it!" one cried out, urging Darcy faster. "Go!"

His idiot horse obeyed the command and galloped hard until there was no hope of catching up to them. Iain ran as fast as he could, hoping to glimpse where they were going, but the boys disappeared into the trees.

He cursed beneath his breath, furious at the way this day had begun. It was bad enough to be robbed, much less by boys. But it wouldn't take long to identify them to the authorities.

His feet were bleeding through his stockings, and his body was perspiring from the hard run. A sight he would be, arriving at Penford like this. He'd have to improve his appearance before arriving, or else they'd toss him back into the road like yesterday's breakfast.

Iain walked the remaining distance to the manor house, keeping off the gravel road. Several of the tenants eyed him as he passed, but he kept walking, his shoulders held back as if it were the most normal thing in the world to arrive at an estate wearing only trousers.

Tall hedges stood beside the house, and a small arbor led into a garden. He hurried toward it, feeling sheepish about his lack of attire. It might be that he could find a footman or a gardener who could help him with clothing. But as he approached the garden, he realized that he had entered a maze of hedges. Curiosity got the better of him, and he began wandering through the boxwood aisles.

At one end, he saw a stone fountain with rosebushes planted beside it. Deeper within the maze, he found a bed of irises, their purple blossoms illuminated by the sun. And when he reached the farthest end, he saw lilies of the valley.

He stood for a moment at the edge of the maze, where it opened onto a green lawn. A lovely woman was seated upon a stone bench, a book lying beside her. Her hair was reddish brown, tucked into a neat updo beneath her bonnet. She closed her eyes for a moment, lifting her face toward the sun like a blossom.

The sight of her stole the words from his brain, and Iain decided that his missing horse could wait, for the time being.

Who was this woman? One of Lady Wolcroft's granddaughters? It was possible, given her white morning gown trimmed with blue embroidery. Every inch of her appeared to be a lady. Iain took a few steps closer, fascinated by her.

The young woman dug her fingers into the stone bench, and her face tightened. Slowly, she eased herself to the edge of the seat, and she hunched her back. She gripped the bench hard, as if every movement was a struggle. Iain tensed, trying to understand her difficulty. It was only a moment later when he realized what she was doing.

She was trying to stand up.

The woman leaned heavily against the bench as she tried to force her legs to bear weight. When her knees buckled, she sat down again, her spirits dismayed.

Iain let out the breath he'd been holding. The pieces were beginning to fall into place. It might be that Lady Wolcroft had asked him here to help her granddaughters. If this young woman couldn't walk, there was no chance of her finding a husband.

And yet, she had a courage that he admired. There was a quiet determination in her eyes, of a woman who would not give up. He understood her.

Softly, he emerged from the hedgerow, wanting to know who she was.

There was a strange man standing in her garden.

Lady Rose Thornton blinked a moment, wondering if her imagination had conjured him. Because he was also half-naked and smiling at her, as if nothing were the matter.

"You'll have to forgive me for being half-clothed, *a chara,*" he apologized, "but I was robbed on my journey here by a group of damned thieving boys."

Now what did he mean by that? Rose shut her eyes tightly and opened them again. No, he was still there. She filled her lungs with air, prepared to scream for all that was holy.

"I won't be harming you," he said, lifting his hands in surrender, "but I would be most grateful for some clothes. Not yours, of course." He sent her a roguish grin.

She gaped at him, still uncertain of who he was. But she had to admit that he *was* indeed an attractive man, in a pirate sort of way. His brown hair was cut short, and his cheeks were bristled, as if he'd forgotten to shave. She tried not to stare at his bare chest, but he cocked his head and rested his hands at his waist. His chest muscles were well defined, his skin tawny from the sun. Ridges at his abdomen caught her eye, and it was clear enough that he was a working man. Perhaps a groom or a footman. Gentlemen did not possess muscles like these, especially if they lived a life of leisure. His green eyes were staring at her with amusement, and Rose found herself spellbound by his presence.

"Do you not speak," he asked, "or have I cast you into silence with my nakedness?"

"Y-you're not naked," she blurted out. Her anxiety twisted up inside her, and she began babbling. "That is, you're mostly covered," she corrected, her face flaming. "The important bits, anyway."

Not naked? What sort of remark was that? She was sitting in the garden with a stranger wearing only trousers, and she hadn't yet called out for help. What was the matter with her? He could be an intruder bent upon attacking her.

But he laughed at her remark. It was a rich, deep tone that reminded her of wickedness.

Rose couldn't help but wonder why on earth a footman was naked in her garden. "Stay back," she warned, "or I'll scream."

He lifted his hands. "You needn't do that. As I've said, I have no intention of harming you. I fear you've caught me in a kettle of pottage. Could you be helping me, if it's not too much trouble?" With a slight lift of an eyebrow, he added, "I am here at Lady Wolcroft's invitation."

That nudged her curiosity. Why would her grandmother summon a stranger to Penford? Mildred loved nothing better than to meddle, but she wasn't even here at the moment. She had gone to Bath only a few weeks ago.

Then again, it was entirely possible that this man was lying. Probable, even.

"Who are you?" she managed to ask. "And why are you here?"

"I am Iain Donovan, the Earl of Ashton," he answered. "At your service." He bowed, and in his grin, she detected a teasing air. An Irishman, she was certain, given his speech patterns. But an earl? Exactly how empty headed did he think she was?

Rose folded her hands in her lap. "There is no need to lie, sir," she told him. "I know full well that you are not an earl."

He blinked at that, his face furrowed. But honestly, had he really thought he could pull off such a deception? She was no country miss, easily fooled. "An earl would travel in a coach with dozens of servants. Never alone."

Before he could argue with her, she continued. "You may go to the servants' entrance, and our housekeeper, Mrs. Marlock, might have some old clothes to lend you. Perhaps a bit of food, and you can be on your way." Though she kept her tone reasonable, she had no way of knowing whether this man was dangerous. Perhaps she should have screamed after all. There was still time to do so.

The man crossed his arms over his chest and regarded her. In an even tone, he said, "I've not spoken any lies, miss."

"It's Lady Rose, Mr. Donovan," she corrected. As far as she was concerned, this man was a commoner with no claim to any title. "I should like for you to leave. Now." Her nerves tightened, for if this man dared to threaten her, she could do nothing to stop him. Especially since she couldn't run.

Even if she did call out to her footman, Calvert, he might not arrive quickly enough. Her gaze seized upon a rake nearby, and she wondered if she could reach it, if the need arose.

"I've no reason to speak untruths," he said. "As I told you before, I was robbed on my way here." He paused a moment, adding, "The axle broke on our coach, and my servants stayed behind to fix it. I thought it best to continue on horseback, since Lady Wolcroft invited me to stay as her guest."

"An unlikely story," Rose countered. "If you really *were* the earl, you'd have brought several footmen with you."

He raised an eyebrow. "And how many footmen was I expected to have?"

"Enough to bring several of them with you. A gentleman never travels alone."

The man's expression turned thunderous. "He does, when there's no other choice." It looked like he was about to argue further, but instead, he tightened his mouth and said, "Lady Wolcroft's eldest daughter and my mother were friends. She wants to marry me off to an Englishwoman, and that is why I am here."

She didn't believe him one whit. No, he had to be a vagrant of some sort, a man down on his luck who was attempting to take advantage by lying. "Well, sir, you do spin an entertaining tale. I've heard that the Irish are excellent storytellers, but you can take your story back to our housekeeper."

"It's not a story, Lady Rose. I *am* here to find a bride." The intensity in his voice was rather strong, and made no secret of his annoyance.

She leaned as far over as she dared and managed to reach the rake handle. It made her feel better having a makeshift weapon.

"What are you planning to do with that rake, *a chara*?" he inquired, taking another step closer. Rose gripped the handle with both hands and drew it closer, using the tool to keep him at a distance.

"Nothing, if you go away." Truthfully, she didn't know exactly what she would do with the rake. It wasn't exactly suitable for stabbing someone. She could poke him with it, but not much else.

This time, she did call out to her footman. "Calvert! I have need of your assistance!" She hoped he would guard her against any threat. Right now, she wanted the strange man gone from her presence.

Even if he was quite handsome. And a charming liar.

The Irishman's mouth twisted, and he bowed. "As you like, then, Lady Rose. I'll be seeing you later, when I've better clothes to wear than these."

She wasn't certain what to think of that, but she gripped the rake tightly. "Be on your way." *Or I'll have my footman remove you.*

But as the stranger disappeared into the maze, she was aware that her heart was beating swiftly, out of more than fear. Although she had seen her brother without a shirt before, never had she seen a man like Iain Donovan. His dark hair had a hint of curl to it, and those green eyes fascinated her. His cheekbones were sharp, his face lean and chiseled. He looked like a man who had walked through hell itself and come out stronger.

There was nothing at all refined about him. She'd wager that he'd never worn gloves in his life.

No. He could not possibly be an earl.

And yet . . . she'd been intrigued by his physical strength, wondering if his muscles were as firm as they appeared. His form could have been carved out of marble, like a statue.

When Calvert arrived upon the path to take her back to the house, she stole a look back at the maze. As soon as she was safely inside, she intended for her footman to follow Mr. Donovan and find out the real reason why he was here.

"Well, now, I don't know as I'm believing ye, lad." Mrs. Marlock planted her hands upon her broad waist. "Lady Wolcroft said naught about a houseguest arriving from Ireland. But if'n I'm wrong, I'd be a fair sight embarrassed to turn ye out again. I suppose ye mun have some clothes, aye?"

"Aye, that is true enough." Iain was well aware of his impoverished appearance, but there was naught to be done about it. "If I could speak with Lady Wolcroft, I'm certain she will sort it all out."

Mrs. Marlock tilted her head to the side as if assessing his story. Her gray hair was bound and pinned up beneath a cap. She reminded him of a soldier, though she had a ring of house keys instead of a sword at her plump waist. "Lady Wolcroft isn't here, and I can't be certain when she'll return from Bath."

Bath? Why had she gone there after she'd invited him to come visit? Well, now this was a fine kettle of fish. He had no clothes, no money, no signet ring, and no one to welcome him to Penford.

The housekeeper continued, "Have ye any other proof of who ye are?"

No, he had nothing at all. He'd been stripped of everything, may the thieves be eaten in tiny pieces, bite by bite. Iain's frustration rose up, but he forced himself to tamp it down. The last thing he needed was to frighten the housekeeper.

He searched for a believable lie. "My servants will be arriving today with my belongings, once my coach is repaired," he said smoothly. "That should be all the proof you need." He spoke calmly, keeping his tone even so as not to intimidate Mrs. Marlock. If he gave her any reason to doubt him, she would throw him out.

He was on borrowed time, and he had no means of proving his identity. If Lady Wolcroft were here, there was some chance she might recognize him. But no one else would.

The housekeeper didn't appear convinced. "Ye say ye've come from Ireland, is that so?"

"I come from Ashton," he answered. "In County Mayo." For a moment, he waited to see if she had other questions. When she said nothing, he added, "I imagine Lady Wolcroft may have spoken of my mother, Moira, has she not? Or my brother, Michael, God rest him?"

Mrs. Marlock folded her arms and frowned. "Nay, she hasn't." She eyed him as if trying to make a decision. At last, she said, "Well, there could be some truth in what ye say, but until Lady Wolcroft returns, I can't be letting a stranger into the house. Ye can return in a few days, and see if she's back home again."

Her refusal didn't surprise him at all. But he didn't want to be turned out in the middle of Yorkshire with no shelter, no money, and no food. Thinking quickly, he decided upon an alternative. "I'll swear to you that I *am* the Earl of Ashton. Allow me to stay this night, and once my servants arrive at Penford, I should be glad to compensate you handsomely for the trouble." He wasn't quite certain how he'd manage it, but he would find a way.

The housekeeper only smiled. "And when the Queen arrives, she'll offer me proof that I'm her long-lost daughter." With a shake of her head, she added, "Nay, sir, ye'd best go now. I'm certain ye can find someone in the village who'll be giving ye a place to bide for a wee bit."

Iain highly doubted it, given his state of undress. No, it was far better to talk Mrs. Marlock into letting him remain at Penford. "And what if I offered to . . . that is—" He hesitated, wondering if it would hurt his cause to lower himself further.

What choice do you have? he thought to himself. *No one knows who you are.*

He bit back his pride and asked, "What if I gave you my assistance on the estate? At least until my servants can prove who I am." It was the best compromise he could give. He'd done his share of menial labor on Ashton, after most of the tenants had left or died. It had been unavoidable, and he would set aside his pride if it meant gaining shelter for the night.

Mrs. Marlock frowned, crossing her arms as she stared at him. "I already asked ye to leave, sir. Ye've no references, and despite yer manner of speech, ye're a stranger among us. There's no place for ye here."

Iain straightened and regarded her with all seriousness. "Mrs. Marlock, what will Lady Wolcroft say to you when she learns that you turned away her guest?"

The old woman hesitated, and her uncertainty made him press further. "All I ask is to remain here for a single day. I need not stay in the main house, if it makes you uncomfortable."

She narrowed her gaze. "I don't know ye, sir. And it's our butler, Mr. Fulton, ye'll have to speak with. I cannot give ye a place to stay within this household. It's nae possible."

"A few hours, then," he bargained. "Just until my servants arrive."

Though he had no desire to sleep outside, if he couldn't convince Mrs. Marlock or Fulton that he was the earl, he'd have no choice. And while he might be a slightly adventurous sort, sleeping on the moors would be colder than the devil's conscience.

He sent her a warm smile, and added, "You do seem to be a charitable woman, Mrs. Marlock. I know you'd not ask a guest to sleep out in the freezing rain when there's shelter to be had."

"There's no rain today, lad," she said. "And ye'll find a place in the village, as I said before. If ye *are* the earl, they'll be glad to help ye." Her tone suggested that she didn't at all believe him. But as proof of her charity, she handed him a large hunk of bread. Iain tore off a piece, devouring the food, since he hadn't eaten in hours.

He wasn't going to give up on gaining a place to sleep. Not when he was convinced that he could prove himself by evening at the latest. All he needed to find was the signet ring that had been stolen.

When he'd finished the bread, he asked, "What of clothing, Mrs. Marlock?" He lowered his arms to his side, giving her a full view of his bare skin. "I can't be going around with naught to wear."

A faint blush rose over her cheeks and she sighed at last. "I suppose ye're right, at that. I'll see what rags we have, before ye gang to the village."

"I am grateful indeed. And thank you for the food." He inclined his head, and she eyed him as if not knowing what to do. In the end, she bobbed her own curtsy.

"Hattie!" she called out. One of the maids hurried inside the kitchen, a *cailín* of about sixteen. The girl sent him a curious look, and her gaze slid over his bare torso in open admiration. Though he rather felt like a roasted goose on display, Iain said nothing, in case the maid turned out to be an unexpected ally.

Mrs. Marlock said, "Stop yer gawpin, Hattie, and fetch the man some clothes."

The maid blushed and gave an embarrassed smile before hurrying away. Though Iain kept his expression masked, Mrs. Marlock moved in front of him and glared. "Once yer dressed, ye'll be leaving Penford. If ye *are* her ladyship's guest, ye'll get a full apology from me at that time." The look on her face said she doubted he would return.

"You'll see," he told her. "I will be dining at your table tonight." Once he had located his stolen belongings, he was confident that they would accept him.

Mrs. Marlock offered nothing more than an indignant "humph."

A few minutes later, Hattie brought him a ragged shirt and an equally tattered coat, along with a pair of shoes. Given the young girl's age and her attire that was slightly better than a kitchen maid's, he surmised she was a maid-of-all-work. And although he doubted if anything would fit, it was better than remaining half-naked and unshod. Iain thanked her for the clothes.

Unfortunately, it seemed he would be spending the next few hours out of doors, wearing servant's rags. A fine day this was turning out to be.

You never expected it to be easy, he reminded himself. *Why should they believe you're an earl? Without any proof, how could they?*

He put on the ill-fitting shirt, coat, and shoes, taking the time he needed to make plans. Although he had hoped his men would join him here, it was beginning to seem that they had abandoned him. And with no servants to vouch for him, his circumstances had become dire indeed.

But he would never give up. Too many people were dependent on him.

After he was dressed, he followed Hattie down the servants' hallway. She turned to him and with a hopeful smile said, "I do wish you well, sir." Pointing to the door at the end, she added, "You can go out that way."

He eyed the door and then regarded the maid for a moment. "Do you believe that I am the Earl of Ashton, though I'm looking as if I'd been dragged through the midden heap?"

Hattie appeared uncomfortable and lowered her gaze. "It—it's not for me to be sayin', sir." With that, she continued leading him toward the back door.

He didn't argue with her, for she was only obeying orders. His mind was already conjuring up where he would stay this night. Possibly in the stables or somewhere sheltered. He hadn't a single coin to call his own, so no one in the village would give him a place.

Iain had only walked a few steps when he heard a woman screaming. The piercing noise made it sound as if she were being attacked. He didn't stop to ask questions, but hurried up the stairs leading to the hall. He found a middle-aged woman running toward the front door, her hair tangled and hanging down her back. She wore a long-sleeved blue serge gown and her eyes were wild. Far too young to be Lady Wolcroft, he guessed, but it could be the woman's daughter.

"Lady Penford!" Hattie exclaimed, rushing forward to her aid. "Please . . . let me help you."

Iain looked around to see what the woman was fleeing from, but there was nothing at all.

The woman's face was deathly white, and her hands shook badly. When Hattie put her hand out, Lady Penford gripped it hard. "Please, you have to help me! The—the wolves. I heard them howling. They're coming for me."

The maid sent a look toward Iain and shook her head in warning. Though Iain wasn't certain what was happening, it was clear that Lady Penford was suffering from visions that weren't real.

The woman started to bolt again, and Hattie tried to stop her, holding her by the waist. "My lady, no. You mustn't leave the house."

Whatever illness had captured her mind, Lady Penford might injure herself if she was allowed to flee. And though it wasn't his business, Iain stepped toward the doorway to keep her from escaping.

"Let me go," Lady Penford insisted, wrenching her way free of the maid. But when she moved toward the front door, Iain remained in place to block her. He sensed that this woman was trapped in a world of her own imaginings, one where reality made little sense.

"Where are the wolves?" he asked calmly. He kept his voice quiet, as though soothing a wounded animal.

His question seemed to break through Lady Penford's hysteria, and she faltered. "They—they were chasing me." Her face held confusion, and she appeared unaware that he was a stranger.

"Would you feel safer in your room?" he asked. "Perhaps Hattie could take you there."

"No." Her breathing grew unsteady. "I can't go back there. The wolves will find me." She gripped her hands together and took another step toward the door. "Summon my coach."

He met Hattie's gaze, and she moved closer to Lady Penford. Iain took another step backward to prevent her from reaching the door.

A slight noise caught his attention at the top of the stairs, and he saw Lady Rose being carried by a footman. "Mother, please wait a moment." Her face paled at the sight of the matron, and she ordered, "Calvert, take me downstairs."

It sobered him to realize how difficult Lady Rose's life must be, having to rely on others to carry her where she wanted to go. The simple act of helping her mother would be quite beyond her abilities.

When she saw Iain standing by the door, her face tightened in dismay. Color flooded her cheeks as if she was embarrassed that he had witnessed her mother's outburst. Hattie brought a chair close to Lady Penford, and the footman set Lady Rose upon it, retreating to a discreet distance.

"Are you all right?" the young woman asked. In her voice, there was the gentle tone of compassion, no censure for the madness. She held out her hand, but Lady Penford ignored it.

At this close proximity, Iain noticed that Lady Rose's eyes were the color of warm sherry. A few tendrils of reddish-brown hair framed her lovely face, and he found himself wanting to ease her worry.

"Did you hear me, Mother?"

Lady Penford gave no answer, but she stared down at her trembling hands.

"I was just talking with Lady Penford about the wolves," Iain said, as if there were nothing at all wrong. He fixed his gaze upon the young woman, hoping she would play along, since the older woman seemed to be caught up in confusion.

But Lady Rose paid him no mind. "Everything is all right now, Mother. I am here." She reached out a hand, but the woman ignored it.

"I'm afraid," her mother admitted. Her eyes welled up with tears, and she twisted her hands together. "So afraid."

He glanced over at Lady Rose and saw her flushed cheeks. The maid and footman eyed one another before casting their gazes downward. Clearly the woman's madness was not a new occurrence.

"Is there anything I can do to help?" Iain asked.

The older woman turned back to him, and her mood suddenly shifted. "I've not seen you before. Do you know my son James? Is that why you are here? Has he returned from India?" Her voice was edged with emotion, and he suspected that grief and worry had led her into this agitated state.

Iain risked a glance toward Rose, who shook her head. It wasn't clear whether her brother was dead or gone, but he decided not to upset the woman any more than necessary. It was simple enough to continue with the ruse. "I might have seen him. Will you remind me of what he looks like?"

A sudden moment of clarity passed over the woman's face, and her expression filled up with sorrow. "James has been gone for a long time. I pray he will return, but he hasn't answered my letters. He must come back, you see. He is the new Earl of Penford." Her voice lowered to a soft whisper. "Now that my husband is . . . gone, there is so much to do. So many decisions to be made, and I can't—I simply can't—" Lady Penford covered her mouth with her hands, panic rising in her expression.

"You needn't worry," Rose reassured her. "Lily and I will manage. Right now, I think you should go into the drawing room and have a cup of tea. Mrs. Marlock might have scones with clotted cream. Would you like that?"

The mention of food successfully diverted the matron's attention. "I—yes, that would be lovely."

"Hattie will take you to the drawing room, and we will join you there." Rose signaled for the maid to come forward, and Hattie guided Lady Penford down the hallway.

When her mother was gone, Rose turned back to Iain, and her expression held sadness. "Thank you for stopping her from leaving. She's been grieving ever since my father died."

He nodded. "She seemed very upset." *And not in her right mind,* he thought, but didn't say so. "Will she be all right?"

Rose sighed and straightened in the chair. "No one knows the answer to that question. There are good days and bad days."

He glanced back at the footman. "Do you need assistance? That is, if you wish to join her, I could—" But he stopped short, realizing how inappropriate it would be for him to carry her.

Lady Rose didn't appear to take offense, but simply answered, "Calvert will bring me there." Then she glanced at Iain's bedraggled clothing with a questioning look. "Do you still claim to be an Irish earl, sir?" Her words held a dry humor, and the look in her eyes said she didn't believe him at all.

Iain's mouth twisted in a smile. "My name is Lord Ashton, *a chara.* And you'll have to wait and see, won't you?"

Chapter Two

Rose wasn't certain what to believe of this gentleman who claimed to be an earl. He lacked the deferential manners of a servant, especially after he'd taken charge of her mother's hysteria and calmed her. Even wearing rags, he *did* appear to be something more. But everything about him was improper, from his speech to his lack of formality. She simply couldn't believe that he was a nobleman—not without his own coach and servants.

Lord Ashton, was he? More like Lord of the Ashes.

Despite his appearance, he intrigued her. And yes, he *was* quite handsome, in a forbidden sort of way. The way he'd smiled at her was both wicked and filled with promises of dark corners and secret liaisons. His dark hair needed to be trimmed, and his cheeks held the stubble of a beard, making her wonder what it would be like to touch it.

Her mind was wandering as badly as her mother's. Why was he truly here? And who was he?

Calvert brought her into the drawing room to join her mother. Her sister, Lily, arrived shortly afterward. Rose met her sister's questioning look, and she shook her head slightly to let her know that this was not a good day. *Tread softly, Lily.*

"Mother, would you like tea?" her sister asked brightly, reaching for the silver teapot.

Iris's face had gone distant, and Lily had to repeat herself twice more before their mother blinked and turned to face them. "What was that? Oh, yes, tea. With milk and sugar, if you please."

Lily prepared the tea and sat beside their mother as she offered her the cup. Iris did appear calmer, but neither of them wanted to say anything to bring back the fearful visions.

"Are you feeling well today, Mother?" Lily poured another cup for Rose and set it before her.

"Yes, I am much better now. But who was that new gentleman I saw a moment ago?"

Dash it all, she'd hoped her mother would forget all about Lord of the Ashes. Her sister sent her a curious look, for she had not seen the stranger who had arrived at Penford. Rose decided it was best to say nothing.

"He's no one, Mother. You needn't worry." She didn't want her mother distracted or afraid of a stranger.

"A new gentleman?" Lily prompted.

Don't, Rose warned her silently, raising an eyebrow. Now was not the time to discuss it.

But Iris turned and sent her a mysterious smile. "He *was* rather dashing. I'm not blind, my dear. Was he here to pay a call on you?" Before she could tell her mother no and attempt to change the subject, Lady Penford continued, "You *are* in need of a husband, after all, Rose."

An unbidden rush of embarrassment gathered inside her, and Lily interrupted them. "Not now, Mother. It's too soon." Her sister distracted Iris with a sugar biscuit, redirecting their conversation to a new gown she planned to have made. *Thank you, Lily.*

But even so, it hurt that her mother would say something so thoughtless when Rose already had a suitor. Her eyes welled up with tears, and she blinked hard to hold them back.

I will not cry. But the very thought of Lord Burkham made her emotional, for she missed him so much. He had been on the verge of offering for her when she had fallen ill in Yorkshire. The terrible sickness had forced her to battle for her life, and when it was over, she was left too weak to move. Thomas had sent letters over the past few months, wishing her well. She was confident that when she could walk again, he would ask her to marry him.

Rose refused to surrender to a life where she had to be carried like a child. No matter how long it took, she would not return to London until she could walk. Perhaps it was her pride, but she didn't want Thomas to see her as an invalid.

"You really ought to return to London for the Season," Iris continued. "You are such a lovely young woman. Any gentleman would be glad to marry someone as sweet as you."

Rose tried to muster a smile, but it felt as if a weight were crushing her chest. Iris seemed to have forgotten all about her inability to walk. "I cannot return for a few more months. But Lily might wish to go."

"No, I—I would rather not attend the Season," Lily stammered. Her sister sat down and chose a large tea cake, stuffing it into her mouth to avoid further conversation. Then she gathered two more and piled them upon her plate, making it clear that she would continue eating so she would not have to speak. Rose raised an eyebrow at the pile of food, but Lily sent her a pained smile. Both of them were in the same dilemma, truthfully. They had already selected their future husbands; it was simply that fate had intervened.

Lily had been avoiding marriage ever since Matthew Larkspur, the Earl of Arnsbury, had gone missing. Rose was certain she was waiting for the gentleman to return . . . if he ever did. Her sister pined for Lord Arnsbury, and she seemed eager to shut herself away from society to avoid choosing someone else.

Iris sipped at her tea, and she suddenly sent Rose a gentle smile. "It will be all right, my darlings. Both you and your sister will one day marry the men of your dreams. I believe that."

In that moment, their mother no longer appeared to be the same woman who was fleeing from imaginary wolves. Instead, the moment of clarity revealed a woman who was once again trying to find happiness for her daughters.

Rose searched in desperation for another topic of conversation. "Do you suppose it will rain today?"

"Now, do not try to change the subject," Iris chided. "You are my eldest daughter, and it's high time you were wed. How old are you now? Twenty?"

"Twenty-three," she murmured.

Her mother frowned. "No, that's not possible." As she began trying to convince her that she was only twenty, Rose pasted a smile on her face and let her thoughts drift. She didn't want to think about the undeniable fact that she was likely to remain a spinster unless she learned to walk again.

She hadn't given up—not at all. Every day she practiced standing, and though her legs would not yet support her weight, she refused to abandon hope. She had to rebuild her strength, and if force of will would move her legs, then she would indeed walk again.

"It is unlikely, but not impossible," the doctor had said. And Rose had held fast to that fragment of hope, needing to believe it.

Outside, she saw movement, and when she focused her gaze, she realized it was the Irishman, Mr. Donovan. It appeared that he was walking toward the stables.

Now what was he doing? Her curiosity was piqued, and more than anything, she wanted to follow him.

But being unable to walk meant that she was never alone. She could go nowhere without help, and she didn't exactly want the footman to think she was infatuated with the man-who-claimed-to-be-an-earl. No, she was merely intrigued by his story—that was all.

"Rose, what is your opinion?" Lily interrupted her thoughts, and she jerked her attention back to them.

"I—that is, whatever you think would be best."

"Excellent." Iris beamed at her. "This will be most splendid."

Now what exactly had she agreed to? When she risked a glimpse at Lily, her sister was wincing and shaking her head. Oh dear.

Rose cleared her throat, waiting for her mother to elaborate. Iris finished her tea, looking entirely too satisfied. "Very well, then. Both of you will go to London as soon as your grandmother returns. And by the end of the summer, I shall expect one or both of you to have a husband."

London? No, not that. She'd rather be devoured by the aforementioned wolves.

Iris rose to her feet and was already talking about the details of the upcoming Season. "I shall speak with Mrs. Marlock about ordering new gowns for both of you. And then . . . I won't have to worry so much." Her voice trailed away softly as she reached the doorway.

The moment their mother was gone, Lily let out a groan. "London? Rose, what were you thinking?"

"I wasn't listening," she confessed. "I was distracted."

"Obviously." Her sister stood and began pacing. "We have to convince her that she only imagined it. We are not going to London to be married off. Especially me."

"Because of Lord Arnsbury?" she ventured.

Lily's face flushed, and there was a flash of grief. "He might come back. And if he does . . ." There were years of hope bound up in that wish, for her sister loved the earl with all her being. But it had been nearly two years since he'd disappeared. The chances of him returning were growing slimmer each day, and she didn't ask what Lily would do if he never came back.

"Whether or not he does, we have a problem." Rose used both of her arms to press hard against the chair, attempting to stand again. "Lily, help me up."

Her sister came to support her waist, and in her expression, Rose saw sympathy. "Are you certain you can stand?"

"My arms are getting stronger." She *would* manage somehow.

But her sister took a step back. "Oughtn't you to ask Calvert? He's stronger than I and could help if you stumbled."

With reluctance, Rose lowered herself back down. "No. Never mind." Though she understood that Lily didn't believe she could stand, it dimmed her spirits. Her throat tightened, and she took a deep breath. "What should we do about Mother?"

"I think we should behave as if she never brought it up. Pretend she never suggested any of it. Like the wolves. She won't remember in the morning."

"I suppose so." Rose risked a glance out the window again, and it bothered her that she had lost sight of Mr. Donovan. Where was he now? She craned her neck, but still could not see him.

"*What* is it that has you so distracted, Rose?" Lily peered outside the window and then turned back. "It's him, isn't it? The gentleman you spoke of."

She sighed. "Well, yes. Mr. Donovan claims he's an earl, but I don't believe him."

Lily wrinkled her nose. "An earl? Why would he say such a thing?"

"I have no idea. But I wonder why he's truly here." The logical explanation was that he was attempting to insinuate himself within their household for a nefarious purpose. And yet . . . she didn't quite believe that.

Her sister's knuckles tightened on the window, and she shook her head. "Oh no."

"What?" Rose couldn't see anything from her vantage point.

"It seems that you were right about Mr. Donovan. I don't think he's an earl at all."

It was maddening being unable to see, and Rose used all her strength to hoist her weight against the arms of the chair. "Why would you say that, Lily?"

Lily turned back with an apologetic look. "Because he's stealing one of our horses."

Iain urged the gelding into a hard gallop, guiding the horse toward the spot where he'd been robbed. Behind him, he heard the sounds of men yelling, "Stop, thief!"

Which was ironic, really, because this was *his* horse, even if no one here would believe him. He'd been shocked to find Darcy inside the stables, where he'd been intending to conceal himself for the night. Someone had put the gelding in one of the stalls, and that meant the boys were nearby. This time, Iain intended to confront them and seize the rest of his missing belongings.

More than all else, he needed that signet ring. Or at the very least, the letter from Lady Wolcroft inviting him to Penford.

He was convinced that the robbery was adolescent mischief. They had somehow knocked him from his horse—possibly with a rope strung between the trees—and had entertained themselves by stripping him of everything.

Iain, however, was not amused. Their trickery had cost him his identity, and he would hunt them down until he had everything back.

He leaned in, searching his surroundings for a sign of the boys. The afternoon sun was blinding, but he found the lake easily enough. The road grew narrower, and at last, he spied one of the boys walking alone. He looked to be about thirteen or so and was wearing Iain's coat. The moment he heard Iain coming up behind him, he broke into a run.

Not fast enough.

Iain leaned down and seized the boy, dragging him atop his horse. The lad was skinny, and though he fought, Iain gripped him hard. "You're not going anywhere. Not until you've returned everything you stole from me."

"I didn't steal anything. I was bringing it back," the boy complained.

"Like the clothes you're wearing? And what did you do with my signet ring?" Iain had no sympathy for him. The lad had questions he was going to answer. "I'm thinking we should speak to your father about this."

The boy sent him a sly smile. "He's not at home." The gleeful expression on his face made it obvious that he *wanted* Iain to take him home.

Perhaps it was better to take a different tack. "Then you'll be coming with me. Unless you want to return my ring first?"

He didn't truly know *what* he would do with the boy, but he wasn't about to let the lad go free. Not until he had answers.

"I don't have it." To prove his point, the boy showed his empty hands.

"Then where is it?" he demanded. The boy's answer was a shrug. His expression remained defiant, as if he intended to hold his silence.

Iain reached inside the coat pockets, and not only was the ring missing, but also the letter from Lady Wolcroft. Damn it all, that was the proof he needed. And the smug expression on the lad's face only irritated him.

Continuing this line of questioning would lead him nowhere. It was unlikely the boy would tell him anything. Iain decided to try a different tactic. He gripped the boy in the saddle and turned Darcy back toward Penford. The servants there might know who he was and what to do with him. Iain could also summon the boy's father if need be.

As they rode onward, the lad remarked, "Are you kidnapping me?" The hopeful tone made it sound as if he was eager to be abducted.

He decided not to answer the question, since it was clear that the boy was unafraid of anything. Threats would do no good whatsoever, and until Iain found out what the boy valued, he would get none of his possessions returned. He continued riding toward Penford and asked, "Why did you and your companion steal my belongings?"

"I didn't steal anything. The horse followed me, so I decided to take him to Penford. It's probably where he came from."

Iain didn't believe that for a moment. "And what about my clothing? You just happened to find it and take it from me?"

"I *did* find it. It was on the ground near the stream where I found the horse."

The boy's story was filled with holes. Someone had knocked him from his horse and robbed him. And he just "happened" to find Iain's horse and coat? No, not a word of his story was true.

"You're lying, lad."

The boy lowered his shoulders and gave a dramatic sigh. Rolling his eyes, he said, "You're right, of course. I dragged you from your horse, and then I stole it and your clothing to trade for food for my family."

"At least your second story is more believable. Aside from needing food." Iain turned the boy's palm over. This was a lad who had hardly worked a day in his life. His fingernails were neatly pared and no dirt was beneath them. Not to mention his speech held the air of nobility. "You've never gone hungry in your life."

"And how would *you* know?"

The boy's taunt awakened the dark memories without warning. Iain had seen far more hunger than he'd ever dreamed of—and those nightmares would be with him always. Too many of his friends had weakened and died. Though Ashton had not suffered as much as other areas, the lack of food had devastated the tenants. Iain would never forget the cries of the children, or the wailing of their mothers when an infant succumbed to starvation.

"Because I have seen people die from hunger. And you're nowhere close to that."

The boy seemed to sense the shift in his mood and said nothing. He also stopped struggling on the horse.

"What is your name?" Iain asked. "And you'd best be telling me the truth because Lady Penford's servants will know who you are, won't they?"

The boy hesitated, but admitted, "My name is Beau." The lad didn't offer anything further, but Iain was convinced that he was a nobleman's son. Everything from the boy's speech, to his disdain for authority, spoke of breeding.

In the countryside, everyone knew everyone. If he caused a stir or demanded justice, they likely would defend their own, for *he* was the outsider here. But the lad appeared to have little respect for consequences, and it was likely that he had played tricks of this nature before.

It took only moments to reach the estate, where he found the coachman waiting for him. The man's face was purple with fury, and other servants had gathered around.

"What the devil is going on?" the coachman demanded. "First ye go off with one of our—" He paused a moment and inspected the gelding. His expression transformed and some of his anger faded. "This isn't one of our horses."

"No. He's *my* horse, Darcy," Iain said. "And I'll be taking him back to the stables now." He dismounted and pulled Beau off the horse, still gripping him by the arm. "This lad stole him from me, along with my clothes."

With that, he stripped the boy of the coat. The fabric was torn near the hem, and it was filthy. He glared at Beau, folding the coat under his arm. "He and his friend thought it would be a lark to steal." An idea sparked suddenly, one that perfectly fit the boy's crime. "And since he stole my horse, I believe he'll be spending the afternoon mucking out your stables as punishment."

The coachman looked uneasy about the prospect. "Well, I don't rightly know. Is this true, Master Beauregard?"

The boy lifted his chin. "I didn't steal anything. I found them."

"I'm certain your parents would be wanting to know of your mischief," Iain remarked. "You and your friend."

"As I've said before, my father isn't here." His tone held a note of triumph, as if no one could hold him accountable.

"Sir Lester should return within a day or two," the coachman remarked.

Iain realized he'd been right about the boy's family. Beau was either the son of a knight or a baronet.

Yet at the mention of his father, the boy grew defensive. "He wouldn't believe any of you. And if I find out anyone has told him, every last one of you will be dismissed." He stiffened and shot a glare at all of them, fixing his final stare upon Iain.

"I cannot be dismissed,'" Iain said to the coachman. "Can I?"

The older man's mouth twitched. It was clear that he found the boy's threat irritating. "Nay, you cannot." Especially since Iain was not employed by the household.

Before the coachman could say anything further, Iain said, "Then there is no problem with him spending the afternoon shoveling horse droppings, as punishment, is there? I will take it upon myself to see that he does a fine job of it." Without waiting for a reply, he guided the boy back toward the stables. He caught a glimpse of amusement from the servants, and not one of them voiced their protest. Like as not, this was a rare chance for the boy to face consequences.

As he glanced behind him one last time, he saw a face pressed up to a window of the house. It was Lady Rose, watching them. Iain sent her a smile and bowed slightly, before he escorted the boy into the stables.

It was nearly sunset when Rose finally got up the nerve to visit the stables. Calvert wasn't at all happy about it, but he had no choice in the matter. "It's too dark to be riding, Lady Rose. I can take you in the morning, if you like."

But she wasn't here to ride. She had waited for Mr. Donovan to leave the stables, fully expecting him to be on his way. Yet hours had passed, and no one seemed surprised that he was still here. It was as if he'd bewitched the servants into believing his tale.

All she knew was that he'd returned with the horse. It seemed that it had been a misunderstanding of some kind, and somehow Sir Lester's son, Beauregard, had been involved.

"I want to know why Mr. Donovan is still here," she said. Calvert shrugged. Her footman had never been much for conversation, and at the moment, it frustrated her to no end. "Well?"

"He's supervising whilst the boy mucks out the stables, so I've heard."

"Why on earth would they be doing that? I thought he'd left hours ago."

The footman seemed at a loss for words. When he couldn't gather up an explanation, Rose waved her hand in dismissal. "Just take me to the stables, and I'll find out for myself."

The footman grumbled about her orders, but he reluctantly obeyed. He carried her through the gardens, and as he walked, Rose tried to think of what to say to Mr. Donovan. She should ask him to leave again, but curiosity was overruling her common sense. Well, that, and the fact that the man was the most handsome servant she'd ever seen.

When they reached the stables at last, the door was ajar. The strong odor of horse manure assaulted her nostrils, and she found Donovan standing beside Beauregard. The young boy wore a furious expression, and he was covered in filth. Perspiration had dampened his shirt, and he shoveled another pile of manure while the Irishman watched.

"Nearly finished, lad. You've paid the price for your folly, I'd say. If you're wanting to tell me where my ring is, you can stop."

Beau didn't respond to the comment, but instead continued shoveling. It was the first time she'd ever seen him engaged in any kind of labor. His face was thunderous, but he had filled a wheelbarrow with droppings. The coachman, Nelson, was busy trimming one of the horse's hooves near the far end of the stable.

Mr. Donovan turned when he heard them enter. "Lady Rose, it's glad I am to see you once again. Although I'm not so very presentable at the moment." He sent her a rueful grin. She noticed, then, that he was wearing a different coat. It was still dirty and a bit worn, but it *did* have more of the look of a nobleman than the rags he'd worn earlier.

"Why is Beauregard working in the stables?" she asked. And why was the Irishman overseeing the boy's efforts? It wasn't his place to do so if he had been ordered to leave the estate.

"This young lad robbed me of my horse and belongings when I arrived here," Mr. Donovan explained. "He agreed to muck out the stables as punishment for his mischief. And in the morning, he will bring back everything that belongs to me. That is, unless he wishes to clean the stables again."

Rose doubted if Beauregard had "agreed" to anything. But strangely, he *had* completed the task. She studied his face, but the boy refused to meet her gaze. Instead, he shoveled another heap of dung, ignoring both of them.

"Where is your father, Beauregard?" she asked the boy.

At that, he turned, and shot her a glare. "He was supposed to return three days ago."

Mr. Donovan caught her gaze, and Rose understood his silent nod. She had the feeling that he had also promised not to tell Sir Lester of his son's misdeeds. For a moment, his green eyes lingered upon hers, and she could almost sense his thoughts: *The boy needs his father.*

They all knew it. Beauregard constantly caused trouble, due to his father's lengthy absences. Most of the folk were thankful when he returned to school after the holidays. Which made her wonder why Beau was here, instead of at Eton. She didn't voice her suspicions, but instead remarked, "Won't your family be looking for you, Beau?"

"There's naught to be worried about," Mr. Donovan said. "I sent word to his household that he was paying a call upon you and your sisters and would be back at nightfall."

Beauregard shot him a sullen look, and rested his shovel against the stall. "My father *will* be angry at you for this when he returns. I told you, I wasn't the one who stole from you." He grumbled beneath his breath, muttering something about a horse that had followed him.

Mr. Donovan ignored the threat and added, "You missed a spot in the corner, lad. Finish it, and then we'll bring you home. After you've washed up, that is."

"We?" Rose asked.

"Aye, *a chara.* You can accompany us when I take the lad home again. Then we'll talk, and you can ask me all the questions you're wanting to." He strode over to the end of the stables and brought out Molly, one of the older mares. "Bring Calvert as a chaperone, if you'd like."

"That would be *Mister* Calvert to you," the footman corrected with a glare. Iain only ignored the man.

But the coachman stepped away from the horse he was tending and intervened. "Lady Rose needn't go anywhere," Nelson argued. "Especially with the likes of you."

At the sight of the mare, Lady Rose hesitated. "I don't know. I haven't been riding in some time, and—" Her words broke away. From the look on her footman's face, she could tell that he had no desire to go anywhere. Nelson also seemed unwilling to condone it.

But then, it was her decision, was it not?

"It's not so very far, is it, lad?" Though Mr. Donovan directed the words to Beauregard, he never took his gaze from hers. His green eyes held interest, and she felt a prickle of awareness toward the man. His shirt was damp with perspiration, and it outlined rigid muscles. She wondered exactly how strong he was, and a blush stole over her face. Even Lord Burkham had never looked at her in such a way . . . as if he were trying to know her intimately. The thought unnerved her.

"It's about three miles," Rose heard herself answer. Her brain argued that she had no business escorting Beauregard home—not with this man. He was an Irish stranger whose flirtatious demeanor was entirely improper.

And yet, she'd felt so trapped in the past few weeks, any outing was a welcome opportunity—even if it was only for a chance to leave the estate. She was so weary of being inside, unable to move or go anywhere without the curmudgeonly Calvert.

"Three miles isn't a long journey at all. And it is a fine evening, to be sure." Mr. Donovan reached for one of the saddles and began readying Molly.

Nelson started to protest, but Lady Rose lifted a hand and shook her head at the coachman. It was not his place to deny her the right to ride.

Once Mr. Donovan had cinched the saddle, he beckoned to her. "Bring Lady Rose here," he told the footman, "and you can return to the house if you've no wish to go with her."

"I won't be leaving her with the likes of you," Calvert countered. And while Rose could understand his reasoning, the idea of a ride tempted her. It *was* a lovely evening, and despite her inner doubts, was there any harm in riding a few miles down the road? She didn't think so.

"Put me upon Molly," she ordered her footman. "I'll be fine."

"But, Lady Rose, you cannot consider this." Calvert appeared aghast at the idea. "You don't even know this man."

"No," she agreed. But she did want to know more about him and why he had come to Penford. It would give her the chance to ascertain whether he was telling the truth. "You are welcome to follow on your own mount, if you wish. Or Nelson can accompany me." The coachman looked uncomfortable at the idea.

Calvert also appeared uneasy. "I can't be leaving you alone with the Irishman."

"Then come with me." She pointed toward the mare. "But help me onto Molly first."

He brought her over to the horse, looking uneasy about her decision. Rose sent him a pointed look, reminding Calvert that he was in her employ. Eventually, he lifted her onto the mare. She sat sidesaddle and guided the animal to the door. "Thank you. I shall wait outside until you decide whether to attend me yourself or send another servant."

The footman sent her a weary look, but nodded. "I know my duty, Lady Rose." With the greatest of reluctance, he went to fetch his own horse with the help of Nelson.

Mr. Donovan clapped his arm on Beauregard and followed. "Come, lad. We'll get you washed up before you go home."

Resentment was written all over the boy's face, but he obeyed. Rose guided the mare out of the stables and toward the path. A moment later, Mr. Donovan led the adolescent boy from the stable toward the water trough, and ordered the boy to strip off his shirt.

Beau looked disgruntled, but did as he was told, washing his face, arms, and torso. Donovan did the same, splashing water on his face and throat. Droplets of water spilled over his skin, while his hair was wet along his forehead and cheeks. He turned to her, as if he'd sensed her watching, and he sent her the pirate smile again.

Rose felt her cheeks warm, unsure of why she was so intrigued by this man. There was a sense of rebellion about him, as if he obeyed no rules but his own. But she felt her own mouth respond with an answering smile.

He's dangerous, she thought to herself. Her skin tightened, as if by an invisible caress. She followed the trail of a water droplet as it slid down his throat to his chest. Never before had she been so entranced by a man. It was better to avert her gaze, to prevent herself from imagining such wickedness.

She didn't understand her own reaction, for she should not be looking at Iain Donovan. He was a visitor, nothing more. Her heart belonged to Thomas, and this was nothing but idle foolishness.

The mare started to graze as she waited. Beauregard finished washing, while the Irishman helped Calvert saddle up their horses.

When Mr. Donovan returned, he was riding the black gelding he'd taken earlier, while Nelson led a second horse outside. The coachman helped Beauregard mount the animal, while Calvert followed on his own horse. Then Mr. Donovan drew his gelding beside her mare. Although their horses were of similar size, he was still far taller than she.

"This is Darcy," he told her. She leaned over to touch the horse, and the gelding snorted.

"He's beautiful."

"He's friendly enough. But I can't say as he's the most intelligent horse I've ever had." He sent her a conspiratorial smile. "Frightened of everything, he is."

"Then why did you choose him?" Most men would take a spirited stallion instead of this one.

"Because no one else wanted him." He gave the horse's jaw a friendly pat. "He may not have the wits of a field mouse, but he's a good sort, is Darcy." With that, he gestured for her to move forward. "Lead on, Lady Rose."

She did, and oh, it felt wonderful to be ambulatory, even if it was only on horseback. Rose breathed in the evening air, sighing with thankfulness. For a moment, she pretended that her legs were whole, that she was not dependent upon others. She held fast to the dream, knowing that it would end as soon as Calvert helped her dismount.

But for now, it was enough.

She wanted to urge the horse faster, to feel the wind against her hair. That would only end the ride sooner, so she refrained. Instead, she drank in the sight of her surroundings, enjoying the sunlight as the last of the day disappeared. The dirt road meandered over hills and by the river, and she felt the breath of spring upon her face.

"You look as if you're starving to be outside," Mr. Donovan said. "How long has it been?"

She stiffened in the saddle. "I sit in the garden every day."

"How long has it been since you've left the estate?" he corrected.

"Since we arrived in early December." They had only a few neighbors who dwelled in the country, and when her mother's mental state had worsened, it had seemed prudent to bring her here, where it was private.

When Mr. Donovan looked as if he wanted to ply her with more questions, Rose patted the horse and urged the mare into a trot. He countered by bringing his horse alongside hers. "Are you afraid of me, Lady Rose?"

"Now why should I be afraid of a groom?" she countered. "That is who you are, am I right? You seem to know your way around a stable."

"You know that's not who I am." He kept his pace even with hers and sent her a dark smile. "I told you. I am the Earl of Ashton, and your grandmother invited me here."

She still didn't believe that. There were too many flaws in his story, most notably, the absence of servants. A peer would never arrive at an estate on horseback. And although he claimed that there was a coach accident and that he'd left his servants behind, she could never imagine an earl doing such a thing. For one, it was dangerous. For another, it made no sense at all.

"My grandmother isn't here," she reminded him. "Why would she invite you to come if she was on holiday in Bath?"

"She told me I was welcome to visit your family anytime this year. I sent word, but apparently my letter didn't arrive."

She glanced at him again, wondering if he might be telling the truth. Letters were frequently missed, so it was indeed conceivable. But she couldn't bring herself to trust him. At least, not yet.

"My grandmother is not a fool. If she does not believe your tale of being the Earl of Ashton, she'll toss you out on your ear."

"As you would like to do?" He shrugged. "You'll see, Lady Rose. She *has* met me, and your mother and mine were friends."

Highly unlikely. "Then why have I never heard of you?"

His expression grew shielded. "I've never been to England before, unlike my older brother."

She didn't miss the hint of pain when he mentioned a brother, but she didn't inquire about the family death. Yet his claim, that he had never visited England, struck her as preposterous. A younger son would have to visit London from time to time.

"So your family neglected you in your training to become the earl."

His hands tightened upon the reins of his horse. "That was their choice, not mine. And I intend to remedy that immediately." He glanced behind him at Beauregard. "This lad stole my brother's signet ring. So *he* knows I am the earl."

The boy let out an exasperated huff of air. "I never saw a ring. He probably *is* a groom. And I'll tell Father how he forced me to shovel dung. If you hadn't come when you did, he might have forced me to eat it."

The boy's resentful words were spoken as if he wanted Rose to be aghast at his misfortune. Mr. Donovan only laughed at the boy and said, "Hardly. But if you don't bring back everything in the morning, I might consider it."

He winked at Rose, and the harmless teasing unnerved her in a way she didn't understand. Even if, God help her, he *was* an earl, he would never spend this much time flirting with a woman like her.

Unless he desired her fortune.

Yes, that was undoubtedly the reason. He hardly knew her at all, and she couldn't even walk. She decided to ignore his flirting, for it meant nothing.

They continued riding down the dirt road, and she grew quiet, savoring the evening light. The sky was transforming from a soft blue into a darker indigo. Upon the horizon, the setting sun gleamed its golden rays.

Beauregard looked as if he wanted to ride on ahead of them, but Mr. Donovan kept him close, holding the reins of his horse.

"I can go home on my own," the young man asserted. "I know the way."

"Children should be seen and not heard," was Iain Donovan's answer. Rose had to hide her smile at Beauregard's indignant glare.

"I'm not a child."

"Aye, you are. Only a child bent on mischief would be stealing a man's shirt and coat. Unless you believe yourself to be a man, in which case I'd have to bring you to the authorities for a more appropriate punishment."

Rose glanced back at Iain, wondering if he truly meant it. But she spied the amusement in his eyes.

"Go and ride alongside Calvert," he bade the young man. "But don't try to flee home without us, else I *will* drag you back."

For a fleeting moment, Beauregard looked uncertain of whether to accept the freedom. But he took advantage of the offer, guiding his mount back to ride alongside the footman. It gave Rose and Iain a slight measure of privacy to their conversation.

"Calvert, if the lad attempts to ride home on his own, bring him back to me," the Irishman ordered. The footman only shook his head and muttered.

"He's not very cooperative, is he?" Mr. Donovan said. "What about you, Lady Rose? If the boy attempts to flee, will you help me hunt him down?"

She started to argue, but then realized it was all in fun. With a serious nod, she said, "I shall send my mother's wolves after him."

A wide, appreciative smile slid over his face. "A fine idea, to be sure."

Though there was an easy tone to his voice, offering friendship, his eyes were watching her with interest. Her cheeks warmed, and she tried to pay it no mind. To shift his attention, she asked, "Where do you live in Ireland, Mr. Donovan?"

"In the west, not far from Connemara. There are mountains there, and green meadows so beautiful, they would break your heart." His expression held love, but there was also a trace of tension in his tone.

"I've heard stories about the famine," she said. "So many have left. Is it as bad as they say?"

His face grew somber, and his eyes remained fixed upon the road. An invisible shadow seemed to pass over him, and his tone darkened. "Worse than anyone could ever imagine."

"I'm sorry." She had heard about the hundreds of thousands of men and women leaving their homes. The workhouses were filled with the poor, and many Irish had sought work in textile mills and factories. Even then, there were not enough positions.

"There's hardly any food left in Ireland," he continued. "No one has money to buy anything. My mother and sisters went to New York to stay with family, while I came here."

"Will you join them there?"

He shook his head. "I made a promise to take care of the tenants at Ashton. I must return to them by the end of summer."

So he still maintained he was an earl. While it was indeed possible that he could possess a title, she didn't quite believe him. Instead, she kept the conversation centered on what she knew to be true. "Did you lose your crops?"

He fixed his gaze upon the road, expression grim. "The blight struck us hard, and a great deal of the land is wasted now. But we will bring back supplies and replant the fields."

"*We*?" Was there someone else who had come with him?

"My wife and I." He cast his gaze upon her again, and this time, *she* was the one who was surprised. Perhaps she'd been mistaken in thinking he had come to England in search of a wife.

"So . . . you're already married, then?" The thought seemed impossible, especially given the way he had been staring at her.

"Not yet. But if you're offering, *a chara,* I'd be glad to accept." He sent her a teasing smile, and it seemed that his mood had shifted from the earlier melancholy.

She sent him a wry look. "I was hardly proposing marriage, Mr. Donovan." She wasn't so desperate as that. "Besides, I already have a gentleman suitor."

"Have you?" His face brightened. "I cannot say I'm surprised to hear it. Any man would be honored to wed a *cailín* as fair as you."

Although his words were kind, she wasn't interested in idle flirting. "Yes, well. You can turn your interests somewhere else."

"Is he here, then? Your betrothed husband?"

"No, he's in London."

"I can't believe that's wise. Leaving a beautiful woman such as yourself at the mercy of the local swains. You might change your mind about marrying him."

She didn't bother to correct him, that Lord Burkham had not yet asked for her hand in marriage. It might be true enough one day soon. She wasn't going to fall prey to meaningless compliments when there were far more serious matters at hand.

"So you intend to find a bride with the help of my grandmother, is that it?" She wondered what sort of woman he hoped to woo. It wasn't going to be easy, for few women would marry a man who wanted her for nothing but money. Only someone quite desperate. Ireland lay in ruins, and it was unlikely that any woman would want to live there.

"Indeed. Unless you change your mind, that is." He reached out and took her gloved hand. His touch lingered upon her, warming the kidskin glove. When he stared into her eyes, she had a sudden rash thought that he was about to kiss her. Right here, in front of her footman and Beauregard.

"Keep your hands to yourself, Mr. Donovan. Or I shall be forced to whack you with a parasol."

"Or a rake," he suggested cheerfully. He winked at her, and she relaxed when she realized that he was only teasing her.

"I could be quite lethal with gardening tools. You don't want to imagine what I would do with a pair of shears."

He winced and made a face. "You terrify me."

Her smile widened. "You *should* be scared. I can be quite fierce when provoked."

"I can easily believe that." His green eyes locked upon hers. "You are a strong woman, Lady Rose. You would tell everyone to go and kiss the devil's backside before you'd turn away from your family or those who need you. Am I wrong?"

Rose blinked a moment at his assumption. No, he wasn't wrong that she would fight to the death to protect her loved ones. "It's true that I will always stand by my family." She straightened in the saddle and regarded him. Though she didn't know why she was telling him this, she felt the need to insist, "But more than that, I also intend to walk again."

He studied her for a moment as if he wanted to ask questions. But he simply gave a nod of acceptance. "You will."

His quiet confidence should have reassured her. But instead, she found herself confessing to him, "I am well aware that no man wishes to marry a woman who cannot walk. I've been trying for months, but no matter how hard I try, I fall. Every time. I just . . . don't know how long it will take for me to rebuild my strength."

"All you can do is get up and try again," he said. "If you want something badly enough, you won't give up."

She turned to look at him, and when she met his gaze, she saw a challenge there. "You're right. I suppose I have to keep trying—no matter how long it takes."

Chapter Three

After they had returned a scowling Master Beauregard to his home, Iain escorted Lady Rose back toward Penford. The boy had been correct that his father was not in residence. Iain learned from Lady Rose that Beau's mother had died four years ago, and Beau had been a hellion ever since.

Although the boy had paid the price for his thievery, Iain wasn't satisfied. He wanted the rest of his belongings returned to him—but that likely meant tracking down the other boy.

Lady Rose had grown quiet and had slowed her pace, taking a moment to look across the land.

"You should ride every day," Iain suggested. The freedom would do her a world of good. He couldn't imagine being bound by the whims of others.

"My sister is afraid I will fall and hurt myself even more." She glanced behind her at Calvert. The older footman had a resigned expression upon his face, and he looked displeased at this short outing.

"It is a risk, aye. But I'd say it's a sight better to be away from Penford and go where you're wanting to. You could take a groom with you instead of the dour Calvert."

She sent him a sidelong look. "Like yourself, were you suggesting?"

He shrugged. "I'm not a groom, but if you're wanting me to ride with you, I could indeed keep you safe." Though he knew she would need a chaperone in that event.

"I do not require anything from you, Mr. Donovan," she said.

"Lord Ashton," he corrected. Though she persisted in believing he was a liar and a beggar, he thought it better to correct her. It didn't matter that he bore little resemblance to an earl, given his bedraggled appearance. And it didn't matter that his mother had refused to have anything to do with him, wanting to hide him away from the world. He was her youngest son, and the heir to the estate.

Lady Rose's sigh made it clear that she still didn't believe him. So be it. He would not spend needless time trying to convince her. The truth would speak for itself.

When they reached Penford, Iain drew his horse to a stop and took her reins. "Shall I help you down?"

"Leave her be," came Calvert's annoyed reply. "I know my duties well enough, and you can let Lady Rose alone."

Iain inclined his head and then asked, "Should I be bedding down in the stable this night, Lady Rose?" The thought wasn't at all welcome, but at this late hour, it was better than seeking shelter from strangers in the village.

He cast one last look at the road, in the unlikely event that his long-lost servants returned. But there was no sign of anyone. In the morning, he would have to travel back to the place where the axle had broken on his coach. At least then, he would have answers.

A flash of something came over Lady Rose's face, but he couldn't tell what it was. Calvert had stepped between them to lift her from the horse. "Don't be troubling the lady over things that don't matter to her. Be on your way and find your own place in the village."

But Lady Rose paused a moment, lifting her hand. "It does matter, I suppose." She eyed him closely, as if wondering about the truth of his identity. "We do have enough room among the servants to accommodate one more."

Calvert looked horrified at the prospect. "My lady, you cannot be serious. We know nothing about this man."

"You could lock him within one of the rooms," she suggested, and Iain spied a hint of amusement in her voice. "Or you could sleep outside his door with a loaded revolver if that would make you feel better."

Her footman appeared unaware that she was teasing, and seemed to be considering the idea. As for himself, Iain was willing to sleep anywhere that wasn't tainted with the odor of manure.

Her decision made, Lady Rose continued, "Tell Mrs. Marlock to find a place for Mr. Donovan in one of the garrets. He need not sleep among the horses."

The footman grimaced and promised to speak with the housekeeper. But the look he sent toward Iain suggested that he would rather have him bide with the pigs.

"Do you believe me, then?" Iain asked Lady Rose, before Calvert could take her away.

She held his gaze for a long moment. "I don't know what to believe." Then, in a softer voice, she admitted, "But I think there is more to you than the others see. I hope that my instincts are not wrong in this."

As she left with her footman, it humbled him to realize that it was the first time that anyone had put faith in him. And he found himself wanting to prove her right.

After nearly an hour, Mrs. Marlock led him up to one of the garrets, far away from the household. She'd also warned that she intended to lock the door behind him. "So ye won't get it in yer head to come and rob us blind whilst we sleep."

It reminded him of a twisted fairytale, one with the earl locked in the tower. All he needed now was a princess to come and rescue him.

To be sure, it had been the most trying day he'd ever had. Iain had attempted to keep his irritation under control—for his hosts were wary enough of him as it was—but now that he had a moment to consider his circumstances, he could no longer deny his frustration. Nothing had gone as planned, curse his damned servants and Niall. Without a coach and a traveling staff, there was little he could do about it.

And now what? Lady Wolcroft was not in residence, and his letter of introduction was missing, along with his signet ring. The others might have believed his story, if Lady Wolcroft had alerted them of his impending arrival. As it was, no one thought of him as anything other than a well-spoken beggar.

Iain lit a candle stub and studied his surroundings. It was a far cry from his estate at Ashton. His father's house boasted twenty-seven rooms, and his own bedchamber had an enormous mahogany bed.

This bed was currently occupied by a cat who did not look eager to surrender his place. The feline yawned, stretched, and sharpened his claws upon the bedding. So be it. It would only be for this night, possibly one more, at worst. And it was a far cry better than the stables.

Iain removed his coat and shirt, then sat down beside the cat to remove the shoes Mrs. Marlock had loaned him. Although he had washed in the trough, he rather missed the simple necessities of soap and warm water. But she had given him another crust of bread with a bit of cheese for his supper.

After he'd eaten, the cat crawled on his lap. Iain he rubbed the feline's ears for a moment, and the sound of low purring filled up the empty space of the room. There was no fire lit in the hearth, but the room was warm, if a bit dusty. Iain guessed he could cross the room in three long paces. The candlelight cast shadows against the wall, and he saw a stack of old paintings on the other side of the room, half-covered by a white cloth. The remaining contents of the tiny room were brooms and tin buckets.

Iain stripped off his shirt, and he leaned back on the narrow cot. He tried to think of how he could prove his identity. Either he had to find out which of the boys had stolen his ring or he had to rely on Lady Wolcroft to help him. He needed to question Beauregard once again. He'd tried earlier, in the stable, but the lad had refused to speak at all. In time, Iain intended to get back everything that had been stolen.

He lay awake, trying to hold back the darker memories of famine. After the first failed crop of potatoes, he had quietly begun hoarding food for his family and the tenants. Careful rations had helped them to survive, but they needed more.

He tried to envision Ashton with green fields and prosperity, refusing to dwell upon the past—only the means of atoning for it. And he had promised Michael that he would see it done.

His mother, in contrast, had fled Ireland, claiming she would never return. She didn't believe for a moment that Iain would succeed, and he suspected she would spend her energy trying to wed her daughters to American millionaires. He hadn't spoken to her in half a year, and rather doubted he would see her again. She loathed the sight of him, and he'd never really understood why. Michael had been the golden saint who could do no wrong—whereas Iain had been the black-hearted sinner.

His mother would find it fitting that he'd fallen into the ranks of the servants in this place. But not for long. He was rather looking forward to seeing Lady Rose's reaction when she learned that he truly *was* an earl.

He did find her entertaining, and he'd enjoyed her company on the ride. After they had brought Beauregard home, Lady Rose had drawn her horse into a slow walk, taking the time to enjoy the night moments.

It occurred to him that this was her only means of moving about. He hadn't seen a Bath chair anywhere and wondered why she chose to rely on servants to carry her. Earlier, in the garden, she'd attempted to stand and failed. Was she avoiding the chair because she did not wish to feel imprisoned by it?

Though he had been partly teasing when he'd suggested that they wed, it wasn't entirely out of the question. Lady Rose intrigued him. She was lovely of face, and he also liked her wit. But then, if she was already spoken for, he would respect her wishes. It was entirely possible that they could become allies and help one another, however.

He let his mind turn over the idea as he lay back on the thin mattress and listened to the sounds of the old house. Outside his door, he heard a slight sound of someone walking up the stairs. He tensed, waiting for a knock.

When none came, he got up and walked to the door. "Who's there?"

Again, nothing.

He didn't bother to put on his shirt, but pushed on the door handle and was surprised to find that it opened easily. Mrs. Marlock had put the key inside, but either she'd neglected to lock it, or she'd only pretended to do so.

Iain pushed it open softly and saw a figure dressed in gray, walking down the narrow staircase. Quietly, he shadowed the person, keeping his footsteps light. It soon became evident that Lady Penford was walking in her sleep.

"Are you all right, Lady Penford?" he asked softly, hoping to gain her attention. She swayed a little, but did not appear to hear him. Slowly, she continued walking toward the second-floor landing. There was a balustrade at the end and the staircase continued down. She lifted one leg up, attempting to climb over the railing.

"Stop!" he called out, not caring who heard him. He ran toward her, knowing she was trapped within a prison cell formed of illusions. When she hoisted herself onto the balustrade, he repeated, "Lady Penford, don't move."

At that, she hesitated, looking back at him. Her eyes were unfocused, her face deathly pale. A long braid of fair hair hung below one shoulder, and her gray wrapper was falling open.

He could seize her and force her back, but if she screamed, the entire household would awaken and believe that he'd attacked her. No—better to save that as a last resort. He was close enough to grab hold of her, if needed.

It seemed that she was too far gone, that she would not heed common sense. Iain struggled to think of something—anything—that would keep her from throwing herself down to the first floor.

"The wolves," he said quietly.

The moment he spoke of the imaginary wolves, she jerked back to stare. "W-where?"

He moved beside her and pointed to the floor below. "Don't you see them?"

She began trembling and lowered her leg from the balustrade. "Oh no. You're right. They're down there, waiting for me."

He let out a breath of relief, not caring that he'd lied. One of the maids came running, and behind her was another young woman who resembled Rose. "What is going on, Mother?" she demanded.

Lady Penford never looked at her daughter, but lowered her head. She gripped her palms together, but Iain didn't leave the matron's side. Her mind was in a fragile state, and he didn't want to risk her trying to flee.

"Lily," the matron whispered. "I do not think you should have left your bedchamber. Not this late and certainly n-not with a gentleman in our presence."

Lady Lily regarded Iain with grave suspicion. She did not appear surprised that he was staying in the house—he guessed her sister had told her—and yet, she eyed him with a dark warning. From behind him on the stairs, the cat padded down and approached, weaving between his legs. The feline nudged his knee, and Iain picked up the animal, stroking its ears.

"I was just telling Lady Penford that it was not wise to climb over the railing," he told her.

She gave a visible wince and hurried to her mother's side. "Mother, please. You should let me walk you back to your room. It's late."

"In a moment," she promised. Her voice was weary, and she regarded Iain once more. He offered his arm to escort her back, but her expression turned confused. "Thank you for saving me from the wolves, sir."

"You are most welcome, Lady Penford."

"And why aren't you wearing a nightshirt? Your attire is most improper."

"I had retired for the night when I heard you needed help," he said. "There was not time to dress." The woman was lucky that he'd been wearing trousers, to be honest. He far preferred to sleep without confining clothes.

"Well. See that you put something on in the future. My daughter should not be exposed to . . . that," she finished, taking Lady Lily's hand.

The young woman's cheeks flushed, but she behaved as if he were fully clothed. She sent him a quiet look of thanks. "I'll walk you back to your room now, Mother."

"And what of Lady Rose?" he asked.

"She is sleeping soundly in her own room, you needn't worry." With that, she took her mother back, followed by the maid. The cat trotted behind both of them, leaving him alone on the stairway landing.

Iain waited a moment to ensure that they reached their rooms safely. He was about to return upstairs when he heard a small voice. "Mr. Donovan."

He followed the direction of the sound and saw a door slightly open, near the end of the hallway. When he reached the room, he saw Lady Rose lying on the ground. "Is my mother all right?"

"Yes. Lady Lily took her back to her room." He crouched down and asked, "Would you like me to help you up? Or perhaps summon a servant?" It appeared that she'd dragged her body across the floor in an effort to reach the door.

"No, thank you," she remarked. She strained, bearing all her weight upon her elbows until she managed to sit up, leaning against the door.

Iain didn't like the fact that she'd struggled so far across the room. Someone would have to carry her back to bed, and he asked, "Shall I call your maid?"

Lady Rose shook her head. "Not yet. Stay and answer my questions."

Iain eyed the door, and then sat across from her on the floor. Although this was not at all proper, he understood her concern. There was no harm in a conversation, albeit a very late one. But there was an underlying intimacy with him not wearing a shirt and Lady Rose wearing her nightgown.

"What happened to my mother?" she asked, turning serious. "Tell me everything."

"She was trying to climb over the railing," he said. "I don't really know what it was she intended, but she was unaware of the danger."

Lady Rose shivered and gripped her elbows. "Dear God. I'm so glad you were there to save her."

So was he, but he merely nodded. He didn't doubt that if he hadn't heard Lady Penford's footsteps on the stairs, the matron would have broken her neck from the fall.

In a low voice, she admitted, "We had to . . . leave London. Because of Mother's illness." She glanced away from him, as if embarrassed by the confession. "It was the best way to conceal what was happening."

He understood that well enough. "How long has she been this way?"

Rose drew her hands together. "Nearly a year. After my father died, she was never the same. I know we ought to find a doctor to help, but I fear he would put her in an asylum. They would lock her away or give her laudanum to make her sleep all the time. She doesn't deserve that sort of life."

"You ought to hire a companion for her and lock her bedchamber at night. It would be safer."

Lady Rose gave a nod and then regarded him again. "I know you are right. But I somehow thought she would be safe. Apparently, I was wrong." She adjusted her wrapper, concealing her nightgown from view.

"I would ask for your assistance in lifting me into bed, were it not so improper," she said softly. A trace of irony crossed her face. "It seems I must drag myself back."

"Do you really believe I'm going to allow you to do that?" He fully intended to help her, but he knew that he would have to leave as soon as he did so. And right now, he wanted to spend a few minutes more with Lady Rose.

"Just ring for Calvert," she advised. "He will assist me."

"I'd rather summon the demons of hell." He drew his knees up, pretending as if he intended to remain on the floor.

"Calvert is not that bad. And at least I can trust him to lift me up. He's old enough to be my father."

"Grandfather," Iain corrected. "And he's as crotchety as a gelded rooster surrounded by hens."

"He is that." She bit back a laugh, covering her mouth. As she gained command of her amusement, her gaze swept over him. "Why is it that nearly every time I see you, you are half-naked, Mr. Donovan?"

He sent her a wicked smile, glancing at the prim wrapper that covered her from chin to ankles. The ruffled garment was shapeless, like a muslin suit of armor. "Why is it that every time I see you, you are always fully dressed, Lady Rose?"

She laughed again, and he warmed to the sound. For a moment, he remained seated across from her, and the air grew charged between them. He liked seeing her brown hair braided across one shoulder, a few reddish strands framing her face. Her legs were folded beneath her, and the snow-white gown made her appear like an angel.

Like the devil, he wanted to lean forward and kiss those lips. He wanted to pull her into his lap and taste the sweetness of her skin. If he were wicked, he would peel back that wrapper and kiss a path down the thin muslin to her breasts. They would harden beneath his mouth, and he would take great pleasure in awakening her desire.

His mouth tightened as he tried to gather up the remnants of control. "Put out your arms, and I'll carry you back to bed."

He got to one knee, reaching out to her. She shied away, leaning against the door frame. "That would be most improper, and you know this, sir."

Iain did, but he hardly cared at all. Without another word, he scooped her up into his arms, rising to his feet. She was aghast at his gesture, but truly, he could see no reason to trouble the stone-hearted Calvert.

"Mr. Donovan, please, you cannot—"

She never finished her sentence before he deposited her back in bed. "Would you like the covers pulled over you?"

"I can manage," she gritted out. "Now go, before my servants believe that we've been having a passionate liaison."

Right now, that sounded very fine indeed. He could easily imagine resting his body upon hers, his erection nestled between her thighs. This time, he gritted his teeth hard, trying to push back the desire. "Are you wanting a passionate liaison, Lady Rose?" He kept his voice teasing, though he didn't bother to hide his interest.

"Don't be silly. You've helped me to bed, and now you can go."

He drew the covers over her, well aware of her body warmth. He tucked her in, sitting on the edge of the bed. "There, now. Would you like a bedtime story?" His voice came out husky, and she glared at him.

"Get. Out." There was no mistaking her annoyance. "Where *is* my garden rake when I need it?" Instead, she gathered up one of the smaller pillows, holding it like a shield.

But in spite of her warning, there was something else in her eyes. Not fear or loathing—but her own interest. In the dim candlelight of the room, her brown eyes were fixed upon him as if she saw nothing else. She leaned forward with the pillow, instead of cowering backward.

He wasn't about to refuse that invitation. "I know what it is we're missing, *a chara.* A goodnight kiss."

Her eyes widened with shock. And yet, her hands relaxed from the pillow, while she supported her weight on her wrists. She looked nothing like a lady who was terrified of a stolen kiss. Instead, her mouth was slightly open, her cheeks flushed.

"Absolutely not. I will scream if you even try such a thing."

He was tempted to lean in and taste her offering. What would it be like to feel her soft body against his own, stroking the line of her back? Would she wind her arms around his neck and open to him like a summer blossom?

Iain moved a breath closer, watching her reaction. For a moment, she held herself in place, waiting. But instead of desire in her eyes, he saw the first trace of fear.

Before she could protest again, he kissed her forehead. "Sweet dreams, Lady Rose." Then he stepped back to leave. It wasn't the kiss he'd wanted, but at least she would not be angry with him.

Yet, he was wrong about that. She appeared angry that he *hadn't* stolen a true kiss. "You are a wretched man," she informed him as he strode to her bedroom door. In one hand, she held the pillow.

But he only paused and smiled. "What was that?" He raised a hand to his ear and said, "You wanted to thank me for taking you back to bed? Oh, aye, *a chara,* you're very welcome, then."

With that, he closed the door gently behind him. A moment later, he heard a soft thunk as the pillow struck the wood.

It was dawn, but Rose lay awake in bed, her mind spinning. It was a miracle she'd slept at all. She could not believe Mr. Donovan had taken such liberties with her—especially when he'd not been wearing a shirt. When he had bent to kiss her, she'd been well aware of the heat of his male skin. Her body had risen to his silent call, gooseflesh prickling over her arms. Over and over, she blamed herself for not calling out for a servant. Someone would have come if she'd only raised her voice.

But she hadn't. Rose closed her eyes, feeling her cheeks burn with mortification. The kiss was branded upon her skin, even now. Though he had done nothing except touch his mouth to her forehead, she could not stop thinking of the way it had made her feel—almost beloved.

You didn't scream. You allowed him to kiss you.

She buried her face in the pillow, feeling the weight of the sinful moment. Lord Burkham had written letters to her, kind words of how he would remain steadfast, believing she would get well. How could she let herself forget that?

She should never have allowed her imagination to sway toward another man. The Irishman had soothed her ego, making her feel desirable. And though he had only kissed her forehead, she'd yearned for more.

That was what bothered her most—her own secret feelings burdened her now.

Her traitorous mind had questioned what it would have been like if he'd kissed her lips. Would he have claimed her like a pirate, kissing her until she succumbed to seduction? Or would he have kept the kiss chaste, similar to those Lord Burkham had given? Thomas had only kissed her hand a few times, and once, he'd kissed her lips when they were out walking. Never had he pressed her for more.

Not like the Irishman. She had a feeling that if she'd allowed even the slightest kiss, he would demand her surrender. All night, she had dreamed of him, imagining the touch of his mouth upon her skin.

Stop. Rose clenched her fists against the coverlet, knowing no good could come of such thoughts. She sighed and hoisted herself to a seated position. There was a bell on the table beside her, for her to ring if she required assistance. But she was tired of waiting on people to help. She wanted to take care of herself.

Using her hands to push her useless legs over the side of the bed, she braced herself. *I am going to get well.* After six months, she had recovered from the violent illness that had left her numb and unable to move. Strange to imagine that food could poison her body in such a way, leaving her immobile.

No matter how long it took, she would continue her daily outings to the garden to enjoy the fresh air and sunshine. It frustrated her that so many things she'd taken for granted were now lost to her. The simple acts of choosing a morning gown and walking across the room were impossible.

Rose dragged her body across the coverlet until she reached the bedpost at the foot of the bed. Her arms had grown stronger with each day, and she felt certain that one day she would manage to stand up. She still had sensation in her legs, even if they would not bear her full weight.

After taking a deep breath, she clutched the bedpost with both arms, hugging it tightly as she eased herself toward the ground. Her legs slid off the coverlet, and once again, they were like the legs of a marionette, collapsing beneath her.

She gripped the bedpost, struggling to hold herself upright. And still, there was nothing she could do. Her legs would not support her body.

Someone knocked at the door, and she hoped it was her maid, Hattie. "Come in," she answered.

Lily entered the room just as Rose's arms gave out and she crumpled to the floor. "Rose, what are you doing?"

"Humiliating myself." It was difficult to be dignified when one was eye to eye with a chamber pot. She wrinkled her nose and lifted her face from the floor. Lily hurried over and helped her sit upright. With one arm around her waist, her sister hoisted her back onto the bed.

"You should know better than to try and stand," her sister chided. "It might have been an hour before Hattie found you. You couldn't reach the bell."

Rose knew that, and yet, she had no intention of abandoning her practice attempts. Instead, she changed the subject. "How is Mother faring this morning?" She swept a lock of hair out of her eyes and tried to behave as if nothing were wrong.

"Did you hear about what happened last night?" A look of guilt flashed over Lily's face.

Although Mr. Donovan had told her, Rose shook her head, feigning ignorance. "Tell me."

Her sister reiterated the story of how their mother had climbed over the balustrade, preparing to jump, when Mr. Donovan had intervened. "I believe he saved her life, Rose."

"I am glad he was there," she agreed. But although she was indeed grateful to him, she couldn't stop feeling guilty about the stolen moment in her room.

"Do you think we should offer him a reward to show our thanks?" Lily asked.

Rose hesitated. "I don't know if that would be wise. He claims to be the Earl of Ashton—which I cannot possibly believe—and he says he is here at our grandmother's invitation."

Lily sent her an incredulous look. "Is that even possible?"

"Judging by his appearance, I don't believe so." And yet . . . she wasn't quite certain. He had the air of a man who was accustomed to getting his own way. It wasn't at all the demeanor of a servant.

Her sister appeared to share her sentiment. "If Grandmother could find an unmarried earl—no matter where he comes from—I wouldn't put it past her. Honestly, she's entirely too desperate to find a match for us."

Rose sent her sister a weak smile. "I know she is only trying to help. But I do not intend to be a candidate for marriage. At least, not until I can walk."

"Are you still hoping Lord Burkham will offer for you?" Lily asked. Her sister sent a glance toward the six letters Thomas had sent. Rose had bound them up in a ribbon, and the letters gave her hope that he would indeed wait for her.

"He was going to, I feel sure of it." And if they hadn't left London because of their mother, she felt confident he would have come to visit her during her illness. She pushed back the uncertainties and took comfort from the letters. Once she learned to walk again, everything would be different. She would return to London, win a marriage proposal, and become Lord Burkham's viscountess. Somehow, she had to believe that it would happen.

"So *do* you think Mr. Donovan is an earl?" Lily was asking her. She began helping her to remove her nightgown, and Rose lifted her arms.

"I don't know what to believe. Either he is an accomplished liar, or he is indeed an earl who has fallen upon difficult times." When she tried to imagine Mr. Donovan's face, all she could think of was last night when he had lifted her into his arms. Although he had done nothing except put her into bed, the intimate gesture had unnerved her. Even now, her face flushed with the memory of his kiss. "He behaves in an improper manner, however."

"He *is* Irish," Lily pointed out. "Perhaps their customs are different?"

"Possibly." But whereas Thomas had waited half a year to kiss her hand, Mr. Donovan had waited half a day to kiss her forehead. He was the sort of man who was dangerous to a woman, for despite her attempts to remain immune, he had provoked an instinctive response. She didn't understand her own reaction or why she still remembered that kiss, hours later.

"What are we going to do about Mother?" she asked, in a pointed means of changing the subject.

Lily began lacing up the back of Rose's corset. "She doesn't remember anything about last night, which is a blessing. Except, she very much remembers our discussion about going to London." Her sister made a face. "I do wish you hadn't agreed to go."

Rose lifted her shoulders in a shrug. "Soon enough, she will remember that I cannot walk."

"Will she?" Lily tied off the corset. "Or will she try to wed *me* off instead?"

"Would that be so terrible?" She sent Lily a halfhearted smile, but her sister was not in a congenial mood.

"Yes it would," Lily insisted. "I am not going to join the debutantes who wear white and send simpering smiles to unwed men. Matthew will return, and then I will wed him." A softness stole over her sister's face, for she had never given up on the man she loved.

But there was something else in her tone that made Rose stop a moment. "Did he already ask you to wed him before he left for India?" This was the first she had heard of such a thing.

Lily paled and straightened her shoulders. Quietly, she reached for a silver chain around her throat and withdrew it from beneath her gown. At the end of the chain was a small gold ring.

But more than the ring was the look of steady faithfulness in her sister's eyes. It was clear that she loved the Earl of Arnsbury with all her heart.

"When did he give you the ring?" Rose asked.

"Two summers ago." Lily returned it beneath her gown, but in her blue eyes, Rose saw the veiled pain. And whether or not Lord Arnsbury ever returned home, her sister would not marry another man. Especially if she was already promised.

"Have you told him that you would marry him?" she asked Lily.

The young woman nodded. "So you understand why I cannot be the one to marry. At least, not until Lord Arnsbury returns."

Rose let out a sigh. "I cannot marry, either. Not until I can walk again." She clung to that wish, for the idea of being unable to walk for the rest of her life was a horror she couldn't face.

Lily reached out to squeeze her hand. "You will. And perhaps we'll find a new physician in London who can help you." She helped lift a morning gown over Rose's head and began buttoning her up the back.

Rose had little faith in physicians and dismissed the idea. "I do not intend to go anywhere until I can walk again." She preferred to remain here, where she could heal in peace and shield her mother from idle gossip. "And Mother isn't well enough to return. You know she would cause a scene."

"The difficulty will be in convincing her that we cannot go," Lily pointed out. "She seems determined to return to London, no matter what I say."

"Tell her I cannot walk or dance," Rose pointed out. "It *is* the truth."

"Which she forgets all the time." Lily sighed. "You do realize that we would not be in this situation, had you not been so distracted by *that man*."

Rose mustered a slight smile. "Forgive me." Though, to be fair, any woman would be distracted by Iain Donovan. Not only because of his interfering, flirtatious manner—but also because he was handsome, in an unrefined way.

And because he'd been half-naked when she'd first laid eyes upon him.

And maybe because he'd kissed her forehead.

"What *are* you going to do about the Irishman?" Lily was asking. "We cannot simply send him away if he truly is an earl."

Rose shrugged. "I don't know. Possibly we could let him stay one more day whilst we make inquiries. And if we find out he *is* lying, then we'll send Mr. Donovan on his way. That will be that." She straightened and reached for the bedpost to try standing up again. This time, she would hold the post closer to her waist, and that might help.

But Lily rested a hand upon her shoulder. "Rose, don't. You already fell once this morning. You're not ready."

Not ready? And when *would* she be ready if she didn't keep trying? Never, that's when.

She ignored her sister, and gripped the bedpost. "Then ring for Calvert. He can help me up after I fall on my face."

"I don't want you to hurt yourself. Especially now, when Mother is so ill. Just . . . wait a little longer before you try again." Though Lily's voice held concern, she caught a hint of impatience. It was as if her sister was taking care of two invalids instead of one.

Rose's fingers clenched and the frustration rose up inside her, spilling over into anger. "Lily, I've been unable to walk for months. Do you have any idea what that's like?"

Her sister's expression softened with sympathy. "I know it must be difficult, but it *will* get better. I promise you that."

Though a part of her knew that Lily hadn't meant to offend her, all her emotions came spilling out. "You cannot make that promise. And telling me I shouldn't even try? What else can I do but try?"

She hated herself, hated the helpless feeling of being unable to move. And she would never consider giving up.

Lily paled and reached out to take her hand. "I'm sorry, Rose. I didn't mean it that way."

And she knew that. Her sister wasn't trying to hurt her, but she couldn't understand what this was like. Rose let go of her sister's palm and regarded her. "I am tired of being reliant upon other people for everything. I cannot even dress myself or put on shoes."

"Neither can I," Lily pointed out with a light smile. "At least, not without Hattie's help. All those buttons can be impossible."

But her sister's teasing didn't alleviate the hurt. Instead, it made her more determined to try again.

Rose hugged the bedpost as tightly as she could, letting her legs slide downward from the bed. But before she could get a firm grip, her sister surprised her by holding her waist. Lily steadied her for a moment. "That's it. Can you straighten your legs?"

Rose tried to move her knees, but they kept buckling beneath her. Lily caught her before she could sink to the floor. "Put your arms around my neck."

"If I do, both of us will fall." But her grasp was already slipping from the bedpost.

"Do it now," Lily ordered.

She obeyed, and her sister half-dragged her over to the chaise longue. It was humiliating being unable to command her lower limbs, and she apologized to Lily. "You were right. I wasn't ready to stand."

Her sister didn't argue. "Why will you not try a Bath chair? At least then you could move among the rooms easier."

"If I do, it feels like I'm giving up," Rose admitted. It had been nearly six months since she had lost her ability to walk. Surely she would make progress soon, now that her body had healed. But despite the fact that she was now able to feel pressure and sensation in her legs, they had grown far too weak.

She leaned against the chaise longue and looked outside at the grounds. Sunlight gleamed over the edges of the trees, and she felt the need to be out of doors. At least there she did not feel like a prisoner within her own body.

"Go and fetch Calvert for me," she bade Lily. Her footman would bring her to the garden bench, but if she asked to go riding, he would find endless reasons why she should not. It was miraculous that he had accompanied her last night to bring Beauregard home, when he hadn't wanted to. A slight flush suffused her cheeks, for it had been Iain Donovan's doing. The Irishman had talked his way into it, and she had a feeling that the man could convince the devil himself to obey his wishes.

Her sister started to leave, but then stopped at the doorway. "Be careful, Rose. Don't try to do too much, too soon."

She only sent her sister a quiet smile.

Chapter Four

Iain had just finished leading his horse from the stall, when the coachman, Mr. Nelson, stopped him. "And just where d'ye think ye're going, lad?"

He hadn't considered himself a lad in ten years, but he faced the coachman. "I am going to find my missing footmen and discover what happened to my coach." It had been long enough, and he needed to know if they had abandoned him here.

The older man sent him a doubtful look. "And will ye be speaking to the Queen, whilst you're there?"

Jesus, Mary, and Joseph, he didn't have time for this. "The last I heard, she was in residence at Buckingham Palace. I've not yet been invited."

Nelson barked out a laugh. "I like you, lad. But I can't say that it'd be wise to let ye go off just now."

Was the man daft? "It's *my* horse," he reminded Nelson. "And I can ride with him whenever I'm wanting to." It irritated him that he was having to explain himself to this man. And by the spittle of Saint John, his footmen had better have a damned good explanation for their absence.

"I'll return with my servants by midmorning," he promised. "Then I can prove that I am a guest of Lady Wolcroft." That is, if they hadn't gone off and abandoned him.

"And what if you're wrong, lad? What if there *are* no servants waiting aboot? Will you simply be on your way, without a brass farthing to buy supper?" The old man reached for Darcy's reins and smiled knowingly. "Ye'll be out on your arse with nowt to show for it."

Iain was about to tell the coachman to leave off, but paused a moment. If harm had befallen his men and if the coach was gone, he'd be left with no means of proving his identity—not unless he could get his brother's signet ring back. He'd managed to talk his way into a garret for shelter, and Mrs. Marlock had given him porridge for breakfast—but the coachman was right. If his servants were gone, he'd have no choice but to return here.

"You obviously have something else in mind." Iain recognized that now was not the time to burn bridges. "What is it you're wanting?"

The coachman leaned against his shovel. "Well, now. The way I see it, ye've fallen on hard times. I could use help in the stables unless ye're too proud to soil yer hands."

Iain stared at the shovel with annoyance. It was clear enough that the coachman didn't at all believe he was an earl. And though he wasn't opposed to hard labor when it was necessary, Nelson was taking deliberate pleasure in offering such a task. It was clearly a test.

"I thank you kindly for the offer," Iain said. "But I must find out what happened to my servants. Until I know for certain if they are gone, I cannot tarry here." He would not dwell upon the alternative.

"They may cast ye out, lad," Nelson warned.

"Not if I find the proof I need." He finished saddling Darcy, and mounted the horse. With a nod to the coachman, he began riding along the main road.

The Yorkshire landscape had a haunted look about it today. Large gray clouds rumbled in from the coast, while the moors were windswept and dreary. With each mile he rode, his mood worsened.

Why had he thought to come here? He was convinced that his men had used him for passage across the sea and had no intention of joining him. Instead of arriving at Penford as the Earl of Ashton, he appeared more like an Irish refugee. And he had no idea what he should do now.

His brother owned a townhouse in London that now belonged to him, but he had never visited it. There was a small staff of a butler and a footman, because his mother refused to dismiss them. Iain didn't know where she'd found the money to pay them or whether his family had any funds within their bank.

Even if he did reach London with the help of Lady Wolcroft, he had little to offer a bride, save a title and a derelict estate with rotting potatoes. He would have to charm the young ladies, tempting them with a life where they would be treated with kindness and affection. His own desires didn't matter. And wasn't it ironic that he should be the one to sell himself into marriage, instead of his sisters?

As the morning waned, he eventually reached the site of the broken coach. The axle was still cracked, and no one had made any attempt to repair it—the coach had simply been moved to the side of the road. His footman Niall's claim that he should ride on to Penford while they sought help now seemed like a ploy.

Iain dismounted and let his horse graze while he searched the wreckage. All his belongings were gone, so it seemed. The rest of the horses were missing, along with the servants. Though it was possible that his men had gone to seek assistance at a local village, there wasn't much to speak of nearby.

He searched the coach thoroughly, hoping the letter had fallen from his pocket. But there was nothing at all.

Iain abandoned the coach and mounted his horse once more, following the road into the hills. Although he understood that his companions had used this journey as a means of escaping Ireland, their betrayal cut deeply. He'd tried everything in his power to save his lands from the blight, spending most of his fortune to help his people survive. And the men had repaid him by abandoning him here.

He turned Darcy back to the road. He kept his pace slow while he deliberated on what to do now.

He supposed he'd have to appeal to the good graces of Lady Rose and her family. There were only two threads of hope remaining—if Lady Wolcroft happened to return, or if he wrote to his sisters and asked them to send assistance. Both would require time he didn't have. Which meant he was trapped in the role of a servant, thoroughly bound to the whims of others.

Well then. He'd clearly gone and twisted his life sideways, hadn't he? His pride ached at the thought of being at someone's beck and call. This wasn't who he was—but it was who he'd become.

His mood turned grim as he rode back to Penford. A fat droplet of rain splashed upon his face. Of course. It *would* have to rain now. He adjusted the hat he'd borrowed and quickened his pace.

His spirits sank lower, and he berated himself for not finding any proof of his rank. It was possible that Lady Rose would demand that he leave. And then where could he go?

It seemed that the Fates were laughing at him. His only consolation was that he'd saved her mother's life. That might give him a roof over his head until he could prove he was Lord Ashton.

The hard rain soaked him to the skin, and there was no escaping it. By the time he reached Penford, his body was drenched. He dismounted Darcy and led the horse back to the stables. Thankfully, Nelson wasn't there to chastise him.

Iain discarded the hat and used one of the horse blankets to dry himself off as best he could. Then he lifted the blanket over his head and went back outside. He walked across the green lawn toward the servants' entrance, when, suddenly, he spied a black umbrella held up by a lady seated upon a bench.

Why on earth would Lady Rose be outside in this weather while the rain pounded around her? Her reddish-brown hair was tucked up in a bonnet, but a few curls had escaped and were wet against her cheeks. Her gown was a deep garnet color, and she wore a darker shawl. Iain hurried toward her, and then saw Calvert standing with another umbrella, near the arched trellis, his face puckered with malcontent.

"It's a fine day, Lady Rose," Iain said, greeting her with a smile.

She tilted back the umbrella to look at him, and in her brown eyes, he saw merriment. "It was fine earlier today. Until the rain came." With a glance at his sodden clothing, she added, "It looks as if you've been enjoying the weather, Mr. Donovan."

Her damp face was shining, and the words grew trapped in his throat. Never had he considered rain to be anything other than an inconvenience. But he found himself struck mute by this beautiful woman's smile. The rain continued to soak through his clothing, despite the horse blanket he held over his head. Lady Rose tilted her face to the side. "Wouldn't you rather go inside where it's dry?"

"I was hoping to speak with you," he managed. To Calvert, he said, "Would you give us a moment?" The old man glowered and looked ready to refuse, but he added, "You could wait just over there with Lady Rose in full sight."

A curious look came over Rose's face at his request for privacy, but she nodded her agreement. When the footman stood on the far end of the lawn, Iain drew closer. He kept the blanket over his head to shelter him from the downpour and confessed, "I went riding back to the place where I left my coach, hoping to find my servants. The vehicle was still there, but there was no sign of them. I think they've gone and won't be returning." Although it evoked more frustration, Iain kept his tone serious without any trace of anger.

He studied her, and said, "I know you don't believe any of my truths, *a chara*. And by all rights, you may be wanting to throw me out. But I would ask for a little more time, until Lady Wolcroft returns."

She was listening to him, seeming to consider this. "You wish to stay here?"

He nodded. "I thought I could find the proof I needed by bringing back my servants. But they apparently did not wish to remain in my employ."

Bitterness sank into him with the realization that he was truly at her mercy. God help him, he'd sunk so low. He lacked the means of returning home or going anywhere. All he possessed was Darcy and a few ruined pieces of clothing.

But he could not give up. Instead, he got down on one knee, lowering himself before Lady Rose. "I would ask to send a letter to my sisters, if I may."

"And in the meantime, you wish to stay with us as a guest?" she mused.

He knew how unlikely that was. But he offered, "Only until your grandmother returns. Then I intend to go to my brother's—that is, *my* house—in London."

She leaned forward, studying him. By all rights, she should toss him out. But Lady Rose kept her gaze searching. It was as if she were trying to strip him down to the bone, to find the honest answers she sought.

"I do not know if it would be wise for you to stay."

He knew she was referring to the way he'd kissed her forehead. The move had been born of impulse, and he should not have trespassed.

"I've nowhere else to go," he admitted. "Believe me when I say that this was not what I imagined would happen on my journey to Penford."

He regarded her while the rain dripped steadily upon the horse blanket he was holding over his head. "If circumstances had been different, I would have traveled here with my sisters. There'd have been four coaches, and fifty servants, to be sure. I would have brought gifts for all of you, as thanks for your hospitality."

Her expression softened slightly. "And what would you have brought me, Lord Ashton?" There was a teasing glint in her eyes when she used his title.

"A bracelet," he answered. "Perhaps made of Connemara marble, polished smooth. The stones are lovely, with streaks of dark and light green."

She tilted her umbrella back. "And for Lily?"

He thought a moment. "A silver comb for her hair, I think."

Lady Rose gave a nod of approval. "She would like that very much." She never took those brown eyes from his gaze, as if deliberating. Finally, she released a sigh. "If my brother were here, there is no question James would demand you go. I shouldn't consider this at all."

He waited while she decided, making no move to rush her. Lady Rose thought for a moment. "Against my better judgment, I let you stay for one night. You could have robbed the household or murdered us all in our beds. Instead, you saved my mother's life."

He softened at her words, understanding that she was hovering on the brink of allowing him to remain at Penford. "I am not the sort of man who would let any woman come to harm."

She tightened her lips and sighed again. "I think I've been reading too many fairy stories, Mr. Donovan."

The abrupt change in subject caught him off guard. "What do you mean by that?"

Lady Rose drew back her umbrella as the rain slowed. Several droplets rolled down her face, but she ignored them. He lowered his own blanket, waiting for her to respond. "My brain warns me that you are up to no good. That you are telling naught but lies and that any man could say the same and ask to live at Penford. I know this, well enough."

He waited, hearing her silent argument.

"But when I look at you, I do not see a servant. I see a man who is accustomed to giving orders. You do not behave like my footmen or even my groom. You do not see yourself as their equal."

Because I am not one of them, he wanted to say, but didn't.

"You may be dressed in rags, but I would wager that your coat once cost a great deal of money. You also do not stare at our household furniture as if you've never seen finery of that kind." She straightened her spine and admitted, "You behave very much like a prince who has lost his kingdom. And perhaps my love of stories has made me lose my wits."

"Or perhaps you are the one who can see past the enchantment," he said quietly. "I may not look like an earl, and my kingdom may indeed be under the spell of a fairy who has cursed my land . . . but I am in grave need of a princess to set it to rights."

Her brown eyes grew intrigued, but she reminded him, "I cannot be that princess. My heart belongs to another."

"Your point is taken, Lady Rose." He wasn't the sort of man to intrude when a woman's heart was already given. But there could be friendship between them . . . and right now, he desperately needed her assistance. "And I would greatly welcome your help until your grandmother arrives."

She thought a moment, adjusting the angle of her umbrella. "If I let you stay, there will be a condition," she informed him.

"Name it." Truthfully, he cared not what she wanted. He was at the end of his rope, and she knew this.

"You cannot touch me again."

He understood what she meant by that, but clarified, "Unless I have your permission." At her wary look, he added, "If you've fallen, I'll not be standing there and letting you remain on the ground."

Her tension dissipated, and she gave a nod of assent. "Very well. I suppose that's reasonable." She paused a moment, as if thinking about how to proceed. "I suppose I can give you shelter and food for a little while. At least, until my grandmother returns." A troubled expression lined her eyes, and she glanced back at the house. "But perhaps it isn't wise for me to allow a stranger to stay with us."

He understood her wariness, though it put him at a disadvantage. "What is it you're wanting from me, *a chara*? Is there a way I can prove myself worthy of your trust?"

Lady Rose thought a moment and shrugged. "In time, perhaps. You did intercede well with my mother when she was having one of her spells. I am grateful for it."

"But you fear something could happen to her."

Rose nodded. "When she has one of her bad days, she is not thinking clearly. And I may not be able to stop her if she decides to do something dangerous." A shudder crossed over her at the memory. "But I cannot lock her away. Not my own mother."

Iain completely understood her fears. To allay them, he added, "I agree. She may be lost within her own mind, but she would only grieve if she were hidden away from others."

The young woman lowered her face, but not before he caught the sheen of tears in her eyes. "I wish we could help her get better. But I do not know how to heal a broken mind. Perhaps when my brother returns . . ." Her words trailed off, and within them, he heard the trace of another fear. James Thornton, the Earl of Penford, had not yet returned from his travels in India, and no one knew when he would take up his duties in Parliament. Undoubtedly, they were all left in a state of grave worry.

"There is a way I could be of assistance, Lady Rose. I could prevent your mother from leaving the estate unless one of you is with her."

She sent him a hesitant nod, thinking it over. "That might be helpful. You need not shadow her, for I can get Hattie to stay with her for most of the day. But if she is not in her right mind, the servants are afraid of losing their post if they dare to seize her."

He gave a slight nod of agreement. It was a reasonable enough request. He could also instruct Nelson not to prepare any means of transportation for Lady Penford unless her daughter ordered it first.

"Let us make a bargain between us," Iain said. "I will remain upon the grounds of Penford, and you can send for me if there is a need. Between us, we can keep Lady Penford safe."

She nodded. "Very well."

It seemed that this arrangement was the best he could hope for, under the circumstances. "And when your grandmother returns, I will prove to you who I am."

She inclined her head. "But if you are not the Earl of Ashton, I shall have you removed from Penford."

The rain began pounding harder, soaking through the horse blanket until his hair was wet, dripping down his coat. "Would you like to go inside, out of the rain?" Iain suggested, glancing upward at the dark clouds. It did not seem that the downpour would relent again.

In reply, Lady Rose put down her umbrella and defiantly removed her bonnet, lifting her face to the sky. "Not really. I haven't had my hour outside yet."

The rain drenched her hair and gown, spattering against her face. Instead of complaining, Lady Rose began laughing. "I think I've gone as mad as my mother."

Her brown hair darkened from the water, until it grew plastered against her face. Droplets rolled down her cheeks, and her smile transformed her into a breathtakingly beautiful woman. Iain was transfixed by the droplet of rain that she licked from her lips, and he forced the idle thoughts away.

"My lady—" Calvert sputtered. "You must come in out of this rainstorm."

"Must I?" She let out a reluctant sigh. The footman hurried forward with his own umbrella, but she waved him away. At that, the servant sent a hard glare toward Iain, as if his mistress's momentary insanity were due to his interference.

But Iain hardly cared. He was fascinated by this uninhibited side to Lady Rose. And when she opened her laughing eyes and regarded him, he winked. Her response was a mischievous smile.

She's not yours, he reminded himself. And yet, he was glad to see she was not a subdued, proper English lady. He rather liked her spirit.

"You may take me inside now, Calvert. As for you"—she turned to Iain—"go inside and dry off. I will speak to Fulton about you and see what's to be done."

"Will I be permitted to leave the garret?" he inquired.

"Eventually," Lady Rose responded. "That is, as soon as I have proof that you truly are the Earl of Ashton."

He gave her a light bow. "I am grateful for the room, Lady Rose. Even if I do have to share it with a disgruntled cat."

"Moses believes he owns the house," she agreed. "But he's quite affectionate. If you're fortunate, he might share his bed with you."

"So long as he doesn't share mice. I've given up rodents for supper."

She sent him an affronted look. "You *are* an ungrateful wretch, aren't you? And here Moses was hoping to bring you a treat."

He walked alongside her toward the house. "Don't worry, Lady Rose. If you're wanting me to, I'll be certain to save you all of Moses's treats."

As Calvert brought her through the house door, she called back, "I shall hold you to that promise."

Chapter Five

Lily reached for the necklace beneath her gown and withdrew it. The gold ring hung from the end of the chain, and she slipped it on her finger. It was still loose, but the weight of the ring troubled her.

Her sister Rose believed it was a betrothal ring, when, in fact, it was her wedding band. No one knew she was already married—not even her sister or brother. Strange to think that she had wed Matthew in secret and then hadn't seen him in nearly two years. But she held no regrets at all. Her fondest wish had been granted.

She traced the outline of the ring, remembering their wedding day. Although it was not a true marriage in a legal sense—for there had been no time to get a license—they had spoken vows before a minister.

At the time, she had believed it was vastly romantic that Matthew wanted to marry her before he left for India with her brother James. The two men had traveled together, supposedly because of Matthew's investments with the East India company, but she wondered if the real reason was because they'd wanted to see the world and find adventure.

On their wedding night, her family had mistakenly believed she'd gone to visit her dearest friend Catherine—and she had never bothered to correct that assumption. Instead, she had spent the night in the arms of the man she loved.

Matthew hadn't written to her in all this time. It terrified Lily to imagine that he'd been killed. She missed him more and more with each passing day. Even her brother had never answered her letters, and she didn't know what had happened. They needed to send someone to India to bring James back, or at the very least, to tell him that he was now the earl. At the moment, their land steward was helping them keep the estate running smoothly, since their mother was unable to do so. But although everything was prosperous on the surface, Lily couldn't shake the feeling that the illusion would shatter.

Her mother, in contrast, was ever cheerful, believing that all would be well. This morning, Iris had been in good spirits, talking of finding Lily a wealthy husband. *I already have one,* she'd wanted to say, but couldn't. Instead, it seemed better to redirect her mother's attention back to Rose.

Her older sister was desperate to walk again before they returned to London. And although Lily didn't blame her, neither did she want Rose to worry about the opinions of others when they arrived—especially Thomas Kingford, the Viscount Burkham.

Quite frankly, the man didn't suit her sister at all. Burkham was too dependent upon his parents—in particular, his mother. Lily couldn't imagine what Rose had ever seen in him, except that Lord Burkham was a safe choice. Everyone knew him as a gentleman with a respectable title and fortune. But she'd always thought her sister could do better.

A knock sounded at the door, and her mother called out, "Lily, may I come in?"

"Of course." She stood, and Iris entered the room, carrying a ball gown over one arm.

"I brought this in to see if it would fit you. You might be able to wear it to a ball in London." Iris held out a high-waisted gown that was twenty years out of fashion. But Lily didn't have the heart to say no when her mother's good days were becoming fewer and fewer.

"Help me with the buttons," she told her. Iris set down the gown and closed the door before returning to assist.

"It's a gown I wore for my debut," her mother admitted. "I had many admirers then." There was a slight catch in her voice. "Perhaps it will bring luck to you or your sister."

"I think Rose should find a husband first, since she's the eldest." That was a good enough reason, Lily thought.

But her mother turned to face her, and there was sadness in her blue eyes. "Do you think she'll ever walk again, Lily?"

"She seems determined to find a way." But inwardly, she didn't believe it. Although Rose claimed she had feeling in her legs, not once had she been able to bear weight upon them.

Now that her mother was in a better state of mind, Lily decided to ask about the mysterious Mr. Donovan. It *did* seem that the handsome Irishman had provoked a response from her sister. And so she asked, "Mother, did you or Grandmother ever know Lord or Lady Ashton?"

"Why yes, of course," Iris said. "I went to school with Lady Ashton. Moira Ryan was her name before she married. And a more lively girl than Moira there never was. The mischief that girl got into . . ." Iris finished unbuttoning Lily's gown and lifted it over her head. "She married the Earl of Ashton and they had several children."

"Were there any sons?" Lily murmured. Her mother's hands stilled upon her corset, and she didn't speak. "Mother?"

She turned around and saw that Iris had gone pale. When she took her mother's hand, Iris's palm was sweaty, and her eyes seemed unfocused. "Are you all right?"

"My arm." Iris's voice was slurred, as if she were intoxicated. "I cannot lift my arm."

Lily guided her toward her bed. "Sit down a moment." She kept her voice calm, soothing her mother by telling Iris to take deep breaths and rest.

The episode passed within a few minutes, and she helped her mother lie back. Within minutes, Iris curled up to sleep.

Lily pulled a blanket over her, wondering whether she should summon a physician or if this was merely part of her mother's illness. She rang for her maid, and when the girl arrived, Lily asked her to watch over her mistress.

She needed to speak with Rose and determine what to do now.

Rose leaned back in her chair, while her bare feet rested in a basin of warmed water. She wore a clean nightgown and wrapper, and she had decided to take a tray alone in her room this evening. Her hair was damp and combed over one shoulder, but she held no regrets about being rained upon. Instead, she had enjoyed her moment of foolishness.

Oh, she knew that Calvert loathed being her personal servant. Though he tried to hide his malcontent, it was very clear that he resented these duties. He preferred to polish silver rather than take her anywhere. More than once he'd tried to convince her to get a Bath chair.

But she refused to let herself be confined indoors or imprisoned within a chair—even one with wheels.

The warm water in the basin was growing cooler, and she attempted to wiggle her toes. There. She smiled at the slight movement, gratified to see that she had managed the feat.

A knock sounded at the door, and she heard her sister's voice. Rose called out for Lily to come inside, and when her sister entered the room, it was clear that something had happened.

"We're not going to London," Lily began without preamble.

"Sit down and tell me." Rose pointed toward another chair, and her sister brought it closer.

Lily hesitated as if she didn't quite know how to begin. "Mother was having a better day until a little while ago. She . . . brought me a gown she wanted me to try on. But then, her voice grew slurred, as if she were intoxicated." Lily went on to describe the strange illness and how their mother was now sleeping in her bed. "I think we should call a physician . . . but I'm afraid to."

The worry in her voice mirrored Rose's concerns. Neither of them wanted their mother to be thought of as mad. And yet, they could not ignore the onset of this spell.

"In the morning," she said. "We will send for one then, if it's necessary. Perhaps a day or two of rest will make everything right again." Rose lifted her feet from the basin and rested them upon a linen cloth.

Her sister looked startled. "Why, Rose. You moved your feet."

"So I did." She beamed at her sister. Though it was such a small movement, it was the first time she'd managed to lift them without using her hands. Hope burgeoned up within her until it felt as if she'd swallowed sunlight. "By summer's end, I hope to dance, Lily."

"With whom?" Her sister laughed and ventured, "Calvert, I presume? Or perhaps the handsome Mr. Donovan, if you summon him back to Penford?"

Rose's smile faltered at the mention of the Irishman. She had neglected to say anything about her agreement. "He . . . hasn't left yet, Lily."

"What do you mean, Mr. Donovan hasn't left? I thought you sent him away."

"Not exactly." She reached down and lifted her feet from the water, drying her ankles and legs. "I told him he could stay until Grandmother returns from Bath."

Her sister's expression grew incredulous. "Why would you do this? We don't even know who he is."

Her sister was right, but Rose couldn't help but think that he was truly an earl who had fallen into misfortune and was in grave need of assistance. "He saved our mother's life," she reminded Lily. "Is that not worth our hospitality for a week or a fortnight at the very latest?"

"We don't *know* him," her sister repeated. "Honestly, Rose, where has your good sense gone?"

"The rain melted it away." But she sent her sister a pointed look. "And it's not as if you haven't behaved in a rash manner before, am I right?"

Lily had the good graces to blush. "Be that as it may, if he dares to harm anyone—"

"I will be the first to send him away." But she believed that Mr. Donovan—or Lord Ashton—was a good man at heart. And she could not deny that he had awakened her sense of adventure, making her want to go riding each morning. He needed help and advice, both of which she could provide.

"Supper will be served within the hour," Lily reminded her. "Do you honestly expect us to dine with him? Or will he eat among the servants?"

Rose hadn't thought of that. Though she was tempted to order Fulton to bring Mr. Donovan to their table, it would likely cause an outcry from the staff.

"I suppose he should eat with the staff or alone in his room," she answered. "Until we know his identity for certain, it would not be wise to disrupt the order of our household."

But, even so, Rose wondered about the mysterious Iain Donovan. Was he indeed an earl? Or was he merely a liar?

The next day, there was still no sign of Lady Wolcroft. Iain learned that Lady Rose's mother had been convalescing after a brief illness. At least there would be no danger of her wandering off today. It would give him the opportunity to seek his belongings from the mischievous Master Beauregard. The boy had been given adequate time to return them.

Iain poured water into the basin and washed his face and hands. This morning, he planned to pay a call on Beauregard's father. But Sir Lester might not receive him, given the state of Iain's bedraggled clothing—that is, unless Lady Rose accompanied him. He decided to invite her along.

After he finished getting dressed, he rubbed the cat's ears by way of farewell. Moses purred and butted his head against Iain's hand.

He left the garret and walked down the narrow flights of stairs until he reached the kitchen. The housekeeper was busy directing the cook on what to serve at breakfast, and the smell of eggs made his mouth water.

For a moment, he closed his eyes, savoring dreams of hot food. In his own kitchen, they'd had to lock the doors and bar the windows, for starving tenants roamed freely across Ireland and would not hesitate to kill those who had supplies. Iain had worn a revolver at his side, morning and night. He'd also ordered the cook to hide a great deal of the food, and he'd kept a tight inventory over what was saved and what was consumed.

His first responsibility was to his own tenants, not strangers. And yet, nothing had been more difficult than turning away those in need. Because of his rationing, they'd survived the first year of famine. It was too soon to tell if this year would be any different, but he hoped the harvest would improve.

Iain bowed to the housekeeper and sent her a warm smile. "Good morning to you, Mrs. Marlock."

"Off wi' ye." She handed him a bowl of porridge and pointed toward a long table, where several of the servants were eating quickly. "When ye've finished with that, go out and help Nelson with the horses."

He didn't bother correcting her assumption that he was here as a servant, but instead accepted the food and went to sit at the table. Hattie was finishing her own dish of porridge, scraping the bottom of the bowl. Her eyes narrowed at him, but she gave him a nod of acknowledgment and passed him the honey. It was a start, he supposed.

"When you help your mistress to dress, would you be so good as to ask Lady Rose if she's wanting to take a morning ride?" Iain ventured.

The maid sent him a curious stare. "She's not going to ride with you, sir."

Iain wasn't so certain, given the way Lady Rose had enjoyed her ride the previous evening. "I need to pay a call upon Beauregard's father, Sir Lester. Tell her that Calvert can accompany us." But even as he offered the words, he doubted if the footman would agree. Calvert seemed to despise him, as if he were responsible for Lady Rose's venture into the rain.

He took a bite of the porridge with honey, and despite it being too thick, he didn't care. Too many families would fight for a bowl such as this. He ate every bite slowly, and the maid stood from the table.

"I will give her the message, Mr. Donovan, but she won't come." Hattie picked up her bowl and brought it over to wash. "Lady Rose needs to rest and take care of her mother. Especially after the spell Lady Penford had. She's not left her bed since, and that's a good thing, to my way of thinking."

"Will she be all right?"

"I suppose." The maid shrugged. "It's best if she stays in bed, but she's not been eating as much as she should. I'm about to bring her a tray."

Iain hoped Lady Penford would indeed improve, though her lack of appetite was worrisome. "Give Lady Rose my message about riding, and tell her if she cannot, that I understand why." He stood up from the table and added, "Would you be having paper and a pen anywhere about? I should like to write to my family."

"In the desk over there," Hattie responded. But her expression turned curious. "You can read and write, then?"

"I can." He'd been educated at Trinity and had studied mathematics, as well as a bit of law. His mother had sent him away as soon as he was of age, but he'd been grateful for the schooling. It had helped him to be successful at managing the estate after Michael died of consumption.

"I can give your letter to Mr. Fulton, and he'll post it for you," she instructed.

"Thank you, Hattie." Iain crossed the room and opened the desk, where he found a pen, ink, and paper. He brought it over to the table and uncorked the ink, dipping the pen inside. He wrote to his sisters, informing them of all that had happened and his plans for marrying an English bride. If necessary, Colleen and Sybil might be able to aid him by sending proof of his identity.

From the corner of the room, he was aware of Hattie staring at him while he wrote. The maid appeared fascinated, and he tried not to be distracted by her presence.

He paused with his pen, wondering if he dared to write anything to his mother. She had made it quite clear that she wanted nothing to do with him. He'd never understood why she hated him so, but in the letter, he ended with: *Give Mother my regards.*

After he finished the note, he wrote a second letter to Lady Wolcroft, in the hopes that she would soon return from Bath. He explained his situation and asked for her assistance in finding an appropriate wife when they went to London.

He blotted the ink and folded the paper, then looked up at the maid. "I thought you were going to take a tray to Lady Penford?"

"I—I was. I mean, I am," Hattie stammered. "But you really *can* write. I thought you were lying, because, well, you're Irish."

"I am, yes." Did everyone believe him to be a liar? And she had spoken of his nationality as if he bore a rare disease.

The maid shook her head in wonder and held out her hand for the letters.

Iain gave them to her, and Hattie put them in the pocket of her apron. He picked up his soiled dishes and stood, unsure of where to put his porridge bowl and spoon. The maid smiled and said, "Put them by the basin and I'll wash them for you, once I've seen to Lady Penford's breakfast."

He agreed and thanked her before leaving the kitchen. The servants continued filling trays and bustling about their duties, hardly casting him a single look as he headed outside.

He walked through the gardens, and on the way to the stables, he spied tulips that were hanging their heads from the rainstorm this morning. He thought of how Lady Rose had lifted her face to the rain, reveling in the storm. It seemed that she was trying to savor every last drop of joy out of life. He decided to cut a few flowers for her, and perhaps some for Lady Penford as well.

Deeper into the garden he wandered, searching for a pair of shears to cut some flowers. At last, he found an ancient shed beside a tall brick wall. Inside, he found an assortment of gardening tools, shears, and a rusted wheelbarrow that looked as if it hadn't seen the outside world since 1775.

The sight of the broken-down cart made him think of Rose—shut away, pushed into a corner, and forgotten. It wasn't right for her to be treated that way, only brought out from time to time. He couldn't understand why she relied so heavily on a servant to carry her everywhere. It seemed that she ought to find a means of being independent, to go wherever she pleased.

He picked up the shears and left the shed. A climbing rosebush covered the brick wall on the outer edge of the garden, and he decided the new budding roses would welcome, if he could find any blooming. He walked over to inspect the blossoms. When he lifted up one of the branches, he was surprised to see a small door hidden beneath the brambles. He turned the knob, but it was locked. At first, he'd believed the wall was simply a boundary between the maze of hedges and the open lawn . . . but why would there be a door? Something must be hidden behind it, but he couldn't tell what it was without climbing the wall.

Did Rose know it was there? Or even Lady Penford, for that matter?

It's not your concern, he reminded himself. He was not here to mind the errant Lady Penford, or give blossoms to her and her daughter.

Jesus, Mary, and Joseph, he was losing himself in this midst of this nightmare. He could not afford to waste any more time. He needed to reclaim his identity, with or without the help of Lady Rose.

Iain set down the shears, striding toward the stables. Within a quarter of an hour, he had saddled his horse, Darcy, despite the protests of Nelson, the coachman. But before he could leave, Hattie came rushing toward him.

"Mr. Donovan, she says she'll come." The maid was out of breath and she took a moment to settle. "Lady Rose. She wants to go riding, if you'll prepare her horse."

"Not with the likes of you, lad," the coachman protested.

Iain straightened and regarded Nelson. He was done with being treated like a servant. "I am not your lad, and if the lady wishes to go riding with me, that is her decision. Not yours."

The coachman's face turned bright red. "Now, see here—"

Iain ignored the man's bluster and returned to the stables, where he busied himself preparing horses for Lady Rose and her chaperone. All the while, Nelson continued blistering his ears about how improper this was and how Iain was going to be sacked.

He ignored all of it, leading both horses from the stable to join his own mount. Soon enough, he spied Lady Rose, carried in the arms of Calvert. She wore a green riding habit and a matching hat with a feather.

"Good morning, Mr. Donovan." She smiled warmly at him, even as her footman glared. "I must thank you for the invitation to go riding. I've been wanting to leave the house for a few hours."

"How is your mother?" he asked.

Lady Rose inclined her head. "Somewhat better. She had some difficulty speaking, after that spell, but today she seems to be feeling more like herself."

"I am glad to hear it."

Calvert brought Lady Rose over to her horse and assisted her onto the sidesaddle. He shot Iain a disgruntled look, but before he could mount the third horse, Lady Rose stopped him. "Calvert, I have asked Hattie to accompany me as my chaperone."

At that, Iain noticed that the maid was leaning against the stable, lurking in the shadows. He beckoned for her to come forward, but she sent a wary look toward the footman, whose eyes narrowed with annoyance.

"Lady Rose, you can't do this," Calvert pronounced. "What if you are invited to take tea? You will be needing someone to bring you inside, and Hattie's not strong enough to carry you." His tone was filled with triumph, as if Lady Rose hadn't thought of that.

Iain intervened and offered, "I can bring Lady Rose inside, if it is necessary. However, I do not anticipate that we will be there for very long."

Lady Rose seemed to be in agreement. "Since I have arranged for Mr. Donovan to stay at Penford for a brief time, I am certain he can help me. Your presence is not required."

Her footman was already protesting. "But it's wrong and improper, Lady Rose. I cannot condone this."

"Then tell my mother," she countered. "I am certain she will arrange for me to be punished for your imagined misdeeds."

At that, Iain turned away to hide his smile. One could tell Lady Penford anything, and she would forget the tale within an hour.

Calvert sent Hattie a dark look as he helped her onto her horse. "If owt goes amiss, Hattie, you ride back as if Hades's demons are chasing you."

The maid nodded.

"Yes, sir."

"I will be quite well, thank you, Calvert." Lady Rose straightened in her saddle, and began leading the way. She guided her horse toward the gravel pathway, and Iain drew his horse alongside hers.

"I am sorry about that." She glanced back at Calvert and admitted, "He has very strong opinions about what I should or shouldn't do."

"You could choose a different footman," he suggested, keeping his voice low. "If he does not care for his duties, then why should he continue as your escort?" Iain didn't feel it was right for the footman to behave like her father.

"Calvert has been a member of our household for many years." She grimaced. "And his duties concerning me should only be temporary, until I can walk again."

The expression on her face dimmed, as if she didn't want to imagine a future where she was bound to the whims of a footman. "Never mind him for now. Hattie said you wanted to speak with Beauregard again."

Iain pointed toward the main road. "Indeed. Or better yet, his father, if Sir Lester is there. I could use your help in speaking with him." He hoped that she would intervene and help him gain entrance to the estate. He was well aware that his tattered clothing would make any butler turn him away.

"Why would you need to return to Sir Lester's house?" she asked. "Hasn't Beauregard already been punished for stealing your clothes?"

Iain rode alongside her in the direction of Beauregard's house, with Hattie trailing behind. "He didn't return my signet ring or the letter I had with me."

She frowned at that. "I thought he didn't have them. He said he found your horse wandering. What if he's telling the truth?"

"I don't think so." Yet he couldn't deny that the boy's actions had been unusual. Iain had no memory of how he had lost his horse or his belongings, but it *did* seem unlikely that a boy of thirteen could manage such a feat, even with the help of another boy.

There was only one way to find out. "I want to pay a call on his father. It's possible that Beauregard knows who has my ring."

Lady Rose sent him a thoughtful look. "And you need me to help you."

"Aye." He glanced down at his attire and admitted, "I cannot say that I look like much of an earl, do I? They wouldn't be letting me past the servants' entrance, much less the front door."

A secretive smile slid over her face, and he felt like a prized bull being inspected. "You should have allowed me to help you prepare for this call. I could have loaned you my brother's clothing."

"It's the lad's fault that I look this way, isn't it?" He flicked the reins of his horse. "The boy stole what belongs to me, and I'll be having it back."

"But what if he didn't steal your signet ring?" she insisted. "You can hardly ask his father to punish him if he never took it. It might be that your servants knocked you from your horse and stole your belongings. They would be more desperate than a thirteen-year-old boy, I should think."

She might be right, and yet, the evidence suggested otherwise. The boy *had* been found with his coat and horse. "I will speak with him and find out more." That was reasonable enough, he thought.

"So long as you do not interrogate him roughly, I suppose that will be fine." She sent him a sidelong look as if she expected Iain to string the boy up by his heels.

"Are you expecting me to have him horsewhipped?"

"No, of course not." But her tone suggested otherwise. Iain slowed the pace of his horse, eyeing her with suspicion, and she added, "Well, you do seem rather angry."

"I can't imagine why." He made no effort to hide his sarcasm. "I've only had my identity stolen."

"I'm certain we will put it all to rights," she said calmly. "Now, then. Instead of worrying about your signet ring, why don't we talk about something else?"

"Like the weather?"

"That would be impossibly boring. No, I think you should tell me about why you've come all the way to England in search of a bride." A sparkle came into her eyes. "Did a woman break your heart?"

She spoke as if she were digging up gossip, and in spite of himself, he smiled. "I am sorry to disappoint you, but no. My heart is still in one piece, to be sure."

"Surely you left *someone* behind," she insisted. "Was there never a woman in your life?"

He shrugged. "Truthfully, I could have married any lady of my choosing in County Mayo."

She blinked at that. "You seem rather confident, sir. Was it because of your vast estate?"

His smile faded slightly. "Ashton is large enough, aye. But no. It was because I had food stored."

Her expression turned thoughtful. "You may find it more difficult in England, I fear."

His crooked smile turned wicked. "Not necessarily." By way of changing the subject, he remarked, "Though I suppose I'm not the sort of gentlemen the ladies of London are wanting."

Lady Rose motioned for her maid to fall back a few paces. Then she drew their horses a little farther from Hattie before slowing to a halt. "You will need help before you are ready for a ballroom, that is true," she agreed. Her updo was damp from the earlier rain, a few tendrils escaping her bonnet. Iain found himself wanting to tuck one behind her ear but he refrained from touching her.

"Many women like a man who is more like a pirate than a gentleman," Rose offered. "Someone not so refined."

He wasn't certain what to make of that. "You're calling me a pirate?"

"Well, no. Not exactly." Her eyes narrowed at him thoughtfully. "It's simply that you may be . . . quite different from what the ladies of London have come to expect. You're a little rough around the edges."

He said nothing, but her words struck an invisible blow. Aye, he didn't know proper behavior. But she surprised him when she reached over to touch his arm. "It wasn't my intent to offend you, Mr. Donovan."

"You didn't." But she had rightfully pointed out that he wasn't at all ready to blend into society. He lacked the social graces of an earl, because he'd been left behind all those years.

"I could help you," she offered. With a warm smile, she added, "That is, if you turn out to be the earl and not a liar."

"And what do you believe, Lady Rose?"

Her deep brown eyes studied him with interest, and she squeezed his palm. "I believe there is far more to you than anyone knows."

Chapter Six

Her words startled Iain, for he didn't believe that. His own mother believed he was hardly worth notice and had hidden him away for years. Yet Lady Rose suggested that there was more to him? Not at all. He was simply the only one left to do what needed to be done. He kept his hand upon hers for a moment, waiting for some sign of teasing.

But no, she was in earnest. Iain didn't know what to think of her remark, for they were hardly more than strangers.

"Next time, don't forget to wear gloves." She smiled before taking her hand from his. Then she let out a slow breath and pointed toward the end of the road. "We are almost there. What do you plan to say to Beauregard?"

Her abrupt turn of conversation redirected him back to the matter at hand. He had given the matter some thought already. "We are inviting ourselves to tea, and if Sir Lester is in residence, I will ask him if he has seen my signet ring or the letter among Beauregard's belongings."

Rose hesitated and gently suggested, "Will you allow me to try it my way first?"

Her way? And what way was that? Iain eyed her with suspicion. "Are you intending to ask prettily in the hopes that he'll give them back?"

"Wait and see." And with that, she urged her mare forward, leading him up the road toward the small estate. The baronet's land was smaller than his own estate at Ashton, but the two-story house was large enough to boast a dozen rooms, he guessed. The lawn was green and a gravel pathway led up to the stairs. A split-rail fence lined the outer property boundary, and beside the house, Iain glimpsed a fishpond and more gardens.

He couldn't help but be intrigued by Rose's interference. Women were, by nature, more cunning. What did she plan to say or do? The serene look on her face gave no indication of her intentions. He had planned to be forthright with the boy, but it seemed that Rose had subtlety in mind.

He wasn't accustomed to relying on anyone but himself. It was unsettling to step back and let her take command, but Iain wasn't foolish enough to ignore her offer. Rose knew the baronet and his son, and she appeared confident that she could get what she wanted.

And if she couldn't, well then, he could step in and demand the return of his belongings.

When they reached the entrance to the house, Hattie dismounted and knocked upon the door. She announced their arrival to the butler, offering a calling card.

"Lift me down from the horse," Rose murmured.

Iain obeyed, lifting her into his arms while a groom came to take their horses. She felt light, though her gown was barricaded with a whalebone corset and blue silk. Even holding her like this was foreign, for the only time he'd ever carried a lady in his arms was when he'd brought Lady Rose back to her bed. This was different. It felt as if he were carrying a piece of porcelain and at any moment, he might stumble and break her. But he couldn't deny that it felt good to carry her in his arms.

"Can you stand?" he inquired softly, and she shook her head.

"Not yet." Frustration tinged her voice, and he supposed he ought to feel guilty. Instead, he was glad for a few moments longer to hold her.

The butler invited them inside, and Iain carried Lady Rose over the threshold. "I have come to pay a call upon Sir Lester," she said. "Is he receiving today?"

"I shall inquire," the butler replied. To a footman he said, "Please show Lady Rose to the drawing room."

There was no mention of Iain, and he wasn't certain if it had been deliberate on Rose's part. Possibly. He followed the footman into the drawing room, and she pointed toward the far side of the room. "I will sit over there, in front of the window."

He deposited her into the chair she had selected. The drawing room was the color of a robin's eggshell, with cream drapes and gilt furnishings. It reminded him of his grandmother's furniture, delicate and ornate.

"Where do you want me to stand?" he inquired. He wasn't at all clear on her plans, nor his role in them.

"You may sit over here." She pointed to the chair beside her.

Iain sat down, resting his wrists upon the arms of the chair. "Why have you taken it upon yourself to speak with Sir Lester on my behalf, Lady Rose?"

She shrugged. "I suppose because I owe you a favor for saving my mother's life. And because I would like to know what happened when you were attacked."

Before she could say another word, the baronet arrived. Sir Lester was taller than Iain had expected, and reminded him of a heron. The moment he spied Lady Rose, his face brightened. "What a wonderful surprise, my dear. It pleases me no end to have you call upon our humble house."

His dear, was she? Iain stood from his chair, feeling the sudden sense that he was intruding upon a private moment.

"May I present to you Iain Donovan, the Earl of Ashton?" She gestured toward him, and Iain inclined his head in greeting.

"Sir Lester."

The baronet's expression turned surprised, and he appeared uncertain of how to respond. "Lord Ashton. We have not met before." His gaze swept over Iain's disheveled clothing.

"No, we have not. Ireland is my home, and I only arrived at Penford a few days ago."

"His coach suffered an accident, and many of his belongings were stolen," Lady Rose explained. "Fortunately, your son, Beauregard, was helping him to recover them. We came to ask if more of his possessions have been found. Some of his friends tend toward mischief, I am afraid." She shot the baronet an apologetic look.

A sly one, wasn't she? Instead of accusing Beauregard of theft, she'd offered a compliment. It was an intriguing line of questioning.

"This is the first I've heard of it," Sir Lester remarked. "Beauregard left school without my permission. He will be returning soon, and I am not certain what he knows." The baronet appeared uneasy, and he frowned.

"Would you be so kind as to bring your son to speak with us?" Lady Rose asked. "I am certain he could tell us whether or not he was able to recover more of Lord Ashton's belongings."

The baronet signaled to his footman and spoke quietly to the man, before sending him away. "I shall, indeed. Would you both stay for tea? I should be glad of your company."

As the man spoke, his eyes rested upon Lady Rose. It was clear that the older man held her in high esteem and was interested in her beyond the level of friendship.

"I would be delighted to join you," Lady Rose answered, "but we did not mean to intrude upon your hospitality."

"It is an unexpected pleasure." He beamed and gave orders for refreshments. Iain returned to his seat, making small conversation about the weather. He avoided any discussion of the troubles in Ireland.

Within a few minute more, Beauregard arrived, a sullen expression on his face. The moment he spied Iain, he glared at him and wheeled to leave.

"Come back here this instant," his father commanded. "Lady Rose and Lord . . ." He paused a moment, eyeing Iain's attire. ". . . Lord Ashton have come to ask questions of you."

Beauregard's attitude made it clear that he intended to tell them nothing at all. He remained standing with one foot outside the doorway.

Lady Rose tried to send him a smile. "Beauregard, Lord Ashton is grateful that you managed to retrieve many of his belongings when they were stolen."

The confused expression on the boy's face was quickly masked. Iain stared at him, giving nothing away, but making it clear that he had best cooperate. "But a good deal of them are still missing," he finished. Taking his cue from Rose, he lied, "We received your note saying that you found more of the lost items. I thought it best that we came at once to see what you have."

His pointed look was not lost on the boy. But before Beauregard could deny it, Rose intervened again. "Sir Lester, I hope you do not mind if we accompany your son back to his room, so that he might show us the remainder?"

The baronet seemed uncertain about this. He narrowed his gaze upon Beauregard. "Not once did you mention this gentleman to me. And what's this about his belongings being stolen?"

His son hesitated, as if wanting to deny it. "I gave him back his clothes and his horse."

Iain crossed his arms and regarded the boy with a stern look of *I know you have the rest.*

"Is there more that I should be aware of, Beauregard Allen Wallace?" Sir Lester asked. His voice had gone hard, as if he was aware of his son's misdeeds.

Beauregard glared at all of them, but finally fumbled in his pocket. "I found this." He held out a gold signet ring, and never had Iain been more grateful to see his brother's ring.

He took it from the boy and slid it onto his finger, no longer caring about the letter of introduction. The ring proved his identity, and that was all that mattered. When he looked over at Lady Rose, her expression remained neutral.

"Thank you," he told the boy. Iain traced the engraved surface, relieved to have it back. "I am glad you found my signet ring. Was there anything else you found?"

"No." Beauregard didn't at all seem pleased, but with a nod of permission from his father, he left the drawing room, retreating for his room.

"Well, I must admit I am surprised," Sir Lester said. After his son was out of earshot, he added, "My son, unfortunately, lacks discipline. Ever since his mother died, he's been difficult. I had no choice but to send him away. This is the first good deed he's done in a long while." The man's expression grew distant, and his gaze shifted back toward the door.

Rose leaned forward and smiled at the man. "He's still a boy, isn't he? And I suppose when he's away at school, he misses his father."

"I rather doubt that," Sir Lester responded. "If he rolled his eyes any more at me, they'd roll out of his head and onto the floor."

"But you're the only family he has left, aren't you?" Rose asked gently. "He may simply want to be at home."

She went on to offer her sympathy, but while she spoke, Iain found himself caught by the softness of her tone. She saw beyond the anger of a young boy to the pain beneath Beau's actions. Whether the boy had stolen Iain's belongings or had merely happened upon them, he couldn't be sure. But Rose appeared more forgiving than the lad deserved.

"Will you be traveling to London for the Season?" Sir Lester was asking Lady Rose. A footman had arrived with the tea and refreshments. Rose poured each of them a cup, and Iain declined cream or sugar.

She turned her attention back to Sir Lester. "My mother wishes to go to London, but she isn't well right now. I do not think it is possible."

"When she recovers, perhaps?" The baronet was clearly wanting Lady Rose to return to the city. "Have you no wish to join the gatherings? Even with your condition, I would think that you would prefer being amid the social circles and the other young ladies."

Rose shook her head, wincing slightly. "I would rather not face society just yet. I am certain you can understand this."

"Of course. But . . . if I may be so bold, does this mean that you have parted company with Lord Burkham?"

Iain's curiosity was piqued. He leaned forward, wanting to know more about Lady Rose's intended.

"No," she answered. "I have reason to believe that he will offer for me, eventually."

The baronet sighed. "Lady Rose, any number of men would be glad to marry you. That is, if it is your wish." The smile on his face suggested that he wanted to be one of them.

"I do not think I shall marry for some time." Her voice was calm, but beneath it, Iain detected an air of frustration.

"Lady Rose, do not let one man's folly dissuade you from enjoying the Season," Sir Lester reassured her. "Were I to have the honor of accompanying you to a soiree, rest assured, I would have no desire to leave your side."

She sent him a weary smile. "You are very kind, sir."

It was doubtful that kindness had anything to do with it. The baronet was besotted with her and made no secret of that fact.

But Lady Rose was not finished. "The truth is, I do not wish to return to London until I can walk again. And I do not know how long it will take."

"Oh." Sir Lester appeared startled by this revelation, but then he brightened. "Then you will be here, in Yorkshire. I would be glad to assist you in any way that I can."

Though it was none of his affair, Iain didn't miss the look of discomfort on Rose's face. He wiped his hands upon a linen napkin and rose to his feet. "I must thank you for your hospitality, Sir Lester. But I should be taking Lady Rose home again before it rains."

"I could drive both of you back in my coach," the baronet suggested. "It would be no trouble at all."

"No, thank you. I enjoy riding." Rose dismissed the idea and added, "Lord Ashton was good enough to escort me here, so I will be fine. But if you would send word to your groom to prepare our horses, it would be greatly appreciated." She sent him a nod, and with that, Iain lifted her into his arms. It gave him a slight satisfaction to note the discomfited expression upon the baronet's face.

"It will . . . take some time for my groom to saddle your horses," the baronet said. "Would you rather wait a little longer, perhaps?"

Lady Rose flushed, but she shook her head. "Thank you, but I really should be going. By the time Lord Ashton brings me outside, I will only need to wait a few minutes."

Iain kept a firm grip upon her as he walked slowly toward the front door. "Please tell your son that I am grateful for the return of my ring. And if he should come across any other belongings—"

"I will have them sent to you," the baronet answered. He walked back with them to the foyer, keeping his steps slow as if to delay their departure.

"Thank you again for the tea." Lady Rose smiled at the man, and Iain took that as his signal to bring her outside. Her maid, Hattie, followed a short distance behind.

Sir Lester escorted them to the steps to bid them farewell, and Iain kept Lady Rose in his arms while he waited for their horses. The sky was brooding with more rain, and he hoped the groom would return before the downpour began. A slight breeze stirred against the moors in the distance, a portent of the forthcoming storm.

Fortunately, they only had to wait a few minutes more before the servant brought their animals. He helped both Lady Rose and Hattie mount their horses before he swung onto Darcy's back.

"We'd better make haste," he warned Rose. "We're about to be caught in a storm."

"Follow me," she told him. Instead of riding along the pathway, she took an eastward direction. He had no idea what her intentions were, but he obeyed. Her maid glanced up at the sky with worry.

The sky grew increasingly darker, and raindrops spattered against Iain's hat. But just as he heard the low rumble of thunder, Lady Rose led him through a forest grove along a narrow path. A brook ran parallel to them, splashing across the rocks. On the far side of a bridge, she pointed to a summerhouse. The stone structure was octagonal in shape with a roof and four window-shaped openings that were exposed with no glass. "We'll take shelter there."

He didn't argue, though they could easily have returned to Penford by now. It seemed that Lady Rose wanted to extend their outing a little longer.

The maid shivered and said, "I'm right scairt of thunderstorms, Lady Rose. Couldn't we go back?"

"As soon as the rain stops, we will."

"But, it's not so very far. We could be at Penford in a few minutes. Inside." Hattie wrung her hands and huddled close to the horse.

"If you're wanting to go back, go on then," Iain told the maid. Though it was not proper to leave them unchaperoned, she was obviously terrified of the storm. He wouldn't force her to stay.

"I can't be leaving Lady Rose," she protested.

At that, her mistress sighed. "We won't stay long, Hattie, I promise you. But I should like to take shelter for a little while. At least until the rain slows."

Iain dismounted and tethered his horse, before helping the women down. He carried Lady Rose inside the summerhouse and set her down upon one of the stone benches inside. The structure was not fully protected, but it was better than remaining in the pouring rain. The wind shifted, blowing a shower directly toward Rose, and she laughed, covering her bonnet with both hands. "This isn't exactly keeping me dry, Mr. Donovan. Or am I supposed to address you as Lord Ashton now?"

He reached down to lift her away from the opening and carried her closer to the center of the summerhouse. Her eyes held merriment and she added, "This was not one of my better ideas."

Iain only shrugged. "It will do for now." He cast a glance over at Hattie, who was seated on the stone floor, her knees huddled up, with both hands covering her ears. Another rumble of thunder resounded, and she muttered to herself, "I don't want to die, I don't want to die."

"You're not going to die, Hattie," Lady Rose reassured her. But the young maid wasn't listening. She appeared terrified of the storm, and she buried her face against her knees.

The rain spattered against the stone walls, and Iain was struck by their situation. He had never before been trapped in a summerhouse with a beautiful woman in his arms, and it wasn't unwelcome. Her slender body was light, though her skirts billowed down to the ground.

"I fear this is rather awkward for you." She sent him a chagrined smile. "I didn't mean for you to hold me until the rain stopped."

"I don't mind it, *a chara.*"

"I must be getting heavy." Her face was flushed, as if she hadn't considered the consequences of the rain. But her slight weight meant nothing at all to him.

He met her gaze, and in her brown eyes, he saw that she was unsettled by his presence. Though he had done nothing at all except hold her, he was well aware of her slender curves. Her gown was damp, outlining her figure, and he found himself studying her closely.

There was no hint of red in her brown hair now, for it was soaked from the rain. Her eyelashes were tipped with droplets, and the deep brown of her eyes fascinated him. Her nose had a slight tilt, and her cheeks held the flush of embarrassment. Even her lips were a soft pink, her upper lip slightly smaller than the lower. She pressed them together for a moment and then whispered, "Why are you staring at me?"

"Because you are a beautiful woman. Why wouldn't I stare?"

He knew he ought to smile to reassure her that he was only teasing and it meant nothing, but that wasn't entirely true. She was lovely, and he saw no harm in telling her so.

"You are making me feel uncomfortable," she admitted. "And I should remind you that my heart is already given to another man."

"Don't worry, *a chara*. I wouldn't be trespassing where I'm not wanted. They're only words."

She still appeared uneasy. "Perhaps you should put me down on the bench again, Lord Ashton."

"If you're wanting me to, I will. But I should warn you that the rain will soak through your gown and make you colder. It might not be wise."

"Nothing I do is very wise, it seems." She lowered her gaze to avoid his. "I know how improper this is. My grandmother would be appalled if she could see you holding me right now. Even though we do have a chaperone." She nodded toward Hattie, who was still cowering from the storm. "I-I should have brought Calvert along."

He didn't deny it. The scent of her skin enticed him, and he was caught up in watching a single raindrop slide down her throat.

Her breathing seemed to shift, and she was staring back at him now. Her eyes passed over his hair and his face. In her scrutiny, he wondered if she found him appealing enough. He'd never given much thought to his looks, but he hoped she was not displeased.

"Why are you looking at me?" he murmured.

Her mouth tightened, but she managed a smile. "I suppose, for the same reason you looked at me."

"Because you find me handsome?" He continued watching her, and the longer he held her, the more it struck him that he liked having this woman in his arms.

"Well, you *are* that," she admitted with a smile. "But I wondered if you might be a pirate in disguise, planning to carry me off. Despite my intentions to wed Lord Burkham." There was teasing in her voice, meant to lighten the mood.

"I thought you were already engaged to marry him."

"Almost," she confessed. "He was going to ask me before I became ill."

Iain didn't respond to that, for an almost betrothal was no betrothal at all. "Why is he not here with you now?"

Rose shrugged. "He has his duties in Parliament. But he *has* written to me often. I received a letter just last week."

"Did you, then? And I suppose he's come to visit you as well?"

There was a shadowed look in her eyes. "No. But truthfully, I didn't want him to visit. Not when I am like this." Her face grew somber, as if she was embarrassed by her inability to walk.

Although he understood her reluctance, he felt compelled to point out, "If I were betrothed to a beautiful woman who fell ill, the demons of hell couldn't keep me away from her."

"It's different between Lord Burkham and me. It's more formal, as is befitting a viscount."

It sounded to Iain as if Lord Too-Busy-Burkham wasn't at all worthy of a woman like Rose.

"Don't you resent him for staying away?"

"Not at all." She behaved as if nothing was wrong. Yet, Iain sensed that he'd struck a nerve. Her expression remained serene, but in her eyes there was a hint of worry.

Iain shifted her position so that his hands were beneath her hips. It was more of an embrace now, and she raised an eyebrow. "What are you doing, Lord Ashton?"

"Adjusting your position." He wanted to see her face when he was speaking to her.

"I knew I was getting too heavy. Just put me down on the bench. It doesn't matter if the rain blows on me. I'm already soaked."

"As I said before, you're not heavy."

"You wouldn't tell me if I was, would you?" she mused. She rested her hands upon his shoulders, her gaze intent upon his.

"No. But it's no trouble to hold you."

He was even more distracted when Rose touched his cheeks. "You haven't shaved in a few days, have you?"

"I've been rather busy trying to reclaim my earldom," he reminded her. "There was no time." But the soft touch of her hands upon the bristled line of his jaw was driving him toward madness. Never had any woman touched him in this way. Her hands seemed to burn through his skin, awakening sensations that drove out common sense. He was aware of every line of her body, the scent of her skin, and the water droplets on her cheeks.

She offered a wry smile. "Pirate."

He growled at her. "Argh." His voice came out rough and husky, and she laughed softly.

The longer he held Lady Rose in his arms, the more he desired her. Iain was captivated by her full lips, and for a moment, their breathing seemed to fall into a rhythm. Rose's arms had softened against him, until they hung loosely around his neck. Her brown eyes met his with awareness and a sense that this should not be happening between them. But he couldn't deny that he wanted to lower her body and claim her mouth. He wanted to taste the sweetness of her lips and give in to his own temptation.

"You should put me down now," she murmured.

She was right. And yet, he had no wish to let go of her. "If you're wanting to stand up, I could help you balance."

Her expression turned wary. "I've been trying to stand up for the past month. It hasn't worked thus far."

"Would you like to try again?" he asked.

She shook her head, as if she'd already given up. "My legs haven't the strength."

"That isn't what I asked."

She hesitated a moment but then nodded. Slowly, Iain lowered her, holding her by the waist as he brought her feet to stand upon the earthen floor.

Her knees wouldn't bear her weight and buckled beneath her, so he held her steady, using his strength to hold her upright. "Keep your legs straight, if you can. I'll help support you until you've got your balance." With both arms around her waist, he kept her upright, being careful not to let her slip.

Once again, her legs crumpled beneath her, and he saw her emotions falter. She was afraid to trust herself. "I can't do this."

"Look at me, Lady Rose," he said. He held her waist, staring into her eyes. "Try again."

Gently, he eased his hands until she was standing on her own. For the barest second, she held her legs straight, until her knees gave out again and he caught her.

"I won't let you fall." He pressed his hands against her waist until she regained her stability. This time, she stood for two seconds before her legs buckled.

Tears rimmed her eyes, and he wondered for a moment if she was upset with herself. But then, she started to laugh through her tears. "I did it. I know it was only for a moment, but—" Her words broke off in a half sob before her laughter intruded again.

The look of utter joy on her face was like a fist to his gut. Never before had he seen such elation, and he continued holding her upright.

"I stood," she managed to whisper, her smile incredulous. "After all these months, I did it. Yes, it was only for a second or two . . . but it was real, wasn't it?"

"It was, aye." He suspected that it had drained a great deal of her strength away. He was supporting all her weight now, and she made no attempt to stand again. "In time, you'll get stronger."

He lifted her back into his arms and brought her over to the bench. He eased her down into a seated position.

"Do you know how long I've been trying to stand?" Rose rested her hands in his, holding both of his palms for a moment. The gentle pressure of her grip was a welcome affection, and he squeezed them in return. Her face flushed, as if she suddenly realized how inappropriate it was for them to hold hands.

Her smile faded slightly, and she pulled back, folding her hands in her lap. She behaved as if nothing had happened and said, "If I can stand, I may learn to walk again."

"You'll need to strengthen your legs." She would have to keep practicing until they could bear her weight again.

"Thank you for this, Lord Ashton. You cannot know how much this means to me."

He wanted to reach for her hands again, but resisted the urge. When he glanced over at Hattie, who was supposed to be chaperoning, the maid was still huddled up, hiding her eyes. "How long has it been since you've walked?"

"Six months." She tried to lift her knee, but she wasn't able to move it more than an inch or so. "I've been trying to recover ever since."

"How did it happen?"

She sent him a chagrined look. "I became sick after eating potatoes, of all things. I was violently ill, but the effects went beyond my stomach. My face went numb, I could hardly see without the room blurring, and I had trouble breathing." Her expression grew somber, and she added, "I nearly died from it, and the doctors couldn't say what my illness was."

"It must have been frightening," he said. But even as he spoke the words, the grim memories of the famine reminded him of others who had died from bad potatoes. She was not alone in her suffering. Though he tried to shut out the visions of blight, of slimy potatoes rotting in the ground, he doubted if he could ever eat a potato again. "It's glad I am that you lived, Lady Rose."

"So am I," she agreed with a faint smile. "But after I recovered, I was never able to regain my strength." Her hands moved back to rest upon his shoulders. "But I *will* walk again, I promise you that. No matter how long it takes."

He met her gaze, forcing the memories away. "And then what? You'll return to London to Lord Burkham?"

A flush came over her cheeks. "Perhaps, if my mother's health improves."

The idea of Lady Rose returning to a man who had so obviously abandoned her made him leery. Yet, there was a softness in her voice, a yearning look in her eyes. Damned if she wasn't still in love with the man.

"I want to believe that if I can walk again, we might one day marry."

Iain didn't reveal his true thoughts. Any man who had ignored Lady Rose during her illness, only bothering to write letters, was naught but a coward. But he wasn't about to insult her suitor. She would learn the truth for herself when she reached London. And if he was wrong about Burkham, so be it.

"You will learn to walk again," he predicted. "But are you certain that you still want Lord Burkham?"

She let out a sigh. "I do. Very much." There was enough of an ache in her voice, that he wished he could help her. Lady Rose had a determined nature that appealed greatly to him. She was quite lovely of face, and he admired her spirit.

He didn't want to see her suffer from a broken heart. She deserved better than that, after all she'd endured.

He could understand her desire to return to London, fully recovered from her illness. And he found himself wanting to help. If he offered for the sake of friendship, she might refuse because of her pride. But he needed her assistance, as well. He had no inkling of how to behave in polite society or how to find a bride. Perhaps they could strike a bargain between them.

"Lady Rose, I've a proposition for you," Iain began. "I wonder if we might help one another."

Her face held curiosity, and she waited for him to speak. He stood by the open window and admitted, "As I've said before, I've come to England in search of a wife. But I have never been to London, and my knowledge is woefully lacking."

"And what would your bride receive in return for handing over her dowry? Besides a pirate for a husband, of course."

"Several thousand acres of land, along with the manor house."

Lady Rose thought for a moment. "Just how particular are you, regarding her looks?"

Her caveat was not lost upon him. "It all depends. Given the choice between a shrewish beauty and a kindly troll, I suppose the troll would be easier to live with."

"There are a few possibilities," she said. "Though I would not call Evangeline a troll. More like painfully shy. A wallflower who hardly talks to anyone. But she is a dear friend of mine."

"That wouldn't bother me, if she has a good heart." He leaned back against the summerhouse wall. "If you will help me find a suitable bride, in return, I could help you learn to walk again."

He wasn't expecting the burst of laughter from her. With a smirk, she added, "Are you from Nazareth, then? Can you turn water into wine as well?"

He ignored the jibe. "You did stand just now, did you not? You've not used your legs in half a year. If they gain strength, it could happen."

Her teasing mood dissipated, and she turned serious. "I want to walk again, and I am willing to do whatever it takes to learn how." She brushed droplets of water from her face and regarded him. "But it could be another year before that happens. You don't have that much time."

He didn't know whether her prediction would be true or not, but he wanted to make the attempt. And there was no question that he needed her help in navigating the complications of London society. "Are you willing to let me help you, Lady Rose?"

She hesitated for nearly a minute, staring outside the stone window of the summerhouse. The rain had stopped, and they could now return to their horses. Hattie had risen from the floor and was standing a discreet distance from them, though she had undoubtedly heard every word.

"Possibly," Lady Rose said at last. "But I am realistic about what progress I might make." She faced him squarely, her mind made up. "I will amend our bargain. If I manage to take two steps on my own in the next few weeks, I'll make a list of the wealthiest heiresses whom I believe would make a suitable match for you. And I will speak to them and to their parents on your behalf."

"Fair enough." He reached out to her hand and kissed the back of it. "I am not from Nazareth, as you said. But we are in agreement."

It was not a contract he had made lightly. For he had a feeling that Lady Rose would indeed walk, sooner than she believed it was possible.

Chapter Seven

After they returned to the house, Rose's thoughts were in turmoil. Now that she had seen the signet ring upon Mr. Donovan's hand, she felt guilty about doubting his identity. They had treated him so badly—he'd slept in an attic room among the servants, for heaven's sake.

She asked Mrs. Marlock to make up one of the guest rooms, and Rose sent some of her brother's older belongings for Lord Ashton to wear.

But that wasn't the only reason she was anxious. No, it was because Lord Ashton had offered to help her walk again. This afternoon, that dream had finally seemed within reach. It had been so long since she'd been able to bear weight upon her legs. Even though it had caused her great fatigue and had barely lasted more than a second, she was so thankful for that fragile moment.

Only days ago, she had wondered if it would ever be possible. And now, Lord Ashton had made it real. Though she was afraid to get her hopes up—for she had no idea how he could help her—she couldn't stop the feelings of joy.

She spent the remainder of the afternoon daydreaming and thinking of possible brides for Lord Ashton. Most of the wealthy heiresses had no need of a penniless Irish lord. They could choose any man they wanted. But surely there was someone.

A knock sounded at the door, and she heard Lily's voice. "Rose, may I come in?"

"Yes, do."

The door opened, and her sister hurried inside. Lily's face held excitement. "I have news. The Countess of Castledon is coming to supper this evening. Along with Grandmother."

"I thought she was in Bath." Rose straightened, wondering why their grandmother had not simply returned home.

"She was. But she stopped to spend the night at Castledon, and the countess thought to send word of her impending arrival."

Rose managed a slight smile. "I imagine it was a warning that we should brace ourselves." Though she loved her grandmother, she had a feeling that the old woman was plotting something. Why else would she stop at Castledon first?

Lily sent her a pained smile. "I suppose we had best prepare ourselves." She sat down on the bed and said, "I hired a man to travel to India to search for James. He needs to come back, Rose."

"I know it." Her deeper fear was that their brother had disappeared somehow or was hurt. All of them were trying to put up a brave front, but what if he didn't return?

"We are having difficulty with some of the tenants," Lily said. "Many of them haven't paid their rents. Then, too, some of our money has gone missing."

"Missing? How?"

"When I was visiting Mother this morning, she confessed that she had given money to the poor." Lily's expression revealed her dismay.

"Oh, dear," Rose sighed. "How much?"

"A thousand pounds, at least. Any time someone asks her for money, she gives it. Apparently someone from a charitable society asked her for a donation."

Rose winced, for she hadn't known of this. "She cannot be expected to handle money. Not anymore."

"Not in her current state of mind," Lily agreed.

"It makes me wonder, what else has she been hiding from us?" Rose hadn't worried about the state of their finances, for everything had seemed fine. But if it wasn't, what then? She didn't like to think about it.

"I don't know," Lily said. "But we need James to return. Once he does, we can unravel all this." She crossed the room and opened Rose's wardrobe. "In the meantime, would you like my help in getting dressed for dinner?"

"If you like." She attempted to move her legs over the side of the bed, but she lacked the strength to do so without lifting them with her hands. "I will wear the violet gown. And please ring for Hattie, so she can help me with my hair."

It was her own vanity, but she wanted to look nice. Especially since Lord Ashton would be joining them at dinner for the first time.

"Your hair does look . . . interesting." Lily grimaced and brought over the gown. "You were caught in the rain, I imagine?"

"Yes." She wanted to confess everything to her sister, about how Lord Ashton had helped her stand while Hattie cowered from the rainstorm. But the more she thought of his calm strength, the more her face flushed. When he had held her in the summerhouse, the heat of his hands around her waist had spread all the way through her body.

The earl had evoked such a feeling of longing, she hadn't expected her senses to awaken in such a way. She could not deny that he had kindled up the fierce need for human touch. She had wanted to lean her head against his broad chest, allowing him to hold her up.

It was so wrong.

She told herself that it was only her loneliness for Lord Burkham that had made her so susceptible to temptation. Once she saw Thomas again, these feelings would fade.

Her sister helped her dress, and Rose decided that it was best to keep silent about what had happened in the summerhouse.

"You are *not* attending supper." Calvert sent Iain a murderous glare and blocked the hallway. "Servants do not dine with the family." The older footman puffed up and said, "I don't know what lies you've been telling, but you're nowt but a charlatan. Someone has to stop you."

Iain stood his ground. He wasn't about to waste time arguing with the footman. Instead, he stared back at the man with the confident knowledge that he was indeed the Earl of Ashton. But before Calvert could speak another word, an elderly woman approached, leaning lightly against her cane.

"Ashton! I am so pleased you could come as our guest." She beamed at him and reached out to take his hand. "My goodness, you're the very image of Moira. I would know you anywhere." Lady Wolcroft peered at him, her face alight with warmth.

Calvert looked appalled, his mouth gaping like a codfish. Iain had to admit, the man's discomfort was gratifying. At least he had the good graces not to speak.

"I apologize that I was on holiday when you arrived." Lady Wolcroft patted his hand and took his arm. "But I want to reassure you that I *did* receive your letter last winter, and I am confident we will indeed find you a bride." She guided him down the hallway, while behind him Calvert sputtered.

"I agree," came another woman's voice. Iain turned and saw a matron who sent him a vivid smile. Her blond hair was arranged into a neat updo beneath her bonnet, and the mischievous expression on her face revealed that both of them had overheard the footman's outburst.

"Lord Ashton, may I present Amelia Hartford, the Countess of Castledon." Lady Wolcroft nodded to her friend as she introduced them.

Iain bowed. "Lady Castledon. It's pleased I am to make your acquaintance." He sent her a smile of his own, glancing back at Calvert, who held the rigid posture of a statue.

The countess exchanged a look with Lady Wolcroft, and he could have sworn the pair of them were plotting. "You were right, Mildred. Ashton will have no difficulty whatsoever finding a bride. He is quite good looking, and that Irish accent will cause many a young lady to fall into a swoon. I, for one, should be glad to offer whatever assistance possible. There is nothing I adore more than matchmaking."

Iain wasn't at all certain whether to be grateful or frightened. Calvert stepped forward to take Lady Castledon's bonnet and wrap, and he cleared his throat loudly.

Lady Wolcroft was ignoring him, but he kept coughing until at last she asked, "Calvert, are you suffering from consumption, or was there something you needed to say?"

The footman stiffened. "My lady, I believe this man to be an imposter. He cannot possibly be lord of anything at all. I wanted to warn you."

"What on earth are you prattling on about, Calvert?" the woman demanded. "I know exactly who he is."

"B-but, he arrived wearing nothing but—"

"It is a story best told over supper," Iain interrupted. "Suffice it to say that I was robbed of my belongings on the journey and arrived here looking like a beggar."

"Oh, that *does* sound like a good story," Lady Castledon gushed. "I do so want to hear all about it. Especially the part where you were wearing nothing."

At that, Iain nearly choked. The mischief in the countess's eyes revealed that she had fully intended the innuendo. "I hesitate to disappoint you, Lady Castledon, but I was half-clothed."

"I should like to have seen *that.*" The matron winked at him. "Do tell me that you will allow us to meddle and choose the perfect bride for you. My husband, David, thinks that I interfere too much, but I say that men need to be managed. Don't you agree?"

He understood that she was only having a bit of fun, and despite Lady Wolcroft's horrified expression, he inclined his head. "I give myself over into your hands. Do with me what you will."

"Oh, I *do* like you, Lord Ashton," the countess sighed. "It's a good thing I'm happily married, or I should have set my cap for you myself."

Iain escorted both ladies toward the dining room, while Calvert glowered. As they walked, Lady Castledon and Lady Wolcroft continually chattered, filling his ears with promises of how they would help him choose a bride.

When they reached the dining room, Lily rose and exclaimed, "Grandmother, I am so glad you've returned." She kissed the woman on the cheek and then offered a greeting to Lady Castledon.

Lady Penford was already seated at the table, her face pale. The matron hardly looked well enough to dine with them, and when her gaze turned to her mother, she did not appear to recognize the older woman.

Lady Wolcroft's expression dimmed at the sight, but she crossed the room and went over to embrace her daughter. "I heard that you were ill, Iris. I am so sorry that I was away and did not receive word until a few days ago."

The woman did not respond to her mother's words, and there came a rise of panic in her eyes. Iain decided to ignore propriety, and he chose a seat beside the matron. Strangely, it did seem that she recognized him, and her eyes seemed to plead with him to keep her safe.

"Are you feeling better, then, Lady Penford?" he asked gently. "No bad dreams are plaguing you?"

"S-some," she stammered. She looked down at the table and clenched her hands together.

"Then it will be good to have your family around you," he reassured her. "Your mother and your daughters."

She nodded but kept her gaze fixed upon the tablecloth. An awkward silence filled up the space while the others took their seats. Rose had not yet arrived, but Iain hoped she would join them soon. He was eager to see her again after their outing in the rain.

The countess sat across from him, and she eyed Lady Penford thoughtfully before choosing another topic to change the subject. "Lord Ashton, how is your family?"

He could have said that they were all fine, but then, was there any purpose to a polite lie? The countess was quite aware of why he had come to Yorkshire. This was about planning a strategy, finding a bride, and saving his sisters' hopes for marriage.

"We have fallen upon difficult times," he admitted. "It's grateful I am, that my mother and you"—he turned to Lady Wolcroft—"have remained close."

The older woman smiled and added, "Moira was like a daughter to me. She came to England for boarding school, and she spent all her school holidays with us. Do you remember Moira, dear?"

Lady Penford shook her head. Her eyes focused upon the wall, distant and unseeing.

Lady Wolcroft's smile grew pained. "Be that as it may, Moira began writing letters to me. She told me I was the mother she'd always wanted, and she was such a bright spirit. Then one day, just before you were born, her letters stopped. I wrote to her for many years, but she never answered. Even after I visited her at Ashton, she remained distant. Your letter was the first I've received from your family in a long time."

"My mother? A bright spirit?" He couldn't imagine her that way. Moira had always been a tyrannical shrew.

The older woman sent him a kindly smile. "Yes, she used to be. It's possible that a broken heart made her bitter, after your father died."

Iain tried to imagine his mother smiling and found it impossible to do so. "She's gone to New York with my sisters," he told her. "It's been dangerous at Ashton in the past year. She thought it would be best to take them away for a time."

"I can understand that," the countess answered. "I've seen many of the refugees from Dublin, and I can only imagine the suffering. Any mother would want to protect her children."

Although it was true that Moira had been eager to leave with his sisters, she had not spared him a good-bye. It didn't seem that she'd even cared.

A gloved hand touched his, and he looked over at Lady Penford. "It must have been hard for her to leave that burden on you." The matron sent him a sympathetic look, and he squeezed her hand in return.

The woman might indeed suffer from madness, but she had a good heart. And perhaps it was for that reason that he held a softness toward her.

While Lady Castledon and Lady Wolcroft began speaking together about their strategy of finding him a wife, Iain lowered his voice and asked, "How are you truly, Lady Penford? Have the wolves troubled you at all?"

Her face paled, and she seemed to blink away her reverie. "No, not today. But I feel them there, circling around me. Without James, I don't know what I can do."

Lady Penford was appeared dismayed, but Iain reassured her, "I will be here for at least the next fortnight. And I promise, I'll allow no one to harm you."

The desperate hope in the matron's eyes was heartbreaking, but she managed to nod. "I do hope so."

Out of the corner of his eye, he noticed Calvert bringing Lady Rose into the dining room at last. He placed the young woman as far from Iain as possible. Then Calvert began assisting the other footman in serving the first course. He gave Iain a bowl of soup, but there was no spoon. No doubt the footman had sought petty vengeance on purpose.

"Rose, you are looking as lovely as ever," Lady Castledon pronounced. "I do believe the Yorkshire weather agrees with you."

Lady Rose sent the woman an amused look. "Because it rains so often?"

The countess laughed. "I beg your pardon. I meant the fresh air, not the damp. There are moments when it doesn't rain."

"Sometimes the rain is welcome," Iain offered. He sent a knowing look toward Rose before he took a sip of the wine. With Hattie as a neglectful chaperone, it had given them a moment alone. He would never forget Rose's triumph in standing for a brief moment. Her face had lit up with such joy, he'd been struck by the hope in her beautiful eyes.

Lady Castledon's gaze shifted from Rose to him, and he realized belatedly that the countess was already determining whether a match could be made between them.

"What sort of wife are you searching for?" Lady Wolcroft asked. "Amelia and I can put our heads together to think of something."

"He wants a bride with a dowry large enough to rival the crown jewels," Rose teased. She raised her own glass in a silent toast, her eyes sparkling with merriment.

"My dear, don't be vulgar," Lady Wolcroft chided. To Iain, she said, "Although, I do understand that a certain . . . pecuniary stability would be welcome. Especially given the famine in Ireland."

Lady Castledon leaned in, steepling her fingers. "Do you want a wallflower or a woman who speaks her mind?"

"Either is fine." He truly didn't care one way or the other. So long as the woman was kind and would understand the challenges ahead—that was all that mattered to him.

Lady Rose sent him a knowing smile. "I think you should be more selective, Lord Ashton. There are very desperate women among the ton."

He set down his spoon. "I am not in a position to be more selective, Lady Rose. There are hundreds of my tenants starving, and I cannot feed them. I would wed any woman willing to help me."

He couldn't afford the luxury of choice. Although he believed he could eventually improve their situation with careful investments, all that took time. The quickest way to bring back prosperity was to marry an heiress. And if it would silence the voices of the dead who haunted his dreams, he would indeed marry anyone.

Her expression shifted into sympathy. "I am sorry. I did not mean to make light of your situation."

Lady Penford reached over and absently patted Iain's hand. "I have a solution. You should wed one of my daughters. I like you, and I would give you my blessing."

Both Rose and Lily's expressions were aghast, and he suppressed a laugh. They were horrified at the idea, which should have been insulting, except that he knew their reasons.

"If either of your daughters would consent to being my wife, I would not refuse. I like your eldest, in particular." He winked at Rose, who shook her head with exasperation.

"Excellent." Lady Penford smiled brightly. "That's settled then. The wedding can be held within a few weeks."

Rose coughed, nearly spewing her wine over the table. "Really, Mother. Why are you so eager to be rid of me?"

Iain leaned back in his chair, rather enjoying the entertainment of Lady Penford's conversation. It was quite possible that she'd taken a tonic before supper and was quite pickled.

Lady Penford's expression turned wistful. "I like weddings. Weddings lead to babies, and I should quite like grandchildren."

Rose glanced at Lily and said, "I am beginning to think I should take a tray in my room. This is not a conversation I wish to pursue any further."

Iain was rather intrigued. The women were speaking freely, as if he weren't there at all. He reached for his wineglass, only to find that Calvert hadn't filled it. When he lifted it and motioned for the footman, he received a furious glare for his trouble.

"Grandbabies *are* marvelous," Lady Castledon agreed. "My stepdaughter, Christine, just gave birth to a new son last Christmas. He is the most perfect child I've ever seen."

"Rubbish," Lady Wolcroft pronounced. "You say that about every grandchild."

Lady Castledon only smiled. "There is no such thing as an imperfect grandchild. You already know this." She glanced over at Lily and Rose, nodding to each of them. Then she turned back to Iain and said, "My husband and I will be returning to London within a fortnight. I will ask my sister, the duchess, to host a gathering at her home and select only the women who would suit you, Lord Ashton."

"He does not require a harem, Amelia," Lady Wolcroft said.

The countess ignored the jibe and added, "And your own perfect granddaughters simply must attend." To Rose, she added, "It isn't necessary to have dancing, so you needn't feel out of place."

Iain thought it was a considerate offer, but Rose was already shaking her head. "Mother has been ill, and I don't think we should—"

"I am much better," Lady Penford insisted. "And I do *so* miss the parties in London. They are truly lovely."

The longing in her voice was not lost on her daughters. "We will go back someday, Mother," Lily assured her. "But not for a little while longer."

Rose met Iain's gaze across the table and sent him a slight nod. He fully intended to keep his part of the bargain and hoped she would do the same.

One week later

"Are you ready?"

Rose looked up from the stone bench and saw Lord Ashton waiting. Every day for the past week, he'd met with her for a few hours so she could practice standing up. Though she still could not balance herself for long periods of time, it was getting easier. He held out his hand, but she had no idea what he wanted from her. "Ready for what?"

"Why, the next step, of course."

Her face furrowed with confusion. "And what exactly is the next step?"

"You'll see." He held out both hands, and she saw that he had again forgotten to wear gloves. His dark hair needed to be trimmed, but she rather liked it. It made him different from all the polished gentlemen she had met.

She reached out for his hands and kept her knees bent, carefully shifting her weight as she attempted to stand. He steadied her, helping her find her balance. It took a moment, but she managed to stand for nearly twenty seconds before he eased her back to the bench.

"You *are* getting stronger, *a chara,*" he said. "But there is something else that would help you progress. If you're feeling daring, that is."

She had no idea what he meant by that. "What do you think would help me?"

"Swimming."

The very idea made her blush. The last time she'd gone swimming was when she was a little girl. She and Lily had taken off their gowns, and had gone swimming in their unmentionables until they were caught by their furious governess.

She could never go swimming with a man watching her. Or worse, swimming with her maid or sister. It was an impossible idea—completely outrageous. And yet . . . she could see his reasoning. It would give her a means of strengthening her useless legs in a way that might hasten her progress. She knew how to float, and kicking her legs would help rebuild her lost muscles.

She couldn't believe she was even considering such an idea, even as warm as it was outside. No. It simply wasn't done.

"I couldn't possibly do such a thing." She shook her head. "My grandmother and mother would never condone it."

"If they learned about it, aye. They wouldn't allow it at all." He shrugged. "But if we went out riding, there's no reason why they would need to know."

"Everyone would know. I would come back completely wet," she pointed out. "My hair would be soaked." She couldn't even imagine a way to conceal that.

"You needn't go with *me*," he said quietly. "You could take Hattie and your sister. Tell them what it is you're wanting to do."

In his voice, she heard the calm tone of a man who had no intention of impropriety or bringing harm to her good name. She shielded her eyes against the sun and studied him closely. Over the past week and a half, Lord Ashton had become a friend, and someone who was genuinely interested in helping her walk again.

"They don't really believe I'll walk again," she admitted. "If I told them of your idea, they would accuse me of trying to drown myself."

He extended his forearms, and helped her to stand again. "If you want my help, that I will give. I swear that I'll do nothing that would bring shame to you. I could help you into the water until you can swim on your own."

She didn't know what to say, except to shake her head. Everything she'd ever been raised to believe told her this was wrong. She had to remain covered from throat to ankle, buried under layers of petticoats and corsets.

Yet, the thought of spending an afternoon floating on the lake, hidden within a grove of trees, was a delicious temptation.

Lord Ashton helped her back to the bench once more. "I would hope, by now, you would realize that I've no intention of accosting you, Lady Rose. I made a bargain to help you walk again, and our time is running short. By the end of this month, I will need to go to London to find my bride."

She knew that. And it was likely that all his efforts would be for naught. How could she possibly think walking again in a month would be feasible? She'd been trapped for so long.

"I will think about it," she agreed. "But I cannot go with you to London. I am not at all ready to walk."

He bowed in understanding, and then eyed her again. "There is something else you could try."

She listened, waiting for him to speak. He reached down for her hands again, and she stood. Each time, it got a little easier. But this time, he commanded, "Step on my feet."

"What? Why?" It would bring her closer to him, and she was uncertain about it.

"Trust me, *a chara*. Now trample my toes, if you don't mind."

A smile twitched at her mouth, but she hid it. Gently, she used all her effort to step on his right foot. Then his left. It was awkward, and she could feel her balance tipping. He sensed it, too, for he caught her waist and held her there. "Walk with me," he said, and began to tread backward.

She kept her feet upon his, and he moved them both toward the garden wall. Rose couldn't help but laugh at the incongruity of him trying to move her across the garden. "*What* are you doing, Lord Ashton?"

"There, now. You've walked." He sent her a roguish grin, and added, "Shall we go to London, Saturday next?"

His green eyes held mischief, and she shook her head in exasperation. "You are a foolish man. I didn't walk at all."

"Aye, but you did. I may have moved you there, but you most definitely walked."

"Not on my own." She eyed him in the manner of a scolding governess. "I only managed it because you had your arm locked around my waist."

She kept her voice chiding but didn't tell him how his embrace had unnerved her. Though it meant nothing and they were only friends, she was fully conscious of his strong arms and the planes of his body. Every time his palms were upon her, her skin prickled with awareness. Even now, she detected a hint of the soap he had used for washing.

"Hold on to my shoulders," Lord Ashton advised her. He moved her sideways, spinning lightly, in a mock dance. He held out one of her hands while the other rested at her waist. "Here you are, *cailín*. You've even danced. I believe I've fulfilled my end of the bargain."

"No, you have not, Lord Ashton." Yet she couldn't help but smile at his teasing.

He helped her back to the stone bench and regarded her. "Have you chosen possible brides for me? I should like to hear about them."

He spoke as if he were selecting a bottle of wine, and she wanted him to be more serious about the matter. "Marriage is quite a decision to make. You will need to meet the ladies to determine whether one will suit."

"It doesn't matter at all what I'm wanting, *a chara*. Only what the lady wants."

She expected his words to be lighthearted, but this time, there was only seriousness in his eyes. "Exactly how bad is it in Ireland?"

He sobered and rested his hands on his knees. "If you'll forgive my language, it's hell on earth, Lady Rose. Imagine an estate the size of

Penford with no crops, no animals, and no servants. If you want food, the price is very dear, and most cannot afford it. Many of our tenants have gone to America, for they cannot survive here. I've received no rents from the people, and with no income, I cannot pay our staff. I've stripped our expenses down to almost nothing, and the rest of my family is gone." His green eyes held a bleakness that troubled her. "Marriage *was* a last resort, Lady Rose. Believe me, I tried to bring in income through investments and selling off whatever I could. But I am out of time."

"What do you mean?"

"I would sell my soul for an heiress, if it meant restoring Ashton."

She eyed him for a long moment. Somehow, this didn't seem to be for the sake of his tenants and his sisters. "That's a high price to pay for land." Tilting her head to the side, she regarded him. "This is about proving yourself, isn't it?"

A hard edge came over his face. "It's about helping those in need. It's my responsibility."

Rose let out a slow breath. "Then I will do what I can to help. But you must give me some guidance about what you want in a bride."

His anger seemed to diminish, and he reached for her hand. "Someone kind. Someone who can look past my pirate ways."

A ripple of nerves washed over her, for she sensed he was talking about her. His fingers tightened over her palm, and she felt the heat wash over her. His green eyes held warmth, but she wasn't certain whether he was teasing or not.

"Don't flirt with me, Lord Ashton. You must be serious about this." She sent him a friendly smile, as if his words meant nothing.

"I am serious. That's what I'm wanting in a bride."

She stood again, but lost her balance. He caught her waist and steadied her. "You know I intend to wed Lord Burkham if he asks for my hand." Surely when he saw her walk—even stand—he would offer for her.

"How many letters has he written to you?"

The question surprised her, for she didn't see how it mattered. "Why do you ask?"

"How many?" he repeated.

"Six. And the most recent one came last week." That ought to satisfy his curiosity. She couldn't see why he cared.

His palm warmed her spine, and he kept his grip around her waist while she remained standing. "Six letters in six months?"

Oh. She didn't miss his raised eyebrow or the implication. "Yes. He writes to me often."

"One letter a month is not often."

The pointed look he sent was irritating. "But he *does* write to me. He wished me well in his last letter and told me that he missed me greatly."

Lord Ashton said nothing, but she could tell that he thought little of the viscount. It wasn't his concern, was it? Without knowing why, she jumped to his defense. "He has duties in Parliament and responsibilities toward his estate. I am grateful for each of his letters."

"All six of them," he noted. "In half a year's time."

"Don't cast aspersions on the man I love," she reminded him. "He does the best that he can."

But Lord Ashton surprised her when he leaned in. "If the woman I loved fell sick, I would be at her side, day and night. And even if my duties took me from her, I would write every day." The roughness in his voice took her aback, and for a moment, she found herself caught up in his stare. She couldn't read his emotions, for his anger was blended with an intensity that stole her breath.

"I cannot understand why any man wouldn't do the same for you." His mouth rested above hers, and she felt the heat of his breath upon her lips. Against her will, her body responded to his nearness, making her soften to his touch. Though he crossed no boundaries, she trembled at the hushed sense of the forbidden.

"You're too good for him, *a chara*. If he truly loved you, he would not have left you when you were ill. And I think you know that."

Her face flooded with color, for he was the first one to openly say this. "Then why would Lord Burkham bother writing to me?"

He hesitated at that. "I cannot say. Except that perhaps he feels guilty for not treating you as he should."

She didn't want to believe it. Not when Thomas represented her hopes and dreams for the future. No, she would take comfort in the fact that he *had* continued to write letters, and she was glad of it. She let out a sigh. "I am tired, Lord Ashton. I think we are finished for today."

He regarded her with solemnity. "It wasn't my intent to hurt your feelings, *a chara*."

"I know." But she couldn't bring herself to smile. His observations had planted the seeds of doubt within her mind. And yet, there was no way to know what Lord Burkham's feelings were until she saw him again for herself.

Without asking permission, Lord Ashton reached for her hands once more. Slowly, he placed them on his shoulders while he rested his own hands at her waist. She wanted to pull back, but his green eyes held her captive. "I hope you know that I am your friend. I want to help you."

She nodded, fully conscious of his arm around her waist. He held her a little longer, and she wondered what it was he wanted. The expression on his face was kindly, but there was something more within his gaze. She didn't understand it but couldn't bring herself to turn away.

Instead, she studied him in return. His dark hair was slightly long, but his face was clean shaven. Her curiosity got the better of her, and she took off her glove, reaching out to touch his cheek. "You shaved."

"So I did."

She traced the planes of his face, fully aware that she shouldn't be doing this. And yet, he didn't seem to mind her touch. He allowed it, and when she touched his opposite cheek, he warned, "Careful, Lady

Rose." His voice held a gruff quality that made her stop. But when she tried to pull her hand away, he covered it with his own, bringing it to his mouth.

Against her palm, his mouth was warm. The heat of his lips made gooseflesh rise upon her skin. Her imagination conjured up the image of his breath upon her body, and her breasts tightened inside her corset. She didn't understand these sensations or why she should feel anything at all. Dozens of men had kissed her hand, though never like this.

"I'm sorry," she murmured and tried to pull back.

"I'm not." The wicked smile returned, and he kept her palm firmly in his own. "But it only seems fair that I should be allowed to do the same."

She was frozen in place when his palm cupped her cheek. His thumb traced the outline of her jaw, moving lower to her chin. Her heartbeat quickened, blood rushing to her face. She told herself that this meant nothing, that they were only friends.

But he was overstepping the boundaries of friendship, reaching for something he couldn't have. The look in his eyes seemed to reach beneath her defenses. This man was taking apart her good sense, tempting her in a way she didn't understand.

"I am going to stay and teach you to walk, Rose." He lifted her hand and stole another kiss that left her reeling. "That promise I've made, and that promise I'll keep. But if ever you change your mind about Burkham, know that you are worth more than one letter a month."

Chapter Eight

Iain rode across the open land, following the curve of the lake. The May sunlight warmed him until he was sweating from exertion and heat. He hadn't stopped thinking about Rose since yesterday. It bothered him that she wanted a man who had abandoned her during her illness. How could she love such a person? Burkham deserved to lose her.

And yet, his own fate remained out of his hands. He knew he needed an heiress—but he was not at all prepared for London. Devil take it all, he dreaded entering such an unfamiliar world. Men and women would judge him by his Irish way of speaking, and he had no idea how to behave. He wished it were possible to avoid London entirely.

They will know you aren't worthy of being the earl. Lady Rose might think he had the difficult task of teaching her how to walk, but hers was the greater challenge.

Iain cursed beneath his breath and urged his horse faster until he reached the secluded part of the lake. He led Darcy over for a drink and then walked along the edge of the water. He wanted to swim, to churn his arms across the surface and release his frustration against the frigid water.

He wished Michael were alive so he could ask his brother for advice. Even though Iain had been the black sheep, the unwanted younger son, his brother had been his best friend. And God help him, he still felt the loss, even now.

No one was nearby, so he discarded his clothing on the shore and walked naked into the lake. The water stole his breath as soon as he stepped into it, but this was what he wanted right now—the punishing cold. He forced himself to begin swimming long strokes across the water, and the longer he swam, the more his body adjusted to the temperature.

He knew his obligations to Ashton and had made up his mind to marry. But he wanted to marry a woman he liked, especially since he would be expected to sire children with her.

The image of Lady Rose's face appeared in his thoughts, haunting him. Here was a woman with determination and courage. A woman who wouldn't turn her back on adversity, but who would meet her challenges without retreating. Although she wasn't tremendously wealthy, she had a respectable dowry.

Rose doesn't want you. She wants Burkham. Try as he might, he couldn't silence the voice of logic. But he didn't believe that the viscount would come up to scratch. And he'd written only six letters in half a year? Mary, Mother of God, the viscount was leading her on. Even if Rose did return to London, there was no guarantee that Burkham would ask her to wed.

Irritation rose up within him, and he told himself it was none of his affair. It didn't matter that Lady Rose's touch lingered within his memory. She didn't know how close she'd come to being kissed. The softness of her fingers upon his cheek had made him want to taste those lips, to show her the danger of one simple caress.

He kept swimming hard, back and forth, until his muscles burned from the exercise. It helped him to clear his mind and think of what to do. He would need a great deal of time to find the right woman to marry, and the longer he stayed here, the more his chances of finding the right woman diminished. Yet, if he stayed another fortnight, he could not only help Rose make progress on learning how to walk again, but he could also use that time to learn more about behaving like an earl.

The sound of an approaching horse made him remain in the water, but when he saw Rose riding closer, he paused. To his surprise, she had come alone this time and was riding along the edge of the lake. Usually she brought Hattie or Calvert with her, but not today. He wondered why.

Her pace was slow, and after a moment, she glimpsed him. Iain straightened in the water, unable to stop his smile. Well, now. Wasn't this an interesting dilemma?

"You have me at a disadvantage, *a chara.*" He took a few steps closer, unable to resist teasing her. Now the water was at his waistline, and Rose put up her hands.

"Stop," she commanded. "I didn't realize you were here. There's no need to . . . leave the water." Her face held a lovely blush, and he rather wanted to see what she would do now. "I'll just go now."

Oh, no. He wasn't about to let this opportunity escape. "I had just finished swimming," he said. "If you'd like to take your turn, the water is all yours. Though, I must say, it's a bit cold now."

"I wasn't planning to swim."

He took another step closer, and this time, the water grazed his hip bones. Rose scrunched her eyes shut. "No, you needn't come any farther."

He rather wondered if she would sneak a glimpse if he were to leave the lake. He took another step forward, baring a bit more of himself.

When she didn't respond, he guessed that she was indeed hiding her eyes. "I do need my clothes," he pointed out. "And they are on the shore at the moment. I'll go and fetch them."

This time, he strode out of the water, fully bared. God almighty, it was cold. He watched Rose closely as he continued toward his clothes, but she kept both hands covering her eyes.

He couldn't be certain, but it almost looked as if there was a slight space between her fingers. Was is possible that she was staring at him?

"Are you enjoying the view, *a chara*?" he asked as he reached for his smallclothes and trousers.

"I am not looking at you."

"So you say." He smiled to himself as he dressed. When he was half-clothed, he returned toward her horse. Aye, he could have finished putting on his shirt and the remainder of his clothing, but he wanted to see her reaction, to tease her a little more. "You can look now."

She did, and promptly shut her eyes again. "You are not dressed, Lord Ashton."

"All the important bits are. And it's not as if you haven't seen me in this state before."

She let out a groan. "Really, now. Must you behave in such a villainous manner?"

"I would only be a villain if I pulled you from that horse and threw you in the lake." He had no intention of doing so, but the slight gasp she emitted made it clear that she wasn't quite so certain.

"Don't you dare."

He approached the horse while her eyes were still closed and reached up, pulling her down to stand before him. Rose squealed, and tried to fight him, but he held her steady. "Now, *a chara*, I wouldn't do such a thing to you."

"You took me off the horse."

"So I did. You were wanting to walk, were you not?" He kept her standing, knowing full well that his body was still wet from the lake.

"Your skin is freezing," she pointed out. "The water was too cold."

"It's England. It will never get warm," he felt compelled to remind her. And he was accustomed to swimming in frigid water, for it wasn't at all warm in Ireland, either.

But the longer he held her waist, the more she had an effect upon him. Her eyes remained closed, her lips slightly parted. Her reddish-brown hair was caught up in a pretty green bonnet, and she wore a riding habit that revealed the dip in her waist and the curve of her hips. Iain kept his arms around her, enjoying the temptation before him. There was no denying that Lady Rose was a stunningly beautiful woman, one he wanted to touch.

Not yours, he warned himself.

But she wasn't fighting his hands upon her waist. And although she gave a slight shiver, she didn't seem frightened of him.

"I'm not going to harm you, Lady Rose," he reminded her. "You can open your eyes."

After a moment, she did. "I cannot believe you were swimming naked in the lake. Did you think no one would come along?"

He shrugged. "I don't suppose I cared if anyone did."

Right now, he was enjoying the feel of this woman in his arms. Her lips were soft, her cheeks blushing at his unclothed state. And though he knew he ought to let her go, he told himself that she would lose her balance if he did.

She swallowed hard and told him, "You may put me back on my horse now. I'll return to Penford, and I won't bother you."

"That wasn't why you came riding out here," he predicted. "You were thinking of swimming, weren't you?"

"I came for the pleasant view. And we both know I cannot swim. Especially not with you."

He wasn't convinced of that, but he wouldn't press the matter. Instead he lifted her up into his arms and walked toward the large boulders that rested on one edge of the lake. "You can dip your toes into the lake, then. There's no harm in it."

Iain balanced himself carefully as he stepped onto the group of boulders, and chose a spot near the water's edge. Gently, he lowered Lady Rose to a seated position and then sat beside her.

"You're too close to me," she protested. "Find your own rock." But there was a hint of amusement in her voice, as if she didn't truly mean it.

"I like sharing yours. And besides, if you fall in, I'll be able to snatch you back out again."

"I am not going to fall in the water." But she did lean back against the largest rock, smiling a little as she untied her bonnet. The ribbons hung down against her bodice, and she adjusted her skirts to hide her ankles.

He remained beside her, acutely conscious of her body beside his. It was entirely inappropriate for him to be half-clothed and leaning next to her. But she wasn't protesting anymore. Instead, he caught her stealing a glance at him when she thought he wasn't looking.

"Are you going to put your feet in?" he asked.

She shook her head. "I don't think so. It would be foolish. Besides that, I'm already breaking too many rules by sitting here alone with you. Though if anyone finds me, I shall claim that I was abducted by a pirate."

"And then you would be forced to wed me to save your reputation," he suggested. "Which is not so very dreadful."

"I disagree," she countered. "You, Lord Ashton, are a very wicked man with no sense of propriety." But her eyes revealed her amusement.

"If I worried about what others think, I would not be sitting with a beautiful woman on a sunny day, now, would I?"

He leaned back with his arms crooked behind his head. He had the feeling that Lady Rose had a rebellious side to her, buried beneath her years of good manners.

She shook her head and sighed. Then she lifted up one foot and began unbuttoning her shoe. "I must be mad."

A rebel indeed. He grinned and helped her with the other shoe, until she was clad in stockings. "No more than I. But it was an invigorating swim."

"You ought to put your shirt on," she reminded him. "Someone will see you and think you are intent on seducing me."

"You *did* accuse me of being a pirate, *a chara*." He kept his voice light, but leaned a little closer. "We aren't known for being gentlemen."

In response, Rose dipped her hand into the water and splashed it at his chest. "Then I'll be forced to defend myself from you."

The frigid water spilled down his bare chest, dampening his waistband. Iain rested his arms on either side of her, trapping her against the rock. "Now that wasn't fair, Lady Rose."

Her smile faded instantly. "I was teasing, Lord Ashton."

"Were you?" He was feeling rather bold at the moment. He drank in the sight of her—those wide brown eyes, the delicate nose and sweet lips. Her hair was hidden beneath the bonnet, and he took it off, setting it aside. "You don't need this."

"My face will be covered in freckles if I don't wear it." But she didn't appear to mind his interference. And instead of shoving him aside, she was watching him with interest. Sunlight gleamed across her brown hair, revealing the hints of auburn. He leaned in, resting his forehead against hers. Her eyes widened, but she remained fixed upon his face.

"Did Burkham ever kiss you?"

"Of course." Her voice held a hint of panic, but she didn't pull away.

He was caught up in the beauty of her. Her breath warmed his mouth, and for a moment, he remained near to her. She was forbidden to him, and he would not intrude where he wasn't wanted. And yet, every part of him was entranced by her.

"Tell me to leave you alone," he said in a low voice.

But she remained silent. Her hand moved up to touch the roughness of his face, and it only deepened the intimacy. She trailed her fingers upon his jaw, and the simple touch undid him.

Iain bent and brushed his mouth against hers. It was the barest hint of a kiss, the promise of more if she wanted it.

He pulled back immediately, searching her expression. He never wanted her to feel threatened by him. "Tell me if you're wanting me to stop."

He leaned in again, nipping at her lips a second time. He waited for a long moment, giving her more than enough time to refuse. She could tell him no at any moment, and he would pull back. Instead, her eyes were wild, as if she didn't know what to say or do.

She tasted of summer, a softness and warmth like sunlight. Her eyes were caught up with his, her expression emboldened by a taste of the forbidden.

Iain bent and claimed her mouth deeply, framing her face with both hands. He didn't stop kissing her, learning the shape of her mouth and drawing her even closer.

Rose's fingers dug into his bare skin, but Lord Ashton's chest was no longer cold. Beneath her fingertips, she could feel his heart beating faster. Her mind was numb to all this, uncertain of what to do.

She ought to shove him away, but the moment he kissed her deeply, every rational thought fled her brain. His mouth was sensual and warm, his tongue reaching out to hers. She heard a breathless gasp that came from her, and her own heart stuttered in time with his.

Thomas had never kissed her like this. She'd never known anyone could kiss in this way. With every stroke of his tongue, Iain was pulling apart her good sense, arousing her deeply. Her breasts were erect beneath her shift and corset, while between her legs, she felt a phantom ache.

My God, the man could kiss. Although it was wrong, she could not bring herself to pull away. Not yet. Instead, she met his kiss with her own, learning what it was to slide her tongue inside his mouth in a daring way.

The primal groan that resounded from his mouth made him take her harder. He threaded his hands into her hair, kissing her soundly until she was breathless.

She needed to tell him no, to shove him back. But she was dizzy from his touch, shocked by the sensation of his mouth as he kissed a path down her throat. He tasted her like a starving man, and every part of her yearned for more.

His hardened muscles were beneath her hands, and she couldn't remember when she'd taken her gloves off. But the need to touch him, to explore his warm male skin, overrode common sense. She allowed him to pull her so close, her skirts grew tangled up, and she was lying atop him.

Sweet God above, she could feel the ridge of his arousal. When her hips pressed against his, the aching between her legs made her restless. She was beginning to understand how a woman could fall prey to a man who wanted her.

His breathing was labored, and when she saw the heated look in his green eyes, she began to come to her senses. She had promised herself that she would go back to London to be with Lord Burkham. Instead, she was kissing another man in Yorkshire. It made no sense at all. What was wrong with her? Why was she allowing herself to fall beneath his spell?

She never should have come here alone. The moment she'd seen Lord Ashton, she should have left and gone home. The man was not to be trusted.

She pulled back from Iain and pressed her hand to his mouth. "No. I cannot do this. Please stop."

Iain did, but she was well aware of his desire for her. She reached for her shoes, trying to put them on, while her fingers trembled. The buttons wouldn't work, and her eyes blurred with tears. She didn't even know why she was starting to cry. She hadn't betrayed Thomas, since they had never been engaged. What did it matter if she kissed another man?

It mattered because she'd felt more in Iain's stolen embrace than Thomas had ever made her feel. And she knew why Iain had kissed her. He needed a bride, and her dowry would indeed be enough to help improve his estate. All he had to do was sympathize with a poor, helpless, crippled woman.

Her broken pride only made it harder to fight the tears. She fumbled with the buttons until the first shoe was back on. Lord Ashton helped her with the other, but his touch upon her foot was more than she could bear.

"Please don't," she said. Not while she was trying to hold her feelings together.

She pulled her foot back and reached for the edge of the stone, trying to hoist herself up to a standing position. Even using all her arm strength, it wouldn't work.

"Allow me." Lord Ashton didn't wait for her to answer, but lifted her back into his arms. He said nothing at all about his actions, but brought her to her waiting mare, placing her on horseback.

"I won't apologize for kissing you," he said at last. He rested his hands upon her mount, his expression serious. "But you should ask yourself if you truly want a man like Burkham after the way he's neglected you."

Or after the way I kissed you, was the unspoken message.

Rose's face burned with humiliation. She didn't know what had possessed her to allow the kiss. But she honestly didn't know what she wanted right now. When Lord Ashton had looked into her eyes, she had lost sight of all the reasons why it was wrong to let him kiss her. Like a pirate, Iain had taken what he wanted. And she could not deny that she had done nothing to stop him.

Why? What was the matter with her? She didn't understand how any of this had happened. This wasn't the sort of woman she was, to succumb to temptation.

But it was as if Lord Ashton had awakened her senses, raising questions she didn't want to face. She'd wanted to believe that once Thomas saw her again, the old feelings would return . . . but what if they didn't?

"You startled me, Lord Ashton," she said, trying to gather herself together. "I apologize if I led you to believe that I wanted you to kiss me. I hope we can return to our friendship with no harm done."

He said nothing, but his thumb stroked her palm. The gesture echoed deep within her very skin, reminding her of the shocking feelings.

And when she rode back to Penford, she was only too aware of her bruised lips and the pounding of her heart.

Chapter Nine

Iain had been invited to join Lady Penford for tea, along with her mother. But before he could enter the drawing room, Calvert barred the way. It was irritating the way the footman took it upon himself to guard the women.

"You, sir, are a *foul* villain. After what you did to poor Lady Rose . . ." The man's face was nearly purple with outrage.

Iain had no idea how to respond to that, for there was no way to know what Rose had said. Instead, he remarked, "And just what am I accused of this time?"

"I saw her when she returned from her morning ride. She was most distraught, and I have no doubt that you were the cause of it."

He supposed, in this instance, the footman was correct in his assumption. And truly, the man's loyalty could not be faulted.

Iain ignored Calvert's remark and said, "The ladies are expecting me at tea. Kindly let me pass."

When the footman did not move, Iain added, "Though I am certain you believe you are guarding Lady Rose, I am no threat to her. Leave both of us alone, or I'll be forced to inform Lady Wolcroft of your interference."

The footman scowled, but was wise enough to retreat. When Iain entered the drawing room, he found Lady Penford standing beside the window. She wore a lopsided crown of yellow tulips over her tangled, unbound hair. At the moment, the matron appeared to be in a state of childish joy.

"Come and see!" she blurted out with no greeting.

Iain crossed the room and stood beside her. Outside, he saw nothing out of the ordinary. It was likely that she was caught up in another of her spells. "What is it?"

She pointed to one of the hedges. "Look, just there. Do you see the bird's nest?"

He peered closer at the greenery but saw nothing at all. "I'm afraid I don't, Lady Penford."

Her expression grew wistful. "They must all leave the nest, I fear. And sometimes their mother has to give them a push." She glanced back at him, and a daffodil slid over one eye.

He asked, "May I?" before he adjusted the crown. "Were you outside in the garden this morning?"

She nodded. "My husband, Lord Penford, used to bring me flowers every day. I do miss him."

"These are cheerful," he admitted. "Did you make the crown yourself?"

"I did." With a rueful smile, she confessed, "I used to make them when I was a girl. I was merely giving into an impulse, though I suppose I must seem like a foolish old woman."

Ian didn't think there was any harm in it. "My sister, Sybil, used to tell me that when she grew old, she would wear whatever she liked, and devil take the consequences." He recalled that on Sybil's fifteenth birthday, she had worn her favorite ball gown inside the house, just because it made her smile. "If you want to wear a daffodil crown, I say you should."

Her face brightened, and she took his hand in hers. "You *are* a kind young man. Your mother must be very proud of you."

My mother loathes the sight of me, he thought, but didn't say so. In many ways, Lady Penford had treated him more like a son than Moira ever had. She took his arm and led him back to the sitting area, patting his hand as they walked. He helped her sit down on a gilded chair. Since they were alone, he decided to broach a different subject. "What are your thoughts on finding Rose a husband? She said something about a Lord Burkham."

Her smile faded. "The viscount is not right for Rose." With a dismissive gesture, she added, "He would bore her within a year."

Good, Iain thought. He was glad to hear it. Though he supposed he had no right to feel possessive of Rose, he couldn't deny that her kiss had affected him. It had been an impulse, misguided by the need to touch a beautiful woman. The moment he'd tasted her lips, he'd known how forbidden this was. And perhaps that was why the memory lingered.

But more than that, he liked Rose. She had wit and humor that made her easy to be around. He genuinely wanted to help her walk again, though he knew how difficult it would be. Every time she stood, her face brightened with such joy and wonder, he felt the echo of pride in her accomplishment. Being around her made him feel that he could have a purpose, and she had never once made him feel inferior.

"What about you?" Lady Penford was asking. "What sort of bride are you hoping to find in London?"

Her question caught him off guard. He didn't quite know how to answer it, and finally said, "Whichever woman will have me, I suppose. I cannot say that I'm much of a catch."

"In that you're wrong, Lord Ashton." Lady Penford smiled warmly and plucked one of the daffodils from her crown. "You are handsome and kind. Any woman would be glad to wed a gentleman like you." She snapped the stem and gave it to him.

He tucked it into his buttonhole. "Even Lady Rose?" Though he'd meant the remark in teasing, the truth was, he did admire the young woman.

But Lady Penford seemed taken aback by the idea. "Why, you hardly know one another. You only just met a few days ago."

No longer did the matron appear to be an ally. Instead, she appeared every bit the protective mother. "No, I would not want Rose so very far away in Ireland. Especially with her difficulty in walking."

She sighed, and her mind wandered back to another topic. "I wish you could see the bird's nest. The babies have only just hatched, and their mother is looking after them."

Iain didn't press the subject, for Lady Penford was right—Ireland would be difficult for Lady Rose, or any bride for that matter. He stood beside the matron, wondering if he had pushed Rose too far already. Despite the neglect of Lord Burkham, she still wanted to marry the man. But he questioned whether she loved the viscount. A woman who had given her heart to another would have rejected his advances . . . but instead, Rose had kissed him back.

She'd accused him of behaving like a pirate, and it wasn't far from the truth. He *had* stolen the kiss without asking. But her skin had been so soft, her scent alluring. He'd been unable to stop himself from the embrace, and he felt no guilt at all. Lady Rose was a beautiful woman, one who tempted him badly.

A good man would stay away from her. Let her win back the heart of her viscount and find happiness. She would never be content in the life he had to offer—even if her dowry was enough to restore Ashton to its former beauty. It was best to let her go.

Iain had already decided to stay a little longer in Yorkshire, helping Rose learn to walk again. And during that time, he hoped she could teach him everything about London society. The mutual agreement would be to their advantage.

"Lord Ashton," came Lady Wolcroft's voice from the doorway. "I am glad you could join Iris and me for tea. We have much to discuss." She turned behind her and said, "Stop lurking in the hall, Lily, and come join us."

Lily sent her grandmother a pained look, but joined them in the drawing room. She chose the seat farthest from everyone else, as if she hoped to make a hasty escape.

"You, too, Rose." She waved at the footman, who carried Lady Rose into the room.

Given the size of this gathering, Iain was beginning to wonder if teatime would turn into an interrogation. He held out a chair for Rose and then one for her grandmother. The ladies sat, and when Calvert passed Iain, he glared at him.

Lady Wolcroft eyed her daughter with exasperation and removed the crown of daffodils from Lady Penford's hair. "Really, Iris, you are no longer six years old. Your hair should be pinned up as suits your age."

The matron appeared confused and troubled by her mother's proclamation. "But I only thought—the flowers—"

Lady Wolcroft tossed the daffodil crown onto the hearth, where the flowers shriveled in the hot coals. "Nonsense. We've no time for such frivolity. We must plan our strategy for London. Rose and Lily need new gowns for the Season, and those will take time. But I daresay we can be ready within a fortnight."

Lady Penford watched the flowers as they burned, her face filled with dismay. But she accepted her cup of tea when her mother handed it to her. Lady Wolcroft had already begun discussing her plans for introducing Iain into society.

"Lady Arnsbury will help us, of course. And my dear friend Amelia, the Countess of Castledon. You met her the other evening. She's already gone to London, but I will send word when we're there."

"London will be wonderful to visit," Lady Penford interjected. "I do so love it there. So many parties, and it's never dull."

"You cannot go with us, Iris." Lady Wolcroft stirred a lump of sugar into her tea. "You would embarrass both of your daughters, and I cannot allow that."

Lady Penford looked down at her tea, her cheeks flushing. In a low voice, she murmured, "No, I wouldn't." But Iain suspected no one heard her.

Though he understood Lady Wolcroft's desire to protect her daughter, he saw the rise of tears in Iris's eyes. He felt bad for her sake, for no one wanted to be left behind. From across the room, he saw the look of dismay on Rose's face. And perhaps he was overstepping his bounds, but he offered, "I see no harm in Lady Penford traveling to London, so long as she is feeling well. She could remain at home and that would allow her to hear all the stories from Lady Lily and Lady Rose." It was a compromise, and the matron sent him a grateful look.

But Lady Wolcroft would have none of it. "And what if she runs into the streets, shrieking about imaginary wolves? How do you think that would affect their chances of marriage?" Her mother grimaced at the idea. "Or perhaps Iris might try to fly off the balcony and break her neck."

"No," Lady Penford whispered. "I promise. I would never do such a thing."

"You certainly tried to, just over a week ago," her mother retorted. "Or so your daughters said."

Lady Penford appeared stricken by the announcement, and she looked down at her hands.

Iain leaned to her side. "Don't let it trouble you, Lady Penford. That matter is over and done with. It won't happen again."

At that, Rose sent him a grateful look. He nodded, holding her gaze with his. *I won't let anyone harm her.*

"Lord Ashton, I understand that you are attempting to be kind," Lady Wolcroft continued, "but my daughter, though I love her, is not fit to be out in society anymore. She cannot go paying calls with a crown of daffodils, thinking herself to be Queen of the May. Nor can she wear her hair down or attempt to speak with any families whose sons might offer for Rose or Lily." With a hard look toward Iris, she added, "It would not be good for any of us."

He disagreed with that. Imprisoning Lady Penford alone without her family might have the opposite effect. Loneliness and grief might push her further over the edge. He glanced over at Iris and could see the anxiety rising in her expression.

"I would never do anything to threaten their chances of making a good marriage," the matron insisted. She tried to tuck in a wayward lock of hair with a pin, but it only unraveled once again.

"It isn't finding a good husband that worries me, Mother," Rose leaned in and admitted. "It's simply that . . . there are far more dangers in London than here." She seemed torn between her mother's wishes and the possibility of Iris hurting herself.

But Lady Wolcroft had not finished. "None of you understands the greatest danger of all. If Iris has even one difficult spell in public, we cannot protect her. She will be taken to a lunatic asylum, where God only knows what would happen to her. It is far better if she remains in Yorkshire where she will be safe."

Iain had heard of the terrible conditions in the asylums, and he glanced back at Rose again. *What do you want to do?*

She could only shrug and shake her head.

Lady Penford pushed her teacup back and stood. Her hands trembled, and her eyes were filled with tears. "Since you have all decided my fate, I suppose there is no reason for me to remain here." To her mother, she added, "Apparently I *am* six years old, for all that anyone else can see."

With that, she departed the room. Rose turned back to her grandmother and frowned. "You didn't have to be so abrupt with her. She was having a good day."

"She'll forget all about it in an hour," the matron predicted. She set her cup to the side and regarded all of them. "I regret, Lord Ashton, that you had to witness our family disagreement."

Lady Lily offered him a sandwich, and Iain accepted it. "While I understand your desire to protect Lady Penford, leaving her behind might cause her to fall into a deeper despair." He hadn't missed the looks of dismay from her daughters.

"Be that as it may, we must leave her." Lady Wolcroft straightened in her chair and sipped at her tea. "Iris is far too ill to return to London. If she were in her right mind, she would agree. There is no sense in harming her daughters' chances at making a strong marriage."

The older woman spoke with the authority of one accustomed to getting her way. But her granddaughters appeared uncomfortable at the notion.

Iain met Rose's gaze. "What are your thoughts, Lady Rose?"

With a resigned sigh, she admitted, "I suppose the best course of action is to delay our travel to London. You may go on without us, but I prefer to wait a little longer. I might be able to walk again, if I keep trying."

Her grandmother grew impatient, as if Rose had suggested that she was learning to fly. "There are many widowers who would not care. Some of the older gentlemen who already have heirs might consider you for a wife."

"I would rather not wed a man old enough to be my grandfather," Rose pointed out. "I am not quite that desperate."

"You *are* three and twenty, Rose," her grandmother reminded her.

"Practically ancient." She rolled her eyes and then turned back to Iain. "But I suppose I *could* get an offer from a gentleman." The knowing look in her eyes held a note of humor.

It was almost a challenge. Iain touched his mouth briefly, never taking his eyes from her. It was a silent reminder of their kiss, and a faint blush stained her cheeks. No, she hadn't been immune to his embrace at all.

"You might gain a marriage offer," her grandmother agreed, "but it will not be from a gentleman of the ton, Rose. It may be a long time before you can walk again, and you will lose out on your childbearing years. You must lower your expectations."

She kept her gaze fixed upon Iain. "I never lower my expectations." With that, she steadied herself and slowly stood up from the chair. The women's conversation ceased abruptly, and they stared at her in amazement. Iain couldn't help but smile. He knew she had stood with his assistance, during the rainstorm, but he hadn't known she could stand on her own now. She must have been practicing every waking hour.

"You stood up!" her sister exclaimed. "When did this happen, Rose?"

She gave a slight smile. "I told you I would learn to walk again. And this is only the beginning. The next time I go to London, I intend to dance with Lord Burkham. Everyone will know they were wrong about my illness."

Her grandmother's eyes held a trace of wonder, and this time, there was a genuine smile. "What a lovely surprise. I am quite pleased for you, darling." With a shrug, she added, "I suppose a fortnight will not matter. We may as well give you the chance to continue your healing. It may make a great difference in finding a man to wed."

Rose eased herself back into the chair, and the relief on her face was evident. Even standing for such a brief period of time had exhausted her. But it was indeed a start.

Iain raised his teacup to her in a silent toast. Over the next fortnight, he hoped she would make further progress, until she could indeed walk again. Even if it was only a few steps, her grandmother was right. It would greatly improve her chances of finding the right husband.

Yet the idea of her returning to Burkham annoyed him. Rose deserved better than a man like him. Iain resolved that when they did go to London, he would ensure that she had every opportunity to find the husband of her dreams.

Even if it could never be him.

One week later

It was just after dawn, and her family was still sleeping. Rose stood beside her bed, holding herself balanced for several minutes. Each day, her legs were getting stronger.

Soon, she told herself. Perhaps even today, she might take her first step. She smiled at the thought, and her gaze moved toward a vase of flowers by the window. Lord Ashton had sent her a new bouquet of roses, and she loved the heady aroma. They wouldn't last long, but the flowers made her smile.

Hattie came to help her dress in her riding habit, and asked, "Am I to ride with you this morning, Lady Rose?"

"No, not today. Just ask Calvert to bring me to the stables."

Her maid nodded, and Rose let her believe that Calvert would be her escort. The truth was, she wanted to be alone.

Her legs needed to be stronger, and she hadn't forgotten Lord Ashton's suggestion about swimming. Although it wasn't possible to immerse her entire body without the risk of drowning, she would try sitting upon the bank and kicking her legs. It might help.

After she was dressed, Calvert carried her downstairs and outside toward the stables. He instructed the coachman, Nelson, to saddle her mare. He also ordered Nelson to prepare his own mount, but Rose stopped him. "I am going alone this morning. I will return by midmorning."

"It's not safe, Lady Rose," he objected. "You must have an escort or a chaperone with you."

Ordinarily, she would agree. But she wanted no one to see her dipping her feet into the lake, particularly Calvert. Even Hattie would balk at the idea.

"I do not intend to leave the grounds of Penford," she lied. "If I have need of anyone, I'll simply shout." She had made up her mind to sit near the water and exercise her legs. She had deliberately not worn any stockings, and her riding boots hid her bare feet. No one need know about this and there was no danger.

Her footman hesitated. "So you intend to ride through the grounds? And that's all?"

She nodded. "Of course. And I'll return when I need assistance dismounting." Truthfully, she was already able to get down on her own. It wasn't so very hard to hold on to the saddle and slide down. Though she couldn't take any steps, she planned to ride toward the shore and sit near the water's edge, near the large boulder. She wasn't entirely certain if she was strong enough to pull herself back onto the horse, but she guessed she could stand upon the tallest boulder and use that for help. At the very worst, she could always call out for help if she couldn't manage on her own.

The voice of doubt edged her confidence, for there were many disasters that could happen. The moment she tried to get off the horse, any number of things might cause trouble. She ought to bring Hattie with her. That was the sensible move, she knew. And yet . . . she was tired of being reliant on others for help. She wanted a few moments to herself to see what she was truly capable of. Only then would she know if walking was even a possibility.

Her time was running out, for they were leaving for London in one week. Rose was determined to take at least a few steps on her own before that time.

"Lady Rose, I cannot say I approve of this," her footman insisted.

But she held firm on her decision. "I do not require your permission to ride, Calvert. If I wish to go, I shall. Now help me onto my horse."

His expression was disgruntled, but he obeyed. The moment she was secure upon her saddle, Rose nodded in farewell, and urged her mare across the estate. She lifted her face into the wind, reveling in the cool air while the morning sunlight creased the edges of the horizon with rose and gold. It felt so good to be on her own, as if the chains of her weakness had shattered.

It felt so wonderful to be in command, to guide the horse where she wanted to go. Being on horseback granted her a liberty she hadn't known she needed.

Undoubtedly, the water would be frigid this morning, but since she had no intention of submerging her body, there was no harm in it. Her feet might be cold, but then, that would be her motivation to move them.

Rose chose a secluded part of the lake where several large boulders lined the water's edge. Then she drew her mare to a stop beside the largest stone. The animal was well trained, and held steady as she gripped the saddle and let her legs slide down to a standing position.

For a moment, she clung to the saddle, fighting for her balance. Then she took one step and promptly lost her footing. She fell hard on her backside, but thankfully, she'd managed to land close enough to where she was wanting to sit.

Using her arms, Rose pulled herself onto one of the flat boulders and leaned her back against the largest one. There. She had made it this far. If she could get her boots off, she could dip her feet in the water and slide down a little until her knees were submerged.

As she struggled with her boots, she thought of what Lord Ashton would say if he saw her now. The man had been polite during the last week, and not once had he treated her any differently than a friend.

Which was as it should be. But she couldn't deny the twinge of disappointment as she remembered that breathless kiss. Was that what it was meant to be like, kissing a husband? Never in her life had she experienced such a heart-pounding moment. She'd felt the kiss over every inch of her body, the tremors rising over her sensitive flesh. It was seductive, beckoning her closer. She shouldn't have allowed it, but she'd been powerless to resist him.

It only proved the point that Lord Ashton was indeed a very dangerous man.

When her riding boots were off, she eased herself down until her toes were in the water. The icy water was numbing, and not at all comfortable. But in time, she adjusted to the cold and moved her ankles back and forth. It was a start.

Rose couldn't see the bottom, but it wasn't surprising. This part of the lake had a steep drop-off. Some of the children from the village liked to dive off the boulders into the pool.

She moved a little closer, until her calves were in the water. Again, she continued exercising her legs, kicking them in the lake. It took more effort than she'd imagined, but she persevered until exhaustion set in. She was beginning to understand why Lord Ashton had suggested it. This was an effective way to keep building up her strength.

When she decided that she'd had enough, she dried her legs and tugged her boots back on. Then she whistled for her mare.

The horse obediently trotted forward, and Rose reached for the reins. She was feeling good about what she'd accomplished, and spoke quietly to the mare as she stood up on the boulder. Her knees were shaking from her earlier exercise, but she held herself balanced as she reached for the saddle. All she had to do was get one foot in the stirrup, and she could pull herself up the rest of the way.

Rose struggled, using all her strength, but still couldn't manage it. She tried to use one arm to lift her leg into the stirrup, but her balance faltered.

She tried again and finally managed to get one foot in. But when she tried to pull herself up, holding the reins, the horse perked up at a sudden sound. The mare jerked her head, and Rose lost her balance, tipping wildly.

"No, oh, no!" she cried out, before she fell backward off the boulder and her back hit the water. The frigid cold took her breath away, and the heavy riding habit and boots dragged her down. The icy lake submerged her, and she fought to stand up.

The water was deeper than she'd remembered, and it came over her head. When she tried to gasp for air, her mouth filled up with water. She could swim, but both the sodden wool and the heavy boots were weighing down her body. With a tremendous effort, she plowed her arms through the water, reaching for the boulder. She wanted to weep with relief, until she realized that she lacked the strength to pull her body out of the water. There was no true handhold, and even the embankment was steep.

This had truly been a horrible idea. Why had she ever believed she could go off riding alone? It had been nothing but foolish pride. And now, she was freezing, soaked to the skin, and clinging to a boulder for dear life.

She didn't know whether to laugh, out of hysteria, or begin screaming. It should have been an easy matter to pull herself up, but her entire body was numb and impossible to move.

You could drown, she told herself. *You could die if you cannot get out.*

She filled her lungs with air and shouted out, "Help me!"

But there was only the sound of her mare grazing and trudging farther away from the water's edge.

Rose shouted again, hoping that someone would hear her. Perhaps Calvert or even the coachman might hear her if she was loud enough. Her voice grew hoarse, and her fingers began slipping from the edge. With a tremendous lunge, she grasped the rock, tearing her fingernails in the process.

Once more, she called out, and when she heard the answering sounds of hoofbeats, she wanted to cry with relief. She hardly cared who it was, so long as they could pull her out of the lake—even if it was Calvert, come to chastise her for her folly.

But when the rider emerged from behind the trees, she saw Lord Ashton galloping hard toward the water.

"Hold on, *a chara,*" he told her. "Don't let go."

That wasn't at all in her plans, but she could feel her fingers slipping. "Hurry, please. I can't hold on to the rock for much longer."

Within seconds, Lord Ashton reached down and lifted her soaked body out of the freezing lake and onto the boulder. The moment she was out, her teeth began chattering, and it felt as if knives were slicing her flesh into ribbons.

"I'm s-so c-cold."

Immediately, Lord Ashton removed his coat and put it around her shoulders. "Here. Warm yourself while you tell me what happened."

"I f-fell into the water. My mare moved back when I was t-trying to mount, and I lost my b-balance." She shuddered, gripping his coat as if she could absorb his body heat from it.

"We had better get you home," he said. "You'll catch your death out here."

She sent him a rueful smile. "I nearly did. I suppose I never should have taken your suggestion, trying to swim to strengthen my legs."

"Not in a riding habit and boots." He lifted her on top of her mare, but her boots were sagging from her feet. He tugged at the first riding boot and emptied water from it. When he glanced at her bare foot, he stopped and held it a moment. "What you did was dangerous." His tone held traces of anger, even as his palm warmed her bare skin.

The gesture startled her, and she felt the gooseflesh rise over her calves and up her thighs. He continued holding her foot, and though she wanted to tug it free of his grasp, the heat of his skin was so very welcome. But she could not allow it. "Put my boot back on my foot, if you please."

"What you did was foolish, and you could have drowned."

"I wasn't *trying* to swim. I thought I would put my feet in the water for a little while. It should have been safe enough."

A flush of chagrin came over her at his quiet rebuke. But the gentle touch of his hand revealed concern that she hadn't anticipated. He replaced her boot and then reached for the other one, emptying out the water. Again, he warmed the bottom of her foot, and warmth spiraled through her skin. "You should not have gone alone."

She knew that, and she could not deny that the danger had been real. "You're right. But I let my pride get in the way of common sense. I had no intention of falling in."

"No one ever intends to drown. But it *does* happen."

The touch of his hand scattered all coherent thought like droplets of water. "I—I know." But when Lord Ashton kept his palm upon the sole of her foot, she imagined his hand moving up her calf to her bare thigh.

Good Heavens, what was the matter with her? Why was she allowing her thoughts to wander like this? Her face reddened, and she begged, "My boot. Please put my boot back on."

He let his hand linger a little longer. "I am glad I was here to save your life." Then he slid her boot back onto her foot.

"So am I." She gripped the edges of his coat and turned her mare back to the trail. "And now, I should very much like to return home and get into dry clothes." Her body was freezing, shuddering violently from the cold air.

"So we will." He mounted his own horse and began escorting her back.

"I promise I won't try that again." She knew how fortunate she was, that he had come along so quickly.

"Not alone," he amended. "But if you're wanting to put your feet in the water, I can accompany you if you wish."

Oh, no. Not with the way he had stolen a kiss in the past. Or the way he had taken liberties with her feet just now. "No, thank you. If I ever decide to return, which is highly unlikely, Calvert will be my escort."

"He might fall into a fit of apoplexy if you revealed your bare ankles or legs," he warned.

"More likely, he will complain at every moment." At this point, she hardly cared what the footman said or did.

The clammy wool clung to her body, and rivulets of water dripped down her hair. Her teeth chattered, and she urged her mare faster along the path back to Penford. All she could think of right now was a warm fireplace and layers and layers of blankets.

"What will you tell your family about this?" Lord Ashton asked.

She shook her head. "Just that my mare lost her balance and tossed me in." The indignity of her fall made her realize that her family would worry about her even more. They might even try to forbid her from riding at all.

But she couldn't give up. Not now, not when she was so close to regaining her strength.

He drew his horse alongside hers. "My offer was real, *a chara*. If you want me to accompany you and ensure that you are safe, I will."

Rose didn't know what to say. It wasn't at all a good idea to be alone with Lord Ashton. Not only because of the impropriety, but because of the way he made her feel. The Irishman had a way of tempting her, of melting away her good sense.

In the warmth of his coat, the scent of his skin lingered. It made her feel as if his arms were around her, even now.

Stop this, she warned herself. *He is not the man for you.*

Rose gripped the edges of his coat and tried to suppress the unwanted feelings. "I don't think that would be wise."

"Not in deep water, no. But shallow water would pose little harm." He slowed the pace of his horse.

He had misunderstood her. She wasn't speaking about exercising her legs—she was referring to being alone with him. Rose wanted him to remain a friend and nothing more. But although he had maintained his distance over the past week, she had not forgotten the stolen kiss.

And she could not ignore that he was a handsome man who wanted to spend time with her.

She let her mare begin walking, though she was still cold. Right now, she needed him to leave her. "Lord Ashton, you ought to go on alone to London and leave me to this task of learning to walk again. I do thank you for wanting to help. But it's something *I* must do."

"I have my own motives, Lady Rose, and this you already know. I have no desire to travel to London and be mocked for my ignorance in society."

She sent him a sidelong look. "You're not completely ignorant. And you'll remember London once you return. It's not so very hard."

He pulled his horse to a stop and regarded her with honesty. "Lady Rose, I've never been to London. Not once, in all my life. My mother took my older brother Michael, and left me behind."

She blinked a moment. It was impossible to imagine it. Why would the countess leave her youngest son behind? It made no sense.

"Whenever our family went to London, my siblings and I traveled together," she told him. "Always." With a curious look, she waited for him to tell her more.

Lord Ashton's expression turned grim. "My mother didn't want me there. It was easier for her to keep me in Ireland, where no one would know anything about me. I was the invisible younger son."

Rose didn't miss the bitterness in his voice, and sensed that she shouldn't ask why. "Is there still a rift between the two of you?"

He turned to face her. "It's doubtful that I will ever see her again. I'm certain she is glad of it."

With that, he urged his mount to continue on, leaving Rose forced to follow him. She'd never imagined that the Earl of Ashton would be so isolated. Surely he had been trained to take on his older brother's responsibilities.

"And so you asked my grandmother for help," she said quietly. "Because you had no idea how to find an English bride."

He shrugged. "I could find one, but marrying her is another matter. I asked to come and visit Penford because I knew I needed to learn about London society."

His confession made sense, and she probed a little further. "Did you spend time with the Irish nobility?" She suspected he must have, but he surprised her again by shaking his head.

"Whatever I learned, I learned from my brother. My mother would have been glad if I'd never returned from Trinity." He paused a moment, then added, "I've no wish to be a burden on anyone, nor do I wish to humiliate myself. Can you see why I want to help you walk again, Lady Rose? It's my way of repaying you, if you can help me to learn what I need to know."

She met his gaze and gave a single nod. More and more, it was all making sense. Although he was the Earl of Ashton, his servants had abandoned him and he had virtually nothing. His title meant very little, and all he possessed was a handsome face and a charming demeanor.

She recognized the challenges that lay ahead of the Irishman. People would talk about him and his family, whispering about the troubles in Ireland. They would wonder why he had been hidden away, speculating all sorts of scandalous behavior. And some would attempt to ridicule him for it.

She didn't want that to happen. Not to him.

"I am getting stronger, but I am nowhere near walking," she admitted. "However, since you *did* save my life, I owe you a favor." She studied him closely, mentally comparing him to the gentlemen of the ton.

Most people would judge him by what they saw, at first, and that was easily remedied. The more she thought of it, the more she wondered if Lord Ashton would know how to conduct himself among the heiresses. Perhaps a rehearsal of sorts might be welcome.

"After we are home, I will change my gown and we will meet in the drawing room to discuss your plans," she insisted. "I can help you with any questions you may have about how to find an appropriate bride."

Lord Ashton gave a nod. "As you wish. But I cannot spend the remainder of the summer in London, Lady Rose. There are people depending on me to save Ashton. I made promises, and I intend to keep them."

She had suspected as much, and both of them needed time they didn't have. "Meet me within the hour," she said. "We will start your training immediately."

And perhaps they could find a strategy that would suit them both.

Chapter Ten

Iain entered the drawing room within the hour, as requested, but Lady Rose was not yet there. Instead, he found Beauregard waiting for him, along with his father, Sir Lester. The boy wore a wary expression, but he nodded in greeting.

"Sir Lester," Iain said. "This is a surprise."

The baronet pointed to one corner of the room, where Iain's trunk stood. "We found the remainder of your belongings, Lord Ashton."

"How?" Iain asked. And more importantly, why had the man taken it upon himself to bring them here? It seemed like a great deal of effort when they were hardly more than strangers.

"I understand that you have delayed your journey to London while you were in search of your possessions," the baronet said. "It wasn't difficult to make inquiries and find them. One of Beau's friends had your waistcoat." He frowned at his son, who kept his attention fixed upon the floor. "Then I sent my servants to inquire among the Irish. With so many seeking jobs in Yorkshire, it wasn't hard to find someone selling a trunk of clothing."

Even so, it didn't explain the man's reasons for helping him. Iain sent him a curious look, and Sir Lester continued, "Now that you have everything, I'm certain you will want to return to London to your family's home."

And then, the meaning became clear. Sir Lester was trying to be rid of him. Although he'd offered a friendly smile, Iain hadn't forgotten the way the man had fawned over Lady Rose.

"Do you remember who sold my clothing to you?"

Sir Lester nodded. "His name was Pádraig, I believe. And he sold the lot to us for three pounds. I'm quite good at bargaining."

A tightness gathered inside Iain like a fist. It shouldn't have surprised him that his own servant would sell off his trunk of belongings for profit. It seemed that loyalty was a trait easily forgotten in the face of adversity.

"Thank you," he said to Sir Lester. "I will be glad to pay you for your trouble."

"Three pounds is naught to worry about," the baronet said. "You can be on your way, and we will consider our Christian duty done." He smiled warmly.

Iain walked over to the trunk and opened it. With a quick glance at the folded clothing, it did seem that everything he'd packed was inside. But he hardly cared about the possessions now. As he surveyed the belongings, a sense of embarrassment came over him. These clothes were meant to ensnare the affections of a rich woman, but they had belonged to his older brother. He now realized that none of them were suitable. They hardly fit him, either.

"My goodness," Rose exclaimed, when she arrived in the drawing room, carried by Calvert. "Are those your missing clothes?"

"They are, thanks to Sir Lester." He nodded toward the baronet, and Lady Rose greeted the man. Her hair was still damp, and her maid had gathered it into a sleek updo. A single pink rose adorned the chignon, and she wore a morning gown in the same color.

"How very thoughtful of you, Sir Lester. I can only imagine how difficult it must have been."

"Not at all, Lady Rose. I was glad to be of service, and truly, it's the sort of thing I like to do. Help out my fellow man and all that." He beamed at her.

"Well, it was very gracious of you." She murmured for Calvert to set her down on a chair. Iain didn't miss the besotted way the baronet was staring at Lady Rose. She, however, appeared not to notice.

"Perhaps, now that your health has improved, we might go out riding one morning?" Sir Lester suggested.

Rose looked from the baronet to Iain, as if she'd not considered this. "I—I do not know, Sir Lester. My mother's health has not been the best, as of late, and I really ought to stay with her." She offered her apologies, and then added, "But I do thank you for the invitation."

The baronet's face reddened, but he mustered a smile. "Another time, then."

Calvert placed her in a chair and then asked, "Shall I bring the trunk upstairs, my lady?"

"Not just yet," Rose said. To the baronet, she added, "Thank you again for bringing Lord Ashton's belongings here. It was very good of you. Perhaps another time, you might stay for tea." She touched her wet hair and added, "I am unfortunately not very presentable at the moment, after my horse threw me off."

At that, Sir Lester's expression transformed into sympathy. "I do understand, Lady Rose. I hope you were not hurt."

"Only my pride," she reassured him, though Iain knew it was not at all true. She'd nearly drowned, and though she put on a false front that all was well, her ordeal had indeed frightened her.

"I suppose Beauregard and I will be on our way." Sir Lester took his hat from Calvert and bowed as he left.

"Thank you again for your trouble," Iain said.

Lady Rose echoed his thanks. Once Sir Lester and Beauregard were gone, she sank back into the chair and pointed toward the trunk. "There isn't very much here, is there? I suspect you sold off a good deal of your own clothing. There aren't many garments inside that you could wear to a ball, are there?"

He gave no answer to that, for he *did* lack proper attire. But it wasn't because he'd sold off his clothing—it was simply that he had nothing else. His mother had never bothered with fine clothes for him, and his brother's coats and trousers didn't fit. He had hoped to purchase a new wardrobe once he reached London, if he could somehow come up with the funds. He had no way of knowing whether Michael or their father had hidden any money within the house.

The very thought of his brother brought a wave of sadness. He missed Michael, for they had been friends as well as siblings. Many times, his brother had been angry at their mother for treating him as the lesser son.

"We're brothers," he'd insisted. "She has no right to behave as if you don't belong."

"Perhaps I'm not her son," Iain had teased in return. "I might be a changeling."

"I was there on the day you were born." Michael shook his head. "And you are *my brother. No matter how she treats you."*

For years, he'd wondered why his mother hated the sight of him. As a boy, he'd tried to ask the servants why Lady Ashton didn't want him. But they had simply sent him a sympathetic look and held their silence.

"Did you hear what I said?" Rose asked, breaking him free of his reverie.

He shook his head. "I'm sorry. My mind was wandering."

"I said that I could have a tailor come and measure you for new clothing. There isn't much time, but it can be done."

He didn't want to be beholden to her and politely refused. "I will take care of it myself, once I reach London."

"It's no hardship to arrange it beforehand," she said quietly. "It will make it easier for you, if you needn't wait on new attire."

He understood her veiled insinuation, that others would judge him by his appearance. "You're assuming that I have nothing suitable."

The soft look she sent him held understanding. "Am I wrong, then?"

She wasn't. If he wore these, he would receive only pitying or embarrassed looks from the ladies. But he still didn't want her to pay for his clothing.

Rose studied him for a moment. "We have a little time before we go. And you *have* helped me a great deal."

"I'm not in a position to pay for a new clothing," he admitted. "At least, not yet."

Using both hands to support her weight on the arms of the chair, she stood up. With her eyes locked upon his, Rose steadied herself and let go of the chair. With a tremulous smile, she asked, "Do you think I can put a price upon this? Before you helped me, I could do nothing."

He understood that, and yet, his pride ached at the thought of accepting her help. "All I did was help you stand each day." Over the past two weeks, he had met with her in the garden every afternoon, gradually extending the time she remained standing.

"And you argued with me when I said I was tired. You refused to let me stop." Her face held the serenity of a woman who was grateful to him.

"Because you're stronger than you look, Lady Rose."

Slowly, she inclined her head. "You're the only one who believed in me. So I will summon the tailor, and you must endure his measurements for your own sake."

He knew she would not be swayed, so he agreed to her decision. "Then I will repay you for the clothes, Lady Rose." No matter how long it took.

She lowered herself back into a seated position. "I am glad you see it my way. If I may be frank, you need every possible advantage if you intend to wed an heiress. Although you may be in a desperate state of poverty now, you *are* a handsome man. For many women, the illusion of wealth would be enough."

He blinked at that, not knowing quite what to say. "Are you suggesting that the women would value my looks over my lack of a fortune?"

"Many would. Particularly a widow, if you would consider it."

He hadn't truly bothered to think of what kind of bride he wanted. Debutante or widow, it didn't matter.

"I hadn't thought about it," he said, sitting beside her when she lowered herself back to her own chair.

"Many women have used their beauty to wed a titled lord," she said. "Your situation is no different, except that you must use your charm to find a bride."

"I suppose I must set aside my pride."

"Indeed. Just as I've set aside my pride in order to walk again." With a look, she added, "It was not my desire to swim in a frigid English lake, I can tell you that. But you *did* save me from drowning."

"I am glad I was there." He couldn't imagine the horror of her falling beneath the water, being too weak to pull herself back out again. Her intent to exercise her legs had nearly resulted in disaster.

And although they were only friends, the idea still haunted him. "Is there somewhere else you could have gone to swim?" he asked. "Some place less dangerous, like a shallow pool?"

Her expression grew shadowed with sadness. He didn't know what he'd said to prompt it, but at last, she nodded. "There is a place I could go, where I can sit on the bottom of a small pond. It's quite shallow."

"Where is it?"

"Inside my father's garden. It's a walled garden where he and my mother used to go and lock themselves away from the world."

The moment she spoke of it, Iain remembered the hidden doorway he had found. It intrigued him, and he wondered what secrets the garden held. "When was the last time you saw it?"

Rose let out a slow breath, her eyes soft with memory. "Just after he died. I went there for a few hours to . . . grieve and say good-bye to him." She blinked a moment and gathered her composure. "Mother hasn't gone there since the day he died. But the gardeners do. I've seen them go inside to tend it."

"Do you want to see it again?" He didn't want to dredge up painful memories, but his curiosity was piqued.

She shrugged. "I don't know. I think I would, but it hurts to remember that he's gone."

"If it wouldn't bother you, I should like to see their garden," he said quietly. The enclosed space might give them a means of practicing her walking without her feeling self-conscious.

"I suppose we could." She eyed him again and said, "But in return, you must allow me to instruct you on proper etiquette. If you've never been to London, you will need my help."

Lady Rose was right, and well he knew it. "Agreed."

She leaned on the arm of her chair and sent him a smile. "You do realize that I will be ruthless in your training. We have so little time, and there is much for you to learn."

Iain reached out and took her palm in his, kissing the back of her hand. "I look forward to everything you intend to teach me, Lady Rose."

Sunlight brightened the sky, and Rose waited for Lord Ashton upon the stone bench where she spent time out of doors each day. Calvert had brought her this far, but she did not want the footman to know of her plans for the morning. She had dismissed him, telling him not to return for her until later.

In her palm, she held the iron key that fit into the garden lock. Though she shouldn't have been uneasy about visiting her father's private sanctuary, it felt a bit like awakening his ghost.

She heard the soft footsteps of Lord Ashton and turned to greet him. He wore one of the unfashionable coats from his belongings, and she noted how the cuffs were too short. The coat itself hung upon his frame, as if it had been fitted to a larger man.

She frowned, wondering if the clothes had ever fit him properly. It seemed as if he were wearing another man's clothing. Why had he brought them, if they did not fit? Were they all he had?

"Good morning, *a chara,*" he greeted her.

"And to you." She held up the iron key. "Shall we go?"

He leaned down, and she lifted her arms up, allowing him to carry her. Although it was a short walk to the walled garden, with every step, she grew more self-conscious about being in this man's arms. He was strong and lean, and he had a way of carrying her that felt like an embrace. With her arms around his neck, she nestled her face against his shoulder.

For a fragile moment, she let herself succumb to the feeling of security, forbidden though it was. She had a strong friendship with a man who needed her help—just as she needed his.

When they reached the door covered with rose brambles, he lowered her to stand. Rose placed the key inside the lock and turned it. The door opened easily, the hinges silent. She stood at the doorway but could not yet see the garden.

"Do you want me to carry you inside?" he asked. She nodded, and he lifted her up once again, bringing her into the walled space.

The moment she saw the flowers in bloom, tears welled up in her eyes. All around her, it was as if her father's spirit remained. She couldn't help but remember how he used to bring flowers to her mother each morning. The loss of him caught her without warning.

Roses climbed across the brick wall, and were only starting to bloom. In another corner, she saw bright red tulips and purple grape hyacinths blooming. A hydrangea bush was budding, and a willow tree hung low over a clear pool of water. A waterfall descended over a few larger stones into the pool, and sunlight reflected in a golden shimmer over the surface of the water. The pool was so clear, she could see the river stones lining the bottom.

Lord Ashton set her down upon a stone bench beneath the willow tree. He walked around the perimeter, studying the flowers. The garden was larger than he'd expected, and soft grass carpeted the open space. She could almost imagine her parents enjoying private moments alone in this Elysium, perhaps sharing a picnic.

"It's beautiful here," he remarked. "But why haven't you come to sit here each day? The gardeners have taken such good care of the grounds."

She raised her eyes to his. "Perhaps because it reminds me too much of Father. The memories are still strong." Though Iain didn't ask how he had died, she offered, "My father grew very ill, and at the end, he was in a great deal of pain. I am glad that he is no longer suffering, though I miss him."

Lord Ashton sat beside her and studied their surroundings. Although the serenity soothed her sadness, she saw the tension in him. In spite of her better judgment, Rose asked, "What happened to your father?"

"He died before I was born. I never knew him." He spoke in a flat voice, as if it didn't matter. And yet, she imagined that life must have been very difficult without any father at all.

"I'm sorry. It must have been hard for you." She leaned closer to him, offering her hand in sympathy. "And your mother."

"The earl was murdered by one of our tenants," he said flatly. "And I've no wish to speak of it."

Dismay filled her heart, and she had no inkling of what to say to him. She had never heard of the tragedy. Yet, she squeezed his hand in silent support. He wasn't wearing gloves like she was, and the touch of his bare hand felt intimate, despite the fragile silk barrier between them. He held her palm, his thumb stroking the back of her hand.

He wasn't looking at her, but she was keenly aware of his caress. Her mind warned her to pull away, but she couldn't bring herself to do so.

After a time, he squeezed her palm. "It was a long time ago, Lady Rose. There's no sense in dwelling upon the past. Only on what lies ahead." He released her palm and added, "Let us enjoy the day in this garden. You can teach me what to expect in London. I will keep you from drowning." His last words were spoken with a hint of teasing.

It was a welcome change of subject. She folded her hands in her lap and said, "Tell me more about what you already know. Surely you attended supper parties in Ireland."

He sent her a chagrined look. "Only once, during the last few months. Michael attended all of them in the past."

Her suspicions rose up again. It was unnatural and uncalled for if both sons were not in attendance. An unsettling feeling came over her, but she held back her uneasiness. "Did you ever attend a ball in Ireland?"

He shook his head. "No, never."

She was appalled to hear it. "I cannot believe your mother would be so shortsighted. Regardless of her personal feelings, it's irresponsible for you not to attend."

It was one matter if he had been too young to attend—but it seemed that the countess had deliberately shut him out. All members of the nobility would have attended a ball, solely for the purpose of learning proper behavior.

"So you remained at home while your brother attended?" she clarified.

He inclined his head. By way of a distraction, he stood and snapped off a twig from the willow tree. Rose turned over the matter in her mind, trying to understand the countess's reasons for isolating her son.

She herself had been taught the rules of etiquette ever since she was able to speak a full sentence. It was as natural as breathing to her, and she understood that this man stood at a great disadvantage if he dared to set foot in a ballroom.

Lord Ashton returned to stand before her. "I know that I lack the clothing and the demeanor of a proper earl. But I suppose you can teach me what I need to know."

"Perhaps." But for a gentleman, London was fraught with the potential of social disaster. She had assumed that he had prior knowledge of proper behavior.

"I may not be there to guide you, however," she pointed out. "And I will not lie. There are gentlemen who would seek to humiliate you if you *did* win the heart of an heiress they wanted to pursue."

He sent her a sidelong look. "I can take care of myself, Lady Rose." His gaze passed over her. "But we could be allies in London and help one another."

"What do you mean?"

"I mean that there is nothing that will attract the notice of your viscount faster than if you were to dance with me. If Burkham's feelings remain, he will return to you immediately to stake his claim."

"You make the viscount sound like a barbarian intent upon hauling me away. I assure you, he is not."

"Never underestimate the power of jealousy."

"If I cannot walk again, jealousy means nothing."

"You will." Lord Ashton brushed the soft edges of the weeping willow branch across her cheek. Although the gesture was only meant in fun, the sensation sent a sudden chill over her skin, particularly when she studied him closely.

Was it possible that the countess had indulged in an affair without her husband's knowledge? To the servants and outsiders, Iain would be a legitimate heir. But what if he wasn't?

It was one possible explanation for his mother's neglect. But Rose pushed the thought back, not wanting to think of it. Whether or not Iain Donovan was a trueborn earl didn't matter. If the outside world and the solicitors accepted him, then the title was his.

She caught the edge of the twig and held it. His green eyes grew heated, and in that moment, her awareness deepened. Iain Donovan was truly a handsome man. His dark hair was slightly mussed, and she had the urge to straighten it. She caught the hint of his soap, a faint aroma that made her want to move closer to him.

"Don't be looking at me like that, Lady Rose." His tone grew rigid, like he was holding himself back.

"Like what?" she whispered.

"Like you're wanting me to kiss you." He moved in closer, and his expression left no doubt that he wanted to. The words made her heart beat faster, and she tried to calm herself.

"We're only friends," she reminded him.

"So we are. It doesn't mean that I'm dead." His pirate smile returned, and she did pull away this time.

"Behave yourself." She rested her hands upon his chest to keep him at arm's length.

"Is that what you want?" He reached out and covered her hands with his own. Her eyes locked with his, and she was conscious of his roughened hands against her gloved ones. She ought to pull away, but she couldn't bring herself to do so.

"O-of course."

Lord Ashton slid his hand into her hair, drawing it down the edge of her cheek. His touch burned through her skin in a path of heat. She felt the echo of sensation coursing through her, and she couldn't have moved away if she'd wanted to. His green eyes held hers captive, and she was intently conscious of his touch.

"Please don't do this," she whispered, while he was staring at her. He let his hand linger upon her chin, sliding it down her throat to her shoulder. A thousand shivers broke over her skin, and she felt herself bloom with arousal. She imagined this man kissing her again, and the very thought made her self-conscious. They had an agreement to help one another, and that was all. She shouldn't dream of letting down the boundaries between them.

"You're worth more than six letters," he said quietly. "I hope you know that."

And with that, he released her, stepping back. Rose rubbed at her arms, uncertain of what to do or say now.

She took a moment to steady herself and then said, "I don't want to talk about Lord Burkham. I would rather try learning to walk."

"Do you want to start beside the water?" he asked at last.

She nodded, needing the distraction. "All right."

He leaned down and lifted her into his arms, bringing her to the waterfall and pool. Though she was acutely aware of his embrace, she tried to push back her wayward thoughts. "While I exercise my legs, you can ask me any questions you like. About London, that is."

He chose a place beside the pool and lowered her to the grassy bank. "I can't say that I really care about London, Lady Rose. I've no questions about a place I've never visited."

"Then I will tell you all about it." She straightened, and he sat on the opposite side of her.

"There are more people there than you can imagine," she broke out, reaching for her shoes. "I suppose it's similar to Dublin, though I've never been there." She fumbled with the buttons, struggling to unfasten them. Lord Ashton reached over and began unbuttoning her shoe without asking permission. She was grateful for the assistance, though she was well aware of how very improper it was for the pair of them to be alone in this garden without a chaperone. Undoubtedly the servants would gossip about her, not to mention that her grandmother would have a fit.

But a part of her didn't care. Soon enough she would have to return to the outside world where others would judge her. Here, she could almost imagine that she was whole and well again.

"Have *you* ever been there?" she asked. "To Dublin, I mean."

"I spent years there," he answered. "When I studied at Trinity, I sometimes walked across the bridge over the River Liffey. There were moments when I liked living in Dublin, but Ashton was always my home."

"Did your brother treat you in the same way as your mother?"

Iain shook his head. "Michael and I were as close as brothers could be. I would give up being the earl in a moment if it would bring him back again. He was my best friend."

When he started to pull her shoe off, she stopped him. "I can manage from here." She hadn't worn stockings—and she did not want him touching her bare skin. The very thought brought a chill of goosebumps over her body.

She handed him the other shoe to unbutton while she hid her bare foot beneath her skirts. He allowed her to remove the second shoe, and then she used her arms to scoot closer to the water's edge. Slowly, she lowered her feet into the water, catching her breath at the cold.

"No stockings again, Lady Rose?" he remarked. "How very scandalous."

"It would be far worse if I *did* wear them," she remarked. "There is nothing worse than itchy wet wool against one's skin."

She began moving her legs through the water. She was well aware of his gaze, and she pleaded, "Don't look at my bare feet. It's bad enough that I'm here alone with you."

He obeyed, but instead of gazing into the garden, he stared at her face. "You've no reason to be afraid of me, Rose."

Which wasn't true at all. She could still remember the temptation of his mouth and the way he'd conjured up a deep response. She wasn't afraid of him—she was afraid of herself and the way he made her feel.

Desperately, she attempted to change the subject. "Let us begin speaking of the proper way to arrive at a ballroom."

"If we must." Iain sat down beside her and began removing his own shoes and stockings.

She blinked a moment and asked, "What exactly are you doing, Lord Ashton?"

"Joining you." With his trousers rolled up to his knees, he slid his own feet into the water. "Jesus, Mary, and Joseph, that's cold enough to freeze the teats off a witch."

She grimaced at his raw speech. "Well, that's . . . not quite the way I would have described it. And you cannot speak in such a manner when we reach London."

He moved his feet in the water and shrugged. "You think I will shock the ladies with my manners."

"Indeed," she agreed. "You must behave with the utmost propriety. Else mothers will allow you nowhere near their daughters."

"I'm not concerned about my bride's mother. Only her." He stood in the pool of water, and it came up to his knees.

"If you do not win her mother's approval, nothing else matters. She won't let you speak to her daughter." Although Rose had a feeling that a besotted young woman might indeed rebel against her parents. Lord Ashton was entirely too persuasive.

His mouth curved in a knowing smile. "Is that so?"

"It is." Her thoughts were scattering like dandelion seeds on the wind, so she began blurting out instructions. His hair was still rumpled and a little too long to be fashionable, but she had no doubt that every unmarried woman would try to catch his eye.

"When you meet the young ladies, be mysterious," she suggested. "Do not tell them anything about your poverty. For now, you are trying to attract possible heiresses, and the less they know about you, the better."

She lowered her legs deeper into the small pool, until the water rose up to her knees. Again, she moved her legs rapidly, attempting to strengthen them.

"Will I be expected to dance with the ladies?" he inquired. "And only once, I presume?"

"Yes." With a slight frown, she murmured, "You do know how to dance, don't you?"

A slight smile played at his mouth. "I do. That was something my brother insisted that I learn. If he had to suffer, then so would I."

That, at least, made it easier. She began talking more about the balls, explaining how to be introduced properly to young ladies and how to maintain good manners.

"You should have supper with my grandmother and me tonight," she said suddenly. Though she had not noticed anything out of the ordinary with his table manners, she wanted to ensure that he knew about the proper silver to use and what to expect at supper parties regarding conversation.

"I should be glad to dine with you, *a chara*." He glanced over at her feet and added, "Aren't your legs getting cold? Would you like me to warm them?"

"They are cold, yes. I should probably go back to the house." She eased herself out of the water, immediately folding her gown over her bare legs. From the way Lord Ashton was studying her, she felt her cheeks flush. "I hope my advice regarding London was helpful to you."

He inclined his head. "If I can remember all of it, I'm certain it will be." Then he stood and reached down to help her stand. She gripped his hands and managed to rise. Beneath her gown, her legs trembled from the cold. She wiped her feet against the grass, trying to dry them.

"Before you go, I've another idea," Lord Ashton said. "Put your feet atop mine."

She frowned, wondering if he intended to walk with her. "No, thank you. We're both barefoot and it would not be right."

"Then how will I know if I was taught properly how to dance?" He kept her hands gripped in his.

She eyed him with wariness. "I cannot dance, and you know this."

In response, Iain lifted her off the ground. He rested his grip beneath her hips so that she looked down on him. "Aye, you can."

She was startled by the sudden motion and blurted out, "This is not how we dance in London, Lord Ashton."

"It isn't?" He opened his mouth as if stunned, and she raised an eyebrow at him. "You can't be telling me the truth. After all those years of suffering through dance lessons with Michael?"

His teasing lightened her mood, and she nodded. "I'm afraid so. Whoever taught you to dance in Ireland was completely wrong." She offered a sympathetic smile. "We are much more formal here."

"My apologies, Lady Rose." Iain lowered her to stand, and as she slid down his hardened body, the closeness unnerved her. He was strong, his body made up of rigid planes and angles. He slid his arm around her waist and took her other hand in his. "I think you should be teaching me how to dance properly."

His palm was warm against hers, and he stood watching her. Those green eyes were the devil's lure, beckoning her toward temptation. "That *was* our agreement, wasn't it? You were going to prepare me for the dangers of London society."

"I am not ready to dance yet." She didn't feel at all ready to attempt it, even resting her feet upon his. And if she was honest, that was what made her uneasy. She didn't want the intimacy of his skin beneath hers.

"Try." He leaned closer, and in his eyes, she saw friendliness and encouragement. "Or are you afraid I'll step upon your toes?"

"I would be stepping upon yours. And I do not think you wish to have them crushed. You would be hobbling for weeks." She gave an apologetic smile. "It would be best if we stop for now."

"Not yet."

Rose could feel the warmth of his breath against her face, and his hand moved to her waist, lightly resting there. She couldn't help but enjoy the heat of his touch. And instead of needing to pull away, she allowed him to continue.

"Put your feet upon mine."

She hesitated, but obeyed. Her feet were still cold from the water, and the moment she stepped upon his, she let out a half shriek. "Your feet are freezing!"

"And now you know my true reason for wanting to dance. You can warm my feet."

"It's like standing upon ice." She wanted to step off, but he began moving, forcing her to dance with him.

As he took her in a slow waltz, she felt reckless in his arms. It did feel almost like dancing, and she couldn't hold back her smile. "My grandmother would be appalled if she could see me right now."

"I would think she'd be glad to see you dance."

"I'm not dancing. Not truly." But for a moment, it was good to imagine it. Perhaps in a few more months it might happen.

"This is another way for you to move your legs," he said. "They will get stronger if you dance with me."

She hadn't truly considered that, but he was right. And it was more enjoyable than she'd thought it would be.

"Next time, you should wear shoes," she advised. "I will do the same."

He inclined his head and spun her around again. All around her, the sunlight warmed her skin, and she caught the faint fragrance of flowers. "Do you suppose your parents danced in this garden?"

"I don't know. But perhaps."

He slowed his pace, watching her closely. "Am I dancing like a proper English gentleman?"

"You are, yes. There's nothing to fear on that account."

Again, he took her across the garden, spinning her in the waltz. She was conscious of his hands on her waist and the way he was watching her.

"Are you growing tired?" he asked.

She was slightly out of breath, but it had felt so good to feel normal for a few moments, she didn't care. "A little."

He relaxed his hold upon her waist. "If you're wanting me to stop, say the word."

She met his gaze and smiled. "I should want you to stop. But it has been so very long since I've danced. You found a weakness of mine."

He kept moving her, though he held back on the pace. His left hand drew her slightly closer, until they were now in an embrace. Though he continued to dance with her, she was well aware of how close they were.

He said nothing, but the unspoken words slipped beneath her defenses. She knew that he was interested in her, and he made no secret of it. What she didn't understand was why he had such an effect upon her.

"Lord Ashton, we should stop now." Her words were the barest whisper, for she no longer trusted herself. She was entranced by his handsome face and the way he was watching her now. If she lifted her mouth even the slightest fraction, she would be kissing him again.

He drew his hand over the line of her jaw and tipped her chin up. "Here, in this place, you will call me Iain. And I intend to call you Rose."

She was trembling in his arms, feeling so lost. When he slid his hands into her hair, holding her imprisoned, she tried to look away.

"What are you afraid of, *a chara*? I would never hurt you."

No, she knew that. But when she was in Lord Ashton's arms, she felt more alive, in a way she'd never before experienced. In hardly more than a fortnight, he'd taken apart her illusions, making her question the feelings she'd held for the viscount.

"Nothing," she lied. The truth was, the earl had made her doubt Lord Burkham's intentions, making her wonder if he'd ever cared for her at all. She had told herself that the six letters were a sign of interest and caring. But now, she wasn't so certain.

"Don't be looking at me like that, Lady Rose," he warned. His eyes had grown hooded, and he moved his hands around her in a true embrace. The warmth of his arms enfolded her, making her feel safe.

"Like what?" Her breathing had shifted and was unsteady, her skin sensitive beneath the fabric of her gown. Though she was trying to behave as if nothing were wrong, her good sense was disappearing before her eyes. She was standing in a beautiful garden, locked away from the world in the arms of a handsome Irishman. If she had never met Thomas, undoubtedly this man would have caused her heart to flutter.

Or pound against her chest, as it was currently doing.

"Take a step back, Lady Rose," he warned. "Or I'll not be responsible for the consequences." Rose lifted her eyes to his and there was no denying the desire in them. He was giving her the opportunity to raise boundaries between them, but she couldn't bring herself to move. She was lost in his gaze, feeling her own forbidden answer. In this place, there was no one to see. No one to tell her how wrong it was.

And when he leaned down to kiss her, she didn't pull away. His mouth assaulted hers with tenderness, flooding her with sensation. Her bare feet rested upon the grass while she clung to him for balance. His breath held the hint of tea, and the kiss became an awakening. It drew out the wilder side of herself, making her yearn for more.

Beneath the onslaught of sensation, she had no choice but to return the kiss. His hands moved over her spine, drawing her so close, their hips touched again. The swell of his manhood rested against her stomach, and she grew fearful of the arousal he'd conjured. She could imagine Iain laying her down against the grass, removing the layers of clothing until they were flesh to flesh. The heat of sin burned through her with reckless intensity.

God help her, she was caught up in his spell, while he drew her ever closer to the forbidden edge of desire. *Tell him to stop,* her brain urged her. But her body silenced her mind, so drawn by his touch.

Iain moved his hand over her bottom, lifting one hip until her leg was raised. Caught up against him, she had to wrap her arms around his neck. Though she knew it was wrong, she didn't push him back.

Her lips were swollen, deliciously bruised as his tongue entered her mouth. He stroked her, even as he moved his hardened length against her. She grew utterly wet beneath her petticoats, breathless at the pressure between her legs. Her breasts were tight against her chemise and corset, straining for more.

"Tell me to stop, Rose," he murmured.

Her brain was disconnected from reality, and she struggled to find her sense of reason. "I-y-yes, you must."

With his arm around her waist and hers around his neck, she felt her breath catch. He was staring at her like a man bent upon seduction. "Don't go back to the viscount," he said quietly.

Lord Ashton traced the edge of her cheek with his thumb. A thousand sensations spiraled through her, and she took a step backward.

"I shouldn't have kissed you," she told him. "It—it was wrong of me." He was making her nervous with the way he was watching her.

"No, it wasn't."

Again, he took another step forward, and she drew away. Only to suddenly become aware of what she'd done. She froze in place, both terrified and stunned that she had taken a step backward. "Iain?"

His sudden smile was blinding, and he held her hands in his. "You've already taken the first steps, *a chara.* Without even realizing it."

She had. For the first time in months, she'd managed to take two steps. Unbidden came the tears over her cheeks, while a shaky smile broke through. "I don't even know how this happened."

Lord Ashton shook his head. "I can't say how it did. But I watched you take two steps away from me."

Certainly, it was because he'd embarrassed her, but she couldn't bring herself to care. Joy flooded through her.

"Can you take a step toward me?" he asked.

She sent him a sidelong glance. "I'm not sure I should. Especially with the way you're looking at me now."

A knowing grin slid over his face. "And how am I looking at you?"

"Like I'm a slice of cake." She sent him a wry look, but he only appeared amused by her observation.

"Perhaps I was wanting another taste of you." He reached out to her shoulders, and she laughed at him.

"Oh, no." At that, she took a step away, suddenly realizing why he was teasing her. "Is this a ruse, meant to make me run away from you?" She faltered but took another step. Her body swayed out of balance, but with her bare feet upon the grass, it was easier to steady herself.

"Is it working, then?" Iain reached out to her, pretending that he wanted to snatch her back into an embrace.

"Yes." Rose stopped walking and gave up trying to hold back her tears of happiness. She didn't care if she was sobbing like a small child. These first few steps were nothing short of miraculous. Her cheeks were wet, but she was smiling so hard, they ached.

Iain closed the distance and brought her back into his arms, holding her tightly. She no longer cared, but dampened the front of his shirt with her tears. He rubbed her spine, his arm around her waist. "Don't cry, *a ghrá*. Else, I'll have to kiss your tears away."

She wiped at her eyes, and a laugh broke free. "Then I suppose I'll have to run."

Chapter Eleven

"Lord Ashton, you have a visitor." Fulton stood at the doorway to the dining room, where Iain was about to have supper with Lady Rose, her mother, and Lady Lily. They had not yet served the first course, and Iain stole a look at Rose to determine the proper answer.

Before she could answer, Fulton continued, "I realize that it is past the time for callers, but this visitor claims to be one of your missing servants."

Iain's mood darkened at the sudden news. He had a feeling he knew exactly who this "visitor" was. Immediately, he stood from the table. "Ladies, please forgive me, but I will return shortly."

"Is anything the matter, Fulton?" Rose asked.

The butler shrugged. "That, I cannot say. All I know is that the man insisted on seeing Lord Ashton. I thought it best, in case there was news from his family."

Iain rather doubted it. He'd believed that all his servants had abandoned him here. Why then, would one return to speak with him? There was more that he needed to understand, and he could not risk Rose and her family overhearing any of this conversation.

"I will meet with him outside," Iain informed Fulton.

"That isn't necessary—" Rose began to argue, but he only bowed to the ladies and hurried out. He strode into the hall and saw Niall waiting.

His gut tightened with suspicion, though the man stood with a bright smile on his face. He started to come forward to greet him, but Iain stopped him with a hand. "We will talk outside."

He didn't wait for a reply but beckoned for Niall to follow him out the front door. Once they had gone down the stairs, he led them across the gravel driveway, turning toward the garden. He never looked back at the man, but heard Niall's light footsteps behind him. Within a few minutes, Iain reached the boxwood maze, and entered it, going deeper into the hedges until they were hidden from everyone else.

"Where have you been?" Iain demanded. "I thought you and the others were going to repair the coach and join me here."

His former footman crossed his arms and leaned back against one of the hedges. There was an unreadable expression on his face, as if he were trying to decide what to say.

"You weren't coming back, were you?" Iain surmised. "You used me for passage here, and you never intended to work for me."

"Aye," the man admitted. Yet there was no trace of remorse on his face—only weariness. "I thought I'd be finding work here and then send for my wife and children later. But no one wants to hire the Irish. There are too many of us."

"Why would you think I'd want to take you back now?" Iain shook his head. "You made your choice when you left. And you sold my belongings off for three pounds." He saw no need to keep a footman who had been disloyal.

The man removed his hat and twisted it. "It wasn't a choice, my lord. Not really. I had no money for food, and no one would let me work." He lifted his shoulders in a shrug. "But I've family waiting on me to send them money."

There was a heaviness in the Niall's voice, and he added, "I watched my daughter die of hunger, and I couldn't save her. I would do anything to save the rest of my children. Anything at all."

Perhaps that was true. But Iain no longer trusted the man. A desperate father might also resort to theft or murder if he had no one to help him.

Before he could refuse, Niall inquired, "Will you be traveling to London as you'd planned, my lord?"

He already knew what the man wanted, but he nodded. "We are traveling there in a week. Lady Rose and her family have agreed to help me find an heiress to wed."

Niall's expression turned thoughtful. "Then you'll be needing a valet or a manservant to travel with you."

Iain didn't like the man's assumption that he would take him back. "I think you should be on your way and find another employer."

But his former footman made no move to leave. "I've nowhere to go, my lord."

"You should have thought of that before you left me." He kept his words cool, though he hadn't missed the drawn look of hunger in the man's eyes. "I've no need of your help now."

Niall's gaze lowered. "I can't undo the mistakes I've made. But there is another way I can atone for it." Iain waited, and the man continued. "There are stories about your mother," he said. "Stories that you should know before you go to London."

No. He refused to listen to more lies. Iain seized the man by his filthy shirt and shoved him back against the hedges. "Leave her out of this."

Niall's expression held pity. "I know you've always wondered why she hated you. Why she never trained you to be the earl, only your brother." He placed his hat back upon his head and bowed. "If you're wanting to know the truth, I can tell you the reason."

Iain had no doubt that the man was lying. He'd already admitted that he would do anything for his family, and undoubtedly that included falsehoods. "Whatever it is you're wanting, Niall, you'll not get it from me. Go," he ordered. "Our conversation is finished."

The man studied him and kept his voice low. "That may be. But what do you suppose will happen when they find out that you are *not* the heir to Ashton? That your blood is no different from mine. And the only reason you had a place to live was due to your brother's mercy."

Lies, his brain warned him. And yet, his blood had turned to ice. He couldn't let go of the feeling that there *was* something wrong. Michael had named him the heir, and all the tenants had accepted him—at least, the ones who had stayed behind.

"Why do you think Lady Ashton never treated you like her beloved son?" His footman spoke in a whisper laced with bitterness. "I think you know the truth. You always have."

His instinct was to release his temper, blackening the man's eyes and beating him until he stopped spreading lies. But the coldness within him was rooted in doubt. He *had* wondered if he was illegitimate, possibly one of his father's by-blows. It was the only logical explanation for his mother's hatred of him. But Michael had been vehement that he was Moira's son, despite her behavior.

He didn't know what to believe.

"You're playing a dangerous game, *Lord Ashton,*" Niall asserted. "And you ought to be knowing the truth before you present yourself as the earl."

Iain straightened and met the man's gaze evenly. "There is no game. I am the heir to Ashton, and the earl. Your falsehoods will not change that."

"They are not lies," his footman said. "But grant me a position with fair wages, and I will tell you everything I know."

"You've gone and pickled your brains," Iain remarked. "I have nothing to gain by hiring you."

"But you have everything to lose." Niall's eyes glittered as he stared at him. "Don't you want to know what happened to Lady Ashton?"

He could ignore the man, but the offer *did* tempt him. It was possible that Niall had only lies to spread . . . but what if there was truth to his words?

The man let out a heavy sigh. "I will return in the morning for your answer, my lord."

He wanted to tell Niall not to bother. And yet, he knew desperation when he saw it. He'd chosen the footman to come to England because the man had a family to support, and Niall had needed the income.

But now, after he watched the man leave, he could only wonder what sort of threat his former servant posed.

During the next week, Rose noticed that Iain seemed more on edge. He had a new valet, Niall, who was deferential and polite. But instead of being thankful for his servant's return, Lord Ashton seemed wary.

Ever since she'd taken her first steps, they had visited the garden each day. Rose continued to have Calvert carry her outside, in order to maintain the illusion of being unable to walk.

But today, before Lord Ashton arrived, her sister approached the stone bench. Unhappiness lined her face, and Lily sat down beside her. "Rose, you cannot keep on meeting him in secret. The servants are already talking."

"I've done nothing wrong," she protested.

"I believe you. But it doesn't look right." Her sister glanced back at the house and asked, "Is he courting you?"

"Not exactly." Perhaps it was her own vanity, but she hadn't yet told anyone in her family of her accomplishment. No, she wanted to keep it a secret, for as long as possible—at least, until she stood up in London and danced in front of everyone. It was a welcome daydream.

She imagined how her family would exclaim their surprise and be overjoyed by the miracle.

"Then why do you spend an hour with him in the garden each day? It's scandalous." Lily appeared worried, her mouth twisted in a frown.

Rose answered her with a soft smile. "You needn't worry. I am only teaching him about London society."

"In a garden with no chaperone?" Her sister lifted an eyebrow at that. "When you could easily do the same thing in the drawing room?"

Her lips tightened, and Rose added, "He is helping me practice standing each day."

"Which, again, you could do in the drawing room."

She studied her sister and saw traces of redness in Lily's eyes. No longer did it seem that she'd come here to lecture her about propriety. "There's something else wrong, isn't there? Is it Mother? Has she been giving away money again?"

"I don't think so. But I received a letter from one of Matthew's friends. He was taken captive by the Sikhs." Lily's eyes filled up with tears, and she clenched her hands together. "I don't know what to do, Rose. He's over there alone, and no one can say if he'll come back alive."

All she could do was reach out and embrace her sister. "We will pray for him. And in the meantime, you can write more letters. Perhaps when he is freed, he will know that you were thinking of him."

"I feel so helpless," Lily whispered. When she drew back, she closed her eyes, trying to gather her strength.

"Was there any word of James?" Her fear deepened when she realized that both of them could be captives.

"He's alive, so far as they know," Lily answered. "But he went after Matthew to try and bring him home."

She gripped her sister's hand. "Then we have to believe that he will. That both of them will come home soon."

A single tear dripped down Lily's face. "In the meantime, Mother and Grandmother are forcing me to try on gowns and talking about all the gentlemen I'll meet in London. I don't want to meet anyone. I'm not going to marry any man. This is an utter waste of time."

"If you want, I will try to distract them," Rose offered. Although her grandmother was spending most of her time on Lily, it might be that she could redirect their attention to her, if needed. No longer did she feel quite so averse to returning to London. Now that she had taken her first steps, there was hope for her future.

The sound of footsteps crunching on gravel caught her attention. Lord Ashton was approaching them from the house, and Rose wished she could warn him away. But her sister's gaze narrowed upon the earl until he stood before them.

"Good morn to you both," he greeted them. "Lady Lily, this is a pleasant surprise."

Her sister sent him a false smile and nodded. "You've been spending a great deal of time with my sister, Lord Ashton. I hope you realize that the servants are gossiping."

He sent Rose a conspiratorial look. "Are they? I suppose they think I am intent upon debauchery and ruining your sister."

"Indeed." Lily planted her hands upon her hips and waited for him to offer an excuse.

"I told her that I was teaching you about London," Rose interjected. "She can't seem to understand why I wouldn't do so in a drawing room with chaperones present."

He turned to Lily and met her gaze evenly. "Your sister is lying."

"I am not."

"Yes, you are. You know full well that not only am I forcing you to kiss me, but we are committing fornication in broad daylight. Which would not be proper in the drawing room." He lifted his own eyebrow and shot Lily a dark smile.

At that, Rose stood up and glared at him. Her knees were shaking, but she would not stand back and listen to this. Already her face was crimson at his insinuation. "Lily, don't you dare believe his lies!"

"Why? It's only now becoming interesting." But the faint smile on Lily's mouth revealed that she didn't believe him at all.

"You are a wretch, when we've done no such thing."

He only winked, and puckered his lips. She couldn't believe his audacity. "If I had a rake right now, I would beat you senseless with it."

"It's a good thing you don't." He smiled again at Lily and said, "The truth is, I am teaching your sister to walk."

His confession deflated her spirits. Why would he tell her sister that when she wanted it to remain a secret? How could he ruin her surprise?

"She's made very little progress and has fallen several times," he continued. "She did not want to alarm any of you. Especially the servants, who would accuse me of trying to harm her."

Some of her anger dissipated, for he'd not mentioned her steps at all.

"Rose, no." Lily urged her to sit back on the bench. "You're going to hurt yourself. You've stood, and that in itself is a tremendous accomplishment. But walking?"

"We have made an agreement," Rose said. "Lord Ashton has promised to catch me before I fall on my face. And I, in return, am teaching him about the complexity of forks."

Lord Ashton joined in, nodding in agreement. "They are quite impossible. Why anyone would need three forks at any meal is wasteful, indeed. It's grateful I am that your sister is helping me to navigate cutlery."

Lily glanced at Rose and then back at Lord Ashton. "Well. That's not quite what I was expecting."

"And you understand why she does not want anyone to know about her lack of progress in walking," he said gently. "Allow her to keep her pride. There's no harm in trying. When I catch her, that is."

"Which you have done often," Rose agreed. She lifted up her arms. "Now, if you would bring me into my father's walled garden, I wish to attempt it again."

Lord Ashton lifted her into his arms easily. "I am at your service, my lady."

As he carried her toward the garden, Rose glimpsed Lily's thoughtful expression before she folded up the letter she was carrying. Her fingers touched the necklace around her throat before she lifted her hand in a wave and walked back to the house.

After she had gone, Lord Ashton asked, "Was that an acceptable lie?"

"I thought you were going to tell her everything," she admitted.

"I know what this means to you. And it was only a white lie. I've caught you every time."

"So you have." Her earlier bad mood was gone as she anticipated taking a few more steps today.

He studied her face and remarked, "It's good to see you smile, Lady Rose."

"I was imagining the look on my grandmother's face when she sees me walk again."

Iain set her down upon the stone bench by the willow tree, and his hands lingered a moment. Rose removed her shoes, standing in her bare feet upon the grass. Although she could take a step or two in shoes, it was still easier walking barefoot. "Will you hold my hands while I practice walking, Lord Ashton?"

"Iain," he corrected as he walked toward her. He held out his hands, and she took them, balancing herself before she took one step.

"Thank you, Lord Ashton." No matter how he'd insisted, she refused to call him by his name. There was already too much intimacy between them with their friendship. And although she had allowed herself to succumb to the temptation of his kiss, she could not allow it to happen again.

Carefully, she set one foot in front of the other, holding on to his hands for balance. He led her across the garden slowly, to ensure she didn't fall. Once, she stumbled but caught herself again.

"Are you looking forward to your travels to London?" he asked her.

She nodded. "And now that you have new clothing, I am certain you are, as well."

Over the past week, the tailor had measured and fitted him for evening wear, clothing for paying calls, and everything a gentleman needed to win the heart of a lady. To any unwed maiden, he would be a dashing figure, an Irish lord worth pursuing.

She wondered how many of the families knew of his past. Surely there were those who had met his father and were aware of how he'd died. Would the scandal follow him there?

"I can't be saying that I'm looking forward to London," he admitted. An enigmatic expression crossed his face. "I am hardly a gentleman whom the ton would want to present to their daughters."

She shrugged off his worries. "Don't be foolish. My grandmother and Lady Castledon will vouch for you." In fact, it was more likely that the ladies would be intrigued by the earl they had never met. "I am certain many women will throw themselves at your feet."

"I doubt that will happen." He sent her a crooked smile. "I cannot say that a penniless earl is attractive at all."

She was about to tease him but realized that he was in earnest. His expression held an uneasiness. And it seemed more than apprehension about a city he'd never visited. It was as if he truly did not believe women would want him for himself, as if he had no value.

Rose considered what to say. If she complimented his looks, he wouldn't believe her at all. Instead, she told him, "A man of kindness holds a great deal of value to a woman. Sometimes that means more than all the money in the world."

"Some would not call me kind."

She met his gaze with sincerity. "What you have done for me goes beyond kindness. I won't forget it, Lord Ashton."

He offered his arm and kept the pace slow. Though each day had brought improvement, she had to lean heavily against him as she took a single step.

"You need to be careful at these gatherings," he warned. "Do not try to do too much, too soon; else, you run the risk of falling." He sent her a sidelong look. "I will attend the same gatherings, and if you have need of me, I can lend my support."

"I should be most grateful for your assistance. Especially if you keep me from falling on my face." The idea of walking again brought a sense of joy, mingled with fear of embarrassing herself.

Ashton released her hands and took a few steps back. "Can you walk toward me alone?"

"I will try." She took a moment to steady herself and then took the first step. Although she walked with a heavy limp, nothing could suppress her smile. It took several slow steps, but eventually, she reached his side. "I fear I'm not very graceful. Rather like a wounded animal dragging herself across the ground."

"That will improve over time."

She wanted to believe it, but it might take months. "I had better not risk dancing. I would fall without question."

"You could likely manage to dance, if you wanted to. If you dance with me, I will never let you fall."

She believed him. When she met his gaze, she saw the quiet reassurance, and it softened a piece of her heart. Men would undoubtedly ask her to dance, for it was expected of her.

And yet, she doubted if the risk was worth it.

"Just try," he urged. "Something slow. What if Burkham invites you to waltz?"

He was right. If Thomas was there, he would indeed offer a dance. She didn't want to refuse her chance to show him what she'd accomplished. Inwardly, she knew how unlikely it was that she would succeed. But here, in this garden, there was no risk at all.

"All right," she agreed. "We'll try it."

Ashton took her hand, resting his other palm against her waist. He moved in a slow tempo, giving her time to pick up each foot in the dance step. But every time he attempted to turn her, her feet seemed to tangle together.

"I'm so clumsy," she apologized. "My feet won't move the way I want them to." She lacked the physical ability to keep the rhythm, and it heightened her frustration. "I don't even know what I was thinking. No one waltzes this slowly."

He didn't deny it, but his hand pressed lightly at her waist, turning her once more. "You knew it wouldn't be easy."

"You're right. And besides that, I only took my first steps a week ago. It could take months before I'm nimble enough to dance."

In answer to that, the earl lifted her up and held her body aloft while he spun her in the waltz step. The sudden motion caught her unawares, and she began to laugh. "You cannot lift me up in a ballroom, Lord Ashton. Please put me down." Her cheeks were flushed with embarrassment, though the Irishman didn't seem to care. He stopped spinning her, but held her up a moment longer.

"Iain," he corrected. But he did not set her down just yet. He kept his arms beneath her hips, and Rose was caught up in his green eyes. He stared at her with unveiled interest, and his dark hair framed a chiseled face. She could half-imagine him carrying her across the garden and laying her down against the grass before he kissed her again.

The thought brought her attention back to his firm mouth. She had enjoyed his kiss, and it had soothed her pride to know that she'd kindled his interest. It had been so long since she'd seen Thomas, she didn't know what remained between them. But it felt good to have a man watching her as if he wanted her.

"Iain," she murmured.

He brought her down, but the entire time, her body was pressed close to his. She kept her arms upon his shoulders a moment longer before she took slow, limping steps back to the garden bench. Why did she allow her imagination to trespass into thoughts of what could never be? He needed an heiress who would return with him to Ireland. Not a woman like her. They were friends, and that was all.

It was better for her to pick up the pieces of her life and renew her relationship with Lord Burkham. Once she saw him again, she would know if his letters had any meaning at all.

Iain remained on the opposite side of the garden, looking around at the flowers. For a moment, his eyes narrowed when he spied a circle of mushrooms in a shaded part of the garden lawn. She didn't understand what had transformed his mood until he bent down for a closer look.

The mushrooms were crushed and slimy. Why on earth did he want to go any nearer?

Rose took a few steps toward him, and the stench of the fungus made her wrinkle her nose. "We should go," she told Iain. "It's been nearly an hour."

And still he remained transfixed. He made no comment about what was going on in his mind, and she finally prompted, "What is it?"

"It smelled like this," he told her. "In Ireland. The potatoes rotted in the ground until the air was tainted with it." He stood, his expression suddenly stoic. "So many were starving."

His mood had shifted so abruptly, and the past seemed to haunt him. "I have to help them."

"You will."

But a cynical look crossed his face, as if he had no right to be wasting time in a garden. "I suppose this was a reminder I needed. They're running out of time, and so am I." He straightened and crossed over to her. "I have to find my bride and soon."

She took his arm in hers. "It will not be easy finding someone who will want to go back with you to Ireland."

"She can remain in England, if she wishes," he said, leading her back toward the garden door. "I can visit her from time to time. It might suit a woman who wishes to be married but have her freedom."

It didn't seem to be a pleasant arrangement; rather, it sounded like a lonely existence. *You're not going to marry him,* she reminded herself. *This does not concern you.* And yet, she couldn't help but think of his future bride. "What about any children you might have?"

Iain didn't look at her. "I have no desire for children." His cold remark startled her, for she'd imagined he would be a very good father.

"But what about an heir?" she pointed out. "Someone will have to inherit the earldom."

He shrugged but said nothing. His disinterest rang false, and she had the sense that he was hiding something from her.

"What if your wife wishes to have a child?" she asked. "Would you deny her that?"

He lifted her through the doorway and then locked the garden door behind him. "I will not deny her marital rights. But no child deserves to be born into a life of suffering. And that is all that remains in Ireland."

London

One week later

"We've arrived!" Lady Penford beamed with happiness as she peered outside the window of the coach. "Oh, I am so pleased to be back in London, Rose. Everything will be so much better now. I can sense it."

Rose wanted to believe it, and she reached out to squeeze her mother's hand. "I am glad you were well enough to come." It had been a journey of mixed-up days, some better than others. But the excitement of the travel had given her mother a new enthusiasm that had been missing for some time. Lord Ashton had traveled in a separate coach and, as far as she knew, had continued on to his brother's townhouse. She had rather hoped he would travel with them, but he had maintained a courteous distance. Which was all well and proper, but . . . a little disappointing.

When the coach stopped, Calvert carried her inside their townhouse. Rose had not yet revealed her ability to walk, wanting to maintain the surprise. But truthfully, she wasn't certain if she could manage the stairs yet. She had continued to practice walking in secret, but she tired easily and knew better than to use all her energy because of pride. Then, too, the exercise had made her legs ache. At night, sometimes she awakened in pain, both in her legs and her lower back. But she would accept any amount of discomfort, so long as she could walk.

Her mother and sister led the way, and the butler, Fulton, ushered them into the sitting room, where he gave orders for hot tea and refreshments. He had arrived earlier with several staff members, and it was clear that he had the household well in hand.

Her grandmother followed them, sinking into a chair with an enormous sigh. "A more ghastly trip I've never taken. I must say, I'd forgotten how much I despise traveling."

"Why *did* you come with us?" Rose asked.

Lady Wolcroft glanced over at Iris, who had her eyes closed and was leaning back against the settee. The silent message was understood. *To protect your mother.* But her grandmother answered, "To help both of you find husbands. And, of course, to assist Lord Ashton in his own quest for a bride. Have you thought about which ladies might suit him?"

"Not yet." A sudden aching caught in her gut when she imagined another woman with Iain. It wasn't jealousy, she told herself. Not at all. It was simply that she couldn't decide which bride would be right for him. Rose had considered her best friend, Evangeline Sinclair, but she was so painfully shy, it didn't seem like a good match.

"And what of you?" Lady Wolcroft asked. "I presume you have no interest in wedding Lord Ashton?"

Her grandmother's suggestion held a knowing air, but Rose tried to ignore it. "I cannot possibly travel to Ireland, Grandmother." She reached for a sugared scone, dotted with currants. "Besides that, what reason would I have to wed Lord Ashton?"

Her grandmother poured out for them, and settled back with her tea, a mischievous look in her eyes. "What reason, indeed?" Then she winked at Rose. "You've been spending a great deal of time in his company."

Blood rushed to her cheeks as she caught her grandmother's meaning. Iain Donovan was indeed a handsome man, one who would tempt any woman. "Nothing happened, Grandmother. We are only friends."

Her grandmother let out a hearty laugh. "That may be. But if you have any difficulty finding a husband who isn't bothered by your inability to walk, I doubt it would bother him. And," she lowered her voice to a whisper, "let us simply say that I imagine Lord Ashton would have no trouble begetting heirs."

Except that he doesn't want any, Rose thought. Even so, her face flushed at the thought of his kisses. He was relentless, a man whose touch made her breathless. She shut down the vision immediately, forcing herself to return to reality.

"Now then," her grandmother began. "Lord Ashton will take residence in his family's townhouse and see what has become of his estates during his time away. While he deals with those matters, he has asked me to help in the matter of finding a bride. I shall pay a call upon Her Grace, the Duchess of Worthingstone. She is hosting a ball soon, and I am quite certain she would be willing to extend an invitation to Lord Ashton with all the appropriate ladies in attendance. Amelia has also promised to help me, if needed."

Lady Wolcroft spoke as if arranging a marriage was rather like choosing a new bonnet. "And as for both of you—" She paused, studying Lily first, before her gaze shifted back to Rose. "I will see what can be done to help you find husbands."

"I think we can manage it ourselves, thank you," Rose responded. "After all, Lord Burkham and I are still corresponding."

Her grandmother's expression turned sour. "He may be a viscount, but he's tied up in his mother's apron strings. You ought to find a kindly older widower who will let you do whatever you wish."

Or an Irish earl with the manners of a pirate, Rose thought, eyeing her grandmother.

It seemed that everything was shifting right now. It wasn't at all wise to turn her attention toward Lord Ashton. She knew the reality of his misfortune, and even her dowry might not be enough to heal his broken estate . . . especially if her mother had been giving away money.

Yet, she could not deny the invisible strings that pulled her closer to him. He was a man who could not offer her a fortune, but he was indeed handsome and kind.

"Lord Burkham would not make a good husband for you," her grandmother continued. Rose said nothing, for she was well aware of her family's doubts. But she had to make her own decision about whom to marry.

Her sister straightened in her chair and changed the subject. "Grandmother, has there been any word on Lord Arnsbury?"

Lily's eyes held hope, but Lady Wolcroft shook her head. "I am afraid not. After the last letter, I believe Lady Arnsbury has hired men to try and find him."

Her sister managed a pained smile. "We did the same for James. I do hope they will return soon." She fingered the silver chain at her throat.

"As do I." Lady Wolcroft let out a baleful sigh and turned to her granddaughters. "In the meantime, I hope both of you will consider that there are many men who would be excellent husbands. We are late in arriving for the Season, but I am certain you will each find the right gentleman to wed."

Rose knew her grandmother was right, but her greater concern was not about finding a husband. She wanted to become the woman she had once been, able to walk like everyone else.

Perhaps then she would find a gentleman who would see her as someone to love instead of a burden.

There were hundreds of Irish—men, women, and children—in the London streets. Iain's mood darkened at the sight of them as he drove through the city. He'd seen countless signs in store windows that read: *No Irish*. His people were homeless, driven out from starvation, and no one wanted them. Especially not the English.

His valet, Niall, was staring out the carriage window as well. Iain hadn't wanted to bring him along, but the man held far too many secrets—and Iain didn't know which ones were true. He thought it better to keep the man close, rather than risk him spreading stories that could threaten his chances of making a good marriage. While he didn't think Niall would blackmail him, it was a chance he didn't want to take.

Although his valet had eaten regular meals since he'd joined Iain, there was still a bleakness and a sense of hopelessness surrounding the man.

"I'd thought of bringing my family to London last winter," the man blurted out, breaking the silence. "I thought we could start over. I'd find work and we'd have enough to eat. But Isla was too sick to travel, too weak. And we had no medicine for her."

Iain remained somber, for though he'd known of the little girl's illness, he hadn't known Niall had planned to leave. The man turned back to face him. "All these people are going to die. Just like Isla did. And there's naught we can do to save them."

Iain held the man's gaze for a moment. "Not all of them." He eyed the streets and added, "I gave *you* another chance when I didn't have to."

He hoped he wouldn't regret the decision. "The question is whether or not you'll offer any loyalty in return."

His valet met his gaze squarely, and his expression held sincerity. "I will, aye. It's very grateful I am for all that you've done for me, my lord."

But Iain still wasn't convinced he'd done the right thing. "Whatever happened to Pádraig or Terence?" He'd heard nothing from his men in weeks.

"They went to Yorkshire and tried to find work in one of the factories, but I cannot say if they found anything."

Niall paused a moment and lowered his voice, although there was no one to overhear him. "I promised I would tell you what happened to your mother. If you're wanting to hear it."

Iain wasn't certain of that, but he said nothing to deny it. At his silence, Niall began by saying, "You *are* Lady Ashton's son. Everyone will attest to that. But there are whispers about your father."

"He was killed by one of our tenants. I know that much." And Iain suspected that somehow his mother held him to blame, though he had not yet been born.

"I was fifteen years old when the earl killed Seán O'Toole," Niall said. "I was there when it happened." His voice turned flat, and he continued, "His lordship broke into Seán's house in the middle of the night, raging at him for attacking the countess."

A strange iciness crawled over Iain at the revelation. He hadn't known that his mother had been hurt by one of the tenants, but he understood what Niall was implying.

"His lordship had a revolver, and he shot Seán in the stomach," Niall continued. "He did it to avenge his wife's honor. But Seán had a gun of his own, and he killed the earl before he bled to death."

The servant stared at Iain with pity in his eyes. "You may have been born to the countess. And it's indeed possible that she could have been pregnant before the attack. But whether or not the earl is your father, you remind Lady Ashton of the night she was hurt. That is why she can't treat you as a beloved son. Because she doesn't know who fathered you. None of us does."

He absorbed what the man had said, and the pieces *did* fit together. If his own mother didn't know who had fathered him, she would have no choice but to accept him as the earl's son.

"What do the tenants say about it?"

Niall shrugged. "They don't care who you are, so long as you end the famine. They'd rather have the devil they know than the devil they don't." He straightened. "It's better for all of us if you are the earl. If you wed an heiress and restore our crops, it's more than any of the tenants can do." He eyed Iain. "But that is why Lady Ashton treats you the way she does."

He turned over the information in his mind, uncertain what to think of it. For all he knew, he could be a bastard. Or not.

Even if he had no right to the title, it didn't change the fact that he held himself responsible for Ashton and for his sisters. He owed it to all of them to somehow find a wife who could quickly restore the estate.

The coach came to a stop in front of his brother's townhouse. He had never been here before, but Lady Rose had promised to notify his London household of his impending arrival.

The coachman came to open the door, and Iain stepped outside. The air was full of mingled odors, of soot and horse manure, food and a scent that was uniquely London. A rise of uneasiness caught him as he remembered all the times he'd been left behind in Ireland. These were his first moments in this foreign city, and the differences were vast.

He twisted his brother's signet ring, feeling the weight of the gold. Regardless of whether he had been fathered by the earl, Moira hadn't believed it.

But perhaps his brother had.

He would never know what Michael had thought, but he had never treated him as anything other than his younger brother. It was Michael who had taught him how to run the estate, Michael who had made him the land steward for Ashton.

Because of his brother, Iain knew every inch of the estate, and he had sworn to make it profitable again. His heart ached at the memory of Michael, for he had died far too young from consumption. And though Iain was the only one left to pick up the pieces, it was for the greater good of Ashton. His sisters needed him, too.

He brushed away a wrinkle from his coat and strode up the front stairs. Niall knocked on his behalf, and Iain did his best to appear like the earl. *Behave as if you own the world and everything in it,* Lady Rose had advised. *If anyone questions you, ignore them. Pretend that you are always right.*

At the thought of her, he wanted to smile. She had tutored him on proper etiquette and all the rules of society during the past week. It was difficult enough being in this city, especially when he had to impress the right people, but he hoped Rose's instructions had prepared him for what lay ahead.

The butler opened the townhouse door and beamed at the sight of them. "My Lord Ashton, it is good to meet you at last. Your brother Michael, God rest his soul, spoke of you often with such fondness. I am Chester Barlow."

"Thank you, Barlow," he managed. He was grateful to learn that Michael had mentioned him. Perhaps it wouldn't be quite so difficult to make his place here in London. He followed the butler inside and gave over his hat and coat, while the man gave orders for a footman to bring him a light supper.

"I will take a tray in my room," Iain said. Though it was still early, he needed time to gather his thoughts and plans.

"Very good, my lord." The butler made arrangements for his belongings to be brought from the coach. There were only two trunks, and he knew that would appear unusual to the staff. It was yet another reason why he wanted to retreat: to avoid the inevitable questions.

He walked up the staircase, following the footman, who guided him to his room. The servant departed quickly, giving Iain time to think.

He recognized this room as his brother's. The large bedroom held an enormous bed, and a fire had been lit in the hearth. Iain sat down in his brother's chair, watching as the coals glowed within the iron grate.

He walked over to Michael's desk and opened it. Inside, he found paper, a pen, and ink. And there, atop a stack of papers, was a letter his brother had written but never sent. The familiar sight of Michael's handwriting made his throat ache and his eyes burn when he realized that the unsent letter had been addressed to him.

> *Dear Iain,*
> *I must say, I do despise London. Mother believes I must try to gain a seat in Parliament and argue for the rights of the Irish, but I would rather be at home and let someone else take my place.*
> *You have no idea how tedious it is or how very fortunate you are. I envy you. But perhaps one day*

Perhaps one day, what? The letter remained unfinished, with no ending. God help him, he missed his brother. He wished Michael were here to guide him and show him how to unravel this mess. But he'd promised to take care of Ashton and their sisters, no matter what it cost.

He'd made up his mind not to let Niall's revelation bother him. He had never known a father, and regardless of who had sired him, outwardly, nothing had changed. He couldn't do anything about the circumstances of his birth, and unless his mother renounced him, his responsibilities were the same.

But it felt as if he had stepped into his brother's shadow, living a life that wasn't his. This room . . . the servants . . .

What right did he have to live in this way when so many were suffering? And why would any woman want to marry him, knowing how terrible it was at Ashton?

No. He could not reveal any of it to the London heiresses. He would have to live a lie of omission and pretend to be someone else, in order to save his tenants.

The image of Lady Rose came to mind, and he rather wished he could see her now, even if only for a conversation and a cup of tea. Although she refused to consider him as anything more than a friend, never would he forget the forbidden softness of her kiss. Or the way she'd smiled at him when she'd taken her first steps.

With her, he could be the man he was—not the man he was trying to be.

But he had to set aside his own desires and think of her needs. He could never destroy her life by asking her to wed a man like him. Lady Rose deserved a life of happiness after all she'd endured—not a life in Ireland.

He folded his brother's letter and set it aside. There was no choice but to do what was necessary and wed a woman who was as desperate as he was.

Chapter Twelve

It took only three days for Rose to slowly begin losing her mind. Her grandmother was under the mistaken belief that three hours of rest were required each afternoon. Or perhaps she thought Rose should spend her time staring at the wall.

Each day Lord Ashton proved that he had not forgotten her. He sent her unusual flowers along with amusing notes. He avoided roses or lilies, but instead sent iris blooms. In one of her replies, she had pleaded, *Help me escape the horror of this prison.*

Today, he had promised to take her out driving in his carriage. Thank heavens.

She told herself that it was the perfect opportunity to strategize about the Duchess of Worthingstone's ball tomorrow evening. In spite of her initial misgivings, she had decided to introduce Iain to her dear friend, Evangeline Sinclair—with a dire warning that he was not to frighten her. Timid and tenderhearted, Evangeline was the sort of friend who reminded Rose of clumsy puppies and pink ribbons. She was quite a bluestocking and adored her books. Were it not for her shyness, she would be surrounded by suitors. She needed a kind man, and it was possible that Iain might do well enough.

Yet, the idea of Evangeline kissing Lord Ashton brought a twinge of uneasiness to her gut . . . almost like jealousy. But then, Rose had no claim upon him. She needed to sort out matters between herself and Lord Burkham. It wasn't her business what happened between Iain and other ladies. She would arrange introductions, and the rest was up to him.

A knock sounded at her door, and Hattie informed her, "Lord Ashton has come to call. Are you receiving?"

"Yes, I will see him." Rose waited in her chair for Calvert to come and carry her downstairs, wishing all the while that she had the strength to go down on her own. But she wasn't at all confident about her abilities.

Within a few minutes, the footman brought her down into the drawing room. When she saw Iain, she smiled with relief. "I feel like a princess being rescued from her lonely tower," she admitted. "I hardly care if we do anything more than drive in circles. As long as I can leave this house."

"I am at your service, Lady Rose." He returned her smile with his own and then sent her a silent question, *Do they know?* With a raised eyebrow, he offered his arm.

Rose shook her head slightly. Although everyone would eventually find out about her newfound ability to walk, she wanted to keep the secret a little while longer.

"Calvert, please bring me outside to Lord Ashton's carriage. Hattie will accompany me."

The footman scowled but followed the earl down the hallway and out to the waiting vehicle. The light curricle was painted black and appeared fit for swift driving with a pair of matched horses. "Is this yours?" she asked, as Calvert lifted her onto the seat.

"It was my brother's." Iain climbed up beside her while Hattie took her place upon the rumble seat as a chaperone. "I am glad that the horses were well cared for, during all this time. In fact, I rather feared that there would be no transportation at all, leaving me to walk through the streets."

In the narrow seat, his body was pressed close to hers. It was a deliberate move, she knew, but one that was not unwelcome. He drove the horses slowly within Kensington Gardens so that she could enjoy the sunshine and the flowers in bloom. But as the minutes passed, she had another urge. "Lord Ashton, if you do not mind, I wish to drive faster."

He sent her a knowing look. "Because you've been feeling like a captive these past few days?"

"Indeed."

He guided the horse away from the gardens, adding, "We'll have to find a larger space." He drove the horses toward the Serpentine, and once they had a clear pathway, he let the horses run. The reckless speed was exhilarating, and Rose was grateful for the feeling of the wind in her hair. The light curricle took the corners easily, and she laughed aloud as the carriage turned along the opposite bank.

"This is wonderful," she breathed. "Like flying."

Lord Ashton continued the speed until the horses appeared to tire. He slowed his pace and inquired, "Was that what you were wanting, Lady Rose?"

"Exactly. I've been going out of my head with boredom. Poor Lily has been subjected to paying countless calls, while I've been left at home."

"And has the viscount come to pay a call on you?" Iain asked.

His question dimmed her mood. "No." But she hoped that Lord Burkham would come at least once. She had sent him a letter, but so far had received no acknowledgment.

"You're disappointed."

"Of course I am. We were nearly engaged, and now he behaves as if I'm invisible."

Iain took the horses down another pathway. "Then show him you're not." He sent her a sidelong glance. "I presume your grandmother has arranged for you to wear a stunning ball gown, along with jewels?"

"Lily has a gown, but my grandmother wishes for me to wear something demure and unnoticeable. Something white or yellow, perhaps." She rolled her eyes and added, "They want me to remain trapped within the wallflower garden."

It seemed an opportune time to mention Evangeline, but before she could speak of her friend, Iain shook his head. "They shouldn't treat you that way."

"It's not your place to interfere," she reminded him. "And I can manage my grandmother." She lifted her chin, adding, "Lord Burkham is expected to be in attendance at the duchess's ball, and I shall confront him then."

He glanced back at Hattie. Dropping his voice low so the maid would not overhear them, he said, "You need to practice walking."

"I know. But Hattie doesn't know. No one does, except you."

At that, his expression shifted. There was a sudden warmth in his eyes that reached out and drew them closer. "I am glad of it, *a chara*."

She grew wary of the closeness between them and the secret they shared. Her mind warned that she was letting down her guard around him, falling into the easy banter of his friendship. But beneath his teasing demeanor, Iain Donovan was very different from Lord Burkham and the other men. Although rough around the edges, he was a man whom she could truly call a friend. If she needed his help, he would not hesitate to give it.

"I have selected a few women who might be suitable as your bride. Miss Sinclair, for instance, is a lovely young woman who will be at the ball tomorrow evening. She is rather shy, however."

Iain gave a slight nod, but seemed somewhat distracted. He pulled the curricle to a stop beside a small pathway. They were secluded for a moment, and he turned back to the maid. "Hattie, I am going to carry

Lady Rose over to sit at the bench over there. Kindly wait here until I return with her."

The maid agreed to wait, and when he reached out to gather Rose into his arms, Iain leaned in to whisper in her ear, "This will give you the chance to walk for a few moments without anyone seeing you."

Thank goodness. It had been a long time since she'd walked in the garden with him, and she needed to practice. The last thing she wanted was to stumble or fall when she attended a public gathering.

"Thank you," she murmured, as he brought her to sit on the bench. She waited until she was certain they were alone and slowly stood up. Iain offered her his arm, and she took it.

"At the ball, I can help you walk across the room, if you wish it."

"Not unless I lose my balance," she corrected. "Else it will look as if we are courting." As she walked at his side, her legs felt stiff and ungainly. Her left leg still had a heavy limp, and she started to laugh. "I look as if my leg is dragging a heavy chain behind it."

"But you *are* walking," he pointed out.

He was right. Her heart clenched with a blend of thankfulness and overwhelming emotion. She had to fight back the tears of relief.

"What is it?" Iain prompted.

She blinked back the rush of feelings and calmed herself. "It suddenly struck me all at once, what I've overcome to be here. I can't quite believe it."

He softened, and his green eyes met hers with warmth. "You have, *a chara.* And in spite of your illness, you have done what you set out to do." He reached out and touched her cheek, and she covered his hand with her own.

"I have, haven't I?" With a smile of joy, she took his arm.

"Is it easier if you slow your pace?" he asked.

She concentrated as she walked and found that moving slowly did, in fact, make it easier to disguise the limp. "A little." It was also a consolation that she would have a long ball gown to disguise her movements.

She leaned heavily against his arm as they walked, and after a few moments of strolling, she began to regain her confidence. He responded to her pace, and when she slowed to a stop, he did the same. "Do you need time to rest?"

She shook her head. Just ahead, through the clearing, she could see the banks of the Serpentine. Though she longed to walk along the edge of the water, she didn't want to be seen by other members of the ton. Not yet.

As they began walking back toward the bench, she urged, "Will you take me out walking each day, so that I may continue to get stronger?"

"If that's what you're wanting, aye." There was an unusual edge to his voice, almost protective in nature. His attention was focused elsewhere, and when she turned her head, her heart nearly stopped.

There, at the edge of the path, stood Thomas Kingford, the Viscount Burkham. The man she'd once dreamed of marrying. He was here with a young lady, and behind them strolled two matrons as chaperones.

The blood seemed to drain away from her face, and a numbness settled over her. Rose felt lightheaded, and Iain tightened his grip on her arm. "It's him, isn't it?"

"Yes." Even her voice sounded faraway, as if she were speaking through a tunnel.

"Look at me, Rose." He locked his gaze with hers. "What are you wanting to do? Shall we stay here, or do you wish to speak with him?"

"I—I don't know." She had to gather her senses. For all she knew, Lord Burkham might not have noticed her. But then again, the four of them were continuing on their walk, while the young lady talked animatedly.

"If it's your wish to speak with him, I will stop. Or we can avoid them if you want to maintain your secret longer."

She took a deep breath, gathering strength from his presence. "Lord Burkham has avoided me for half a year. I think it's time we spoke again."

Though her words were spoken with courage, Iain knew how much it cost her. Lady Rose had likely wanted to make a grand reveal of her ability to walk. Instead, that dream had been taken away.

It was clear, from the way the young debutante was holding on to Lord Burkham's arm and giggling, that she was delighted to be walking with him. The knowing looks from the matrons behind them spoke of their ambitions for marriage.

Rose was trying to maintain a brave face, but beneath her serene expression he could see the underlying pain. She squared her shoulders and began to walk toward them. Iain held her gloved hand within his arm, hoping she would take comfort from that. As far as he was concerned, the jackanapes could take the silly girl and leave Rose alone. If Burkham didn't see the value in the woman he'd left behind, then he deserved an empty-headed miss.

The viscount had taken little notice of Rose, but abruptly, his companion's giggling stopped. The young miss had caught sight of her and leaned in to whisper.

At that, Lord Burkham turned, and stopped walking immediately. A sudden rise of joy came over his face, and he sent Rose a blinding smile. "Lady Rose," he breathed. He appeared to forget entirely about his companion and left the young woman standing there. Iain's hand tightened upon Rose, and he wanted to knock the smile off the man's face.

You left her, he wanted to remind Burkham. What kind of man would abandon a woman he was courting when she became ill?

But if he escorted Rose back to the curricle, she would be angry with him. She needed to face Burkham and see him for what he was.

When the viscount reached her side, his gaze swept over her, and Rose straightened. "You are a wonder, Lady Rose. I cannot tell you how glad I am to see you walking again."

The composure upon Rose's face faltered, and she glanced back at Iain with uncertainty. He squeezed her hand lightly in a show of support. Yet, he'd never expected the strong surge of jealousy that rose up within him like a fist to his gut. He had no right to feel possessive of Rose . . . but when he saw the viscount, he couldn't control the response.

There was no denying the look of utter happiness in the man's eyes. Burkham genuinely appeared pleased for Rose's sake.

"I am without words," Burkham said simply. "How miraculous this is."

Iain couldn't hold silent any longer. "It is, indeed. I am certain you are well aware of how hard she has worked to recover from her illness. You must have been quite eager to pay a call upon her to see for yourself."

He thought he did rather well holding the sarcasm back from his voice. To his credit, Lord Burkham did appear slightly embarrassed.

Rose squeezed Iain's arm and sent him a warning look. He only smiled.

She extricated her hand from his and introduced them. "Lord Burkham, may I present a friend of the family, Iain Donovan, the Earl of Ashton."

Burkham nodded in greeting. "It is good to see you again, Ashton. I seem to recall speaking with you at length, last season."

Iain only sent the man an amused look. Whether it was a lie spoken to give the illusion that they'd met before or whether Burkham genuinely thought they had met, he didn't know. But before he could respond, Rose interjected, "No, Lord Ashton has never been to London. You must be thinking of his older brother, Michael Donovan."

The viscount's smile dimmed. "Forgive me for the mistake. If you are now the earl, then I must offer my condolences."

Iain could only nod and shake the man's hand. "Thank you." It occurred to him that there was no way of knowing what connections Michael had made in London. His brother might have friends here, and that might prove useful.

Burkham turned to his companion, likely with the intent of introducing the young lady, but one of the matrons approached first. The older woman eyed Iain from head to toe before she introduced the girl as Miss Everett. Iain bowed and spoke the necessary courtesies, but he didn't miss the stiff expression on Rose's face when she met the debutante.

"Will you be attending the Duchess of Worthingstone's ball tomorrow evening?" Lord Burkham asked Rose.

She is, and if you dare to break her heart again, I'll be breaking every bone in your body. Iain took every effort to keep from revealing his annoyance.

Lady Rose only nodded. "I am. But please, Lord Burkham and Miss Everett—" She sent a pleading look toward the chaperones as well. "My family does not know that I've begun walking again. It was my intention to surprise them at the ball."

"Then may I ask that you save your first dance for me?" the viscount asked with a warm smile. "For old time's sake?"

When I'm cold in the grave, Iain thought.

But Rose blushed and answered, "Of course."

Miss Everett's cheeks reddened, for the viscount was now behaving as if she were invisible. She couldn't have been more than nineteen, Iain decided. And her chances of wedding the viscount were disappearing before her eyes. He felt rather sorry for her.

"Until tomorrow," the viscount said, and he bowed to Rose before escorting Miss Everett back to the pathway.

Rose kept a smile fixed upon her face until they'd gone, and afterwards, she groaned. "I cannot believe I was so foolish."

Iain didn't know how to respond to that. "What do you mean? You had your moment of triumph."

"Not in the way I imagined it." She watched Lord Burkham as he departed with Miss Everett and their chaperones. "I doubt if he will keep my secret. And furthermore, those women will go and spread gossip that we were seen walking together unchaperoned. Especially Mrs. Everett."

"We weren't precisely unchaperoned. Hattie is only standing over there."

"No, but she will make it sound as if you were kissing me within the bushes, ready to defile me. Mrs. Everett is a notorious gossip, and she made Lily's life miserable last Season. She wants her daughter to marry a titled lord, and she will denigrate anyone who stands in her way."

Iain took her arm in his. "I wouldn't let it trouble you, *a chara*. Or are you planning to fight Miss Everett for your viscount?"

"I don't know." Her face fell, and she regarded him. "Right now, I feel so uncertain about everything. I know I said I would save him my first dance . . . but all I could think of was how he said what I wanted to hear. He only wrote to me six times in half a year. And even those letters were only replies to letters I sent to him." Her expression furrowed, and she added, "He has already replaced me . . . as if he believed I would never get well."

There was bewilderment in her voice, and he took her hands in his. But instead of heartbreak, there was frustration in her eyes. "Iain," she murmured. "What am I to do now?"

A strand of reddish-brown hair had fallen loose from her bonnet, and he envisioned untying the ribbons and tossing it away, kissing her hard. He wanted to release her hands, for he didn't trust himself right now. She was beautiful and vulnerable, and God help him, he wanted to console her wounded feelings.

"You should hold your head high and know that you deserve better."

"I thought I knew what I wanted," she murmured. "I thought everything would be different once he saw me walk again. But Thomas wasted no time in finding someone else." Her face tightened with anger, and she bit her lip. "You were right about him. I just didn't want to admit it."

He guided her off the path, away from anyone who might intrude. Her eyes gleamed with unshed tears, and he couldn't stop himself from tracing the edge of her face. "He doesn't deserve your tears."

She closed her eyes, gathering her composure. Then she leaned in and rested her cheek against his chest. He put his arms around her, holding her close. The embrace was unexpected, but he would never turn her aside when she needed him. It was as if she took strength from him, and he inhaled the fragrance of her hair.

Don't do this, his conscience warned. He was letting himself trespass beyond friendship when he had no future to offer Rose—nothing, save poverty. She was a good woman, but he didn't want to bring her suffering.

At last, she pulled back from him. With a chagrined look, she confessed, "I apologize for throwing myself at you. I don't even know why I did."

"It's naught to worry yourself over, *a chara.* But we should return to the carriage." *Before I lose myself and kiss you again.* He reached down and lifted her into his arms.

Her face flushed. "It does feel wrong, allowing you to carry me, when I can walk now. Someone might see us."

"If anyone does see me carrying you, then I shall toss you into the bushes," he teased.

She sent him a weak smile and sighed. "I know I'm being silly. It's just that I don't want there to be a misunderstanding. It would hurt your chances of finding a bride if others believed we were more than friends."

Iain walked exceedingly slow, wanting to hold her a little longer. He studied her face, watching her skin flush. "Will it?"

"It might," she answered. But he heard the slight note of hesitancy in her voice. He stopped walking for a moment, studying her expression. She appeared flustered, almost afraid to speak.

And when he looked into her brown eyes, he saw that she was not unaffected by him. God help them both.

Damn it all, he liked Rose. She was beautiful, resilient, and passionate. He had a feeling that no other woman in London had half of her resourcefulness. But there would be no safety, no steadiness at all in Ireland—only ruins. He didn't like to admit it, but it was the truth.

Better to hold the distance between them than to imagine a life where he would cause her misery. He never wanted to see those eyes fill up with pain or resentment.

He changed the subject and asked, "Are you wanting to return home or would you prefer to drive a little longer?"

Rose sent him a sidelong smile. "I want to avoid that prison for as long as possible."

He brought her back to the carriage and helped her inside. Then he offered her the reins. "Would you like to drive the horses, then?"

She appeared startled, but her eyes gleamed at the prospect. "I've never driven a team of horses, but yes. Yes, I would like to try."

He instructed her on how to guide them, and it was the perfect distraction. Within moments, they were driving along the banks of the Serpentine once more. She kept the pace steady instead of racing them, and from the delight in her expression, she was enjoying herself.

After the third time they circled the lake, she handed back the reins. "Though I don't want to, I suppose I have no choice but to return for luncheon. Unless you brought food?"

He hadn't, but that didn't mean he couldn't remedy the situation. "I can send Hattie to fetch some for us," he offered.

Rose shook her head. "It's all right. I'll return home and my grandmother will send me off to my room to rest. Then I'll be able to stare at the wall a little longer."

"There's no need for that." He turned the curricle back toward the road. "I will invite myself to luncheon, and afterward, we can play whist or another game, if you're wanting company."

Her lips tightened. "No one could ever accuse you of subtlety, Lord Ashton."

"I don't know the meaning of the word."

She laughed at that, and he directed the team in the direction of her family's townhouse. "You seem overly confident that I would want you to stay."

"Why wouldn't you be wanting me to stay? It is preferable to staring at the wall, I hope."

"I would welcome your company," she said. "But again, I worry that others will believe you are courting me."

"Don't be so concerned about what others think." He drew the horses to a stop when they reached her townhouse. "Is there any harm in spending an afternoon playing cards with me? Your sister can join us, along with your mother."

Her spirits lifted for a moment. "My mother would like that, I think. Grandmother has been keeping her behind closed doors as much as possible. I think she is becoming more melancholy each day."

Before the footman could come to help her disembark, Rose turned back to him. "Thank you for taking me for a drive." With a soft smile, she added, "And you may stay for luncheon, before you suffer the indignity of losing to me in cards."

He only shook his head. "Nay, *a chara.* We're to be partners in the game. It is your mother and sister who must prepare to lose."

Rose stared into Iain's eyes when she laid down the ace of spades. His mouth tightened, hinting that he had very few of that suit. She lowered her gaze and then looked back at him to let him know she understood.

"Stop cheating," Lily warned. "I know the pair of you are up to something. You keep staring at one another."

"I don't know what you are talking about." Rose smiled sweetly at Iain. "We haven't said a word."

"You've trounced us in three games. Mother, forgive me, but I think we should switch partners."

"Only if I get *him,*" Lady Penford said. She sent Iain a brilliant smile. "My dear husband and I were quite good at whist, I must say. George adored cards."

"It's not my fault I've had three hands of rubbish cards," Lily moaned. She twisted her necklace in despair, and Rose nodded toward Iain, glancing at the necklace. He gave a nod, and she led with the ten of diamonds.

He trumped Lily's queen with his own king, while her mother threw away a ten of clubs. "Oh, well done," she told Iain.

"Thank goodness we aren't wagering anything," Lily said. "I would be a pauper by now."

"A wager sounds like a grand idea," Iain countered. "If I win this next hand, I'll claim a prize of my choosing and then switch partners by way of thanks."

Oh no. Rose didn't like the wicked look in his eyes. "And what about me? What if *I* win the trick?" She had a few high cards remaining. "What if I don't want to switch partners? We *are* winning, after all."

"Do be fair, Rose," her sister said. "The two of you have beaten us enough. It's time to give me the Earl of Ashton." To the earl, she asked, "Lord Ashton, exactly what did you want for your prize?"

"The first dance with your sister at the Worthingstone ball," he answered quietly.

The room fell silent, and Rose paled. Neither her mother nor her sister knew of her ability to walk, much less dance.

"I cannot promise that," she answered. "You ask too much."

Lily attempted to intervene. "While I'm certain Rose would be delighted to grant that to you when she walks again, I fear it may be some time yet before she can."

Rose couldn't bring herself to speak. Although she had already promised her first dance to the viscount, both of them knew it was unlikely that Lord Burkham would offer. But why would Iain want her first dance? She suspected there was something more behind the wager. Almost like . . . jealousy.

When he'd embraced her in Kensington Gardens, she had felt safe and comforted. His strong arms had held her, and she had nestled against his chest. They had a good friendship, and she couldn't deny her attraction to him. If she were truthful with herself, she'd wanted him to kiss her. She'd wanted to feel as if someone desired her, as if he cared.

The thought of dancing with this man in front of the ton filled her with apprehension. Not only because she was afraid of humiliating herself . . . but also because the very thought made her heartbeat quicken. His hands would be upon her again, those green eyes watching her with interest.

You're trying to help him find a wealthy bride, she reminded herself. *He's not courting you. His offer means nothing.*

Lord Ashton was watching her, revealing none of his feelings. She tried to tell herself that one dance would pose no harm at all. It might be that *she* would win the wager and could redirect his attention elsewhere.

And so it was that she made a wager of her own. "All right, Lord Ashton. If I win the trick, you will ask Miss Sinclair for the first dance. If you win, I will grant you my first dance when I am able to walk again. However long it takes."

He met her gaze with a sudden intensity that made her stomach flutter with nerves. "I accept the wager."

Very deliberately, she chose his weakest suit and laid down the king of hearts. She never took her eyes off him, but let him see that she had taken this quite seriously. He was not going to defeat her.

"Oh dear," Lady Penford said, following suit with a queen. "Lily, can you help?"

But Lily only discarded a ten. "I'm sorry, but *someone* dealt me a rubbish hand once again." She glared at Rose.

All eyes turned to Iain. He withdrew a single card from his hand but did not lay it down. For a moment, they all waited for him to make his move. He didn't smile at all, but locked his green eyes upon hers. She couldn't read his expression, for he offered neither defeat nor triumph.

"Go on, Ashton," she urged. "If you have a card to play, then set it down. Admit your defeat."

With that, he turned over his card and laid down the ace of hearts.

Chapter Thirteen

Victoria Nottoway, the Duchess of Worthingstone, greeted them with a warm smile. Rose had arrived earlier than the other guests, so as not to attract attention when the footman carried her inside.

"Where would you like to sit?" the duchess inquired. "Your chair can be placed anywhere."

"By the wall will be fine," Rose answered. She wanted to remain somewhat out of the way so that no one would notice her.

Her sister drew up a chair beside her. "I'll join you here." Lily cast a glance at the corner, toward a large fern. "Or perhaps, if Grandmother tries to match me up with someone, I'll go into hiding over there."

She fingered the chain at her throat once again. Tonight Lily wore a ball gown the shade of lilacs, trimmed with lace dyed the same shade. Her hair was pulled into an updo and she wore hot house gardenias tucked into the brown strands. There was no doubt that her sister would attract a great deal of notice with her beauty. Rose didn't understand why Lily insisted on waiting for Lord Arnsbury when she could have any man she wanted.

"Lily, do try to enjoy yourself tonight," Rose urged. "Her Grace has gone to a great deal of trouble to make us feel welcome. It would not do for you to remain a wallflower."

Sadness crossed over her sister's face. "I know it. But it doesn't mean that I've given up on Matthew."

Beneath her skirts, Rose moved her feet and ankles. "I'm going to stand for a moment." She wanted to gain her footing, to ensure that she could keep her balance. A flutter of nerves caught her stomach.

Tonight was the night she'd been dreaming of for so long. She had practiced walking in the privacy of her bedroom, and now she felt confident she could manage it—so long as she kept her steps slow.

What she didn't know was how to handle Lord Ashton. Why had the earl asked to claim her first dance? Was it because he wanted to help her in front of everyone?

It was because of him that she'd learned to walk at all. Iain had been ever patient with her, catching her before she could fall. He had helped her to strengthen her legs, encouraging her with every step. Her mood softened, and she realized that she owed him the first dance, after all that he'd done.

"Grandmother is approaching," Lily warned. "And . . . oh dear, she has her battalion with her."

Rose wasn't certain what Lily meant by that, but when she saw the women alongside her grandmother, she relaxed and sat down once more. "It's only the duchess's sisters. Lady Castledon, Lady Falsham, and Mrs. Sinclair."

She brightened when her friend Evangeline crossed the room to join the ladies. Mrs. Sinclair's youngest daughter was the prospective bride she hoped Lord Ashton would court. Her friend was indeed wealthy, though her riches were steeped in scandal. It was bad enough that Mrs. Sinclair and her husband were engaged in commerce, but to own a business empire that was built around ladies' unmentionables had made it quite difficult for their daughters to find appropriate husbands.

But that wouldn't matter a whit to Lord Ashton. Miss Sinclair had one of the largest dowries in London, and that was what he needed. Her only problems were her immense shyness and her father, a notorious Highlander who made it clear that no man was good enough for Evangeline.

Lady Castledon extended her hands and came to greet them. "Lady Rose and Lady Lily, it's been ages." She beamed at them with a sly wink. "I believe you've met my older sisters already. I've told Margaret and Juliette all about your requirements for husbands, and I am quite certain we can find men who will suit. I am eager to begin matchmaking."

The eldest sister, Mrs. Sinclair, had dark blond hair with faint streaks of gray. "What Amelia means is that she is eager to begin meddling." The matron extended her hand in greeting. "It is good to see you again, Lady Rose. Evangeline was so glad to hear that you'd returned to London."

"I've been dying a slow, painful death of shopping," Evangeline admitted. She fidgeted with her gloves. "Mother, may I please sit with Rose and hide behind the draperies?"

Mrs. Sinclair exchanged a look with her sisters. "Certainly not."

"Then I shall wait until you've left my side and go hide within the library." With that, Evangeline planted herself beside Rose. She studied the room of arriving guests with an anxious eye. "I don't know why I came tonight. This was a mistake." With a pained expression, she added, "I can only imagine the spectacle that will take place if my father arrives."

"He won't be here this evening," Mrs. Sinclair told her daughter. "I made Cain promise." Dropping her voice to a low murmur, she confessed, "Evangeline is worried that my husband will threaten to kill any prospective suitor."

"Father told me that if any gentleman asked me to dance, he would slice him into ribbons and feed his remains to the dogs." The young woman appeared uneasy by the thought. "He *means* it, too."

"Cain is only a worried father," Mrs. Fraser reassured her. "He believes it's his God-given right to torment his daughter with threats pertaining to her virtue. My husband unfortunately shares that sentiment. And until you have found a man whom your father likes, I fear you'll have to endure it, too."

Evangeline sent a pleading look toward Rose. "Save me."

"I'm afraid I've done worse." Rose sent her a weak smile. "I found a possible husband for you. You'll meet the Earl of Ashton tonight."

"Traitor," Evangeline moaned. "I thought you were my friend."

"Oh, but she *is* looking after your best interests, darling," Lady Castledon interjected. "Lord Ashton is an Irishman, and he is positively delicious. We'll need to bring extra smelling salts, for half the ladies here will swoon."

While Lady Castledon sang the praises of Lord Ashton, Rose searched the arriving guests for a sign of Lord Burkham. It didn't seem that he was anywhere to be seen. Had he somehow fallen ill? Or was he not coming at all? Her spirits sank, and as the minutes turned into an hour, her sister Lily went with Lady Castledon and Mrs. Fraser to meet the other guests. Evangeline stayed behind, and it granted Rose a measure of comfort to have an ally at her side. Several of the guests began dancing, and she wondered if she would have the opportunity to join them. Or whether she should try.

"Dear God," Evangeline breathed suddenly. "That's not *him*, is it?"

Rose glanced toward the opposite side of the room and saw that Lord Ashton had indeed arrived. He wore the new clothing she had arranged for him, and it fit him like a second skin. His black coat was tailored across his broad shoulders, revealing a cream waistcoat and dark trousers. His black hair was combed back, and when his green eyes rested upon her, she knew that this battle was lost. He fully intended to pursue her.

"Yes. That is Lord Ashton, the Irishman I spoke of."

"He's looking at us," Evangeline blurted out, fanning herself suddenly. The young woman's face reddened. "No, I'm wrong. He's not looking at us. He's looking at *you.*"

And he was. Iain's green eyes held a knowing look, as if Rose were the only woman here. His stare was filled with warmth and a sense of mischief.

"He knows we are only friends," she managed. "But I've told him about you. I think the pair of you should get acquainted."

Her friend's expression turned curious. "I think I might just go find the library, Rose. It looks as if he wants to speak with you."

"Don't go. I've been meaning to introduce you to him. Lord Ashton is—"

"—entirely interested in you," Evangeline finished. "And I am quite certain that I should leave the pair of you alone. Oh, Heavens, he's almost here." She stood up, and promptly stepped on her gown, lurching forward before she caught her balance.

Iain was suddenly standing before them. Evangeline straightened, wincing as she adjusted the hem. "Rose, I'll . . . just be going now."

"Not yet," she said, catching her friend's hand. "Lord Ashton, may I present Miss Evangeline Sinclair."

"A pleasure it is, to make your acquaintance, Miss Sinclair." Iain offered the young woman a kind smile, and Evangeline blushed, fanning herself more rapidly. Then he bowed and greeted her. "Lady Rose, I am glad to see you once more."

The look in his eyes reminded her of what it was like to be in his embrace. Rose was well aware that he was here to claim the dance she owed him. She wanted to refuse, and yet, she was not one to break her promises.

"Would you grant me the honor of your first dance, Lady Rose?" *Can you manage it?* he seemed to be asking.

She looked around the ballroom once more, trying to decide what was best. She supposed she could either dance with Lord Ashton and show everyone that she was no longer an invalid . . . or she could remain in a chair beside the wall.

"Only if you dance with Miss Sinclair next," she countered with a smile of her own. It was a reasonable enough request.

"If Miss Sinclair is willing, I should be very glad of her company." He sent her a charming smile, which made Evangeline's fan flutter faster.

"Of course, I would be happy to dance with you, Lord Ashton," the young woman agreed. Her expression turned worried, and she continued, "But as for Lady Rose, I fear that—" She stopped abruptly, and looked perplexed, as if to remind them both, *She cannot walk.*

But the moment Iain extended his hand, Rose took it and stood slowly. He gave her a moment to steady her balance, and then she leaned against him when she took her first step.

Her eyes fixed upon his with a silent plea, *Keep it slow.* At least then she could hide her heavy limp.

She heard Evangeline give a soft gasp, and there were murmurs all around them. It took all her concentration to walk, but Rose leaned against Iain, determined to keep her balance.

"There's a lass." He smiled at her, allowing her to set the pace. Her heart hammered faster, and she felt the eyes of every guest staring at her. Never in her life had she felt so self-conscious. Though she had longed to take her first steps with Lord Burkham at her side, now she was beginning to reconsider.

Iain was the man who had helped her to walk again, and of anyone here, she trusted him not to let her stumble. He knew the limits of her endurance, and she could confess when she needed to stop and rest.

"You look grand this night." He gave her hand a gentle squeeze as they moved closer to the dancing.

"Thank you." She had worn a sky-blue gown with a full skirt and a lace shawl to cover her bare shoulders. It wasn't the most fashionable gown, but her grandmother had deemed it quite appropriate for the evening.

Because she expected me to remain in a chair, Rose thought. *No one expected me to dance.*

"Do you think you can manage this?" Iain asked. His expression revealed the sincerity of a man who didn't want her to be embarrassed.

"Only if it's a waltz." A quick-paced dance would be quite beyond her balance. But right now, this was about proving herself to others. She wanted everyone to see that she had overcome her illness and could walk again.

She took one step that was too heavy, and stumbled forward. Iain caught her immediately and halted, waiting for her to regain her balance. Her cheeks burned, and she blurted out, "I am sorry."

"Don't be." He brought her to the edge of the dancers, nearest to the wall. They would be away from the others, and yet, she could join in. The music shifted into a lilting waltz, and he rested his hand against her waist. "If you begin to tire, step on my feet. Your skirts will hide it, and no one will notice," he advised.

He'd worn gloves tonight, and she took his hand, feeling braver. She lifted her gaze to the onlookers and saw both her sister and grandmother watching. Their faces revealed shock and joy. Lily was beaming at her, while the matrons spoke in excited whispers. Behind them emerged Lord Burkham.

He, too, was watching. But there was no warmth in his expression. She didn't know what that meant, nor did she care. This was no longer about him; it was about all that she'd done to overcome her illness.

"Lord Burkham is here at last," she informed Ashton. "Just behind you."

"Good. I hope he regrets leaving you behind and realizes his mistake," he admitted. "If I were you, I'd not dance with him at all."

"It wouldn't be polite to refuse him," she said. "After all, we were nearly betrothed. I cannot refuse to dance with him."

"Of course you can. And 'nearly betrothed' means nothing at all." His hand squeezed her waist lightly.

There was something about Iain Donovan that drew her close, tempting her to surrender. She was intimately aware of his touch, of his palm upon her spine, pulling her near. If they were alone, she had no doubt that he would kiss her again. And it would unravel her senses if he did.

He led her gently into the dance, moving slower than the other couples. She tried to follow him, but her footsteps were not light at all. It was far more difficult than she'd ever imagined.

"Don't be nervous, *a chara.* I won't let you fall." True to his word, Iain cut their pace in half, moving slowly as he turned her. Her skin warmed, her cheeks growing flushed. But she trusted him implicitly, knowing that he spoke the truth. He would never let her go.

His hand tightened against her waist, and the heat of his palm warmed the silk of her gown. "I know you won't." She could feel herself softening, transfixed by his gaze. His green eyes burned into hers with an undeniable intensity. The rest of the world seemed to fall away, and her wayward thoughts imagined his mouth upon hers, coaxing her to want what she could not have.

His thumb rubbed a slight caress against the base of her spine as he moved her in a circle. Though he spoke not a word, she never took her eyes from his.

"You look as if you belong here," she murmured. "Our lessons helped."

His mouth tilted slightly. "I don't belong here, and we both know it." He lowered his voice and added, "I find myself not wanting to obey any of the rules."

"What do you mean?" Her voice came out breathless as the music slowed to a stop.

Iain led her away from the dancers, back toward the wall. "I know I should lead you back to your chair and behave as if nothing happened. But that's not what I'm wanting."

Her pulse quickened at his words. "What are you wanting, Lord Ashton?"

His gaze was penetrating. "I want to kiss the soft skin of your throat and take out the pins of your hair until it surrounds your shoulders." He tucked her hand into his arm and added, "And I'm wanting to unfasten the buttons of your gown, one by one. To kiss every part of your bare skin. But I can't."

Goosebumps erupted over her skin, and she felt her cheeks burning with the wanton desires he'd conjured. The invisible heat burned between them, and an ache resonated over her body with his words.

She didn't know what to say or do, but Lord Burkham was suddenly standing before her, breaking the spell. "Lady Rose, I am very glad to see you." He sent her a warm smile and added, "I came to claim my promised dance. I did not realize that Ashton would steal you away first."

The earl only shrugged. "Lady Rose is far too beautiful to leave standing against the wall."

"Then I shall claim the next dance," Burkham insisted. "Lady Rose?"

She saw that the next one was a country dance, and the speed of the movement would be far too difficult. "Not just now. When another waltz is played, perhaps—"

But he only took her hand and pulled her forward. She nearly stumbled, barely catching her balance. "Nonsense. I missed out on the first, so I shall dance the next set with you."

No, not a set. She hadn't the endurance for that, and there was no doubt she would fall and make a fool of herself.

But she didn't want him to know how fragile her walking skills were. "In a little while," she promised. "Once I've had a moment to rest." She wanted him to believe that all was well, that she could do everything the other ladies could.

"If I do that, someone else will steal you away," he teased. And before she could deny him again, he was lined up across from her.

"I am sorry, Lord Burkham. But not now."

"Have pity on me, Lady Rose." He took her hands and forced her to stand across from him. A moment later, Lord Ashton claimed another young woman as his partner, and the two of them lined up beside Burkham and her. She could see the warning in Iain's eyes. He knew, as she did, what a risk this was. And though he did nothing to reveal her weakness, she understood his silent offer to take her away.

She curtseyed to Lord Burkham, and he smiled as he bowed to her. Though she had known these dances since her childhood, her feet refused to manage the steps. Her movements were ungainly and stiff, though she tried to mask them beneath her long skirts.

Dear God, what had she been thinking? She could never manage to dance at this tempo. It was a catastrophe waiting to happen. Within a few seconds, she found herself paired up with Lord Ashton. Beneath his breath, he muttered, "Tell him you're feeling faint, Rose. It's your best hope to get out of this."

He was right. She nodded in understanding and turned back to Lord Burkham when they switched partners.

The speed of the dancing grew swifter, and before she could protest, Lord Burkham spun her in a circle. She started to lose her footing, and the room tipped.

No, please, she thought to herself. She swayed violently and tried to bring herself closer to her partner. She reached out to grasp his arms, but at that moment, Lord Burkham stepped back.

Without warning, she fell forward, sprawling on the ballroom floor. The pain of her face striking the wood was nothing compared to her humiliation. The soft exclamation of the guests and nervous titters only made her wish she could disappear, never to be seen again.

For a moment, she remained on the floor, dimly aware of Burkham asking if she was all right. Then, someone lifted her from the floor and carried her away.

It was Lord Ashton. Within seconds, he'd brought her to the opposite side of the room. She remembered his earlier suggestion and kept her eyes closed, as if she'd fallen into a faint. But inwardly, she wanted to die.

This was supposed to be her moment of triumph, of proving what she could do. Instead, everyone had seen her failure. She had embarrassed herself, and a hard lump of disappointment caught in her throat.

"It's all right," Iain murmured. "I'm bringing you to the terrace where you can get some air. Your sister and grandmother are following us."

Against her eyelids, the tears spilled out. It had been a disastrous night, and now, she only wanted to go home.

Her tears were dampening his coat, but she kept her face pressed against his chest, not wanting anyone to see her. Only when she felt the cool breeze of the night air did she dare to open her eyes.

"Are you hurt?" he asked when he gently set her down on a stone bench.

"My pride is shattered," she admitted, wiping at her eyes. "He wouldn't listen when I told him no."

There was no sign of Burkham anywhere. He didn't seem to care that another man had taken her away. But her sister and grandmother hurried forward.

Lily sat down beside her and put an arm around her shoulders. "Rose, I'm so sorry this happened." She embraced her hard and then pulled back. "But I was so overjoyed to see you walking again. You surprised all of us with this miracle."

"It was too soon to dance, and I knew it." She'd simply wanted to try, to see if there was any hope of becoming the woman she had once been. "I should have insisted that Lord Burkham let me go. I just . . . didn't want to cause a scene."

Her sister gave her a gentle squeeze. "You tried to do too much too soon." With a nod to their grandmother, Lily added, "Grandmother, please tell the duchess that Rose was feeling faint and let everyone believe it was the heat of the room. I'll take her home."

It was the logical move, and oh, how she longed to escape this humiliation. And yet, if she left now, it would feel like giving up. She needed to pick herself up again and overcome her failings. Only then could she hold her head up among the others. If she left now, her only memory would be falling on her face.

"What are you wanting to do, *a chara?*" Iain was asking.

"I can't go home. Not just now." She needed to face all those people with her head held high and walking, yes *walking*, back to the ballroom.

Rose took a deep breath and stood up. "I want you to escort me back to the ballroom."

Iain hesitated, and it didn't surprise her that he had doubts. Lily was already protesting, "Why would you want to, Rose? Surely you ought to rest. It's been a difficult night."

"And it will be far worse if I leave. You would have to go with me, and everyone will only remember my fall." She paused a moment. "And that isn't the memory I want to take from this night. I'd rather remember walking. Feeling like a normal woman."

Although her legs protested, she forced herself to stand up. "I can do this, Lily. I must, for all our sakes."

Lord Ashton drew her hand into his arm. "Then I will walk with you, in case you need to lean against me. And you *will* wait a few moments, until you're steady once more."

She knew it was unwise, for others would gather their own opinions about their relationship. But she did trust Iain to keep her safe.

With great effort, she managed to limp toward the open doors. Candlelight glowed from the ballroom, and the low buzz of conversation continued as he helped guide her back inside.

"I would have caught you, had I been beside you earlier," he said. "We were at the far end of the dancers when you lost your balance."

"I know you would have. I don't blame you for my fall." She forced a smile onto her face and nodded toward some of the guests she knew.

Lady Arnsbury came forward to greet her, and she offered a sympathetic look. "My dear, you had us all frightened when you fell."

"Yes, it was quite sudden. The last thing I expected was to swoon during the dancing. It was very hot within the room." She fanned herself and saw the Duchess of Worthingstone approaching. Several other women stepped closer in an effort to eavesdrop. Rose pretended as if she didn't notice them. "Your Grace, I am so sorry for causing a scene. I don't know what came over me. I suppose it must have been the heat."

The duchess took her hand and gave it a gentle squeeze. "I'm so relieved to see that you are feeling better. All of us were worried about you."

"I am, now that I've had some air. But I think I shall avoid dancing for the remainder of the night." She braved a smile and leaned against Lord Ashton. After she left the duchess, he took her in a slow walk past the others.

"Take me to the far side of the room," she pleaded. "Near the food and lemonade. I can pretend to be thirsty."

"And what about Burkham?" he asked. "The man is watching you."

What about the viscount indeed? she thought. He'd done nothing to catch her, but had stepped back just as she'd fallen. A twinge of resentment caught her. "I don't want to speak with him."

Thomas should have prevented her from falling. It was almost as if he'd *wanted* to humiliate her. But why? And did he intend to keep his distance, behaving as if nothing had happened?

A moment later, the viscount crossed the room. Immediately, Iain stepped in front of her. "Were you wanting something, Burkham?"

The viscount appeared discomfited by his presence. "Ashton, if you don't mind, I would like a word with Lady Rose."

"To apologize, you mean." The earl's voice held resentment, and she didn't at all disagree. She hadn't wanted to join in the country dance, but Lord Burkham had insisted.

"I am sorry she fell. And if you wouldn't mind giving us a moment alone . . ."

"No." Iain crossed his arms over his chest, and she nearly smiled. It looked as if he wanted to pummel the man senseless. "But I will allow you to apologize before you slither away."

Burkham cleared his throat and sidestepped so she could see his face. "Ashton is right. I do owe you an apology. I didn't expect you to fall."

"I told you I didn't want to dance. You wouldn't listen."

He sent her a crooked smile, one that would have caused her heart to soften, a year ago. Now, she saw it as an empty gesture. "Forgive me. I was jealous of Ashton because I thought we had agreed you would save the first dance for me."

Jealousy would imply that he actually cared about her, and she simply didn't believe it. "You weren't here."

"I was late, and that, of course, was my fault," he finished. "But I didn't expect to find you dancing with another man."

She gave a shrug. *Of course not. Because you thought no man would want me.*

"Did you want to dance with Lord Ashton?" he asked. There was a thread of annoyance in his tone, one she didn't like.

"Yes," she answered honestly. Although she'd danced with Iain primarily because of the wager she'd lost, it was also because she trusted him. He understood her limitations and hadn't tried to push her past them. Iain went to stand beside her, and he rested his hand upon the back of her chair in a silent mark of possession.

"I think you should be returning to Miss Everett now," Iain suggested. "Be on your way."

The viscount appeared to consider it, but then Lady Castledon arrived, holding Evangeline's hand in hers. She smiled warmly at Iain and said, "Do be a darling and dance with Miss Sinclair. I've told her all about you, Lord Ashton."

There was no way for him to refuse without embarrassing Evangeline, but he sent Rose a questioning look.

"I will be fine," she told him. "Go on and enjoy yourself."

Iain bowed to Evangeline and tucked her hand in his arm, but his expression held an open threat toward Lord Burkham.

The viscount appeared pleased to see them leave. "Once again, I apologize for your fall. I should have guessed that the reason for your refusal was because you were unable to move so swiftly." He reached out to her hand and asked, "Can you forgive me?"

She saw no reason to be petty, but gave a brief nod, pulling back her hand from his. "I accept your apology. And now, I think you should go."

Once again, he wasn't listening. "I want to begin again. I know that I've made mistakes, dearest Rose. I want to set aside the months we lost and rekindle what there was between us."

Dearest Rose? Why on earth would he call her that? And she was now well aware that there had been nothing between them. Nothing at all.

"You sent me six letters in six months. I hardly think there was much between us, Lord Burkham."

"But we were good friends. That is, we *are* good friends," he corrected. His smile broadened. "I still believe we would suit each other quite well. You are a beautiful lady, and friendship leads to a strong marriage, I believe."

No, love does, she corrected silently. But now she had the answer she'd anticipated. And while it saddened her to think of the young woman she'd been, who had given her heart so freely to this man, she was glad that she hadn't married him.

"We can remain friends, my lord. But that is all."

He appeared oblivious to her refusal and beamed at her. "I am so glad to hear it, Lady Rose." With a glance over at the refreshments, he inquired, "Would you like a glass of lemonade? Are you thirsty?"

Rose wasn't, but she nodded. It gave her a way of sending him off, leaving her to be alone with her thoughts.

She stood up again, watching the dancers as they moved across the floor. Lord Ashton spun Evangeline in a circle, catching her when she stumbled. Her shy friend appeared overwhelmed, and yet, she appeared to be enjoying herself.

A twinge of envy caught Rose within her heart at the sight of them. *She* wanted to be dancing a lively reel, whirling down the rows of dancers. But it was far too soon for that. Perhaps in a few more months it might be possible. *By Christmas,* she promised herself.

"Are you all right?" came a female voice from behind her.

Rose turned and saw the Duchess of Worthingstone standing there. The matron gave her a kindly smile. "I wanted to be certain you suffered no injuries after the fall."

"No. Only my pride." Rose folded her hands and ventured a slight smile.

The duchess stood beside her and remarked, "I admire your bravery for returning to the ballroom. When I was your age, I would have run away."

"I wanted to. But I thought it might make the gossip worse." She tried to muster a smile. "Even now, I suspect they are discussing my lack of grace."

"Not at all." The duchess lowered her voice. "That is why I asked my sister Amelia to intervene. She is a notorious gossip, and everyone adores her." She leaned in and added, "She is telling everyone how miraculous it is that you learned to walk again, and how no one ever dreamed it would happen."

When she looked around the room, Rose realized that the duchess's assertion was indeed true. Many people *were* smiling and nodding at her. The Countess of Castledon had most assuredly interfered.

"Please tell your sister that I wish to thank her."

"I will." Her Grace gave Rose's hand a squeeze. "Now I must go and speak to my guests. But I *am* glad to see you walking again."

Soon enough, Lord Burkham returned with the glass of lemonade, and Rose drank it dutifully. "Forgive me, Lady Rose, but I did promise to dance with Miss Everett." He nodded in the direction of the young girl whom he'd escorted in the park. "I shall return to you shortly."

"Of course," she murmured, though she wanted to tell him not to bother.

Once he was gone, her mind blurred with thoughts of Iain. He had danced with four different women, and she had no doubt that all of them were enthralled with him.

But by the end of the last set, she caught him watching her. He was standing near the terrace with his own drink in hand. Although three other ladies stood nearby, conversing and flirting with him, his attention was not fixed upon them at all.

Instead, he was watching her.

Rose flushed beneath his attention. She remembered the wicked words he'd spoken during their dance, and her body was imagining Iain's touch upon her bare skin.

For a fleeting moment, she wondered if it was possible for *her* to become his bride. He needed a bride to help him restore Ashton. And while her dowry was not as large as Miss Sinclair's, it was respectable enough.

It was irrational to even consider marrying him, when it meant leaving her homeland and living in dangerous conditions in a country torn apart by famine. But she let herself envision it, wondering whether it was as bad as he'd said it was.

Rose decided to walk in the garden once again. The terrace wasn't so very far away, and she could sit down on a bench and breathe in the night air. She hobbled her way through the throngs of people, stopping to tell Lily where she was going. Her sister promised to accompany her, but Rose waved her away. Instead, she signaled for Hattie to join her as a chaperone.

Before she reached the doors, Iain was waiting for her. It seemed that he had guessed her intentions. Though he didn't smile, his expression revealed a man who wanted her fiercely. The moment she reached his side, he took her hand and tucked it underneath his arm. "It's never wise for a lady to be alone at a ball."

"I'm not alone. Hattie is just over there." She nodded to her maid, who kept a discreet distance. But her cheeks warmed at the touch of his gloved hand upon hers. He guided her away from the open doors toward a stone bench.

"I am glad you came to join me," he said. "I was about to abduct you from your chair."

"Would you have dragged me across the room?"

"I would never drag you anywhere, *a ghrá*. I would lift you into my arms and carry you off."

And what would you do then? she wanted to ask, but didn't. Instead, she shifted her attention from his handsome face and looked out at the garden. The moon grew obscured by a cloud, and she saw a man and a woman slip behind a very large lilac bush. She frowned, wondering what was happening. Iain caught the direction of her gaze and took her hand in his.

"Are they . . .?" She didn't finish the question, but Iain caught her meaning.

"Aye." His green eyes held a trace of his own wickedness. "There are many places within this garden for a man and woman to be alone. Were you wanting to walk with me?"

Rose closed her eyes, not knowing what to say. She ought to inform him that no, she would never consider such a thing. And yet . . . she missed the rough bristle of his cheeks when he had kissed her. She missed the softness of his mouth and the way his hands awakened such feelings inside.

"You need to stop looking at me like that, *a ghrá,* or I'll kiss you right here."

I want you to. But she only smiled instead.

Iain let out a soft curse in Irish. "You're killing me, *a mhuírnín.*" By way of changing the subject, he asked, "So, did Burkham grovel for what he did?"

"He didn't *do* anything," Rose felt compelled to point out.

"Aye, and that was his own idiocy. He should have caught you before you fell."

Rose studied the lilac bush, which was rustling slightly. She rather wondered if she should say something, since the pair of lovers obviously were engaged in an illicit moment.

Iain followed the path of her gaze. "Is something wrong?"

She nodded toward the bush and remarked, "I do hope the woman *wanted* to go with him."

Iain took her hand and guided her to stand. "We could go and find out."

"No!" Her words came out in a loud whisper. "She was smiling at the man when she went behind the bush, but—"

All of a sudden, the rustling grew louder, accompanied by a woman's moan. Rose frowned. "Is he hurting her, do you think?"

Iain's face turned amused. "No, *a chara,* I doubt he's hurting her. Quite the contrary."

"But she's making very strange noises. It might be that you should make certain they're all right."

"Only if you come with me," he said.

She didn't think that was a good idea at all. It wasn't her place to judge what others chose to do, but if the woman was unwilling or had changed her mind about kissing the man . . . well, she wanted Iain to do something about it.

"You can go on without me," she urged. "I'll just stay here."

But he pulled her back to her feet, holding both hands. "We won't intrude," he told her. "Believe me when I say, they won't even know we're there."

She wasn't certain what he meant, until he led her down a brick stairway toward a small fountain.

"Stop here," he murmured against her ear. For a moment, she didn't quite know why he'd stopped, but then she realized there was a bare spot in the lavender bush that gave her a clear view of the couple. She didn't know either of them, but the man was kissing the woman wholeheartedly. His hands skimmed the woman's bare shoulders, and she tilted her throat back, letting him kiss her there.

When Iain leaned in close, she felt his warm breath against her own neck and shivered. She could almost imagine herself in the woman's place, while he kissed her. But then the man bent lower, kissing the woman's bare bodice.

"Let us leave them alone," Iain whispered. "Are you satisfied that he's not hurting her?"

She was, but the scene before her was fascinating. The woman's breathing had come faster, and she was panting and moaning as the man continued to kiss her.

A light wind grazed the trees, scattering lilac blossoms across the lawn. Rose frowned a moment. Was the man putting his hand beneath the woman's skirt? Surely she was only imagining it.

But Lord Ashton took her hand and drew her back up the stairs and toward the bench, away from the couple. The woman's moans were rhythmic now, and Iain was shaking with suppressed laughter.

She couldn't understand what was so funny, but he took her hand in his again. "You're looking worried. I can only assure you that the woman is fine."

"Are you certain?"

"Quite." Iain sent her a lazy smile. "So did your viscount propose to you?"

"He wanted to start again." She leaned back, enjoying the night air. "But I told him no."

A look of satisfaction crossed his face. "Good."

His answer lifted her spirits, and she decided to probe him for information. "And how goes your quest for a bride? Miss Sinclair seems quite taken with you."

"You were right about her shyness. But I do like her."

The prick of jealousy was irrational, and she forced it back. Iain gave her hand a friendly squeeze. Undoubtedly others would chastise her for letting him show such affection, but she didn't want to pull away. And anyway, the couple had emerged from the shrubbery at last.

Rose pretended not to notice them, though she was well aware of the young lady's swollen lips and rumpled bodice. She was attempting to repair her mussed hair, and the gentleman helped, tucking a long strand of hair into her updo. She sent him an adoring look, and her companion kissed her hand.

"They appear to love each other," she murmured. "How beautiful."

"Unless he refuses to offer for her. Which is an unfortunate possibility."

She didn't like to think of it, but of course, Iain was right. "*You* would never do such a thing," she pointed out. "It would be dishonorable."

"I am not in a position to refuse any bride," he admitted. "But don't be trying to make me into a saint, Rose. I've had my share of dishonor."

She was afraid to wonder what that meant. But she amended her words, saying, "But you would never ruin a young woman's reputation. You would marry her first."

"I might. If she would have me."

She tensed as he took her hand in his. Deftly, he unbuttoned her glove, sliding his thumb beneath the kidskin. He removed the glove, and his caress warmed her, echoing in other places. As he stroked her palm, he locked his gaze upon hers.

"What are you doing?" she breathed.

"Giving in to temptation." He continued to touch her, and she couldn't understand why such a simple gesture was undoing her senses. Her breasts tightened into hard nubs beneath her gown, and for a moment, it felt as if he were stroking her nipples.

"I didn't like seeing you with Burkham. He isn't the right man for you."

Her heart pounded, the heat spreading over her skin. Right now, her brain was muddled with confusion, and she could hardly gather a sensible thought.

Are you the right man for me? she wondered. This time, she gave in to impulse and stroked his cheek. His face was smooth, and he turned to press a kiss against her palm.

She didn't want to think of the way her skin had responded to his touch or her lips had melded to his. But each time she was with this man, he evoked cravings she didn't understand.

"You don't even know what you do to me," he said roughly. "If you were mine, I would touch you until you cried out in ecstasy. I'm wanting to touch you again, *a ghrá.* Right now."

He stood from the bench and held out a hand to her. "You can walk back to the ballroom with Hattie. Or you can come with me."

She understood that he was offering her a choice. If she returned to the ballroom, he would leave her alone. But with Iain, she lost sight of all propriety. He had awakened her desire, making her crave his hands upon her. If she went with him now, he would kiss her until she could scarcely stand.

And right now, she needed him. After this difficult night, she wanted to surrender to her desires and feel beloved. She rose from the bench and took a single step toward him. Glancing at Hattie, she shook her head in a silent command for her maid to remain where she was.

Without another word, Iain took her hand and led her down the brick steps toward the lilac bush. He moved slowly, giving her all the time she needed. But in her attempt to hurry, she stumbled.

He caught her in his arms and brought her into the shadows. She wanted him to kiss her, needed the touch of his mouth upon hers. When they reached the garden wall, he pressed her back against the brick.

"You're driving me into madness, Lady Rose," he murmured. With his hands, he framed her face, touching her cheeks, then letting his fingers trace her silhouette. She didn't protest, but lifted her arms around his neck.

"Kiss me," she breathed. "Please. I need this."

And heaven help her, he did. His mouth was heated, ravaging her lips in a kiss that was both gentle and filled with intensity. She tasted the sleek wetness of his tongue, and when he stroked her mouth, she clung to his neck.

Iain was murmuring endearments in Irish as he kissed her. His hands moved to her bare shoulders, and he kissed her throat, sending shivers over her skin. "I'm not going to ask why you came to me. But I'm going to give you what both of us need."

He drew one hand over her bodice, and he paused, watching her. She was so deeply aroused, she didn't want him to stop. He took her silence as an invitation, and he slid his hand over the neckline of her gown. Though her corset prevented him from touching her, she couldn't stop the gasp that escaped her.

She kissed him hard, clinging to him as he embraced her. And she knew, God help her, that the grounds of friendship had crumbled, shifting toward desire.

He pulled back, and a faint smile edged his mouth. Then he reached out to her hair and plucked lilac blossoms from the strands. She answered his smile and teased, "What are you doing, Lord Ashton?"

His answer was a roguish grin. "Deflowering you."

Chapter Fourteen

Guilt flooded through him for touching her. Iain knew that Rose deserved so much more than a man like him, but he'd taken advantage of her sweet offering. God help him, when she'd welcomed his kiss, his primal instincts had flared like a Celtic barbarian: *Mine.*

During the weeks they'd spent together, he had come to care about this woman. He'd watched her overcome adversity and stand tall. She was brave and resilient, and when he looked into her face, she made him want to become something more. He wanted to be worthy of someone like her.

After he'd brought her back to the ballroom, her lips swollen and her eyes shining, he realized his mistake in kissing her. She was looking at him with new eyes, as if she were contemplating a match between them.

It wasn't right. After everything she'd endured, after all she'd fought for, how could he ask her to wed someone like him? He was worth nothing at all, and he couldn't imagine bringing her to a famine-ridden country. She would be miserable in such a place. And if he were truthful with himself, he'd rather walk away than risk hurting Rose.

He'd returned home later that night, turning over the situation in his mind. Although he'd come to London in search of a wealthy bride, now he questioned the practicality of his decision. No woman would want what he was offering. It wasn't right or fair to make her believe he was prosperous, when he had hardly a tuppence to his name.

Unfortunately, there was no time to earn the money swiftly. Better to choose a painfully shy wallflower like Miss Sinclair and allow her to live in England, giving her freedom, while he tended to his poverty-stricken estate.

Rose was not at all desperate. Any man would be glad to wed her, and she had choices. And despite the hope in her eyes last night, he could not imagine putting her through the hell that was Ireland. It was better to distance himself now, to choose a bride who would not care where he lived or what he did.

He ignored the tightness in his chest, shoving aside his personal wants. None of that mattered. He rubbed at his eyes, feeling bleary, for he hadn't slept at all. Instead, he'd secluded himself in the study for hours, searching for another solution.

Iain sat at his brother's desk and opened up the ledgers, turning back to the earlier entries. An ache caught his heart as he read unfamiliar handwriting. Undoubtedly, it had belonged to his father. Or at least, the man he'd wanted to believe was his father.

The earl had written detailed entries, documenting his investments, profits, and losses. The numbers blurred together, and toward the end of the ledger, his brother's handwriting replaced the earl's. Michael had become the new Earl of Ashton at the age of seven, though he hadn't begun taking on his father's duties until he was sixteen. In many ways, neither of them could remember having a father.

Their mother, Moira, had taken great pains to help Michael assume the role of earl. She had hired solicitors and countless experts to advise him, and Iain remembered his brother complaining about the endless hours of studying.

Often, they had escaped together, running off to go fishing in the river or swimming. And when he was old enough to help Michael, Iain had taken on the responsibilities of the land steward. He'd enjoyed talking with the tenants and solving disputes among the families. For once in his life, he'd been needed.

And when Michael had died, those families had turned to him. He couldn't fail them now.

Iain closed the ledger, considering possible investment options. Although he had stripped Ashton of most of its funds, he might be able to sell off land that wasn't entailed and use that as a means of rebuilding their fortunes.

The butler interrupted him with a knock at the door. "My lord, you have a caller. A Mr. Cain Sinclair is here to see you."

It took him a moment to make the connection, but he realized this was about Sinclair's daughter, Evangeline. "Take him into the drawing room and have Cook send up refreshments."

He left the study and walked into the drawing room. There, he found Sinclair waiting for him. The Scotsman wore a kilt and linen shirt, and his long, dark hair hung well below his shoulders. Had Sinclair been alive two hundred years earlier, Iain would have expected to find a claymore strapped to his back.

"Mr. Sinclair," he greeted the man, extending his hand.

The older man crossed the room, a hint of a smile upon his mouth. Without warning, he threw a punch toward Iain's head.

Raw instinct took over, and Iain ducked the blow, seizing the man's arm and pinning it behind his back. He'd nearly thrown his caller to the ground, but Sinclair was strong, despite his age. He twisted his way free and stepped back.

"A crow's curse upon you," Iain spat out. "What in the hell was that for?" He hadn't touched a hair on Miss Sinclair's head.

The Scotsman crossed his arms and regarded him. "You've been in fights before. No' like the baw-heided Sassenachs who think they'll be courting my Evangeline."

"Aye." He'd learned to fight as a boy, and he and Michael had practiced often. "But would you care to be telling me *why* you tried to hit me?"

"I wanted to see if you could defend my daughter, if need be. I'll no' let her be courted by a man who canna keep her safe."

In a strange way, it made perfect sense. "I only just met your daughter last night," Iain pointed out.

"And she was walking around with her bonny head in the clouds this morn, dancing by herself and smiling." Cain Sinclair remained standing, and he eyed Iain as if he were considering how to best kill him.

"Don't you think it's a bit too soon to be reading the banns?" Iain offered. "I danced with her a time or two, but no more than any other gentleman."

"Aye, but she didna care about them. You're the first one who's caught her eye since Lord Penford left for India." Mr. Sinclair clenched his fist in a silent threat.

"You've nothing to fear on that account." Iain was glad to reassure the man. "Miss Sinclair is a lovely young woman, and—"

"You don't think she's good enough for an earl, is that it?" Sinclair took a step closer, his face holding fury. "Because she's no' a nobleman's daughter?"

I may not be a nobleman's son, either, Iain thought drily. He knew that Sinclair would do everything in his power to protect Evangeline. The man had been little more than a Scottish outlaw when he had married the Duchess of Worthingstone's sister, Margaret. Their family had fought to make a respectable name for themselves, but there were still whispers of scandal surrounding their business. Because of it, Evangeline was a wealthy heiress with few suitors.

He sent the man a half smile. "What I was *going* to say was that your daughter deserves better than the likes of me."

The older man let out a rough sigh and sat down. "I don't ken if I should be offended or pleased. For you're right."

It might not help his efforts in wooing Evangeline by being honest, but he sensed that Cain Sinclair would accept nothing less. And while the man had a fortune that rivaled the English monarchy, in many ways, they were similar.

"Any gentleman would be lucky to marry your daughter," he began, "but I do not think Ireland would suit her."

At that, Sinclair agreed. "Aye. And a godforsaken place it is now. The puir wee bairns shouldna be starving."

"Most of my tenants left," Iain said. "But I owe it to the rest of them to help. We have no crops, hardly any food at all." He met the Scotsman's eyes evenly. "I am seeking a bride whose dowry can restore Ashton. If Evangeline is willing, I would consider it; however, I doubt she would want a life like that."

Cain Sinclair leaned forward, his eyes alight with interest. "I ken what it is to have nothing. I came from that." There was a glimmer of understanding in his demeanor. "Tell me more about what is needed."

"I am looking to rebuild Ashton," Iain admitted. "Our crops have failed, and even if we had sheep, there's hardly enough to feed them. I thought about selling off one of the properties and investing in the railroad. But it would still take time we don't have."

"Don't be doing that," Cain said. "I know men who've lost everything."

"And there were men who made more money than they ever dreamed of." Iain wasn't afraid to take a risk if the rewards were there.

The Scotsman shook his head. "Every fool thinks that. In the beginning, aye. There was indeed money to be made with the railroad. But no' now. Too many have invested, and that means fewer profits for everyone." His brow furrowed as he thought it over. "I like your honesty, Ashton. And I understand what it is you need. But I've not decided if I'll let you court Evangeline."

"I understand that. But I would welcome your advice on what to do."

The gleam in Sinclair's eyes revealed that he welcomed the challenge. "Indeed." A footman arrived with tea and refreshments. Sinclair took a cup and ate a sandwich while he thought about the dilemma. "You can't be growing more crops until the soil improves. And if it's food you're needing, you'll have to get that here."

Iain agreed with that assessment. "I can send supplies back for now, but eventually we'll have to grow our own food." He had no idea where he would get the money for supplies, however.

"Later, perhaps. You should find a way to bring work to your tenants. I'll speak with Margaret about it, but if the women can sew, it might be they could help our business."

He'd heard rumors about the Sinclair "business." It involved sewing sensual undergarments for young ladies. Aphrodite's Unmentionables was a scandalous concept, and many men had voiced their disapproval while secretly purchasing silken petticoats and corsets for their wives.

"I could ask the tenants' wives," Iain said. "But many are strong Catholic women who might think they'd be going to hell if they were to sew unmentionables. Still, it's better than starving to death."

Cain studied him for a moment. "I'll let you know. In the meantime, I will donate food and supplies for your tenants."

"I'm very grateful for it. It's kind of you."

"My brother and I suffered through several winters in poverty. I wish that someone had tried to help us," was all he said. "In return, I want you to help Evangeline. Whether or not I let you court her, don't let her hide from the world. Make her feel that she is lovely and that she can have her choice of suitors."

"I should be glad to," Iain agreed. "For it is true enough."

Her father seemed appeased by it. "Good. But there is something else you should know." Cain lowered his voice. "There has been talk about why your family never brought you to London. Everyone knew of your brother Michael, but not you. Some are whispering about why you were hidden away."

Iain had prepared himself for that. He straightened his shoulders and met Sinclair's gaze. "Let them whisper all they like. Suffice it to say that my mother and I never got along. She made certain that I stayed behind."

Cain shrugged at that. Then he said, "Evangeline will be attending Lady Arnsbury's supper party tomorrow. I would expect you to dance with the lass a time or two." He drained his cup and reached for another sandwich.

Iain understood the man's reasoning. Sinclair was asking him to help prevent his daughter from being a wallflower. Iain welcomed the opportunity to help the shy young woman.

And yet, inwardly, he was comparing her to Rose. Miss Sinclair reminded him of a sweet younger sister, while it was Rose who held him captivated. He wanted to dance with the woman who struggled with every step, watching her face light up with joy. He wanted to kiss her in the shadows, breathing in her soft scent while their bodies touched.

He was dimly aware of Cain Sinclair speaking about more investment opportunities and ways to rebuild his earnings, but Iain's thoughts were tangled up in Rose. Although he was grateful for the man's suggestions and his offer of supplies and food, he questioned whether it was right to accept the assistance. Logically, Miss Sinclair was the best choice—he knew that.

But deep in his gut, it felt wrong.

"Lord Burkham wishes to know if you are receiving," the butler asked. Rose glanced over at her mother, who was twisting her hands and staring out the window. Iris had remained quiet during the past week, but her anxiety had heightened with each passing day. She spent her time reading, but nothing appeared to give her comfort.

"I suppose so." She didn't know why Lord Burkham had any reason to pay a call. But there was no need to refuse him, either.

Rose eyed her mother, wondering if she should send her away. It wasn't likely that Iris was even aware of anything surrounding her. If she tried to remove her, it was possible that her mother would cause a scene. She decided it was best to simply leave matters alone. "I will see him here."

When Lord Burkham entered the drawing room, Rose stood and took two steps to greet him. It was a matter of pride, of wanting him to see how she had overcome her illness. Though she had fallen on her face at the last gathering, she pretended as if it hadn't happened.

Lord Burkham's face brightened when he saw her. "Lady Rose, I am delighted to see you." He then said, "And, of course, Lady Penford. It has been many months since I've seen you last."

Her mother behaved as if he hadn't spoken a single word. She continued to stare out the window with her hand pressed to the glass. The viscount sent her a questioning look, but Rose simply shook her head. It was best to leave her be.

He cleared his throat and asked, "I spoke at length with my family yesterday. They were quite surprised to hear that you had regained your ability to walk."

Rose had never particularly liked Thomas's parents, for they only cared about appearances.

"Pleased, even," he added. "And I was glad to tell them that they were wrong about you."

She thought about pretending that she was happy, that all was forgiven. But no longer did she yearn for Thomas's approval. Iain had been right about him—Burkham was little more than a puppet whose strings were pulled by his parents. What did it matter if they now believed they were wrong about her?

"Why didn't you come to see me, even once, when I was ill?" she asked. "I mistakenly thought you cared about me."

"I did. That is, I mean, I do. But I didn't want to disturb you. I thought you would wish to convalesce in peace with no one to bother you."

"Did you never think that I might need comforting and encouragement? Or was it simply that you thought I would embarrass you if I could only sit or be pushed in a Bath chair? You didn't want a cripple for a wife."

He sighed and colored at her accusation. "You're right, of course. I should have come."

Thomas drew his chair in closer and lowered his voice. "I wronged you, and I deserve all this." He reached out to her gloved hand. "I know it's too much to ask for your forgiveness. All I would ask . . . is that we might start again."

Start again? Was he serious? "Lord Burkham, I am sorry, but no. At one time I thought we might suit one another, but not anymore."

The viscount appeared confused. "But . . . Lady Rose. Whyever not?"

"Because you don't love me. You never have."

"What has that got to do with it?" There was genuine bewilderment on his face.

A soft sound caught her attention, and her mother was now walking toward them. "He only wants your fortune, Rose. If you were penniless, he'd have nothing to do with you." She sat down and in her hands, she held several pieces of paper. "But it no longer matters. It's all gone now. Gone. Every penny given to help bring him back."

"What is gone?" Lord Burkham asked.

A chill slid through Rose, a premonition of something terrible. "Mother, what are you talking about?"

Iris held out the papers and Rose took them. "Lord Burkham, I think you should go. I must speak with my mother in private."

"Perhaps I should read the letters," he offered. "I may be able to offer you help."

But there was no way of knowing if this was another moment's madness or something real. It wasn't his concern, and for that reason, Rose shook her head. "Thank you, but no."

He cast another look toward the folded paper, but acceded to her wishes. "Let me know if you have need of me."

She thanked him, inclining her head when he bowed and departed. The coldness inside her had intensified, and she opened the letter, reading its contents. It was from their land steward at Penford, telling them of an audit that went badly. He wrote that Lady Penford had taken a great portion of the rents and given them away once again—only this time it was far more than a thousand pounds. No one knew what she'd done with the money, and there was little left to pay the bills.

Her heartbeat pounded, and Rose forced herself to keep her voice calm. "Mother, did you give the rents to someone?"

Iris paled and confessed, "He said that he would help us. That he would keep the money safe for me." Her voice grew distant, and she said, "I think he's going to bring George back. He's not dead, you see—he's being held captive in India."

Rose closed her eyes, feeling sick to her stomach. "Mother, we buried our father. You were there at his funeral."

"No, no. It was someone else. George isn't dead." Her face tensed with unshed tears. "I promise you, we'll bring him back from India."

Dear God, now she was confusing James with her deceased husband. How could this have happened? Their land steward was responsible for collecting the rents and depositing the money. She didn't understand how their mother could even have access to the funds. "Mother, tell me who took the rents. Who was he?"

"I—I don't remember. It was several weeks ago."

"Tell me what he looked like." Rose was trying to keep the panic from her voice, for she had no idea how much money had been lost. "How old was he?"

"I don't know." At that, her mother began to cry. "He was kind to me. I gave him all the money I could find. Every penny. I don't know if it was enough to save George."

Rose sank down in a chair, wondering how dire their situation was. She needed to return to Penford immediately, to find out their financial state and alert the authorities.

"Mother, is there anything—"

"Wait." Iris's face brightened. "There is something I do remember about the gentleman who promised to help us find George."

Rose paused, allowing her mother time to speak. Iris straightened and admitted, "He was Irish. I'm sure of that."

Iain drove his curricle along the banks of the Serpentine, toward the stone bench where Lady Rose had asked to meet him. Her unexpected note had been terse, stating only: *I need to speak with you.*

Instinct warned him that he would not like what she had to say. And when he found her waiting for him, her expression revealed that she had been crying. A footman stood nearby, and Iain wondered what was the matter.

"Lady Rose." He greeted her with a slight bow and helped her into the curricle. "Is everything all right with your family?"

Her lips tightened, and she shook her head. "We have much to discuss. But not here."

Her footman took his place upon the rumble, once Rose was seated. Iain drove along the water's edge, waiting for her to speak. Rose's face held tension, as if she couldn't quite decide how to begin. At last, she stared at her hands and said, "My mother gave away a large portion of our rents to a stranger. And now that our debts must be paid, we have very little remaining."

Iain slowed the pace of the horses. Rose's voice was quiet, as if she were trying to hold her emotions under control. But beneath her serene façade, he suspected a storm was brewing.

"What can I do to help you?"

"Nothing. You haven't any money, either, and both of us are helpless to fix this mess. Someone preyed upon her weakness and stole our rents." She stiffened and turned. "She said it was someone Irish."

The words were like a whiplash, cracking between them. "And you somehow think I'm involved in this?"

"No, of course not." She covered her face with her hands, her shoulders lowered. "But you might know who it could be. Perhaps one of your servants who didn't return."

His anger softened when he realized that she had come to him because she needed his help—not because she believed he was responsible for the losses. For a moment, he was dumbfounded that she would believe in him. That her instinct had been to reach out for him instead of laying blame at his feet.

No one in all his life had done that. They saw him as a worthless bastard, not a man of strength. Her brown eyes studied him with worry, as if he would know what to do. And he warmed to her trust. Though he didn't know how to help, he would try.

She was waiting for him to respond, and he reached out to take her hand. "It could be one of my servants. Or it could be any of the hundreds of Irish who left my country," he pointed out. "Desperate men will do anything to help their families survive. Even lie." The weight of his own words lay against his conscience, for he was among the desperate.

"I can't believe this happened, Iain. I don't know what to do." Her voice was thick, as if she were holding back tears, but her fingers laced with his. "If my mother gave the rents to an Irishman as a gift, no one can accuse him of theft."

Iain wasn't so certain of that. Taking advantage of Lady Penford was indeed as good as theft. "We'll think of something. Trust in me." He was certain they could track the culprit fairly easily. And while the most likely candidate was his valet, Niall, it did seem strange.

Iain glanced back at the footman, wanting a moment of privacy. "Walk with me for a few moments," he said to Rose. The words were an order, not a question. He drew the curricle to a stop and gave the reins over to her footman, offering his arm. He was grateful she hadn't brought Calvert, for the man would likely protest.

She took his arm, and Iain led her through the grass, allowing her to lean against him for balance. Today, it seemed that she was struggling to walk. Though she held her head high, he didn't miss the emotion in her eyes. He moved slowly, guiding her toward a large fir tree on one side of the gardens. Only when they were out of public view did he pull her into his embrace.

She wept, clinging to him. "I'm sorry," she sobbed. "It's just that it feels as if everything has fallen to pieces. My brother hasn't returned, our debts are mounting, and my mother gave away half a year's worth of rents." He held her, welcoming her into his arms. She felt right there, and he let her cry, doing nothing more than holding her.

"It's going to be all right," he murmured against her ear. "I'll find a way to help you."

Her hands tightened around his neck. "Thank you, Iain." She drew back, and he wiped her tears away with his handkerchief. In her eyes, he saw the sudden yearning, and it tore his conscience apart. She had never looked at him like that before, with a nameless emotion in her eyes. One he was afraid to hope for.

A faint blush stole over her, and she confessed, "Lord Burkham came to call, just a few hours ago."

The very mention of the man's name raised his hackles. "Why?"

"He wanted to start again." A furtive smile crossed her face, and his gut tightened.

It's not your business. Let her make her own decisions.

"And what did you tell him?"

"I told him no." Her smile widened, and she said, "I wanted to tell him he was half-potted and there was nothing on earth that would make me say yes. But I didn't." The softness returned to her face and she added, "I thought of telling him that there was someone else."

God help him, he needed this woman. He wanted to kiss her, to feel the sweetness of her embrace. But how could he bring her down into the darkness that was his life? How could he dare to break her heart and make her regret every moment spent with him? The tightness in his gut spread up to his heart. "Rose, I have nothing I can give you."

"You stood by me, when even my own family doubted I would walk again. You helped me stand on my feet and take my first steps. And when you kiss me, you cannot deny what you feel."

"I don't deny it." He would give her that much. "But you are too far above me, Rose."

"How can you say that when my mother has given away everything? I'm not above you at all." Her face turned bitter and she added, "We are equals now, I would think."

She wasn't going to see reason. And the longer he held her, the more she was undoing his resolutions. With regret, he extricated her arms from around his neck and stepped away. "We are not, and never will be equals."

Her tears broke free again, and it was killing him to see her like this. Didn't she know how much he cared for her? She meant everything to him.

"You cannot be with a man like me, Rose."

"Why? Is it because my mother gave away any dowry I might have had?"

He wouldn't care if she were penniless. But he felt he owed her the truth. "You couldn't live in Ireland, Rose. You're not strong enough to survive a place like that, and I wouldn't want to put you through it."

She paled and took a step back. "Because I can hardly walk. That's what you believe, isn't it?"

No, it wasn't. But he didn't want her to hold out hope for him, building her dreams on a life that would shatter her. "I believe that you would be miserable with me. And I don't want to watch you throw away your life."

Her face turned red, and she took a steadying breath. "So that kiss last night meant nothing to you. You were using me."

Her accusation flared his anger. "I've never used you, *a ghrá*. But if I wed you, I'd bring you nothing but sorrow. I know it."

For a long moment, she held his gaze with a discerning look. "Take me back to my own carriage." Her voice was weary, and she added, "Find whatever heiress you want. I won't stand in your way."

He wanted to pull her back into his arms, to show her what she meant to him. But it was better for both of them if she didn't put her hopes and beliefs in him.

"I will help you recover your dowry," he promised. "I'll do everything I can to help."

But when he saw the hurt in her eyes, it was clear she had lost faith in him. She had come to him in an hour of need, offering her heart, and he'd pushed her away.

Inside, it felt as if his veins were frozen, his heart turned to stone. It was better this way, he tried to tell himself.

But even he didn't believe it.

This woman was the best friend he'd ever had. He'd enjoyed every moment spent at her side, and she had given him a reason to smile each day. And what had he done in return but break her heart?

"I am sorry, Rose," he said, as he helped her back into her carriage.

Her eyes gleamed with tears, and she met his gaze. "No. You're not."

As she departed, he wanted to kick himself for the words he'd spoken. He might wed an heiress and save Ashton, but in the end, for what purpose? *He* would be miserable without her. And he would make another woman's life miserable, simply because she wasn't Rose.

Iain watched her drive away with her footman, knowing he had hurt the one person he cared about. Once, he'd believed it was for the greater good. But now, it made him feel like a coward.

He returned to his curricle and guided the horses back to the main road. Inside, he grew irritated with himself. All he could remember was the stricken look on her face.

Let her go, his conscience warned. *She's too good for you, and you know it.*

But Rose mistakenly believed that he valued wealth over her, and that was the furthest thing from the truth.

He sped through the London streets, passing vehicles as quickly as he could. Though he couldn't say why, the need to see her again overcame all common sense. He couldn't let her walk away without knowing the truth—that she meant everything to him.

And damned if he would be a martyr about it.

Chapter Fifteen

All through the drive home, Rose wept in silence. Thank Heaven, she was alone in her own carriage, with only a coachman and footman. She didn't think she could bear it, if Iain had driven her here.

She'd been so stupid, offering herself to him. After he had kissed her, she'd mistakenly believed that there would be more between them. She had allowed her heart to soften beyond friendship, and it had brought her nothing, save rejection and humiliation.

Her carriage slowed down in the street, their pace grinding to a halt. Rose glanced around to see what the trouble was. Dozens of men and women were walking, their faces drawn and tight. When she asked her footman what was happening, he admitted, "It's the Irish, Lady Rose. A boat arrived from Dublin just this morning, and the people have come here to look for work."

She could hardly count all the refugees. Rose held a handkerchief to her nose and mouth, as the overpowering stench of human misery passed them. Their filthy clothes hung upon them, and many were coughing and sick. All around them, the police swarmed, trying to keep order as they pushed the people through the streets.

"You're not strong enough to survive a place like that, and I wouldn't want to put you through it," Iain had said.

This was the Ireland she would face. She would witness suffering like this, every day, knowing she could do nothing to change it. It was one matter if only a handful of people were impoverished at this level. It was quite another when the entire country was starving to death.

Her heart bled for these people—especially the young children clinging to their mothers' skirts. Something had to be done, but she had no understanding of how to solve their plight.

It was little wonder that Iain had journeyed here in the hopes of saving his tenants. But she simply could not imagine that any amount of money would help. She studied them as her carriage passed, and she wondered if he truly believed she couldn't survive in Ireland. The more she thought of it, the angrier she grew. How dare he push her away, claiming she would only be miserable with him?

In the past year, she had traveled along her own path of darkness and had emerged stronger. Iain had stood by her, helping her overcome her weakness until she could walk again. And now he didn't believe she was able to live with him under circumstances such as these?

Inwardly, she was seething. She had told him to find another heiress, but the idea of standing in a ballroom and watching Iain court another woman made her clench her fists.

The carriage pulled to a stop in front of her townhouse. To her surprise, she saw that Iain was standing on her doorstep waiting. She had no idea how he'd managed to outpace her, but his expression held an unfathomable intensity.

Her rage flared again, and she considered storming past him and telling him to go to the devil. But then she wouldn't know why he was here.

Her footman helped her disembark, and the moment she stepped out of the carriage, Iain was at her side.

"I don't want to see you right now," she lashed out. "You've already decided what our lives will be. There's nothing more to say."

"I have a great deal more to say." He put an arm around her waist and lifted her to the top step. He set her down at the threshold, and she suspected that he would not air their disagreement in front of the servants.

Without a word, he waited for the footman to open the front door. She sensed a tension in him, one that held an invisible warning. Something had caused him to ride like a demon from the gardens, ensuring that he reached her house first.

But she would not stand down and listen to all the reasons why he did not want to be with her. Fury burned inside her that he was treating her like a delicate flower who would wither in the face of adversity. That wasn't who she was at all.

The footman offered to take his hat and gloves, but as soon as Iain gave them over, he walked toward the drawing room as if he owned it.

"Would you . . . care for tea?" the footman called out, but Rose refused. Neither she nor Iain had any interest in refreshments. Instead, she followed him into the drawing room and folded her arms, waiting for him to speak.

Iain crossed the room and stood before her. "Don't you ever be believing that I *want* to choose another heiress," he began. "I can't let you think that."

"And that is the reason you came all this way? To convince me that you still want me, even though you've said I'm too weak to endure hardship." She made no effort to hide the frustration in her voice. She was stronger than any woman he would find. Most London heiresses would faint at the sight of starving children.

"I never said you were weak. I said that I didn't want you to be miserable because of me. You deserve a better life, Rose." In his voice, in his demeanor, she saw a visible pain. He took her face between his hands, tracing the edge of her cheek. "I've wanted you from the very first moment I saw you."

At his touch, her anger came roaring back. Why would he say this, after he'd claimed he could never marry her? Was he trying to offer sympathy or toy with her feelings? She didn't want his pity.

Rose was so weary of being the crippled woman left behind in the corner. She had fought hard to walk again, and now the man she cared about was leaving her. A surge of resentment filled her, and she wanted to seize her own power. She wanted him to know what he was walking away from, and God help her, she wanted him to hold regrets.

She pulled away from him and walked to the door. Then she closed it and turned the key, locking them inside. It was a move so scandalous, her grandmother would die of mortification. And Rose simply didn't care.

She tossed the key on an end table and strode toward him. Words would not convince Iain to stay with her. She could give him a thousand reasons why his claims were rubbish, but he would never listen.

Instead, she intended to show him all the reasons why he would regret leaving.

Rose took three steps back to him, and when Iain tried to speak, she pulled his mouth down to hers, silencing him. She poured all her anger into the kiss, showing him exactly what he was leaving behind.

Iain answered the kiss with his own fervor. It was as if he needed to touch her, like a craving he'd never managed to satisfy. Her body reacted to him with a searing response. She clung to him, and the intensity of the kiss made the rest of the world fall away until there was nothing but him.

No man had ever made her feel this way, and she touched her tongue to his, letting propriety be damned. He drew his hands over her shoulders, and she wished there were not so many layers between them. She wanted to feel his touch against her bare skin, and when he lowered his mouth to her throat, she moaned.

"We should stop," he murmured. "Someone will discover us."

"And you would never want that," she said drily. "God forbid that my family would try to force you into marrying me."

He traced his hand down the dozens of buttons that lined the back of her gown. "If the choice were mine, I would marry you now. I would take you upstairs to my bed and spend every hour loving you."

His words made her heart beat faster, and she ached between her legs. She imagined him above her, kissing her until she couldn't breathe. "But you'd rather wed a stranger with a fortune instead of someone like me."

"Is that what you think?" He didn't wait for a reply but conquered her mouth, sliding his tongue inside. The shocking sensation made her grip the edges of his shirt. Rose surrendered to him, opening herself and taking the immense pleasure he offered.

He drew her hips against his, despite the layers of skirts between them. She could feel his arousal, and yet, she did not push him away. Her hair was tousled, her lips swollen.

And then a voice broke through from beyond the door. "Lady Rose, are you all right?"

It was the footman. She closed her eyes, feeling the disappointment of his interruption. Iain continued kissing her neck, and she gripped his hair, fighting against the intrusion of reality.

She was aware of the need to stop. This had never been an attempt to trap him into marriage. She'd simply been so angry with him, wanting him to see that he was making a mistake.

And now, she was the one making a mistake.

"Yes," she called out to the footman. "I am fine."

But every word fled her brain when Iain knelt down, slipping his hand beneath her skirt. His hands moved over her ankle and up her stockings as he stroked her calf. In a low voice, he asked, "Do you want me to stop?"

She closed her eyes, resting her hands upon his shoulders. *I should never have let him kiss me. Especially when he's only going to leave.*

This man had slipped past her defenses, stealing her heart. He was relentless, bold, and more than that, he'd been her friend.

His hand paused upon her thigh, and despite the barrier of linen, she felt the heat of his touch. He started to pull away, and the thought left her bereft.

Don't stop.

To the footman, she raised her voice and ordered, "Leave us, if you would."

Through the door, he called out, "If you should have need of me, Lady Rose, I can—"

"No!" she answered the servant. "Please go. Truly, I—I am fine."

In silent answer, Iain slid his hands back into place, moving his palm until he touched her pantaloons. There was a slit between them, and he commanded, "Look at me, Rose."

He was offering her the choice of what would happen now. She felt as if her emotions had gone through a whirling storm. He had given her all the reasons why he couldn't marry her . . . and yet, he had come back to her.

She didn't know what to think of this. It seemed he was powerless to resist the attraction between them. And from the unfettered desire in his eyes, she could not deny him either.

Rose leaned down and touched his face. His expression tightened with need, and when she touched her lips to his, he moved his hand between her thighs. The linen was damp, and when he found the slit within the fabric, she was startled by her response.

He dared to stroke her, and sensations rolled over her with such exquisite pleasure, her knees buckled. Iain stood again, grasping her waist to lend support. "Let me touch you, Rose."

Her fingers dug into his shoulders, and she couldn't bring herself to refuse. He rubbed his fingers against her slick entrance, and the raw sensations made her convulse against him. She had no choice but to hold on to him, her arms around his neck. Her body's needs overrode all common sense. She knew this was wrong.

He wasn't going to marry her—for he saw her as too weak to survive Ireland. But when he brought her to the edge of a precipice with his caresses, she didn't want to pull away. There was a sense of power in this, and she wanted him to continue.

She kissed him hard, knowing that she was forcing him past the brink of control. And though it was a wicked thing to do, she pressed herself close to him, glorying in the groan that erupted from his mouth.

His eyes were hooded with desire when he slid a finger inside her. She shuddered at the unfamiliar sensation, her nails digging into his back.

"You're mine, Rose. No matter what happens to us in the future, you'll know that at this moment, you belong to me."

He kept his finger inside her while he nudged her hooded flesh with his thumb. She bit back a gasp as he began to work her. "You're the only woman I want."

He was merciless in the torment, keeping up a rhythm while her body writhed against him. It had become a game of control, each trying to command the other. She was losing this battle and hardly cared. Her breath erupted in a shattering cry as he thrust against her. As he kept up the rhythm, she arched her back and the sensation transformed.

God above, she was mindless to the rest of the world. Never had she known that it could be like this between a man and a woman.

Iain plunged his tongue within her mouth and then added a second finger. She tightened around him, half-sobbing his name. There were no words for this, only savage feelings.

With every stroke, he mastered her, and she surrendered to him, craving fulfillment.

"I could touch you like this for hours," he murmured against her lips. "*A ghrá*, do you know what you do to me?"

She was breathing in short gasps, and it suddenly felt as if they were joined together. In her imagination, she thought of his strong shaft plunging inside her.

"You're driving me into madness." Dimly, she was still aware that someone could try to unlock the door, and the very thought of discovery deepened the intensity.

He slowed his fingers, forcing her to hover on the brink of ecstasy, prolonging the pleasure.

"Iain, please. I can't, I—" Her words broke off when he kept his thumb pressed against her center while his fingers invaded and withdrew. She was straining against him, and he tormented her, slowing his pace and then driving harder.

"I want to be inside you," he whispered against her ear. "I want your legs wrapped around me while I thrust and take you. Until you can't bear it any longer."

With that, she shattered in his arms, kissing him hard while her wetness coated his fingers. She was squeezing him, and he continued the stroking until she came apart a second time. Her violent response was more than she'd ever imagined, and she was unable to stand any longer.

Iain supported her weight as she trembled, her body sated as he withdrew his hand and lowered her skirts. Her lips were swollen and bruised, her eyes holding back tears.

"Did I hurt you?" he asked.

She shook her head and closed her eyes. A thousand questions rolled over her, but she didn't want the answers. She didn't want him to look her in the eyes and leave her again. Not after this.

Gently, he lifted her to sit upon the chaise longue, and she fumbled for a pin to straighten her wayward hair.

For a moment, he watched her, and his expression held tension and frustration. "I won't apologize for this."

She felt the physical and emotional exhaustion wash over her. "I was the one who started it." It had begun as a means of proving to him that he was wrong about her. And in the end, he'd torn down her defenses, leaving her vulnerable.

He touched her chin and leaned down to kiss her. His gentleness stole away another piece of her heart.

And yet, she still didn't know if there was any hope for them.

It took hours and half a bottle of brandy to regain control over his sanity. God, he didn't know what had possessed him to barge in on Rose and claim her. But when he'd seen her face, so broken and lost, he no longer cared about anything else. He needed her to know that he didn't have a choice in this, that *she* was the woman he wanted, despite all else.

His original plan of wedding an heiress had been a sound idea—but he no longer knew if it was the right choice anymore.

Iain poured another glass of brandy, wishing he could pickle his insides enough that he wouldn't feel the dull aching. A soft knock interrupted, and he saw his valet, Niall, standing at the door. "You asked to see me, Lord Ashton?"

Iain nodded, thinking about how to begin. If he directly accused the man of stealing the rents, Niall would only deny it. Instead, he said, "What do you know of Lady Penford?"

The question gave his valet pause. "Her mind has gone soft," he said at last.

"It has," Iain agreed. "But she has good days and bad days." He waited a moment, wondering if Niall could have been the one to steal from her. When the man said nothing further, Iain added, "Some of the rents from Penford have gone missing."

Niall's face darkened. "And you think I took them, somehow?"

"She said it was an Irishman." Iain shrugged. "And I know it wasn't me." He folded his arms across his chest and waited.

Niall straightened and eyed him. "Do you honestly believe I would still be working for you if I'd stolen the rents? I'd be back in Ireland with my family."

That much was true. If Niall had hundreds of pounds, he wouldn't be here now. Iain asked, "Who do you think stole the rents, if it wasn't you?"

Niall shook his head. "I can't be knowing that, but I wish I'd thought of it. Maybe it was Terence or Pádraig."

Iain pondered the man's revelation and decided that it was best to question Lady Penford. She might remember more about the Irishman who had taken the rents. "Thank you, Niall, that will be all."

But his valet paused a moment. "And why is it you're so interested in the rents? Is it because you're going to wed one of the Penford daughters?"

"Why would you ask this?" He still suspected the man was hiding something, and no answer at all might bring about more information.

"Because if their rents have gone missing, then the ladies are no better off than us." Niall sent him a sidelong look. "And what will the tenants say if you return with a penniless bride? How will you help them when you've brought nothing?" He shook his head. "They'll say you're not the rightful heir."

"The law says I am."

"Tell that to those who are starving. When you see their children dying in their arms, will you tell them that you're going to save them?" Niall's tone turned frosty. "I held my daughter when she took her last breath. I gave her what food I could, but it wasn't enough. She wasn't strong enough to survive."

His valet sent him a hard look. "You might be thinking of your own happiness, my lord. But it's your people you should be thinking of now."

With that, Niall left, closing the door behind him.

Rose had no interest in attending another ball, but her grandmother insisted. Lady Wolcroft had the demeanor of a battlefield commander, and she informed Rose, "You have two choices, Rose. You will attend Lady Arnsbury's supper party . . . or you will attend Lady Arnsbury's supper party."

And so it was that she found herself wearing a gown the rich color of garnets, while her hair was bound up with sprigs of wild roses. "Grandmother, there is no need for this. Really, I would much rather spend time at home." Staring at the wall was preferable to seeing Iain. Even the memory of that afternoon made her blush.

Despite the stolen moment between them, she knew he needed an heiress for a wife—it was why he had come to London. But how could she sit in a chair and watch him court another lady? The very idea filled her with fury, making her want to tear the imaginary woman's hair out. She lacked the serenity to stand aside, when she had fallen in love with Iain Donovan.

No matter what happens to us in the future, you'll know that at this moment, you belong to me.

His words haunted her, for in her heart, he belonged with her and no one else. But it might never be possible.

"There is someone I want you to meet," Lady Wolcroft insisted.

Not another suitor, she pleaded inside her head. But she forced herself to ask, "Is it one of your friends?"

"One of your mother's dearest friends," Lady Wolcroft said. "She has been traveling for several weeks, but she decided to bring her daughters for the Season."

"Are you wanting me to befriend them?"

Her grandmother's expression remained neutral. "I am certain you will want to. Especially since you have become close to their brother, Lord Ashton."

Her nerves tightened when she realized what Lady Wolcroft was saying. "Do you mean that Iain's mother and sisters have traveled from New York?"

"I do, yes. I wrote letters to Moira, inviting her here. She arrived just this morning."

Rose managed a smile, though it felt as if her insides had turned to ice. "Then I should be glad to greet all of them. Especially Iain's mother."

Because I want to meet the woman who dared to hide him away all these years. And she rather hoped for an opportunity to speak her mind about it.

Her grandmother abruptly shook her head. "Do not mention Iain to Moira. I have my own reasons for meddling, but there is a strong rift between them. If you do mention Iain, she'll cut you off. Let her get to know you first."

Rose didn't argue, but she couldn't help but feel offended at this woman's behavior. How could she treat her youngest son like an outsider? It took all her years of training to paste a calm expression on her face.

When the women arrived at last, Rose was startled by the striking resemblance Iain bore to his mother. They both had the same dark hair with a hint of curl to it and the same firm chin. His sisters attracted immediate attention because of their beauty. The older sister wore a butter-yellow gown, trimmed with creamy lace, while the younger sister wore a white gown with violet embroidery along the hem.

"Come, I will introduce you to them," Lady Wolcroft said.

Rose followed her grandmother, and Lady Wolcroft presented them to her. "Moira, I am so glad you could come this evening. I would like you to meet my granddaughter, Rose."

She offered the older woman a warm smile and said, "I am happy to meet you, Lady Ashton." Iain's mother returned the smile, but there was a distant look in her eyes, as if years of sadness lingered upon her shoulders.

Her daughters, Sybil and Colleen, both greeted her with more enthusiasm. The younger girl, Colleen, was nearly bursting with excitement. "I am ever so glad to be here tonight." Her eyes sparkled with mischief. "I cannot tell you how awful it was to spend nearly a fortnight traveling here from New York. I was ready to throw myself off the ship out of boredom."

Sybil sent her sister a dry look. "I was ready to help you overboard. She would *not* stop talking. You'd think her tongue had a hinge in the middle."

With that, her grandmother waved them on. "Rose, go introduce the girls to your sister. Moira and I would like a moment to speak in private."

She nodded, but the distance toward Lily seemed impossibly far. Though she tried to keep pace with the girls, it only heightened her limp.

"Are you all right?" Sybil asked her, slowing down so that Rose could catch up to them.

"I need to walk more slowly," she admitted. "I've only just recently begun to walk again." On a whim, she added, "Thanks to your brother."

Colleen's face broke into a smile. "You've met Iain? Is he here tonight? I've been wanting to see him, but Mother—"

"Shh—" Sybil cut her off with a dark look of warning. "We will keep our walking slower, then." But she glanced around the room as if to determine if Iain was there.

There was something strange happening, Rose realized. Surely they would have seen Iain already. To Colleen, she asked, "You did arrive at Lord Ashton's townhouse, I presume? Were you able to settle into your rooms this morning?"

The young woman exchanged a look with her older sister and then nodded. "Yes, of course." But she offered nothing else. Whatever she'd been about to say, Sybil had pressed her into silence.

"I do not know if Lord Ashton is intending to come tonight," Rose said. And given all that had happened, she rather hoped he wouldn't.

Sybil was watching her, and her gaze turned curious. "You said my brother helped you learn to walk again. How did that come about?"

Rose was about to explain, when suddenly, Lord Burkham emerged from the crowd of people. "May I have a word with you, Lady Rose?" He nodded to Sybil and Colleen. "Ladies, please excuse us."

Rose's mood dimmed, for she wasn't at all certain she wanted to speak with Thomas. However, neither did she want to cause a scene. To the young ladies, she said, "Forgive me, but I will only be a moment."

Lord Burkham offered his arm, and this time, he kept his pace much slower. In fact, it was a bit *too* slow, but she understood that he was trying to apologize for his earlier mistakes.

"I thought about you at length last night." He touched her fingertips, which were resting upon his arm. "Your recovery has been simply miraculous, and I am so glad for you. Nothing would make me happier than to make you my bride."

She stared at him in disbelief. Did he truly believe she would say yes? "Lord Burkham, while I am flattered by your offer, my answer stands. I am not going to marry you."

"But . . . I thought you would be pleased." His voice held a trace of disquiet, as if he'd never expected her to refuse.

His bewildered demeanor was almost comical. Rose didn't want to insult him, but instead offered a sympathetic smile and tucked her arm into his. "You are a kind man, but you and I are not suited at all to marriage. I would suggest that you speak with Miss Everett again. She *does* think you are wonderful."

"And you don't." There was a hopeful note in his voice, but she only laughed.

"No, I'm afraid not. But you should not marry a woman who does not love you. And you ought to consider loving her in return."

He appeared to consider it. "You're certain you won't change your mind?"

She patted his hand in farewell and took a step away. "I am definitely certain. But I will offer you a suggestion." He met her gaze and waited. "Go and ask Miss Everett to dance. And if she loses her balance, whatever happens, do not let her fall." She didn't wait for his reply, but instead began the arduous walk back to her sister.

Before she reached Lily's side, Mrs. Everett intruded. The matron looked like she'd smelled something rotten before she put on a simpering smile. "Well, Lady Rose. I am surprised that you and Lord Burkham appeared so fond of one another. I overheard him telling his mother that he intended to ask for your hand. I, however, think that would be unwise."

Rose rather agreed with the woman, but before she could speak, Mrs. Everett plunged forward. "If I were you, I would let the viscount go. After all, everyone is gossiping about you and Lord Ashton. You were seen together in the park, and he was carrying you. Have you no thought for decency?"

The woman's audacity angered her. "I've only just learned to walk again, Mrs. Everett. Lord Ashton was helping me return to my carriage, because it was difficult to manage."

The matron sniffed. "Humph. I should think a footman would be a less scandalous choice. As it is, I thought I should warn you away from the viscount. He belongs to my daughter. Stay away from Lord Burkham, or you will regret it."

"Are you threatening me?" She was aghast at the woman's vitriol. Perhaps she ought to warn Thomas, for this woman's manipulation was even worse than she'd imagined.

"Indeed. If I catch you speaking to Lord Burkham again, or worse, *dancing* with him, rest assured, I will not hesitate to besmirch your name."

Oh, will you? She was so irritated by Mrs. Everett's meddling, she decided no response was best. Instead, she walked away, leaving the matron to fume and scheme on her own. *Good riddance.*

A few minutes later, she spied Lord Ashton arriving. The moment he saw her, his eyes locked upon hers. He crossed the room like a barbarian bent upon claiming his woman. The very idea sent a flare of heat through her, followed by frustration. She didn't doubt for a moment that if she had Evangeline's money or if she were stronger, he would have offered for her.

A surge of anger rose up within her. Why did he insist on pursuing her, when he'd claimed he could not wed her? Was she not good enough?

She straightened her spine, awaiting the confrontation. But before he reached her, Lord Burkham intervened. "He looks rather menacing, Lady Rose. Shall I guard you from the Irishman?"

"I'll be fine, Lord Burkham. But thank you."

As Iain pushed his way past the other guests, he didn't seem aware that his family had arrived. He never saw the shocked expression that came over Lady Ashton's face or the delight upon the faces of his sisters.

Instead, he appeared ready to knock the viscount to the ground. He was angry, and that was quite clear when he reached her side.

"Lady Rose, would you care to dance?" Lord Burkham asked. She recognized his invitation as a means of avoiding Iain. But it was like tossing oil upon Iain's fury.

"Thank you, but no." She appreciated the viscount's offer, but she was more curious about why Iain was here.

"May I speak with you, Lady Rose?" There was a slight tic in Iain's clenched jaw, and his eyes narrowed upon her.

"Of course." She waited for him to continue, but he sent a hard glare toward the viscount.

"I'll just . . . go now, shall I?" Lord Burkham ventured, appearing discomfited by the earl's hostility.

"Yes, do," Iain answered. Once the viscount had left, he lowered his voice and said quietly, "Follow me. We need to talk in private."

She rather agreed with that, though when she passed Mrs. Everett, she didn't miss the matron's visible annoyance. "Go toward the library," she said in a low voice. "I will meet you there."

But Iain wasn't about to let go of her. His grip tightened upon her hand, and he cut a path through the crowd of people, leading her away from everyone.

"Wait," she started to protest. He needed to know that his mother and sisters were here. She was about to tell him, when he suddenly spun back.

The look in his eyes was primal, like a man bent upon his needs. "I haven't slept since the last moment we were together. I'm going to kiss you until you can't stand up," Iain said roughly. "I can do it here in front of everyone, or you can let me take you somewhere no one will see us."

Dear God. His words burned through her, heightening her own desire. She didn't care about anyone else or anything now. His fierce need echoed within her body, until she felt her heartbeat quicken.

He moved her through a doorway, leading her away until he located Lady Arnsbury's library. It was unoccupied, and he took her inside, closing the door behind them. The moment they were alone, he kissed her like a starving man, devouring her lips. Rose clung to him, helpless to do anything but ride out the storm of his touch. His hands were everywhere, moving over her bodice. She could hardly breathe for wanting him, and reckless needs swept over her.

What was she doing? Why did he think he could simply storm through a ballroom and carry her off?

She broke free and shoved him back. "Stop behaving like a pirate. You cannot treat me like a tavern wench you can haul off to your ship and have your wicked way with."

His mouth curved in a predatory smile. "Why not?"

"Because I don't deserve to be treated like this."

At that, his demeanor shifted instantly. He stepped back from her and raked a hand over his hair. "You're right, *a ghrá*. You don't."

He kept his distance from her and rested his hands on a wingback chair. "I know what I am supposed to do to save Ashton. But when I see you, there's no one else in that ballroom for me. I want to kill any man who so much as looks at you. And the thought of giving you up is tearing me apart. I can't do it."

She grew very still, her heart quickening. There was shadowed torment in his green eyes, but she felt the need for honesty. "But if you wed me and your people continue to suffer, you'll grow to hate yourself."

"I already hate myself," he murmured. Slowly, he crossed the room and stood before her. "It's not right for me to rely on someone else to save Ashton. I need to find a way, using my own means." His green eyes held hers with sincerity. "I want to give you the life you've dreamed of. A house. Children, if you want them—though I wouldn't make a good father. But more than that, I want to be with you each day. Even if we have no money at all."

He took her hands in his. "I thought I could walk away, but it's killing me, Rose."

In his eyes, she saw an emotion that echoed her own heart's desire. She had fallen hard for this man and couldn't bear to hurt him. "What do you want to do?"

"First, I want to marry you. I'll find another way to save Ashton. If I have to sell every last possession I own, I will do it."

She reached up to touch his cheek, feeling the warmth of his skin. He kissed her palm and the gesture undid her.

But then, the unexpected sound of a key turning in the lock suddenly broke through the tension.

"What was that noise?" Rose turned toward the door, and Iain's expression tightened. He crossed the library and turned the knob.

"Someone has locked us inside."

She gaped at him. "But why?" The moment she spoke the words, she wanted to groan. "Oh no. I think I know who's done this." She told him about Mrs. Everett and her threat. "If we are caught together, I'll be ruined." This was the matron's way of ensuring that she could not possibly wed Thomas. Not that she wanted to, but this would indeed force Iain and her together.

"We don't have to be caught," Iain started to say, but then he looked around. There was not a single window in the library, nor other way to leave the room. There was no avoiding what would happen. If they pounded on the door and shouted to be let out, everyone would know that they'd been alone. If they waited until they were discovered, no one would care that they had done nothing at all. Everyone would believe the worst.

"Are you proposing to hide in the bookshelves?" she teased.

He shrugged. "You might fit, though I wouldn't." His mouth twisted in an ironic smile. "I've already asked you to marry me, Rose. This may simply hasten our wedding." But then Iain sat down and drew up a chair for her to sit across from him. "Have you an answer for me?"

She wanted to say yes, but was afraid of all the obstacles between them. "You still don't think I'm strong enough to endure Ireland, do you?"

"No. You would not be happy at Ashton as it stands now. But I could marry you and let you stay here, in England. At least until it's safer for you to join me, or until I've restored order to our lands."

His offer was meant to protect her, she was certain. And yet, she didn't feel it was right to live apart. "How long do you imagine that would be?"

He shook his head, lifting his shoulders in a shrug. "I cannot say, Rose. All I know is that the thought of watching you wed another man is something I can't endure. And if I tried to wed an heiress for her money, I would regret every moment. It's not fair to her. Or to you."

Iain removed her glove, edging her palm with his thumb. The caress echoed through her body, and she warmed to his touch. His green eyes locked on hers, and he knelt down before her. "Marry me, Rose."

"I do care about you Iain," she murmured. "But there are many decisions we need to discuss. Like how you will get food for your tenants when you have no money. I don't even know how much money our family has or if I have a dowry at all." Every time she'd tried to speak with her mother, Lady Penford could give her no answers. Lily had written to their land steward but had no more information than before.

"Cain Sinclair has offered to donate some food and supplies. We also spoke of other ways to restore Ashton."

Though his response should have reassured her, she hadn't missed the uncertainty in his tone. And though she did want to be with Iain, she worried about their future.

He rose from his knees and sat down across from her. "If you are asking all these questions, I can only assume you are considering it."

She was, but she couldn't quite dispel her fears. "I might." With a daring smile, she added, "Perhaps you should convince me."

He pulled his chair closer so that their knees touched. Then he cupped her face and kissed her softly. Yearning awakened within her, and she responded, kissing him back with all her unspoken feelings. She did love this man and wanted to be with him. But never did she want him to look upon her with regret.

Her heartbeat pounded, and when his mouth moved to her throat, shivers broke over her skin. She tried to hold on to her senses, fearing she might lose control of herself. Quickly, she grasped for a means of diverting his attention.

"Iain, there's something else you should know. Your mother is here tonight. I met her and your sisters."

The expression on his face transformed instantly. But it was not joy or gladness at their arrival. It looked, instead, like he had turned into stone.

"*A ghrá,* are you certain it was my sisters and Lady Ashton?"

She nodded. "My grandmother introduced me to them before you arrived. You were so busy dragging me away, I don't suppose you saw them."

His mood didn't improve. "And what did she say about me?" He spoke of his mother with bitterness in his voice.

"Nothing at all." She hesitated and admitted, "My grandmother warned me not to mention you."

Iain gave a nod. "She was wise, then. She knows how much Moira hates me."

"But it's not right. You're still her son." Regardless of Lady Ashton's feelings on the matter, she ought to be grateful to Iain for taking care of them.

"My mother would have been glad if I had died instead of Michael. Happy, even."

A cold chill encircled her heart at that. "I hope you're wrong."

His mouth twisted. "I don't suppose she'd be glad of a marriage between us. She would do anything to stop it."

Rose stood from her chair and moved in front of him, resting her hands upon his shoulders. There was no denying her need to bring him comfort and reassurance. Iain pulled her down to his lap, and she rested her head against him. "It's our decision. Not hers."

The feeling of his arms around her was welcoming, and she nestled close.

"I need you, Rose," Iain murmured, kissing her forehead. "I cannot imagine marrying any other woman but you." His hands moved over the back of her gown, pausing over the buttons.

She was aching for him, needing his skin against hers. "Touch me now," she pleaded, turning to give him easier access to the buttons. Though Rose knew how scandalous this was, she hardly cared anymore. If they were going to accuse her of wantonness, it might as well be true.

Iain took his time with the buttons, releasing them one by one. When he lowered the bodice of her gown, she felt the chill of air over her skin. Then he worked at the laces of her corset, loosening the tight binding until it slackened. He bent his mouth to the bare skin revealed above her chemise, his hand moving beneath the layers until he cupped her bare breast. Desire roared through her, and she was aching, needing him with a desperation she couldn't understand.

He stroked her nipple, and she let out a shuddering cry. Her nails dug into his shoulders, and she felt herself growing damp between her legs. She couldn't forget the last time he'd touched her intimately, and already her body was eager for him.

But when his lips covered her erect nipple, drawing it into the heat of his mouth, she lost control. A bolt of heat rushed between her legs, and she writhed against his lap. "Iain," she gasped. She craved him inside her, and the forbidden danger of discovery only heightened the passion. Although the door was still locked, dozens of people would be aware of their disappearance. There would be vicious gossip, and Mrs. Everett would not hesitate to humiliate her.

Iain's eyes were hooded with raw desire, and in spite of her innocence, she wanted to touch him, too. She moved her hand to his chest, and he caught it with his hand.

"Let me touch you," she pleaded. "I need to, even if just for a moment."

He let out a curse in Irish, but let go of her fingers. "Only if I can do the same."

There was a chaise longue in one corner of the study, and he brought her there, seating her upon it. Her heart was pounding, and she couldn't help but look back at the door.

"They're going to find us."

Iain rested both hands on either side of her. "The devil himself could set the door on fire, and I wouldn't care, Rose." He bent and kissed her neck. "I want you beneath me. I need to see your face and watch you while I pleasure you."

The words stole her breath, and she understood, then, that there was no stopping him.

Boldly, she brought her hand back to his chest. "Iain, look at me." She touched her lips to his in the softest kiss. "I don't know when they will find us, or what will happen next. But I do know that I want you. More than anything I've ever imagined."

He closed his eyes and took her in a deep, sensual kiss. It was a kiss of relief and thankfulness, and she felt the tension easing from him.

With that, he moved his hand up her stockings, beneath her petticoats, until he touched her bare thigh. He fumbled with her undergarments until he found the slit between them. The moment he touched her intimately, she shuddered as he caressed her wet opening.

"God, you're perfect," he breathed. "I could die right now if I were buried inside you like this."

The thickness of his fingers was a caress that bloomed deep within, and she trembled at the onslaught of his hand stroking her. She could only imagine what it would be like if he made love to her.

Rose pulled at his clothing until she loosened his shirt from his trousers, searching for his bare skin. His body was warm, his muscles well formed, as she traced his abdomen. Iain loosened the buttons of his trousers with his free hand, pressing her hand downward.

"Touch me," he commanded. "The way I'm touching you."

His words broke the spell between them, making her worry about the others outside the room. She grew nervous and admitted, "I've never . . . done this before, Iain. I'm afraid of what we've begun." Her cheeks burned with embarrassment, and she suspected that this would end up in marriage, no matter what doubts she might have.

And perhaps that was why she wanted him so badly. Because, in her heart, she wanted to be with this man, no matter the obstacles.

Iain never took his gaze from hers as he removed his hand from her body. He guided her palm to his velvet erection. The moment she touched him, Rose felt a sense of power. She was fascinated by the soft heat, and when he closed her fingers around his stiff column, she understood what he wanted . . . to be pleasured in the same way he was touching her. The thought was overwhelming, and she moved her hand upon him, caressing his length.

A low hiss escaped him, and he sent her a wicked smile. "That's it, *a ghrá*. Just like that."

She let out a moan when he moved his hand back between her legs, sliding two fingers inside. As she drew her fist upward, he began to thrust his hand until they found a similar rhythm. He nudged his thumb against her secret flesh, and the spiraling caress intensified her arousal. She did the same to him, circling her thumb upon the head of his manhood. Beneath her fingers, she felt a bead of moisture, and her own body ached to receive him.

"I want to be in you, *a ghrá*. I want to thrust within, over and over." He underscored his words by suckling at her nipple while he worked his hand between her thighs. She was so wet, craving more from him until she arched her back. She couldn't stop herself from squeezing at his length, fisting him with her palm until it, too, was wet.

"More," he demanded, and she obeyed, quickening the tempo. He rewarded her by flicking his thumb faster, pushing her closer to the edge in a rhythm that drowned her in the tidal sensations of sexual need. She felt herself rising, coming apart as he thrust and withdrew his fingers. When she reached the brink of ecstasy, she squeezed her hand around his erection, crying out while his tongue swirled across her nipple. Her body clenched the fingers he had buried within, and a rush of shimmering release unfolded, making her buck against him. Her body quaked with a violent shudder, and she felt his own answer while her hand grew wet with his seed.

"You belong to me," Iain murmured against her mouth. "Just as I belong to you."

She was utterly sated and didn't believe it was even possible to move. Iain gave her a handkerchief, and she cleaned her palm while he helped her repair her clothing. She didn't doubt that, to anyone else, she would appear as if she'd allowed Iain the most intimate of liberties.

"I don't think I can return to that ballroom," she admitted. "I don't think I can walk anymore." She sent him a languid smile, but his expression had turned serious. For a while, they sat in silence, and she contemplated her answer to his proposal. Was it right to accept, when she was not the heiress he needed?

Moments later, the intrusion she'd been expecting took place. Someone unlocked the door, and it swung open. Lady Wolcroft was waiting for them, along with Lady Arnsbury and Lady Ashton. All three women entered the room, and Rose felt her cheeks flame.

Lady Ashton stared at Iain, and the frost in her eyes held quiet hatred. Instinctively, Rose reached for Iain's hand, but his face remained stoic. He behaved as if his mother was not here. But there was no doubting the tension in his posture and the invisible walls between them.

It was Lady Ashton who spoke first. "Whatever Iain might have said to you, Lady Rose, he spoke falsely."

"He has asked me to marry him." She tried to conjure up a smile, but the disapproval on the women's faces made that impossible.

Her grandmother's expression turned disappointed. "There was a time when I would have been glad to hear of this, Rose. But I am afraid that it cannot be."

She gripped Iain's hand, feeling as if a trap were closing in on her. "And why is that?"

Lady Ashton sent her a look of sympathy. "Because whatever Iain may have told you, he is not a legitimate heir. Nor is he the earl."

Chapter Sixteen

His mother's revelation was not a surprise, since Iain already knew about the night she'd been attacked by Seán O'Toole. But the look of hurt on Rose's face bothered him far more. In his mind, he hardly cared about whether or not he was the earl. Did it matter so much to her?

"The villain who fathered you is dead," Moira said. "And not a day goes by that I don't thank God for it."

"That's why my father died, wasn't it?" he asked quietly. "He found out about the attack and went to kill the tenant who hurt you."

"He wasn't your father," Moira corrected. "But yes. Aidan was filled with rage, and he shot the man who hurt me. And then that bastard didn't die fast enough. He killed my husband and now both of them are dead."

A single tear rolled down her face. "I should have rid myself of you when I learned I was with child. But it would have been a mortal sin." She stared at him, and in her eyes, he saw nothing but hatred. "I've suffered every day you lived. And I will not stand by and let you ruin another woman's life."

He expected Rose to speak, to say something to defend them. But her silence was damning. Though she continued to hold his hand, he could feel her grip loosening.

She didn't want him any more than his mother had. He should have expected it. And although he ought to let her go, now that she knew he was a bastard, damned if he wanted to. His only thread of honor had snapped in front of a truth he didn't want to face.

Iain stared at the women with no regrets for what he was about to do. He tightened his hand upon hers. "Most of the men and women in that ballroom will believe that I have compromised Lady Rose," he said coolly. "I intend to marry her, no matter what anyone says about me."

"I cannot allow that," Lady Wolcroft interrupted. "My granddaughter believed that you were an earl, a man who could provide a future for her. *I* believed that, too." To Moira, she admitted, "I am sorry for my interference. You never told any of us about . . . why you hid him from the world. I thought you were merely estranged."

"I kept Iain away so that this would never happen," his mother admitted. "I could not bring shame upon my husband."

It was as if he weren't in the room at all. Iain refused to remain silent while they discussed his future. Ignoring all of them, he turned back to Rose. "Before all this happened, I asked you to marry me. Have your feelings changed, now that you know the truth?"

The frozen expression on her face revealed her own doubts. "I feel as if I've stepped into the midst of a storm. I need a moment, Iain." With that, she let go of his hand.

The women closed in on her, and Lady Wolcroft sent him a dark look. "I think it's best if you leave now, Ashton." She opened the door and waited.

Iain didn't move. Instead, he locked his gaze upon Rose. "This is about what *you* want, *a ghrá*. They don't matter."

She still wouldn't look at him. But her hands were trembling as she gripped them together. "I—I need time to think."

It was as if he'd been imprisoned within panes of glass. He'd wanted to believe that she would be different. That she would love him enough to overlook the broken shards of the life he had.

He didn't want to leave her here with these vultures who would tell her how to live her life and what to do now. But when he saw her pale expression, his worst fears were confirmed.

Love wasn't enough to overcome the revelation that he was worth nothing. She'd wanted an earl, not a bastard. And no matter how much it broke him, the right thing was to let her go.

Rose had barely slept since the evening of the party. While her grandmother had been upset about the scandal, her own emotions felt numb and closed off from the world. For a moment, she had let herself believe that Iain loved her, that they would find a way to be together.

He wasn't the Earl of Ashton, according to his mother. And from the look on his face, he hadn't appeared surprised at Moira's revelation. Had Iain known he was not the earl all along? Had he come to England, trying to trick an heiress into marrying him so he could seize an innocent woman's fortune? After all the weeks they'd spent together, she couldn't imagine him doing such a thing. It wasn't the sort of man he was. His devotion to Ashton was real, whether or not the earldom belonged to him.

She had suspected the possibility of him being illegitimate when he'd spoken of his mother's hatred. And yet, she had set aside her doubts, trusting him when he'd said he was the earl.

She didn't know what to believe. She needed to confront him and find out the truth. But the thought of losing Iain was breaking her heart into pieces.

Today, she'd chosen a demure gown the color of a thunderstorm. The dove gray suited her somber mood. She took the stairs slowly, gripping the banister. When she neared the first landing, she saw her mother bidding farewell to Cain Sinclair, along with his wife, Margaret, and their youngest daughter, Evangeline. No one had told her that the Sinclairs had come to call.

"Evangeline, can you stay and talk with me awhile?" she called out to her best friend. Right now, she needed someone to give her advice. Her friend's honesty might help her put everything into perspective.

"Of course." After bidding her parents farewell, Evangeline asked, "Would you like me to go up to your room, or shall we sit in the drawing room?"

"I'm almost downstairs, so let's go into the drawing room." She held on to the railing as she eased each foot down the stairs, feeling the ache in her legs. Though each day was easier, her muscles burned with the exertion.

Her mother was beaming as she opened the drawing room door for them. "He's coming home tomorrow, darling."

"Who is coming home?" She glanced at Evangeline, who shrugged.

"George, of course."

Rose's smile grew strained, and she exchanged a look with her friend. "Give us a moment, won't you?" Evangeline acquiesced and stepped into the hall.

Her mother's face was radiant, and she sighed happily. "I knew it would work. I gave him all our money, and now he's coming home."

"Mother, it can't be. Father has been . . . gone for years." Her throat constricted with fear, and she added, "How much of our money did you give away?"

Lady Penford's expression grew distant, and she strode to the door. "He told me we would have profits enough for strong dowries for all of you. You can marry your earl, Rose. I do like him."

"Mother, listen to me." She caught Lady Penford by the shoulders, trying to make sense of it. "Are you saying that we do have money?"

"He's coming home soon. His ship may arrive any day now." Her mother's face was filled with joy. "I've missed him so much."

A strange thought occurred to her, and she probed further. "Did you mean James is coming home?"

"Yes. And George, of course. Both of them will be home in time to see you married." She raised an eyebrow, and her mood shifted to disapproval. "I did hear about what happened at Lady Arnsbury's party the other night. I do hope Lord Ashton is getting a special license, as we speak."

Her mother's conversation kept shifting from one topic to another, and Rose could hardly tell what was real—especially regarding news of her brother.

"I don't know if I'm going to marry Lord Ashton, Mother. I have no dowry." She ought to regret what she'd done, but the truth was, she didn't. No matter how scandal shadowed her now or how little money there was, her heart still belonged to Iain.

"Yes, you have a dowry. And everything will be fine. I've seen to that." Lady Penford's smile brightened again. "My little birds will fly their nests, and all will be well." She squeezed Rose's hand and said, "Now, I am feeling tired. I want to rest."

The moment her mother was gone, Rose sank into a chair. Evangeline stepped inside the room and asked, "Did you still want me to stay?"

"Please." She rubbed at her temples and said, "My mother is having a difficult day."

Evangeline nodded. "Yes. Your grandmother asked my family to help her, and that's why we were here. She gave permission for my father to assist your land steward. He'll find out what has happened with your finances, and I know he's made some investments already to help. You needn't worry."

Deep inside, a flutter of hope emerged. "Truly?" The thought of a successful businessman like Mr. Sinclair and his wife intervening and helping her family was a welcome one.

"Yes." Evangeline closed the door and pulled up a chair. "But that's not why you wanted to talk to me, was it?"

She shook her head. "It's Lord Ashton."

A slight flicker of disappointment crossed Evangeline's face. "I thought that might be what you wanted to speak with me about. But the earl only has eyes for you."

"I truly was hoping the two of you would end up together." She felt sorry that her matchmaking had backfired in such a way.

Her friend settled against her chair. "I'm used to it, Rose. Men never have eyes for me—only my father's wealth. Sometimes I wish I could meet a man who believed I had nothing."

"Well, I *am* sorry. It wasn't my intention to steal him away from you."

"Nonsense. There was nothing between us, for he's in love with you. And all London is talking of how he seduced you in the library."

Rose was about to blurt out, *He did not*—but then realized that yes, he'd done exactly that. She buried her face in her hands. "What am I to do, Evangeline?"

"Marry him, of course. The talk will die down. It did for my parents when they wed." She got up from her chair and crossed the room. There was still a leftover tray of sandwiches and tarts from the tea earlier with the Sinclairs. Evangeline picked it up and brought it over to share.

"Unless . . . you don't want to marry him?"

Rose let out a heavy sigh. "I do want to marry him, though. In spite of what everyone thinks." She poured out the entire story to her best friend, knowing she could trust Evangeline not to say anything. "Am I a fool to still want him?"

Her friend thought a moment. "Even if he was not the earl's son, he was born within the time the countess was married. She never claimed he was illegitimate, did she?"

"No. At least, not yet."

"Then, legally he *is* the earl, blood or not." Evangeline took a sandwich and eyed her. "The only question is, do you love him? Do you want to marry him?"

Rose didn't answer her friend at first. If love meant that being without Iain was a physical ache, then yes. In spite of everything, she *did* want him.

"Let me say it another way," Evangeline offered. "If I told you *I* was going to marry him—"

"I would want to claw your eyes out." Rose took a sandwich from the tray and ate it. "I suppose that answers my own question."

Her friend smiled warmly. "Don't worry, Rose. Go to Lord Ashton, and you'll find a way to be with him. Whereas I shall remain a spinster, content to bury myself in poetry and books." She smiled happily at the thought and took another bite of her sandwich.

"And what if James returns?" Rose teased.

Evangeline coughed and sputtered, whacking herself in the chest. "Lord Penford? Are you mad?"

"He might be returning. Unless, as my mother claims, it's the ghost of my father, back from the dead." It was a morbid comment, but sometimes it was easier to handle her mother's eccentricity with humor.

"Forgive me, but your brother left me and went to another country for the better part of a year without so much as a by your leave. He is a horrid man, and I wouldn't let him court me if the alternative was being eaten alive by eels."

The vehemence in her friend's voice was stronger than she'd imagined. "Well then. I'll tell him not to call on you."

Evangeline bit her lip and smiled. "I much prefer to plot and scheme on your behalf. I could go with you to Lord Ashton's townhouse to distract his mother and sisters."

She thought about it and said, "No, as nice as that sounds, I must speak with him myself." Having her friend here had lifted her spirits.

But even more, she longed to see Iain. Only then could she separate the truth from lies. And when she saw his face, she hoped to discover whether there was any hope for a future together.

"I want you to leave London."

Iain glanced up from the desk. It was well after midnight, and while he didn't know what had inspired his mother's fury at this hour, it didn't surprise him. There was no sign of his sisters, and he supposed they had retired for the night.

Iain stood, his neck aching from the hours he'd spent pouring over the investments and potential profits. "Of course you want me to leave. But I was here first, if you recall."

"The house doesn't belong to you. Nor do you have any right to behave like the earl. You aren't the heir to Ashton. Michael was. You must depart from London so you don't harm your sisters' chances of finding good husbands. Go anywhere else, except Ashton. And if you dare to set foot upon my land, I will—"

"You'll do what?" he interjected. "Have me shot for trespassing?" Anger flowed through him, roaring with the force of twenty-five years of being made to feel unworthy. He crossed the room and stood before her. "I am the only man capable of looking after Ashton. It's my home, and the tenants trust me."

"There *are* no tenants!" she cried out. "They've all left. We have nothing. Nothing, do you understand?"

She was wrong, for there were a few tenants who had stayed at Ashton. But he realized this was about her fear and loss of pride. Moira had taken his sisters to another ball tonight, and it was likely that they were ashamed of their poverty in the face of all the wealthy families. She wanted someone to blame for their misfortune, and Iain was the likely scapegoat.

He took a moment to gather command of his own temper. "I understand that you blame me for the famine and the rotting potatoes. You think that if Michael were alive and I were dead, everything would be different. But you're wrong." He knew that arguing with her was a mistake, one he might regret. His position was tenuous, and if she renounced him publicly, telling everyone he was not the earl, it would cause more trouble.

"You can curse me all you like," he told her. "But the truth is, I would lay down my life to save Ashton. I'm the only man who would."

Her posture remained ramrod straight, her hatred palpable. "Then go back, if that's what you're wanting. Try to save it, if you believe you can. But you'll fail." A sudden gleam came into her eyes, and she added, "You might as well be gone by morning, for there's nothing left for you here. Lady Rose is not going to wed you. Her grandmother won't allow it."

She doesn't want to wed a bastard like you.

Of course she wouldn't. The broken look of shock in her eyes was still branded upon his mind. She'd been devastated to learn that he wasn't a true earl—only a poor substitute for his brother. He'd wanted to talk to her again, but he didn't know what to say.

A numb feeling settled in his stomach, but he faced his mother. "The decision is hers to make."

"Don't be ridiculous. If she married you, her family would cut her off without a cent. She would grow to despise you." His mother shook her head. "No, they will find someone else for her. It will be a swift wedding, you can be sure. Especially after the gossip you caused."

The idea of Rose marrying any other man was unthinkable. He'd sooner disrupt the wedding and steal the bride away.

"Now that she knows you're a bastard, she doesn't want you," Moira continued. "Let her go. Let her wed a man who can bring her happiness, if you truly care about her."

He did care, more than he'd realized. But he wasn't about to run away from Rose. He'd sent her a note this morning, asking her if they could meet and talk about what had happened.

"I cannot leave London yet." Not only because of Rose, but also because he and Cain Sinclair had begun working together. The businessman had asked him to help interview a few Irishwomen who were talented seamstresses. They spoke Irish Gaelic, and their English was limited.

And though Sinclair could have hired any number of men to translate, it gave Iain a means of repaying the Scot for the supplies and food he was donating to Ashton.

"You don't belong here," Moira insisted. "You should go. Leave Ashton behind and make a new life for yourself somewhere else."

That was what she wanted, he knew. But he refused to walk away. "I made a promise to Michael. And that promise, I'll be keeping." Over the past week, he'd begun gathering the supplies Sinclair had ordered. He planned to sail back to Ireland with livestock, grain, and other necessities.

"The estate isn't truly yours. Not by birthright."

"Why do you care?" he demanded. "If I restore it and give you, Sybil, and Colleen a place to live—why does it matter whether or not I was born from the earl? Do you really want a distant cousin to come and claim the title, someone who won't listen to a word you say?"

"You don't listen, either," she pointed out. But it did seem that she was considering his argument.

Iain softened his tone and offered, "There is no reason why you could not continue living here in London. The three of you can stay as long as you want." She seemed to think about it, and he added, "You need not return to Ashton until I have rebuilt it. There's no cause to face bad memories."

Moira's face turned cold. "I suppose it's fitting that the estate should fail. It's been cursed ever since Aidan died."

It was clear that she believed the superstition. And before she turned her face aside, he caught a glimpse of her tears. God help him, he hated seeing a woman cry, even one who despised him.

"I will take responsibility for Ashton," Iain offered. "Just as I've done over the past year." It was his home, the only one he'd ever known. And whether or not he was the earl, he would never stand aside and let it crumble.

Moira remained silent, but he knew better than to take that for her assent. The tension stretched between them, and he voiced another question that had troubled him. "Was it true, what you said? That my father was killed by the man who . . . attacked you?"

The color fled her face, but she nodded. "They both died that night." She leaned against the wall, lowering her head.

Moira's earlier words haunted him—that she'd wanted to rid herself of him before he was born. And yet, he dared to suggest another possibility. "Is there any chance at all that the earl fathered me?"

He wanted to believe that there was a grain of hope for legitimacy. But the moment he spoke the words, she was already shaking her head. "No. It wasn't him." She paused and continued, "Your eyes are green—not blue, like his were. And mine are brown. I have no doubt who your father was, may he rot in hell."

There was nothing Iain could say to that, so he approached her and opened the door to the study. "Go and get some sleep."

Moira let out a sigh, but didn't leave yet. For a long moment, she studied him, the worry creased on her face. In her eyes, he saw the years of sorrow that had hardened her. There had been a time when he'd badly wanted her approval. But he'd come to accept that nothing would ever change. They would never be mother and son, but if his investments with Cain Sinclair paid off, he might provide for her and his sisters. And one day, there might be peace between them.

Chapter Seventeen

Rose's nerves tightened, as she reread Iain's note. He had asked to pay a call on her, but she preferred to go to him. After the way she'd reacted in shock at the revelation that he was illegitimate, she thought it better if she humbled herself.

She'd missed him more than she'd thought possible. And although there were a thousand reasons why they should not stay together, she needed to see him. More than that, she wanted to feel his arms around her, holding her close. Last night, she had hardly slept, for she'd been going over all the words she wanted to say.

There were only three that counted: *I love you.*

But would it be enough? He'd already said he didn't think she was strong enough to endure Ireland. And now that her grandmother was against a match between them, it felt as if the outside world was locking away any chances of happiness.

This morning, she had chosen a sage-green morning gown with long sleeves and a bell curve to the skirts. The color was one of her favorites, and she waited while Hattie finished tending to her hair.

A light knock sounded at the door, and her sister opened it without waiting. "Rose, oh Rose! You'll never believe what's happened!" Lily was almost breathless with excitement. From the joy on her face, Rose had no doubt what it was.

"Matthew has returned from India," she guessed.

"And James, as well! I have a letter that both of them are on their way home. I found it on Mother's dressing table, and it was from two weeks ago." Her sister was practically dancing with excitement. "They might arrive any day now."

The thought of her brother's return brought about a wave of joy. Rose's eyes filled up with tears. "Thank God."

She stood, and Lily hugged her, smiling. "You don't know how long I've waited for him to come back."

When her sister pulled away, Rose found the slender chain around Lily's throat and pulled it gently. At the end of the chain was a small ring. "Will you marry him now?"

A smile broke over Lily's face. "I hope so. It's as if a lost part of me has returned. You cannot know what that's like."

But Lily was wrong. Rose *did* know what it was to feel empty, as if she couldn't bear to go through each day without the man she loved. "I am happy for you. And I hope that you are very happy together." She leaned against her sister, walking toward the door. "Mother and I are going to pay a call upon Lord Ashton today after breakfast."

Her sister squeezed her hand. "Go to him. I am planning to pay a call upon Lady Arnsbury. I hope . . . I hope all is well with Matthew."

"When he sees you, it will be." She followed Lily outside the bedroom and into the hall. It took some time to descend the stairs, but she was determined to manage it alone. By the time she reached the drawing room, she was slightly out of breath.

Her mother was waiting, and there was an air of excitement about her. "Are you ready?"

"Yes. Thank you for accompanying me." Although she'd been wary of bringing Iris along, it did seem that her mother was having a good day. She might provide a buffer, in case Lady Ashton tried to interfere.

For a moment, her heart ached as she took her mother's arm. It was like having Iris back again, and she resolved to enjoy every moment she could.

"You needn't worry, darling. Everything will be all right now. You'll see." Her mother guided her outside to the waiting carriage and helped her inside.

All during the ride, Iris made bright conversation, as if she was enjoying the outing. Rose answered, though inwardly, her stomach was churning with fear. And when they reached Lord Ashton's townhouse, her heart was beating in time to the horses' hooves.

"You look pale," Lady Penford said. "Are you certain you want to pay a call on him?" A furrow lined her mother's brow, and she added, "He really ought to have come to you."

"Not after the way I treated him," Rose said. She wanted Iain to know that she did love him, in spite of everything. He deserved that much.

The carriage pulled to a stop, and the pair of them disembarked with the help of a footman. With every step, her pulse pounded harder. What would he say when he saw her? What if he wasn't there?

Her mother gave her a reassuring smile as their footman knocked upon the door. They were invited inside, but it was Lady Ashton who met them. A startled look crossed her face, before it was replaced with a genuine smile. "Why, Iris. I haven't seen you in years."

Her mother beamed and embraced Lady Ashton. "I am so glad to see you, Moira. I believe you have met my daughter, Rose."

At that, Lady Ashton's smile grew strained. "I suppose you are here to see Iain."

"Indeed we are," Iris answered. "Would you tell him that we've come to call?"

"He is not here at the moment, but you are welcome to wait." She guided them into a small sitting room. There were few furnishings and no paintings upon the walls. The sparse surroundings only emphasized the family's financial troubles.

"Forgive me, Lady Rose," Moira apologized, "but I feel you have been a victim in all this. My son took grievous advantage of you."

Rose sat down, resting her gloved hands in her lap. "Lady Ashton, your son helped me learn to walk again. We became very close, and I do love him very much. Whether he is the earl or not."

Moira's face tightened, and she turned back to Iris. "Your daughter deserves so much more than this. I am so sorry for the scandal. Mrs. Everett was responsible for locking them in together, so I've learned. But nonetheless, I must caution both of you. Iain let you believe he was someone he was not. He has no inheritance to offer, nothing at all. It would be best if you walked away before making a terrible mistake."

"Love is never a mistake," Lady Penford said softly. "And I support whatever decision my daughters want. Just as you should support your son."

"I cannot think of him as my son," Lady Ashton insisted. "He never should have been born." The hatred in her voice startled Rose, and she reached out for her mother's hand. But Lady Penford faced the matron with serenity.

"Every child is a blessing. And if I had a man like Iain Donovan as my son, I would count myself fortunate indeed." Iris smiled. "Now, tell me about your daughters while we wait upon him."

"What do you want to know?" came a young woman's voice from beyond the door. The two women entered the sitting room, and Rose recognized them as Iain's sisters, Colleen and Sybil. Both had long dark hair, and the elder sister appeared ready to do battle.

"Were you eavesdropping?" Lady Ashton frowned at the two girls.

"Of course we were," the young woman admitted. Her gaze narrowed upon Rose. "What exactly are your intentions toward my brother? Were you intending to cause a scandal and force him into marriage?"

"Sybil, you were not invited to this conversation," her mother said coolly. "Both you and Colleen can return to your embroidery."

"I loathe sewing," Colleen muttered. Rose guessed she was near seventeen, while Sybil was a year or two older. She remembered that Iain had spoken of both of them with affection. It sounded as if they had come to defend him, and she thought it best to reassure them.

"Mrs. Everett decided to lock us in the library together," she admitted. "It was not a choice, really."

Colleen gaped before she collected herself. "Well. I should hope not." She eyed Rose with a warning. "I should tell you, if you break my brother's heart, I will rip yours from your body."

Rose bit back a smile. "I don't intend to break his heart." *But he holds the power to break mine.* "I need to speak with him. Do you know when he will return?"

"I thought I saw his carriage approaching," Sybil said. "I should think he will be here very soon."

Lady Ashton intervened again and guided the girls back to the doorway. "Go back to your rooms, and do not interfere with matters that do not concern you."

But Colleen would not be deterred. She studied Rose with a fierce expression and added, "Iain is a good man, no matter what our mother says."

Only after the young women were gone did Lady Ashton return to her seat. Her composure had been shaken, but she calmed herself. Then she faced Rose and said, "You don't deserve the life Iain would give you. And believe me when I say, you would never be a countess."

"I never cared about a title," Rose said.

Her mother leaned forward in her chair, and interrupted. "Moira, I realize that you are unlikely to bestow your blessing upon my daughter and your son, if they choose to marry. However, you should be aware that we have a great many friends in London. Friends who could be very helpful to your daughters, by introducing them to the right men. We are good friends with the Duchess of Worthingstone, not to mention Lady Castledon."

Rose's throat tightened as she realized what her mother was doing. Not threatening Lady Ashton . . . but offering her an alliance.

The countess didn't miss the insinuation, and she paled. In the end, she lifted her shoulders in a shrug. "I am still surprised that you are not against this match, considering how little Iain has to offer."

"He loves my daughter," Lady Penford countered. "And I rather think his heart is worth more than all the gold in England."

Iain walked into his townhouse, and was nearly attacked by his sister.

"You're back!" Colleen squealed, embracing him hard. "You'll never guess who's here." Before he could get a word in, she burst out, "Lady Rose and her mother. Did you know that Lady Penford went to school with our mother? They've been talking for nearly an hour. And she's promised to help introduce us to suitable men in London. Lady Penford knows *everyone*."

The moment she spoke Rose's name, he hurried toward the sitting room. He didn't know what tales Moira had been filling her head with, but he saw that Colleen was right. Rose was surrounded by her mother and Lady Ashton. He recalled Lady Penford's earlier fear of invisible wolves, and it rather seemed true at this moment.

"Lady Rose," he said, his eyes locking upon her. God, she stole his breath away. She was wearing a green gown, and the color favored the red tints in her brown hair. When she saw him, she didn't smile. Instead, her gaze was searching.

"Why don't we leave them alone to talk, Moira?" Lady Penford suggested. She stood from her chair and walked over to Iain, patting his shoulder. "I'll wish you luck, my dear. Rose, I will await you in our carriage."

Moira said nothing but murmured a farewell and departed, leaving the door open. Iain could hardly believe his mother had obeyed Lady Penford's wishes, but she appeared thoroughly confused.

Rose stood from her chair, and every word fled Iain's brain when he was alone with her. He couldn't tell her that he'd barely slept these past two nights or that he was trying to find a way to earn money for both of them. He drank in the sight of her, hoping to God that she had not given up on them.

"Rose, I—" he began.

But she cut off any words when she stumbled across the room and flung herself into his arms. He gripped her hard, so relieved to have her in his embrace. There were no words to say what was in his heart. It was all meaningless. All he could blurt out was, "I'm sorry for all this." He buried his face in her hair. "I missed you."

Her arms were around his neck, and she whispered, "I need you, Iain. So much more than I ever realized."

He framed her face in his hands, and she closed her eyes, covering his hands with her own. He brushed a kiss across her lips, and she pulled him nearer, deepening the kiss. The embrace joined them together in a way that felt right. She held him close, feeling as if the broken pieces of herself had come back together again.

"God, how I love you, Rose." He tasted the salt of her tears, but he wouldn't let her go. "Does this mean you're going to marry me?" he murmured.

"Yes." She kissed him again, and he wished he had a ring to give her. "And whether you're the Earl of Ashton or Lord of the Ashes doesn't matter. You're the man who stood by me and taught me to walk again. I love you."

He reached below her hips and lifted her up, smiling at her. "I will find a way to give you the life you've dreamed of, Rose. Even if it means we have to live apart for a while."

Her expression turned wary. "We are *not* living apart, Iain."

"You're daft if you think I'm taking you back to a place where there is no food." Slowly, he lowered her back to stand before him. He couldn't stop touching her, and he rubbed the small of her back.

"We will argue about it later. But I do have news that may affect my dowry. Evangeline said that her father will help us sort through our finances and set them straight. We don't know how much money my mother gave away, but—"

At that, Iain's smile broadened. "Actually, I did learn what she did with the rents." He'd spent the morning with Cain Sinclair, and it was then that he'd discovered the truth. "Apparently, she didn't give the money to an Irishman. It was a Scotsman. She gave the rents over to Sinclair a month ago, so he could invest them for her. They made a fine profit for you and your family."

Rose shook her head and a laugh escaped her. "So I do have a dowry, after all. Not that it matters anymore."

He leaned to kiss her again, and added, "You could be penniless, and I wouldn't care, Rose. I'm marrying you because I love you. Because you make me want to become a better man. And because I cannot be living without you."

She leaned in and rested her nose against his. "I love you, Iain. Earl or not."

"I'll be the earl in name," he agreed. "There will be a great deal of work before I can restore Ashton. But with you at my side, I think we can manage it." He stroked his thumb against her palm, and she let out a soft sigh. Then he came up behind her and drew both arms around her waist. Her body nestled against his, in the most natural feeling in the world. "You are the bride I'm meant to have. Ever since you threatened me with a rake."

She let out a soft laugh. "You're fortunate that I didn't use it against you."

He pressed his mouth against her temple. "I need to speak with your mother and ask permission to marry you."

"We can go now." Rose smiled and took his hand.

Iain led her back to the hallway, only to find that his sisters had been eavesdropping again. Colleen sent him a dreamy smile that nearly made him laugh.

But when they opened the front door, the carriage was gone. Lady Rose's smile faded. "She . . . said she was going to wait."

Iain squeezed her hand. "Stay here, and I will find your mother. She may have gone home again."

"I am going with you," Rose insisted. "She's *my* mother, and if she isn't there—" Her voice broke off, revealing the sudden fear.

"I will find her," Iain insisted. "Her carriage can't be far."

"I am not staying behind. Not now." The iron look in her eyes warned that she would not be deterred.

And yet, he was well aware that this search would lead them from place to place with no guarantee of finding Lady Penford. He lifted her palms to his mouth. "Wouldn't you rather stay here and wait for me to bring her home?"

"Not in the slightest," she insisted. "*When* you find her, she will be very upset. If she sees me, it will calm her."

He leaned in and kissed her hard. "We will find her again. This, I promise."

She met his gaze with a single nod. "We will go together. And pray God, we'll find her."

Rose clenched her hands together, trying to calm her wild nerves. They drove around the nearby streets first, but there was no sign of the carriage. Then they had traveled back home, only to learn that Lady Penford was not there. Heaven only knew where she was now. Rose had let herself believe that her mother would come to no harm, since Iris had been so lucid today.

And yet, she'd known how quickly her mother's mood could transform. She couldn't stop blaming herself. Beside her, Iain's expression was grim. She was fighting back tears, so afraid that they might not find her mother. There were so many places she could have gone.

They drove for nearly an hour, past all their acquaintances and friends, while Rose tried to think of where her mother might be. Iris hadn't gone on foot, since the carriage was still missing. That, at least, was somewhat safer.

"Dear God," she breathed, as it suddenly came to her. Her mother had been talking about George for days now, claiming that his ship would soon arrive. "Iain, I think I know where she is. Take us toward the East India Docks."

He started to shake his head. "Rose, I can't be taking you there. It's no place for a lady. I'll have to take you home first."

"We haven't time. My mother could be there now, lost and in danger." She told him about how Iris had been expecting James's ship. "Please, Iain. We have to hurry." He urged the horses faster, taking the curricle across town toward the waterfront.

And all the while, Rose continued to search for a sign of her mother's carriage, hoping they would find her before she came to any harm.

It was late afternoon when they reached the water's edge. Rose leaned closer to Iain, feeling exhausted and afraid.

"Whatever happens, do not leave my side," he warned.

She raised a handkerchief to her nose, trying to blot out the harsh odors. "I wouldn't dare."

They continued down the narrow street, and she saw men and women huddled together. One woman held a child's hand, and she eyed Rose with interest. One by one, she saw more people beginning to follow them.

"Iain," she murmured, nodding toward the gathering crowd. "We need to find her quickly."

His expression grew wary, and he cursed in Gaelic beneath his breath. "I know it."

For the next few minutes, she gripped his hand while they rode through the streets. Her spine prickled with unease, and she wished Iain had a weapon to defend himself. As it was, he had only his fists.

Right now, his demeanor was nothing like an English gentleman. Upon his face was the hard stare of a man who would kill any man who dared to harm her. She saw the outline of his muscles as his hands gripped the reins, his eyes searching the crowd.

"There." He nodded toward the far end of the docks, where the figure of an older woman stood near one of the ships. Men were busy unloading a cargo of tea and spices, and the woman continued to stare at the water as if she didn't see them. Her bonnet was untied, and she was gripping her hands.

But before they could reach her, someone grabbed Rose by the arm. She gasped, and caught the glint of a knife. Iain shoved her back, just as the man slashed it downward.

He dodged the blade, but another man pulled her from the carriage while Iain was distracted by his assailant.

Rose fought hard, screaming and struggling to escape. She jabbed her elbow against the man, and he dropped her onto the cobblestone street. Her hands broke her fall, but her legs tangled up in her skirts. On the opposite side, she saw Iain fighting against three more opponents.

"Rose!" he called out.

"I'm all right." She tried to get up, but her knees buckled beneath her. Fear overwhelmed her, and when the man seized her again, she reacted out of instinct and slammed her fists into him. He let out a howl, and she realized she'd struck him between his legs.

I won't be weak. And I won't let anyone harm the ones I love.

Despite her lack of strength, she was enraged that these men would dare to attack them. She refused to remain on the ground, useless. She started to get onto her hands and knees and spied the riding crop upon the stones. The moment she touched it, she felt resolution rising within her. Iain had once predicted that she wasn't strong enough to survive a rougher life in Ireland—but he was wrong.

She could cast aside a lady's manners and defend herself when needed. She would stand tall and fight alongside the man she loved.

Rose got to her feet and when someone else tried to grab her, she sliced the riding crop against his face. Before he could reach for her wrist, Iain seized the man and tossed him to the ground. "Are you all right, *a ghrá*?"

She nodded. Blood stained his white shirt, and his sleeve was torn. The look in his eyes was wild, and before she could say another word, he shoved her behind him while he dropped into a fighting stance. Iain moved like a wolf when he fought. His fists crunched against a man's face, then he punched another opponent in the ribs. Several larger men tried to attack him, but when Iain held up a knife covered in blood, the crowd scattered.

"Anyone else?" he demanded.

Rose went to stand beside him, the crop in her hand. She felt as if her gentility had been stripped away and in its place was pure survival. If anyone dared to harm them, she would fight alongside Iain.

"Let's go and get Mother," she murmured.

After that, the crowd dispersed. Iain helped her back into the carriage. Then they drove the carriage over toward the dock, where Iris was wandering. Iain pulled the vehicle to a stop, and helped Rose disembark.

Her mother was pacing back and forth, and when Rose touched her arm, Iris let out a shriek. Then recognition slid over her face, followed by confusion. "Rose, what are you doing in a place like this? You shouldn't be here." Her mother's hands were ice cold, and she was trembling.

Rose exchanged a look with Iain, who removed his coat and put it around Iris's shoulders. They guided her back to the carriage, and Rose said, "Come, Mother. We need to go home."

"But James's ship. It's here, don't you see?" Iris pointed toward a Blackwall frigate, which was swaying in the evening twilight. Three tall masts rose from the ship, and the sails were tied down. "I need to know if my son is all right."

Rose held her mother's hand and waited a moment. "If James was on board, he's not anymore, Mother. All the passengers must have left hours ago. He might be waiting for us at home, even now."

But her mother would not be dissuaded. "I thought I heard his voice, Rose. I've been waiting for him. Won't you ask and see if he's there?" Agitation and worry edged her tone.

Iain glanced at both of them, and Rose shook her head. The risk was too grave. "Not just now, Mother."

Before they could help her into the carriage, Iris broke free and hurried toward the ship. Rose was about to follow, but Iain caught her hand. "Wait."

There, on board the ship, stood her brother. He looked as if he hadn't shaved or cut his hair in months, but Iris was laughing and weeping as she embraced him.

"He's alive." Rose could hardly believe it. James looked as if he'd been to the ends of the earth, but seeing him here made her throat constrict with happiness. An invisible burden of worry lifted from her shoulders, and Iain helped her up the gangplank.

Her brother embraced her, and after a good hug, Rose pulled back, wrinkling her nose. "James, I do love you, but you need a bath."

"I am so thankful you are home," Iris murmured.

Her brother's gaze passed over to Iain, and he offered a questioning look. Rose smiled and said, "James, this is Iain Donovan, the Earl of Ashton. The man I am going to marry."

Hours later, Rose felt as if her life had been upended and scattered like marbles rolling across the floor. James was home now, but only after he'd delivered Matthew Larkspur, Lord Arnsbury, back to his own residence. It wasn't clear what had happened to his best friend, but Rose had caught whispers of imprisonment and torture. James had made her swear not to tell Lily.

"I don't want her to intrude upon his reunion with his family. She needs to let him acclimate to being home again. He's not the same man she remembers." James's tone held weariness, and he sent a kindly smile to their mother, who was still holding his hand.

"She'll go to him, no matter what you say."

Her brother shrugged. "Not until the morning. Grant the man a night of sleeping in his own bed." He eyed Iain. "Just as you should go to your own bed. And not my sister's."

"Do *not* act like a beast, James." She didn't like his insinuation.

In answer, Iain took Rose's fingers in his, rubbing them lightly. "In due time, *a chara*."

The sensation sent an unexpected ripple of warmth within her. She stood from her chair and was startled when her knees swayed.

Iain caught her and held her steady. "I can see myself out, Rose."

She knew she should say yes. But there was still blood upon his shirt, and his lip had swollen up from where he'd been struck at the docks. She felt the need to tend his wounds and delay his departure a little longer.

She took his arm as they left the drawing room. Iain started to walk down the hallway, but she redirected his path to the servants' staircase. His face turned questioning, but she guided him to follow her up the narrow stairs until they reached an empty room. It held a small basin, and she brought him inside.

"Sit down, and let me wash away the blood," she bade him.

"This isn't wise, Rose." Even so, he obeyed and sat upon the wooden stool.

She knew that. But she poured water into the basin and pulled out a handkerchief, soaking it. She touched it to the dried blood on his face, wishing she could wipe away the pain as easily. "You were hurt this afternoon."

His expression was rigid, and she tried to be gentle. Then she leaned down and touched her mouth to his in a soft kiss.

"I would never let any man hurt you, Rose. I would die first."

"I know. And that is why I am going back to Ireland with you." She stroked his hair, and he pulled her onto his lap. "When that man pulled me out of the carriage—"

"—I was going to kill him," Iain finished.

She touched his mouth with her finger. "No. What I meant was that I realized something about myself. When I saw those men fighting you, I wanted to tear them to pieces." She smiled at the incongruity of it all. "I will be fine in Ireland, despite all the hardships. Because it means I will see you each day. No matter what happens, I will love you. And I am strong enough to face anything, so long as I am with you."

"My rose has thorns when she needs them." He kissed her gently and traced the edge of her cheek. "I will be glad to make you my wife, *a ghrá.* And I promise that I will work myself to the bone, to give you everything you want."

She wrapped her arms around him and held him close. "Iain, you needn't bother. For everything I want is right here."

Ireland

One month later

"Rose, you look beautiful," Lily proclaimed. Her sister bent down and smoothed an invisible wrinkle from the ivory gown. Lady Ashton had loaned Rose a long veil made of Irish lace. The woman had been quiet and pensive ever since she had returned to Ashton.

Honestly, Rose was surprised she had come, but perhaps it was because her daughters had insisted. There was a truce between them—likely because Lady Ashton knew that Rose's connections in London were stronger than her own. Both her mother and grandmother had already begun introducing her daughters to wealthy gentlemen, and Moira had accepted the help.

Both Sybil and Colleen had thought the wedding should be a grand affair, but Rose simply wanted the people to have a feast and a reason to celebrate.

There was no doubt that Ashton lay in ruins, and the people were starving. Never in her life had she witnessed such hardships. But the tenants had welcomed her, so grateful for the food and supplies donated by the Sinclair family and those she and Iain had purchased with her dowry. When the news had spread among their neighbors, more than a hundred people returned.

"It's almost time for the wedding," Lily interrupted. "Are you ready?" They had decided to hold the ceremony outside, so all the tenants could witness their union.

She nodded. But then, Lady Ashton spoke up. "May I speak with you a moment?" The woman's expression held wariness, as if she was uncertain whether Rose would agree.

"Of course." She nodded for her sister and mother to go on without her.

The door closed behind them, and Rose waited for Moira to begin. The woman's face was flushed, and it seemed that she didn't know how to start. She wore a gown of deep mauve, and her dark hair was pulled into a knot. There were no jewels, for she had sold most of them to pay for her daughters' Season. But even so, she was a beautiful woman.

Rose smiled at her and touched the long veil. "I wanted to thank you for this veil. It's exquisite."

Lady Ashton's troubled look did not diminish. "It belonged to my grandmother."

Rose reached out a hand to her. "I am very glad to wear something that belonged to Iain's family." Although Moira had appeared uneasy about the wedding, the gesture was a welcome peace offering. Rose felt certain that in time, she could build a good relationship with her mother-in-law.

The matron lowered her gaze but took her hand. Rose squeezed the cold fingers and added, "I know that you have suffered a great deal, and nothing I say can ever change it. But I hope that you will find a way to live in peace with Iain and leave the past behind."

Moira appeared worried. "I don't know if I can. Not after all that's happened."

"Go to him," Rose said softly. "He will want to see you."

"I'm not so very sure about that."

"He will forgive you," she insisted. "You have time to make it right. Go now, before the wedding."

Rose didn't know what had caused the woman to have a change of heart, but there was regret in Lady Ashton's demeanor. And whether or not Iain was born from the earl or another man, she strongly believed they could begin again. On impulse, she hugged the woman.

And Lady Ashton offered a tentative smile.

Iain could not have been more surprised to see Lady Ashton at his door. "Have you come to stop the wedding, then?" His words were half-teasing, but the sadness in her eyes caught him unawares.

When she shook her head, he added, "Then why have you come?"

His mother was holding something behind her back, and eventually, she withdrew it. Iain saw that it was a small oil painting of a man and his wife.

"When I went into the attic to find the veil for Rose, I discovered this painting," she began. "This is your great-grandfather, the third Earl of Ashton."

He wasn't certain what to make of it, but then the weight of her words struck him. She'd said it was *his* great-grandfather.

"He had green eyes," Moira whispered. "You can see it for yourself."

Iain accepted the portrait, and when he took a closer look at the man, his blood ran cold. It was like looking into a mirror. There was no doubt at all that he was a blood relation to this man. He set down the portrait, and the hair stood up on his arms.

Moira spoke first. "You have to understand how broken I was after I was violated by a man who was not my husband. And because Aidan sought revenge, he died. I found myself with a living reminder of that night." Tears rolled down her cheeks. "Every time I looked at you, I could only think of the violence. I couldn't see that you were a gift that Aidan left to me, so I wouldn't be alone."

Moira turned away, her shoulders slumped forward. He couldn't answer her, though he knew what she was saying. She finished with, "There is nothing I can say to undo the years I mistreated you. I neglected the only son remaining to me. The last piece of my husband, because I was too blind to see the truth."

For a time, he was frozen, not knowing how to respond. He was the Earl of Ashton in truth. By blood and by birthright.

"I will leave, if you ask it of me," she whispered. "I deserve to be cast out for what I did."

A part of him wanted to lash out at her, for the years she'd made him feel like a shadow worth nothing at all. But what good would it do? She had aged into a fragile shell of a woman who had based her life upon misery and bitterness.

He had Rose now, the woman he loved more than life itself. He had brought her here to help him rebuild Ashton . . . but perhaps she could help him rebuild more than the estate.

With a heavy sigh, he placed his hand upon his mother's shoulder. "Will you walk with me when I meet my bride?"

Moira took his hand and pressed it to her forehead. Against his fingers, he felt the wetness of her tears. "I will, yes. Thank you."

It would take time to let go of the past. But it would begin with a single step.

The wedding ceremony was a blur, and Rose could hardly remember anything that was said. She could only look into Iain's green eyes, feeling as if her heart would burst from happiness. When he kissed her, the crowd erupted into cheers. Bagpipes sounded in a merry tune, and Iain lifted her up, turning her in a slow circle so she could see the revelers.

"I'm so happy," she murmured, as he let her slide down his body. The crowd parted, and he kept their pace slow as they walked toward the elaborate feast that was waiting.

"'Tis a good thing we have men guarding the food," Iain admitted. "Else there would be a mad rush toward the tables."

"What will we do when the food is gone?" she asked.

"I have been thinking," he said. "Our family owns property in Wales that has land for farming. I may send half of our tenants to farm the land and then bring them back with the harvest, until our own crops improve. I will pay for the ship's passage with a portion of the harvest."

It was a good plan, and she believed it would help all of them. "The tenants can return for the winter and stay in their homes."

"Aye." He leaned down and kissed her again when they reached the long table with seats prepared for them. "But I'm not thinking of the tenants just now. I'm thinking of how I'll steal you away during the *céilí*." He whispered of how he would carry her off during the dancing.

She sent him a soft smile. "Do we have to wait that long? I was rather hoping my pirate husband would abduct me right now."

He laughed and pulled out her chair, seating her on it. "Soon, *a ghrá.*"

In the end, they stayed until nightfall. So many of the guests came forward to offer their thanks, it was impossible to slip away. Finally, Iain brought Rose down to join in the dancing. He took both of her hands in his, while the others circled around them. It overwhelmed him to think that this woman would now share a life with them. Even Lady Penford had joined in the dancing and was laughing when a large Irishman picked her up by the waist and swung her in a circle.

"Are you ready, *a chroí?*" he asked.

She squeezed his hands in silent answer. With that, he lifted her into his arms and strode toward the edge of the circle. Laughing, the men and women let them through, while they continued the celebration.

"I've a gift for you, Rose," he said quietly, when they reached the front door at Ashton.

She sent him a curious look, and asked, "Does it have anything to do with the stone walls they've built over the past fortnight?"

"It does. It's not finished yet, but in time, perhaps."

He carried her around the side of the house, back toward the new stone walls that stretched twelve feet high. When he reached the doorway, he lowered her to her feet. "I thought I should bring a garden to my Rose."

He unlocked the door and guided her inside. Though he was still conscious of the rotting odor that lingered at Ashton, he'd done what he could to bring flowers into the space. Most of them were potted. There were urns of climbing roses and he'd brought heather and gorse. It was a wild cacophony of color, with little order to it. But it was the best he could do with so little time. He let her look for a moment while he locked the door behind him. Here, they would have complete privacy with no one to intrude upon them.

In the center of the space, he'd piled several blankets and pillows. Her gaze went toward them, and she raised an eyebrow. "Is this meant to be our garden of Eden?"

Iain shot her a wicked smile and nodded. "I've been wanting to make love to you for so long, I thought we should return to the moment I first loved you." He reached for one blanket and spread it over the green grass. Then he set down a pillow, making a bed for her beneath the stars.

Rose turned her back to him, and then whispered, "I need you, Iain."

He took his time about it, unbuttoning each of the buttons along the back of her gown, pressing his mouth against her skin. Gooseflesh rose over her nape as he continued kissing her. And despite how he ached for her, he would do everything to make this first time last.

He removed her gown and set it on the ground. Then he began unlacing her corset, slowly loosening the barrier that hid her skin. He saw that her hands were trembling and soothed her, "Don't be afraid, *a ghrá*."

"I'm not," she whispered. "But I want to please you."

"You do this already." He set aside the corset and cupped her breasts. Her shift was of the finest linen, and he felt her nipples harden at his touch.

God help him, she was lovely. He wanted to rend the fabric in half, but that would only frighten her. Instead, he turned her to face him. She sent him a wry smile. "You need to remove your clothing as well, Iain."

She helped him remove his coat and waistcoat, unbuttoning the two buttons on his shirt before she lifted it away, baring his chest.

"Now you," he urged. But instead of allowing him to finish undressing her, she untied her petticoats and stepped out of them, leaving only the shift. And when she removed that, he was staring at the most exquisite woman he'd ever seen.

Her breasts were slightly more than a handful, tipped with pink. A light dusting of darker hair covered the triangle at her hips, and he couldn't stop himself from closing the distance. He needed to touch her with a desperation he'd never known.

But she held him off, keeping her hands at his waist. Her fingers moved toward the buttons of his trousers, and he overpowered her. "Not yet, Rose. I won't be able to control myself if you touch me."

He lowered her to rest upon the blanket, and she shivered, her nipples bared and erect. "I'm cold, Iain."

"When I'm through with you, you won't feel the cold at all."

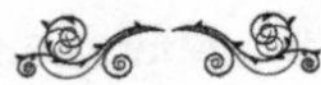

His mouth covered her nipple, and Rose arched up in shock. The aching warmth of his mouth suckled against her, and she felt the echo between her legs. She clenched her knees together, unable to bear the relentless needs that he'd conjured. When he kissed her other nipple, he continued tormenting the first, rolling it between his fingers.

And he was right. There was a heat she'd never imagined before. She dug her fingers into his hair, feeling a delicious sense of the forbidden. Though the garden was locked, she had never imagined her wedding night would be outside. And yet, all around them, she could smell the roses blooming. It was a heady sensation, to feel this man touching her while the moon rose above them and her body was cradled upon a soft blanket. He pushed her wrists back, using his mouth to kiss her lower, and lower still.

"Keep your hands there, *a ghrá.*" He reached down to part her legs, and when she did, he touched her intimately.

"I love you, Rose. And I will treasure you all the days of my life."

"I love you, Iain." Against her center, his warm breath hovered. She was terrified of the wild feelings coursing through her, but she trusted him. Her heart was beating rapidly, and when he tasted her wetness, her fingers dug into the grass. It was a sweet torment, feeling his tongue caress her hooded flesh. He cupped her bottom, lifting her hips as he tasted her. She was utterly helpless, letting the feelings sweep over her. The gentle pressure continued in a rhythm that would not stop. She strained against him, while his tongue stroked. And yet, it seemed that he brought her to the edge, only to pull back. Her body was shaking with desire, and she begged, "I need you inside me, Iain. I can't bear it."

His eyes were dark with passion, but he nodded. Within seconds, he had removed his trousers and underclothing and was naked. She opened her arms to him, and he lay upon her, skin to skin.

Against the juncture of her thighs, she felt the blunt head of him. And she couldn't help but arch, reaching down to guide him where she needed him.

"You're not ready for me yet, Rose," he protested. But she refused to let him leave her. He bent to take her mouth, and she kissed him hard, opening as he slid his tongue within her mouth. She moved her hips, fighting against him as she tried to take him inside.

Instead, he reached down and began stroking her with his fingers. Gently, he circled, while his thick erection was poised to enter her. From deep inside, a shimmering sensation began to take hold. It brought her back to the edge, and his fingers pushed her toward a release that shattered through her body, past every inch of her naked skin. She convulsed against him, the wave pulsing through her. And when he entered her body, there was no pain at all. Only the sense that he belonged inside her.

He remained motionless, letting her grow accustomed to his size. When he began to withdraw, she murmured a protest, only to feel him slide back into place.

"My God that feels good," she whispered. "Do it again."

He did, and it felt as if he were caressing her on the inside. Her body quivered around him, her breasts tightening even more. He entered her slowly, grasping her hips as he thrust. She opened her eyes to look at him, and it was wondrous to watch her husband making love to her.

She tilted her hips as he continued, squeezing his length inside her depths. The husky groan that erupted told her that he liked that. She experimented, trying to find a rhythm that suited both of them. And as she continued to squeeze him, she found that it brought another wave of pleasure.

"I need . . . to go faster, *a chroí,*" he gritted.

She opened her legs wider, and he began to pump harder. The heat of his flesh, the intense pressure, was shocking, and she felt every inch of him caressing her.

She had done this to him. And God above, the power was intoxicating.

Against his thrusts, she pushed back, and he grew consumed by it. He murmured endearments in Irish, kissing her while he palmed one breast.

She came apart again, and squeezed both legs around his waist. Sweat made their bodies slippery against one another, but she didn't care. Iain let out a low growl and she gasped when he thrust hard and shuddered against her as his own release came.

He stroked a few more times, and then collapsed atop her. Rose held him until his shaking abated. Then he rolled onto his back, taking her with him. He drew one of the blankets over their bodies, cocooning their joining.

She rested her head against his chest, feeling beloved. Never had she imagined that a half-dressed Irishman would walk into her life and steal her heart. But he was hers, now and evermore.

He rested his palm upon her spine. "Are you wanting to go back to London, Rose? You could leave all this and return later."

But she shook her head. "My place is with you. There is so much to be done, you'll need my help."

"There's one thing in particular that I'll be needing your help with," he admitted.

"The tenants, I know, and the supplies. We should—"

"Not that." He bent in and nibbled her ear. "I'll be needing your help to make children, my darling wife."

A deep ache caught her at his words. "So you've changed your mind, then."

"Aye." He kissed her deeply. Above them, the darkening clouds threatened rain. He had begun touching her again when suddenly, the skies opened up, the droplets soaking through them.

Rose let out a stifled cry. "I suppose we'll have to go inside now, Iain."

"We will. And I'll have to dress you in warmer clothes before you get cold."

She drew him to her and kissed him hard. "You won't allow me to get cold, Iain, and we both know this."

He traced the outline of her jaw. "Shall I take you somewhere and warm you, *a ghrá*?"

She put her hand in his and smiled. "Anywhere at all."

Epilogue

Three years later

Iain walked through the fields of barley and wheat, while the summer sunlight illuminated the golden crops. He held the hand of his young son, Aidan, while he stopped to talk with several of the laborers.

They had stopped growing potatoes and had kept a portion of the wheat to help feed the workers. It filled him with a sense of pride to know that they were not dependent upon the potato. He had used Rose's dowry to buy seed, and in time, the estate had become self-sufficient. The tenants had returned to help farm the land, and no longer did he see hunger in the faces of the children.

His mother was walking along the road, accompanied by a footman. When she saw the two of them, her face brightened. "Now there is my wee grandson. How is my Aidan?" She held out her arms, and Aidan went skipping into them. Moira dug through her reticule and gave him a sweet. She ruffled the boy's hair, and then met Iain's gaze with a gentle smile.

Her demeanor toward him had transformed over the last three years, with Rose's help. His wife had bridged the distance, asking Moira for advice, and helping Colleen and Sybil find husbands. And in time, his mother had let go of the anger born out of fearful memories.

They began walking back to the house together, and his mother lifted Aidan onto her hip. She adored her grandchildren and spoiled them at every opportunity. When they reached the house, Iain opened the door for both of them. Inside, they heard the sound of a baby shrieking.

Rose was pacing the halls with their infant daughter, Deirdre, against her shoulder. She was murmuring to the baby, and Moira went to them, setting Aidan down.

"Let me take her," his mother urged. "You look as if you've had a dreadful night."

There was no doubting that. Iain had taken turns with Rose, getting up with the baby, but neither one of them had slept well.

His wife handed the baby over, and smiled gratefully. "I think she's getting teeth, and it hurts her so."

Moira placed her finger against the baby's mouth, and Deirdre gnawed at her. "Why don't you both go and have a lie-down while I look after them?"

"You are a saint," Rose proclaimed.

Iain took her by the hand, and his mother took both grandchildren toward the library. Aidan, come and show Granny your blocks." With a wink to Iain and Rose, she departed with the children.

"I feel as if I could sleep for a fortnight and never wake up," Rose admitted.

Iain took her by the hand and guided her up the stairs. "I think my mother is right. We should take advantage of our opportunity to escape."

She smiled sleepily at him. "I am so glad to see her happy. She truly loves our children."

"She does." And he rather thought it was Moira's way of trying to atone for the past. There was no doubting that she would do anything for her grandchildren.

When they reached their bedroom, he lifted Rose into his arms and carried her over the threshold. She laughed. "Now what are you doing, Iain? You know perfectly well that I can walk."

"I wouldn't want you to be overtired, *a ghrá.* Not when you'll need your strength." He kicked the door closed and brought her to their bed. He laid her down and sat beside her, marveling that this woman was his.

"And what will I need strength for?" she teased, her brown eyes warming to his invitation.

"I intend to ravish you, my wife. I've heard that it helps with sleeping." He bent and kissed her deeply, while she twined her arms around his neck.

"I don't think I'll need any help falling asleep," she answered. "But if you do . . ." She let her words trail off while she unbuttoned his shirt.

He captured her wrists and pinned them to the bed. "I do indeed." He lowered his mouth to her throat, kissing her until she arched against him.

"I love you, my Rose."

She smiled at him, reaching up to touch his hair. "I love you, too. Now are you going to ravish me like you promised?"

And he did. Most thoroughly.

EXCERPT FROM WHAT THE EARL NEEDS NOW, *BOOK TWO IN THE EARLS NEXT DOOR SERIES*

LONDON, 1846

Lily reached for the doorknob and turned it. Inside, the room was dark, save for the fire in the hearth and a single candle burning on the mantel. The drapes were closed, as if he was trying to shut out the world.

"Matthew," she said softly. "May I come in?"

There was no answer. She opened the door a little wider, uncertain of whether she should enter. If he was wounded and lying in bed, it was not at all proper for her to visit.

But he is my husband, she reassured herself. Even if no one else knew it but them, she had every right to see him. She took a single step into the darkness, wondering why he would not speak. Was he sleeping?

But no, Matthew was seated in a large wingback chair a short distance away from the fire. In the shadows, she could not see his face—only the outline of a man with his head lowered. In his posture, she sensed pain, mingled with frustration. Tension stretched out in the room, and she waited for him to speak. Long moments passed, and still, he said nothing.

"Matthew, it's Lily," she murmured. "Will you not look at me?"

She prayed that when he heard her voice, it would break the spell of melancholy and bring him back. The silence grew heavier, and for a moment, she doubted herself.

He is not the man you once loved.

Lady Arnsbury had tried to warn her, but she hadn't believed the countess. She'd wanted to trust that it would be different when she saw him. But it seemed that he was locked in his own prison of nightmares, one for which there was no key.

"Matthew," she repeated. "Look at me." *See me. Know that I love you and always have.*

At last, he raised his head. There was no sense of welcome in his demeanor, and it felt as if she were facing a wounded tiger.

"Go away." His voice was raw, and she heard the traces of pain in it. Upon an end table beside the chair, she saw a glass. Had he been drinking? Or perhaps he had taken laudanum for his injuries, whatever they were.

She ignored his command and pulled a chair across from him, sitting so close he could touch her. Her heart was beating hard, and her emotions were tightly strung up inside her. With a glance toward the door, she saw that Lady Arnsbury and the footman had retreated into the hall, allowing them a measure of privacy while still chaperoning her.

In the softest whisper she spoke, not wanting anyone to overhear her. "I am so glad you've returned," she said. "I've waited so long for you."

But again, he said nothing. It was as if he were a stranger, a man haunted by visions she could not see. His hands clenched the arms of his chair, and he repeated, "I want to be alone."

"I am your *wife*," she whispered. "How can you ask me to go? After all that we've meant to one another."

"I *have* no wife," he gritted out.

His head dropped forward, and for a breathless moment, she knew fear. The silver chain holding her wedding band seemed to weigh against her throat. She withdrew it from her bodice and showed him the ring. It was *his* ring, the one his grandfather had once given him when he was a boy.

"How can you say such a thing?" Tears gathered in her eyes, and coldness flooded through her. "After the vows we spoke to one another."

He leaned forward and stared at her. His blue eyes were chips of ice in a face made of stone. Gone was the man she knew, and in his place was a fighter filled with rage. She searched his expression for some sign of affection, some glimmer of hope for them. But there was not even a hint of recognition.

"Go away," he demanded.

The logical response would be to obey him, to surrender and wait another day. But she had waited endless months for his return. And somewhere in this man was the husband she had yearned for. She didn't know what had happened to him, but she would not step aside and fade into the shadows. They would face this together and overcome it.

"No," she answered, reaching out to cup his cheek. "I am not leaving you." She stroked the dark bristle of his beard, not caring that he appeared so rough and unkempt. He had been to Hades and back again. Even his hair was longer than usual, and she suspected he hadn't cut it. Across his left cheek was a slash, a healing wound that seemed to have been cut with a curved sword.

"I promised I would never leave you," she said, tracing the outline of his face. "And you promised to love me forever."

At that, he caught her wrist. "How could I promise such a thing?" A faint trace of irony creased his expression. "Especially when I have never seen you before in my life."

Author's Note

I hope you've enjoyed *Good Earls Don't Lie* and that you'll try the other books in the *Earls Next Door* series. If you'd like to get an automatic e-mail when my next book is available, you can sign up at my website, www.michellewillingham.com. Your information will never be shared, and you can unsubscribe at any time.

Also, please consider leaving a review at Amazon, even if it's only a sentence or two. Your feedback is always appreciated.

If you were wondering about Lady Rose's illness, she suffered from botulism poisoning after eating potatoes that had gone bad. The effects of botulism include muscle paralysis and can last for several months.

Also, to translate a few of the Irish Gaelic terms used in this book, *a chara* means "my friend"; *a chroí*, "my heart"; *a mhuirnín*, "my darling"; and *a ghrá*, "my love." *Cailín* is a young girl, and *céilí* is a celebration, with dancing.

About the Author

Bestselling author Michelle Willingham has written more than thirty-five novels and novellas. Her stories have been translated into sixteen languages around the world and released in audiobook format. She has consistently received four-star reviews from *Romantic Times* magazine, and *Publishers Weekly* has called her stories "genuinely funny and thoughtful." In 2010 she was a RITA finalist for historical romance. She has also been nominated for the Booksellers' Best Award and the National Readers' Choice Award.

She lives in southeastern Virginia with her husband and three children. Her hobbies include baking, reading, and avoiding exercise at all costs. Visit her website at www.michellewillingham.com for more details.

About the Author